A SAVAGE WAR OF PEACE

A SAVAGE
WAR OF PEACE

MR CHRISTOPHER G NUTTALL

http://www.chrishanger.net
http://chrishanger.wordpress.com/
http://www.facebook.com/ChristopherGNuttall

Cover by Justin Adams
http://www.variastudios.com/

All Comments Welcome!

Text copyright © 2015 Mr Christopher G Nuttall
All rights reserved.
Printed in the United States of America.
No part of this book may be reproduced, or stored in a retrieval system, or transmitted in any form or by any means, electronic, mechanical, photocopying, recording, or otherwise, without express written permission of the publisher.

ISBN: 1511828196
ISBN 13: 9781511828192

AUTHOR'S NOTE

As always, comments, spelling/grammar corrections and suchlike are warmly welcomed. I trade cameos in exchange for all such suggestions.

CGN

PROLOGUE I

From: Professor Scott Nordstrom, Dept. Of Xenobiology, Edinburgh University
To: Admiral Percy Finnegan, First Space Lord
Subject: The Vesy, Political Implications
Classification: Top Secret, Eyes-Only UK

Admiral.

As per your request, the Department has composed a long report based on our analysis of the reports from HMS *Warspite*. Data was, of course, limited; neither *Warspite's* crew nor the Russian refugees (or their slaves) were trained observers, let alone alien research specialists. However, our conclusions have been filed and forwarded to you and the working committee.

That said, there are certain political implications that must be brought to your attention.

We believe the Vesy are not, by any definition of the term, a threat to humanity. As far as can be determined from the orbital observations of their homeworld and the limited studies conducted on the ground, they were at roughly 1400s-level when contacted by the Russians and literally had nothing more advanced than swords, pikes and spears (they *had* invented the wheel). The Russians introduced gunpowder and, perhaps more importantly, human-style military tactics and political institutions, but nothing that could allow the aliens to pose a threat to their colony, let alone the rest of the human sphere. It is, of course, impossible to be sure just how quickly they would develop, with the knowledge that certain technologies are possible. We believe, however, that we will have around 200 years before the Vesy start experimenting with crude rockets, assuming they remain isolated from the rest of the galaxy.

I do not believe they will be permitted to remain isolated for long.

Their system represents a treasure trove for human exploration, research and development. It is well known, thanks to the World Court hearings in Geneva, that their system possesses no less than seven tramlines, three alien-grade. As the Vesy lack both a unified planetary government and a space-based presence of their own, they are literally unable to prevent human factions (or the Tadpoles, for that matter) from passing through their system at will. Furthermore, studies of the Vesy themselves (and a biosphere that is very different from Earth's) may bring huge rewards to the nations and corporations that start long-term research programs. Indeed, their viewpoints on technology may suggest new ways to expand and refine our own technological development, in much the same way as direct contact with the Tadpoles helped us to progress around perceived roadblocks and develop new technologies. There may be a considerable demand for Vesy researchers to work in human labs; if not now, then soon.

This will, obviously, lead to charges of exploitation. We have already seen demands, most notably from the Friendship League, that we should basically start a massive knowledge transfer program to assist the Vesy in learning to use modern technology. Many such NGOs have already committed themselves to preventing human exploitation of the Vesy. Others have seen their living conditions, which may be described as primitive, and insist that it is our duty - the so-called 'Human Race's Burden' - to uplift the Vesy, on the grounds we know better than themselves what is good for them. Given that the basic tests determined that the general level of Vesy intelligence was comparable to human intelligence, it is unlikely they will take such a condescending attitude in good part. They may be primitive, but they are not children.

However, the introduction of relatively minor pieces of technology by the Russians caused a considerable amount of upheaval in their society. Introducing everything from modern medicine and weapons to computers and starships would turn their society upside down, literally. Their system of government would probably be shattered, all the more so if human social ideas are introduced. We might see disasters along the lines of Cortez's invasion of the Aztec Empire, the Pakistani Uprising or even the European Winter.

Ideally, we should make no further contact with the Vesy. No matter how well-intentioned, contact between an advanced society and a primitive one is often disastrous for both. The former becomes smug and arrogant, confident in its own superiority; the latter falls apart or collapses into a society-wide depression and inferiority complex. I do not believe, however, that humanity will leave the Vesy alone. Even if the British Government bans all further contact with the aliens, the remainder of the world's governments may have other ideas (and, of course, our NGOs will demand action and involvement in 'assisting' the Vesy).

With that in mind, sir, I have the following recommendations...

PROLOGUE II

The bunker was buried ten miles below Delhi, so deep that nothing short of a major asteroid strike could hope to disturb the bunker and its inhabitants. There was no chance, General Anjeet Patel knew, of any outsiders being able to spy on the nerve centre of Indian Government, not given the sheer level of security built up around the bunker. The government could muster its forces, direct its military and hold secret diplomatic discussions, all in total secrecy. Indeed, it was hoped that hardly anyone outside India even knew of the bunker's existence.

He stopped outside a mirrored door and waited, knowing he was being observed, his body scanned for bugs, implants and other surprises. His face looked back at him; dark skin, a short neatly-trimmed beard, a green uniform and a dagger hanging from his belt, a tradition the Indian military had adopted during the Age of Unrest, when an attack could start at any time. There was a long pause, then the door hissed open, revealing a barren conference compartment. It was empty, save for a table, a set of chairs, a drinks machine and a holographic projector. He stepped inside and saluted as the Prime Minister came into view.

"Prime Minister," Anjeet said.

"General," Prime Minister Mohandas Singh said. "Welcome to the lair."

He tapped a switch and the door hissed closed behind Anjeet. "Take a seat," he added, briskly. "We don't have much time."

"Yes, sir," Anjeet said.

He sat down and took a moment to study the Prime Minister. Singh was an old man, having served in the government for most of his adult life, but his mind was clearly as sharp as ever, despite the calamities that Earth had suffered over the past decade. Who would have believed that there was such a thing as *aliens*? Who would have believed that a powerful interstellar race would wage war on humanity? Even now, with a second alien race known to exist, Anjeet still had trouble getting his head around it. The once-boundless immensity of space, just waiting for human expansion, now seemed confined and restricted.

"I assume you've read the classified reports from Vesy," Singh said, without preamble. "The existence of a second alien race offers us an unexpected opportunity."

"Yes, sir," Anjeet said.

"The Great Powers," Singh added, "are seriously considering declaring the entire system under quarantine. This is not, of course, acceptable to us."

Anjeet nodded, bitterly. India had done well to survive, when the Age of Unrest had washed over the planet, but she hadn't kept up with the Great Powers. Britain, France, America, Russia, China…they'd dominated the march into space, then the quest to settle as many worlds as possible. They'd set the rules and, deliberately or otherwise, they'd made it almost impossible for any of the smaller powers to match their expansion. The sheer mass of power they'd accumulated for themselves made them the masters of the universe.

But the Great Powers had been weakened, badly.

India had fought in the war, of course, fought on the human side. But India had had fewer ships and fewer colony worlds and so the Great Powers had taken the brunt of the conflict. It hadn't taken long for the Indian Government - and the other nations that bitterly resented being relegated to second-class status - to see how this situation could be turned to their advantage. For the first time in fifty years, there was a very real chance of catching up and surpassing the Great Powers.

They still have more ships, but most of them are old, Anjeet thought. *We have newer ships built with technology we learned from the Tadpoles. The balance of power may even be in our favour.*

"It is critically important that we weaken the bonds between the Great Powers," Singh continued, "and Vesy provides a unique opportunity to drive a wedge between them. The Russians are already crippled; a dispute over the finer points of interstellar law can only make matters worse for the Great Powers. Their alliance was not exactly based on mutual trust and respect."

Anjeet smiled. The Chinese and Americans had almost gone to war twice, before the Tadpoles had materialised out of the depths of space to wage war on humanity. It wouldn't take much to set them at each other's throats, at least outside the Sol System itself. No one really wanted to violate the Solar Treaty, not now. There was simply too much at stake... and besides, the Solar Treaty actually worked in India's favour. How long would it last, he asked himself, when the Great Powers realised they'd tied their hands behind their backs?

"The first part of your mission is simple," Singh told him. "You are to do whatever is necessary to take control of Vesy, preferably by working with alien factions on the ground and assisting them to secure their grip on the planet. Our long-term objective is to enter into an alliance with the Vesy, one that will be upheld by the body of international law that has developed since we started our advance into space."

"Yes, Prime Minister," Anjeet said.

He smiled, coldly. If half the reports were true, the Vesy were in a permanent state of war - and the Russians had made matters worse by introducing everything from gunpowder to metalworking and human military tactics. It would be simplicity itself, particularly with the aid of the Russian files, to find a faction that wanted human assistance. And once that faction was firmly allied with India, they'd have the weapons and supplies they needed to conquer the entire planet.

"The second part of your mission is much more complex," Singh continued. "When the time comes, you will take the first steps in forcing the Great Powers to grant us - and our allies - a seat on the table. Your orders have already been prepared for you, General. Ships have been assigned to your command. All you will need to do is open your sealed orders and proceed as planned."

Anjeet took a breath. He'd taken part in the planning sessions, when the original scheme had been conceived and developed. The Vesy hadn't changed much, he knew; their existence merely serving as the trigger for a confrontation that could see India raised to the ranks of the Great Powers or plunged down into a second Age of Unrest. It was always hard to predict which way the Great Powers would jump, after all, and if they *all* allied against India…

But Russia is already broken, he thought, coolly. *China and France licking their wounds after the war. That just leaves Britain and America… and their allies.*

"I understand, Prime Minister," he said. "When do I leave?"

"As soon as possible," Singh said. "And good luck."

Anjeet nodded. He'd need it.

CHAPTER ONE

"Go," the coordinator ordered.

A single starship - a light cruiser - hung in front of the observers, illuminated by the pulsing light of a holographic star. Suddenly, a dozen starfighters appeared out of nowhere, spinning down towards their target. The cruiser brought its point defence online and opened fire, spewing out thousands of bursts of plasma fire at the starfighters as they closed in. One by one, they vanished from the display until only a couple survived to launch their missiles at the cruiser. Both missiles were picked off before they had a chance to do any harm, then one of the remaining starfighters was vaporised. The sole survivor turned and fled into the endless darkness of space.

"Simulation complete," the coordinator said. "Victory; Blue."

Captain John Naiser sucked in his breath as the handful of military officers watching the display started to babble amongst themselves. He'd been a starfighter pilot, back before the war, and he'd never seen any cruiser defend itself so effectively against a conventional swarm attack. But then, neither had the human pilots who'd fought in the Battle of New Russia, where the entire Multinational Fleet had been obliterated by the Tadpoles. They'd been caught by surprise - no human fleet had been able to put out so much point defence - and never had a chance to recover.

"The starfighter is doomed, I believe," Admiral Yeager Soskice said. The head of the Next Generation Weapons program rose to his feet as the room lightened, his face glowing with triumph. "There is simply no way a swarm of starfighters can punch through the defences of a capital ship, not now."

John felt his eyes narrow as he peered at Admiral Soskice. The man was a genius, of that there was no doubt, but he'd never seen action in his life. And he was the man who had foisted an unqualified XO on *Warspite*, when she'd left the Sol System on her mission to Pegasus. There was a very real danger that Soskice and his followers believed their own simulations, while any experienced officer would have known that real life was rarely so cut and dried. What would happen, he asked himself, if the cruiser's sensors weren't so effective at tracking incoming starfighters? Or if the ship's plasma cannons overheated in combat and exploded, depriving the ship of some of her point defence?

"The simulation was rigged," Vice Admiral James Montrose Fitzwilliam said. "You deliberately slanted the advantages in favour of the cruiser."

"The simulation was *not* rigged," Admiral Soskice snapped. "I programmed it to reflect the tactical realities…"

"As you see them," Admiral Fitzwilliam cut him off. "I don't think real life is so cut and dried."

He muttered orders to the coordinator, who hastily reprogrammed the simulation. The lights dimmed as the simulation reset, then the starfighters zoomed down towards their target for the second time. John watched, feeling a pang of bitter regret, as they zipped from side to side, making it impossible for the cruiser to target them with any real accuracy. Nine starfighters survived long enough to salvo their missiles at the cruiser, four missiles survived long enough to strike home. The cruiser disintegrated in a blinding series of explosions.

"Target destroyed," the coordinator said. "Victory; Red."

"That simulation was rigged," Admiral Soskice said, sharply. "Change enough variables and even *you* could win."

"The variables change constantly, depending on the situation," Admiral Fitzwilliam said. "I will happily concede that, under ideal circumstances, the plasma cannons make life hairy for starfighter pilots. That's what happened at New Russia, after all. But *Ark Royal* and her flyers managed to adapt to the new threat and deal some pretty effective blows against the Tadpoles. The day of the starfighter is not yet over."

John smiled, feeling a flicker of admiration. Admiral Fitzwilliam had been *Ark Royal's* XO, then her commanding officer, during the war. He would have gone down with the ship if he hadn't been badly wounded at Alien-Prime and sent home to muster reinforcements. Since then, he'd commanded the MNF that patrolled the border between human and alien space, watching for signs the uneasy truce was about to come to an end. Unlike Admiral Soskice, no one could say he didn't have any experience.

And he served under Theodore Smith, John thought, wryly. *He wouldn't have stayed on Ark Royal if he'd been incompetent.*

"We must advance our own weapons and defences to ensure that we can never be caught by surprise again," Admiral Soskice insisted. "Your... fixation with the glory days of the starfighter is holding us back."

"I believe there are very real dangers in advancing forward too far, too fast," Admiral Fitzwilliam countered. "You have read *Superiority*?"

John - and most of the other officers in the compartment - nodded. The short story had been required reading at the Academy, even though not all of them had agreed with its premise or the outcome. One interstellar power had thrown its resources into developing newer and better weapons of war; the other had continued to build the same old starships and weapons, even when the first power accomplished some remarkable achievements. But the newer weapons and innovations had never quite worked out in practice and there had been no time to get the bugs out. The first power, which should have won the war handily, had suffered a humiliating defeat.

"We are not talking about taking a new device and sticking it on every ship in the Royal Navy," Admiral Soskice said.

"But you *are* talking about cutting starfighter squadrons and redirecting resources to smaller ships," Admiral Fitzwilliam pointed out. "We still have a need for starfighters and fleet carriers, Admiral. And we cannot assume that we should cut a whole spectrum of weapons systems because conditions for deploying them are no longer ideal."

John sighed, inwardly. The hell of it was that both admirals had a point. Starfighter pilots had taken the brunt of losses during the war - John had heard that only ten percent of the Royal Navy's pre-war pilots had survived the fighting - and most of them had died because the Tadpoles had changed the rules. But, at the same time, humanity's starfighters *had* managed to adapt and fight back. The starfighters hadn't been remotely useless.

"We are not the only ones developing new weapons and tactics," Admiral Soskice said, coldly. "The Americans, the French, the Chinese… they're all working on developing new weapons they can use against the Tadpoles - or us! We should not allow ourselves to become complacent!"

"We're not becoming complacent," Fitzwilliam said. "The problem is introducing newer technology without causing major problems or accidentally creating new weaknesses in our ships and defences. Like *Warspite's* first cruise."

John cursed under his breath as all eyes turned to him. "*Warspite* lost power when she jumped through a tramline," Fitzwilliam continued. "How many other problems would be caused by a failure to anticipate the demands of real life?"

Admiral Soskice glowered. "Captain Naiser, just what happened when *Warspite* lost power?"

Asshole, John thought, crossly. He'd known the admiralty was divided between those who wanted to experiment with newer weapons and those who wanted to rely on tried and tested technology, but he hadn't wanted to get caught in the middle. *Is there an answer I can give that will satisfy both of you?*

"A problem developed that would have been caught, if there had been more time to test the drive," he said, smoothly. There was no point in going over the full details, not now. One of the people responsible was dead and the other trapped on Pegasus. "I don't believe it proves or dis-proves either of your positions."

Admiral Fitzwilliam's eyes narrowed. "Explain," he ordered.

John winced, inwardly. When would he learn to keep his mouth shut?

"*Warspite* should have had several weeks to run proving trials before leaving the Sol System," he said. "That would have given us the time to catch all of those problems, as well as testing the tactical systems under combat conditions. We would have been able to integrate the newer systems into both the ship herself and the crew's awareness of just what they can do."

He took a breath, then went on. "There's nothing wrong with newer technology," he added, slowly. "But we need to test it thoroughly, to see how it works in combat and discover the flaws, before we can integrate it fully into our tactical planning. In this case" - he waved a hand towards the holographic simulation, which had frozen just after the cruiser exploded - "the *first* encounter with plasma cannons was a nasty fright and the enemy scored a victory, but we adapted our tactics to compensate. It would be unwise of us to rely solely on plasma weapons to defend our ships."

"Indeed," Admiral Fitzwilliam said. "Do go on."

John had the uneasy sense he was being allowed to gather rope to hang himself, but he pressed on regardless. "Starfighters also do more than merely strike at other capital ships," he continued. "They do long-range recon, dog-fighting with other starfighters and a number of other tasks. There is no reason to remove every starfighter from the fleet just because the rules of the game have changed. They may change again tomorrow."

"They will change again," Admiral Soskice said. "Change is the one constant in the universe."

He nodded towards the simulation, sharply. "As a starfighter pilot yourself," he added, "how would you handle such a situation?"

"Keep moving randomly," John said. "Use decoys and drones, if I had them; spoofing software and ECM, just to make it harder for the enemy to target me. All tactics that we used against the Tadpoles."

"Thousands of starfighter pilots were killed," Admiral Soskice said.

"They knew the risks," Admiral Fitzwilliam said, cuttingly. "We *all* know the risks."

John grimaced as Admiral Soskice glared at his nemesis. It was a non-too-subtle reminder that Admiral Soskice hadn't seen any real action, not outside simulators. And simulators could be altered to tip the balance in favour of one side or the other, if someone was prepared to take the time to try. God knew there were hundreds of trainees who enjoyed flying down the Death Star trench in the simulator, pretending to be Luke Skywalker or Darth Vader, even though it wasn't particularly realistic.

"Five years ago, we were taught that our technology was not the best in the universe," Admiral Soskice said. His voice was under tight control. "Since then, we have struggled to catch up with an enemy who showed a remarkable skill in producing newer weapons and tactics at terrifying speed. We dare not allow them to get past us again."

"And I say, again, that we are not opposed to new technology," Admiral Fitzwilliam said. "We are just opposed to rewriting doctrine and decommissioning whole weapons systems because of the latest shiny thing. And that is what you are planning to do. You want us to stop building fleet carriers and starfighters and concentrate on small cruisers. Which is all well and good, until we run into a threat that requires fleet carriers and starfighters to handle!"

They're both right, John thought. Assuming the Tadpoles hadn't started building their superdreadnaught until they'd run into *Ark Royal*, they'd put a colossal starship into service in less than a year. Given that it took humanity five years to build a fleet carrier from scratch, it was not a pleasant thought. The Tadpoles might be quietly rebuilding their fleet and developing newer weapons even now. *But neither of them will admit the other has a point.*

He listened as the argument raged backwards and forwards, neither Admiral conceding a point. It was deeply frustrating, as well as worrying, that the tension had actually exploded into an argument in front of a small army of junior officers. The First Space Lord had told him, before *Warspite* had left Earth for the first time, that the disagreement between the two sides was already affecting operational readiness, but he hadn't really believed it was so bad.

You should have known better, he reproved himself, as he glanced wistfully at the hatch. Several smaller arguments had broken out between various junior officers, all of whom looked prepared to bicker like children for their superior officers. Military protocol seemed to have gone out the airlock. *You had to relieve your XO because she was utterly unsuited to the post.*

His wristcom bleeped. "Captain Naiser," a voice said, "report to the First Space Lord at 1500."

John glanced at the time - it was 1430 - then made his way towards the hatch, which hissed open at his approach. Behind him, the argument had gotten louder; he sighed in relief as he stepped through the hatch and it closed behind him, cutting off the sound. Outside, a dark-haired woman was waiting, wearing a Commander's uniform. John smiled, despite himself, as he recognised Juliet Watson, *Warspite's* former XO. Unlike other officers who had been effectively demoted, she didn't seem to bear any resentment.

"Captain," she said. She definitely looked happier, now she was in the labs on Nelson Base, rather than a cruiser in deep space. "It's good to see you again, sir."

"Thank you," John said. Someone had evidently been coaching her in social graces; absently, he wondered who and why. "It's good to see you again too."

"I'm just waiting for the Admiral," Juliet said. "Is he going to be long?"

"They've probably started throwing chairs and tables by now," John said. He couldn't help being reminded of a bar fight he'd been caught up in at Southampton, years ago. "Is it anything important?"

"Just to brief him on the progress of our latest experiment," Juliet said. "There should definitely be a way to generate a tramline from scratch."

John frowned. "Isn't that meant to be highly classified?"

Juliet shrugged. John snorted, inwardly. Admiral Soskice's inexperience was showing; Juliet should have been assigned to a lab somewhere in deep space, rather than a warship or even Nelson Base. It was a great deal more secure than the Admiralty on Earth, true, but there were still too many officers and crewmen with low-level security clearances passing through the space station. And Juliet herself would have been happy with a large computer, a simulator and a handful of trained minions to help her with her research.

"I need to visit the First Space Lord soon," he said, instead. "You'll probably have to wait for the Admiral. Do you want to wait in the officers' lounge?"

Juliet nodded, vaguely. They walked along the corridor and through a large metal hatch. Into the officers' lounge. It definitely looked nicer than anything set aside for enlisted personnel, John decided; one wall bulkhead covered with medals, while another held a large portrait of the King and Princess Elspeth. A third held a porthole that showed Earth rotating below the giant station. A steward materialised from behind the bar, data-pad in hand, ready to take their order. John ordered tea for himself; Juliet hesitated, then ordered water. The steward bowed and retreated.

"I heard from Mike," Juliet said, as they waited for their drinks. "He was asking if I wanted to meet for drinks."

John concealed his amusement with an effort. Mike Johnston was *Warspite's* Chief Engineer...and one of Juliet's few supporters on the ship. It was alarmingly clear he was sweet on her, something that would have upset the Admiralty if they'd ever found out about it. John rather doubted that anything had happened, but it was another sign that Juliet had been completely unsuited for her post. On the other hand, he had to admit, she would probably have had more trouble if she hadn't had Johnston's support. Very few people would have risked pissing off the Chief Engineer.

"You should," he said, finally. The steward returned and placed two mugs in front of them, then retreated behind the bar. "It would do you good to get out of the lab for an hour or so."

Juliet smiled, vaguely. "That's what they told me when I was sent to your ship," she said.

"I suppose they would have done," John said. He'd always hated being told that suffering was good for his character, if only because he doubted it was true. "You've been doing better here?"

"There aren't so many distractions here," Juliet said. "I can keep poking away at the problems that interest me, without having to worry about anything else."

And as long as you stay productive, the Royal Navy will be happy to take care of you, John thought. He'd heard all sorts of rumours, most of which were unbelievable, about just how carefully the Royal Navy looked after its tame geniuses. *And if you do come up with a way to create a tramline, they'll remember you longer than Einstein or Tesla.*

"I'm glad to hear it," he said, instead. "Are you going to see Mike?"

Juliet blushed like a schoolgirl. John couldn't help thinking she looked pretty, even though he played for the other team. It was hard to imagine her having a serious relationship with anyone, but maybe it would be good for her. She simply wasn't very experienced at relating to other people; indeed, she preferred machines to her fellow humans.

"I might," she said. "I don't know. When are you leaving the system?"

"I don't know yet," John said. *Warspite* had been held at Earth for six months, since her return from Vesy. He'd spent most of the time defending himself against various admirals, all of whom seemed intent on second-guessing every decision he'd made. "I think the First Space Lord might be about to tell me. I'll let you know so you can make up your mind about going for drinks."

"Thank you, sir," Juliet said. "I'm supposed to remain here for the foreseeable future."

"We won't be," John predicted. He glanced at his wristcom, then rose. "I have no doubt something is about to change, yet again."

CHAPTER
TWO

"Bloody protesters," the driver swore.

Ambassador Joelle Richardson leaned forward as the government car turned the corner and almost ran into a mob of protesters blocking the gates to Downing Street. She'd heard reports of protests, but she hadn't really believed them, not since large parts of London had been rendered uninhabitable by the alien bombardment. And yet, there were clearly two groups of protesters marching up and down in front of the centre of British Government; one carrying signs demanding access to Vesy, the other demanding that British resources be lavished on Britain, rather than alien scum.

She sucked in her breath as a line of policemen worked to clear enough of a path through the crowds for the car to reach the gates. Political protest was far from unknown in Britain, even after the bombardments, but there was an edge to the protests that worried her. The British population hadn't felt truly threatened since the Troubles, since all hell had broken loose on British streets; now, with large swathes of the country in ruins, it looked as though the public was torn in half. She hoped - prayed - that both protest movements weren't much larger than they seemed, because if they were...

It could be the end of us, she thought, bitterly. Hundreds of thousands of people had been displaced by the bombardment, their homes destroyed by tidal waves; no one really knew for sure just how many people had been killed outright. No government could take the risk of sending aid to foreign countries, let alone non-human creatures. *It could lead to civil war.*

She peered at the nearest signs as the crowds parted to allow the car to pass. One read HELP OUR STAR BROTHERS, while another read GET THEM BEFORE THEY GET US and NO BLOOD FOR VESY. Joelle sighed, then glanced at a third sign. NO MORE DEAD CHILDREN. A fourth read DOWN WITH THIS SORT OF THING. She puzzled over what it meant for a moment, then put it aside. It probably wasn't important.

The car passed through the gates and came to a halt outside Ten Downing Street. Joelle braced herself as the driver opened the door, breaking the soundproof seal and allowing the two intermingled chants to reach her ears. It was hard to be sure what they were saying - both groups were shouting loudly enough to deafen an elephant - but she was quite sure that everyone in the area could hear the racket. They'd definitely know the protesters were upset about *something*.

She sighed to herself, then picked up her briefcase and walked through the door into Ten Downing Street. Silence fell as the door closed - she allowed herself a moment of relief - then passed her briefcase to a uniformed officer waiting just inside the door. He took it, waved a scanner over her body, then motioned for her to pass through the inner door, where a young man dressed in a pinstripe suit was waiting. Joelle nodded to him - she recognised the Prime Minister's latest assistant from the news - and allowed him to lead her up a flight of stairs and down a long corridor. Ten Downing Street might *look* like a small house from the outside, but inside the old houses had long since been merged together.

"It must be a relief to move back here," she said, as they passed a long series of portraits, each one showing a previous Prime Minister. "I thought it would be longer before Downing Street was reopened."

"The PM was insistent that we move back as soon as possible," the aide said. "He thought it would demonstrate the resilience of the British Government."

Joelle frowned, inwardly. She had her doubts; London wasn't what it had been, any more than the rest of the country. And yet, she had to admit it was a powerful symbol. Britain was a country firmly rooted in the past, in a history that was long and richly detailed; returning to the very roots of parliamentary democracy was a sign that all would return to normal.

But after the bombardment, and the discovery of alien life, was anything ever truly going to be normal again?

Her briefcase was waiting for her as they walked into the antechamber. It would have been searched by a security officer cleared for classified materials, although in truth there was little inside that wasn't public knowledge. The week she'd spent in Geneva, before being recalled, was already the subject of endless discussion on the planetary datanet, as well as hundreds of programmes discussing the pros and cons of working together to confront the Vesy. Not that the Vesy really *needed* confronting, it was true. In the end, talks had floundered on the very simple fact that the Vesy were no threat to humanity. Or, for that matter, to the Tadpoles.

The aide checked his wristcom. "The PM is currently on the hot line to Washington," he said, shortly. "Do you want a cup of tea to catch your breath before you enter his office?"

"No, thank you," Joelle said. "I can wait."

She looked at herself in the mirror, hanging from one wall. Her long brown hair fell down over a pinched face, one that showed too much of her age. The suit she was wearing was tailored to showcase both professionalism and her femininity, a subtle message to rogue states that should know better, by now, to show any disrespect to a British Ambassador. Her lips twitched in droll amusement as she remembered some of the more interesting moments of her long career. There was definitely something to be said for agitating the rulers of states which regarded women as second-class citizens and kept them trapped in ignorance and slavery.

It might not be very diplomatic, she thought, as the aide's wristcom bleeped, *but it needs to be done. We no longer need to pretend that such states are actually important.*

The aide opened the door and showed her into the Prime Minister's office. Joelle smiled as Prime Minister Steven Goodwill rose from behind his desk to greet her, then held out her hand for him to shake. He looked tired, compared to the man she'd met briefly before her assignment to Geneva, but grimly resolved to move ahead, whatever the cost. It was an attitude, Joelle thought, that suited him in his role.

"Prime Minister," she said. "Thank you for recalling me."

The Prime Minister smiled. "Things keep changing, as you know," he said. "Did you manage to get a few days of holiday?"

"Yes, thank you," Joelle said. The Foreign Secretary - her immediate superior - had told her to take a few days off to relax, but not to leave the country. It hadn't been hard to deduce that she was either in trouble or they had a new assignment for her. "I ended up going to Edinburgh for a few days of rest and relaxation."

"There are fewer places to go for a rest these days," the Prime Minister said, dryly. "Too many beaches utterly destroyed; too many lives completely ruined."

"Yes, Prime Minister," Joelle said.

It was true, she knew. A proper holiday was a luxury afforded to few these days, not when most of the cheap holiday destinations had either been destroyed or turned into refugee camps. Even going to Edinburgh had made her feel vaguely guilty. But she had the feeling she was about to earn her vacation.

"And I trust you have nothing preventing you from leaving Earth?" The Prime Minister asked. "No lover? No long-term commitments?"

"No, Prime Minister," Joelle said. In theory, she could be sent well away from Earth at any time and she would just have to suck it up. But, in practice, the Foreign and Commonwealth Office understood that a distracted ambassador was an ineffective ambassador. But it had been years since she'd had more than a quick fling with anyone. Her work ensured she rarely had time to meet anyone on a personal basis. "I'm as free as a bird."

"Good," the Prime Minister said. "We have a job for you."

He sat back down and motioned for her to sit facing him. "You will, of course, be familiar with the talks in Geneva," he said, once she'd taken her seat. "Tell me; what are your impressions?"

Joelle took a moment to organise her thoughts. "There isn't going to be any international consensus on how to proceed," she said, carefully. "The Vesy don't represent a threat to us, so the Solar Treaty doesn't come into play. I don't think there will be any agreement to leave them strictly alone, Prime Minister. It's much more likely that everyone else is going to make a bid for power."

"Probably," the Prime Minister grunted. He cleared his throat. "Do you have any other thoughts?"

"Several parties were suggesting, quite seriously, that we destroy the Vesy now, before they can become a threat," Joelle said. "I think such suggestions need to be shot down as quickly as possible."

"That might be difficult," the Prime Minister said. "Planning to commit genocide would have been unthinkable, five years ago. But now, with the damage the Tadpoles did to Earth fresh in everyone's memory, it may be hard to keep politicians from putting it forward as a serious option."

"Earth First," Joelle said.

"They're not the only ones," the Prime Minister said. "There are quite a few groups out there proclaiming the need for human unity in the face of alien threats…and extreme measures *against* such alien threats."

He sighed, loudly. "But that's not why I called you here today," he continued. "The failure to come to any sort of agreement on a joint approach to the Vesy, even just leaving the planet completely alone, has led to a major problem. Everyone and his dog is currently trying to make their way to Vesy, from governments intent on trying to secure influence among the aliens to NGOs and religious groups keen to influence the development of Vesy civilisation - and, perhaps, steer it in a human-approved direction. I've been trying to stop them, but I have little authority outside the British Commonwealth. It has led to a rather nasty political argument."

Joelle remembered the demonstrators and frowned. "They want to *help* the Vesy," she said, thoughtfully. "The protesters outside, I mean."

"Yes, they do," the Prime Minister said. "We could keep a lid on it, Ambassador, if we had the agreement of the other Great Powers. As it is, we won't be able to prevent them from heading to Vesy for much longer. They'll cause no end of damage to the local civilisation…which they wouldn't actually consider a disadvantage. By our standards, the Vesy are barbarians. *Primitive* barbarians."

"We have barbarians on Earth too," Joelle pointed out.

"We gave up nation-building a long time ago," the Prime Minister said. "Let them redeem themselves, we said, or remain forever in squalor. The Vesy, on the other hand…it's easier, somehow, to see them as children in need of help."

He took a breath. "There's another problem, of course," he added. "The tramlines. Vesy holds no less than seven tramlines, including one that leads to Pegasus. Whoever controls the Vesy System will be in an excellent position to dominate the surrounding systems for the foreseeable future. Simple common sense tells us, Ambassador, that just about every nation on Earth is going to try to take control. They'll cut whatever deals they have to cut with the Vesy to gain control."

"The Vesy will be cheated, Prime Minister," Joelle said.

"Almost certainly," the Prime Minister agreed. "Although, seen from their point of view, even relatively primitive human tech would be a marvel. A working painkiller alone would be worth billions to them...coming to think of it, so would something that suppresses their mating scents, allowing their women to enter the workforce in large numbers. But the point is we cannot allow others to gain an advantage. We need Vesy allies of our own."

"We may end up with another Terra Nova," Joelle said. "A planet without the united government or the firepower to enforce its control over the tramlines."

"That would be better, from our point of view, than having a single power in control of the system," the Prime Minister said. He shrugged, expressively. "Not that everyone will agree, of course."

Joelle considered it. "We can't claim rights of first discovery?"

"I don't think we can reasonably claim to have beaten the Vesy to their homeworld," the Prime Minister said, dryly. "Besides, it was a rogue Russian ship that stumbled over Vesy, not us. The Russians don't have the strength to back up their claim, but they're trying hard to leverage it to gain advantage elsewhere. I've been hearing rumours about them talking to the Turks and the Indians, perhaps even the Brazilians."

"The Indians have a colony in that direction," Joelle recalled.

"They do," the Prime Minister said. "It adds another problem to the morass."

He cleared his throat. "I'm assigning you as our Ambassador to Vesy and Special Representative to the other human powers active within the system," he explained. "You will have authority to open discussions with the Vesy and trade with them, although there will be some limits on precisely *what* you can offer. Ideally, you are to tie as many Vesy groups as possible into an alliance with us. We need influence on the planet's surface."

Joelle remembered the reports and winced. "We could just offer them weapons," she said, frankly. "It would make them our friends for life."

"I'd prefer not to supply weapons if it can be avoided," the Prime Minister said. "The Russians caused a great deal of problems for them, simply by introducing gunpowder. I would hate to see them trying a mass charge against machine guns or even soldiers armed with modern rifles. Their population might take a sharp drop."

"They will want weapons, Prime Minister," Joelle said, flatly. "It won't be unlike negotiating with groups in North Africa or the Middle East. Weapons come first, or they won't be able to hold on to whatever else they get."

"I know," the Prime Minister said. He looked her in the eye. "If you have no alternative, then yes; you may offer them weapons. However, it would probably look better if you offered them other items first. We have a list of possible options for you to consider, although - as the person on the spot - you will have to make the final call."

Joelle couldn't help feeling a flicker of excitement, mixed with apprehension. On Earth, she could call her superiors at any moment to get their approval; in deep space, she would be completely alone, unable to receive an instant answer to her messages. If she sent a message from Vesy to Earth, if she needed support, it would be months before she could receive a reply. Before then, the situation would probably have changed for the worse.

"Thank you, Prime Minister," she said.

The Prime Minister gave her a humourless smile. "You may want to wait before thanking me," he said. "This won't be an easy task."

He frowned. "In addition, you are to try to build a local agreement with any other human powers operating within the system," he continued. "Again, ideally, we want limits on tech transfer and a general understanding that the system is to remain neutral. I don't think anyone will accept the idea of limits, but I think there will be some support for leaving the system neutral in human politics."

"Because that would give us all access to the tramlines," Joelle said.

"Without having to pay," the Prime Minister agreed.

Joelle nodded, thoughtfully. The Tramline Treaty enshrined open passage through the tramlines, but agreed that whoever owned the system was owed a small fee from anyone who wanted to use the tramlines. However, precedent suggested that whoever owned the system had to be capable of policing their space before they could collect their fee. Terra Nova's inability to patrol space beyond its atmosphere was a constant headache for the diplomats, all the more so as other settlements within the system continued to grow. Sooner or later, Joelle considered, one of them would make a definite bid for system ownership - and marginalise Terra Nova once and for all.

"We could always try setting up a bank for them," she mused. "Have the fee saved until they're ready to access it for themselves."

"It's a possibility," the Prime Minister said. "But who would you trust to run it?"

"The Vesy themselves," Joelle said. It was the simplest solution. "They're not idiots, Prime Minister. We could educate them, couldn't we?"

"And what," the Prime Minister asked, "would that do to their society?"

He shrugged, then leaned forward. "You will be attached to a naval squadron being dispatched within a fortnight," he informed her. "You may choose your own staff - under the circumstances, I think that's the least we can do for you. The squadron CO will have orders of his own, but will generally follow yours as long as they don't put the ships into danger."

Joelle nodded. She would need to read the orders very carefully, then sit down with the CO and have a long talk. She'd known some naval officers who'd regarded diplomats as worse enemies than reporters; she hoped, grimly, that whoever was assigned to Vesy wouldn't be one of *them*.

"Good luck, Ambassador," the Prime Minister said, rising to his feet. "Your orders and supporting documents will be delivered to your office within the hour. I believe you will be invited to board the ship in ten days, but that will be confirmed. We'll try not to leave you behind."

"Thank you, Prime Minister," Joelle said, smiling at the weak joke. It *was* one hell of a challenge - and if she succeeded in hammering out an agreement everyone could live with, she would be able to write her own ticket. "I look forward to it."

CHAPTER
THREE

"Captain Naiser," the First Space Lord said, as John was shown into his office. "I trust you had a pleasant few days?"

"Sin City no longer lives down to its reputation, sir," John said. It was no surprise. The original Sin City had been destroyed during the Battle of Earth. "But at least no one recognised me there, thankfully."

"There is that, I suppose," the First Space Lord said. "Take a seat, please."

"Thank you, sir," John said.

He sat on the comfortable chair, resting his hands in his lap. The First Space Lord's aide appeared and offered tea or coffee, but John declined them both. He'd need all of his wits around him while talking to the uniformed head of the Royal Navy. The First Space Lord waited for the hatch to hiss closed behind his aide, then nodded politely to John.

"I understand that you were attending the simulated battles," the First Space Lord said, casually. "As someone who both flew starfighters and commanded capital ships, what did you make of them?"

John hesitated, thinking hard. Was the First Space Lord trying to break the ice, as if he *needed* to break the ice, or was it a genuine question?

"I think that both sides rigged the simulations in their favour," he said, finally. "The starfighter squadrons shouldn't be counted out just yet, sir."

"Explain," the First Space Lord ordered.

"Real life isn't the same as simulations," John said. "To be realistic, the simulation would need to account for sensor distortion caused by the plasma cannons, the loss of several cannons due to exploding plasma containment fields and the existence of various countermeasures to fuck… ah, *spoof* ECM. One simulation was, therefore, an idealized outcome for the point defence; the other was an idealised outcome for the starfighters."

He paused. "We may need to rely more on smaller carriers, perhaps armoured escort carriers, rather than the giant fleet carriers," he added, "while putting together superdreadnaughts of our own."

"The *Vanguard* project," the First Space Lord noted. "Admiral Soskice's pride and joy."

"Yes, sir," John said. He'd been asked to consult, during the months he'd waited in limbo for a decision on his future in the Royal Navy. "She's an impressive design, sir, but she will wallow like a pig in mud. And she would be alarmingly vulnerable to mass drivers, despite her improved armour. The Tadpole superdreadnaught wasn't perfect either."

"It still took a giant carrier ramming her to put her out of commission," the First Space Lord said. "Both ships were destroyed in the blast."

"Yes, sir," John said.

He felt a sudden stab of sympathy for the First Space Lord. The man was caught between the traditionalist and reformist parties; one wanting to adopt the latest shiny thing, the other wanting to stick with technology they knew worked. But both sides were wrong…keeping the balance between them couldn't be the easiest job in the world. It made him wonder just what would happen to the Royal Navy when the First Space Lord retired.

"But that is a minor issue at the moment," the First Space Lord said. He sat upright, elbows placed on the desk in front of him. "I didn't call you here to discuss the simulations - and how well they reflect real life."

John nodded. It was finally time to face the music.

"Good news first," First Space Lord said, briskly. "The World Court in Geneva has provisionally agreed that you are not culpable for anything the Russians did on Vesy, particularly before you ever knew there was such a world. Your own actions caused more doubt, but it has been generally agreed that you did the best you could under the circumstances. As such, you don't need to worry about either a court martial or war crimes charges from Geneva."

"Thank you, sir," John said, relieved. He hadn't worried about a court martial - any Captain's Court would have upheld his decisions - but the World Court was a political beast. Guilt or innocence wasn't a matter of fact, not when politics were involved. Someone in London might have had to do a great deal of horse-trading to ensure a favourable verdict. "That's good to hear."

"There were a couple of attempts to bring private prosecutions against you," the First Space Lord added, "but the House of Lords threw them both out. It helps, I suspect, that the image of the gallant space captain rescuing helpless women and children is so prevalent. They didn't want to convict a national hero."

John kept his mouth firmly shut. It was unlikely that anyone could successfully bring private charges against him for carrying out his duty, not when military officers were generally excluded from such proceedings. But it would be bad publicity for the Royal Navy and he suspected his superiors had privately breathed a sigh of relief when the decision was handed down. Having an NGO or charity try to convict him of meddling in alien affairs would be embarrassing.

"The Russians may want you to give testimony at the trial of the surviving renegades, John," the First Space Lord added, "but we would prefer to see you out in space as soon as possible, so they may be disappointed. In any case, there is more than enough evidence to convict them of desertion, breaking several treaties and causing the Russian Government a considerable amount of embarrassment, which is a shooting offense in Russia."

"Yes, sir," John said.

"I would still prefer you to remain on Nelson Base or Luna City until you return to your ship," the First Space Lord said. "The court rulings will probably not satisfy *all* of your new enemies, I'm afraid. At last report, the Society of Interstellar Brotherhood was offering a large reward for evidence that could be used against you, while the more militant wing of Earth First has publically condemned you for *not* bombing Vesy into radioactive ruins and exterminating the aliens before they could pose a threat. They will not be happy to hear about your new assignment."

John narrowed his eyes. "Can they prevent me from returning to Earth?"

"Probably not, but it will attract attention from the media," the First Space Lord said. "I authorised you to visit Sin City because the media is permanently banned from the complex, no matter the situation. Earth... it's quite likely you will be hounded as soon as you step out of a military base. I advise you to avoid that sort of attention."

John sighed inwardly, but nodded. The media had swarmed over him once before - the last survivor of HMS *Canopus*, before *Ark Royal* had returned with a captured alien battlecruiser in tow - and he hadn't enjoyed it, not even slightly. Now, with half the population considering him a hero and the other half demanding his immediate execution, it would probably be worse. Much worse.

"Yes, sir," he said, finally.

"Good," the First Space Lord said. "I'm afraid your next posting will make the Society of Interstellar Brotherhood even *more* pissed at you."

He smiled, rather thinly. "You may have heard that talks about keeping Vesy in strict quarantine have broken down," he continued. "The Russians tried to insist they had a claim to the system, the Indians flatly refused to honour an agreement that cut them out of a quicker route to their colonies, the French and Chinese started considering which way to jump...right now, in short, there is no legal barrier to anyone going to Vesy and trying to make contact with the natives. This is likely to be utterly disastrous for them, Captain."

"Yes, sir," John said. He'd *seen* Vesy - and he'd seen the damage caused by a handful of Russian-supplied weapons. Even if the Vesy were cut off from all further human contact, they knew how to make gunpowder and everything from basic muskets to cannons. The slaughter on their home-world would rise rapidly until their society managed to integrate the new weapons. "They don't need our encouragement to slaughter one another."

"It gets worse," the First Space Lord said. "The Brothers" - the Society of Interstellar Brotherhood - "were barred from trying to communicate with the Tadpoles. No one in their right mind wanted the Brothers lecturing the Tadpoles about how their reproductive systems are dangerously immoral, not when the Tadpoles could easily have won the war. It would be a really *stupid* reason to restart the war."

"Yes, sir," John said, again.

"However, it has made the Brothers more determined to approach the Vesy and start transferring technology to them," the First Space Lord warned. "Not all of the Brothers are keen to supply weapons, but medical science and building materials will do real damage to their society in the short term. The influx of human ideas and ideals will probably do worse damage. They're not human, they're not men in rubber suits, but I don't think the Brothers grasp that point. And they may succeed in turning the Vesy into a threat to humanity."

"Sir," John said doubtfully, "the Vesy aren't much more advanced than...than the Elizabethans. Even gunpowder was unknown to them five years ago."

"They will have the advantage of knowing that more is possible," the First Space Lord said, darkly. "Our most optimistic assessment suggests that the Vesy might start experimenting with primitive rockets in four hundred years, perhaps less. It would depend on just how much technology - and ideas - have already slipped into their system. If the Brothers actually start guiding the Vesy down the right path, they might get into space in a much shorter time."

"It seems unbelievable, sir," John said.

"We would prefer not to take chances," the First Space Lord said. "Unfortunately, with a lack of general consensus on the issue, it is impossible to prevent other nations from making contact with Vesy factions and working with them to take control of the entire planet."

He leaned forward. "You will return to *Warspite*, Captain, as CO of the squadron assigned to Vesy," he continued. "Unfortunately, this is something of a poisoned chalice. On one hand, you have orders to prevent cultural contamination, either with ideas or technology; on the other, you are required to support Ambassador Richardson as she makes contact with Vesy factions and attempts to woo them into an alliance with Britain."

John frowned. The only way to woo Vesy factions was to offer them more than anyone else, particularly to the factions which had little to no contact with humans prior to the arrival of *Warspite*. And they would want weapons to defend themselves before anything else, no matter what other goodies the humans could offer. Failing to give the Vesy weapons would practically throw them into the arms of other human powers, the ones less concerned with the long-term impact on the Vesy themselves. They would have no choice, but to act in self-defence.

And yet, handing over weapons and other goodies would *cause* cultural contamination…

"I don't see how we can balance the two requirements," he said, slowly. It seemed impossible to avoid it. "Mere contact with us will cause cultural contamination."

"I don't think you can either," the First Space Lord admitted. "Overall, we would prefer you to block the NGOs from setting up shop outside our direct control, Captain, but we concede that won't be easy. They think they have a mission and they won't let you stand in their way."

"So let them set up where they can be supervised," John mused. "Maybe ensure that they know they can talk to the Vesy, but if they give offense they can be yanked out at any moment."

He groaned, inwardly. The Vesy were aliens. Who knew *what* would cause offense? Hell, for all they knew, wearing pink shirts would be enough to trigger a declaration of war.

"Precisely," the First Space Lord said. "They want contact; they can have it, under supervision. That will make it harder for them to claim we're blocking them from talking to the poor helpless aliens."

John shrugged. "I saw them butchering one another with a fervour that would impress Genghis Khan," he said, tartly. "I don't think they're helpless."

"They might as well be, against orbital bombardment," the First Space Lord said. He sighed, meaningfully. "NGOs and the media aren't the only parties interested in going, John. The Vatican is sending a ship, as are a number of religious factions from America. Hell, the Archbishop of Canterbury is planning to dispatch a ship too. They hope to find new converts among the Vesy, it seems."

"Shit," John said, remembering the religious war the Vesy had been waging. Humans hadn't killed so many of their own kind in the name of religion since the Age of Unrest. "That's going to end badly, sir."

"Probably," the First Space Lord agreed. "The Vesy may take strong offense to being told they're worshipping false gods. And not all of the factions sending ships are trustworthy either, not now. They may start dropping thunderbolts from high orbit if the human god isn't worshipped at once."

He paused. "And the hell of it is that we have only limited authority to intervene," he added, darkly. "Try and get those factions to work from the base on the surface, Captain. It would make it easier to pull them out if the shit hits the fan."

"Aye, sir," John said. He had a sneaking suspicion he should have asked for the court martial instead. He'd escaped one session in front of the World Court, but he might not get so lucky the second time. "The Vatican would presumably have diplomatic immunity..."

"Presumably, but you have authority to override it if they're working from a British base," the First Space Lord said. "It will be a long time before *anyone* truly trusts the Vatican again."

John nodded, slowly. It wasn't his area of expertise, but he knew just how badly the Vatican had squandered a considerable amount of goodwill just before the Age of Unrest. There were still states that had laws allowing them to peer into the church's activities, just to make sure they weren't trying to cover up more sexual scandals and financial malpractice. Hell, there were laws in Britain allowing *any* religious group to be watched, if they seemed likely to pose a threat to the state. Being too trusting had led directly to the Troubles.

The First Space Lord tapped his keyboard, activating the holographic projector. "You will have *Warspite*, John, and a pair of older destroyers to serve as escort," he said. "The Ambassador and her staff will travel on *Warspite*, which will allow you to confer with her about the best way to proceed. Attached will be five freighters crammed with potential trade goods and prefabricated garrison components, as well as HMS *Stuart Tootal*."

John blinked. "I'm getting 3 Para?"

"And two additional sections of Royal Marines," the First Space Lord said. "Do try to keep them apart, when they're not on active duty. We can't afford to keep replacing the bulkheads when they start fighting."

He sighed. "I'd prefer to send more, Captain, but we have too many other commitments at the moment," he added. "The PM has been talking to the Americans and French about a local alliance, but the Yanks are having an election year and the French, as always, are playing their cards close to their chest. I'm pretty sure they're looking for ways to gain advantage in the coming proxy struggle for Vesy."

John nodded, grimly.

"If the shit hits the fan, try to secure the base on the surface and protect our personnel," the First Space Lord concluded. "Ideally...well, the PM wants free access to the tramlines, but little else. But we would prefer to avoid utterly shattering Vesy civilisation if it could be avoided."

"I doubt it, sir," John said. "They've seen too many changes in too short a space of time."

"We will see," the First Space Lord said.

He glanced at his datapad. "You're expected back on *Warspite* in two days, Captain," he added. "By then, your official orders will be cut, along with a set of sealed orders you are to open if the shit really *does* hit the fan. The ambassador will join you and your crew eight days later, giving you long enough to knock *Warspite* back into shape. Until then...go to Sin City or stay here, whichever one you please. I don't think we'll need you before you return to your ship."

"Aye, sir," John said. Returning to Sin City, finding a partner for a day or two and spending time in bed seemed a wonderful option. But, on the other hand, he knew he'd be worrying too much about the coming ordeal. Life had been much easier when he'd been a mere starfighter pilot. "I think I'd be better off reading papers and doing my research."

"There's a whole crew of researchers going with you to Vesy," the First Space Lord said. "They were trying to hire a luxury liner for the trip, I believe, rather than endure passage on a warship. Anyone would think they didn't like it."

"It is an acquired taste," John agreed, deadpan. He well remembered cramped quarters on HMS *Canopus*...although Colin and he had never complained. "I have been told it compares favourably to going to jail..."

"Not these days," the First Space Lord said.

John nodded. Prisoners these days were sent to work gangs, where they worked six days a week in the Reclamation Zones. It wasn't a pleasant task and the reoffending rate had dropped sharply, or so he'd been told. There just weren't the resources to keep prisoners penned up indefinitely, not any longer. The truly serious criminals were simply hung and then buried in unmarked graves.

"You'll find out soon enough, I wager," the First Space Lord said. "Good luck, Captain."

John rose, recognising the dismissal. "Thank you, sir," he said. "I won't let you down."

CHAPTER
FOUR

"There she blows, sir," the pilot said.

John nodded, leaning forward as HMS *Warspite* slowly came into view. She was definitely sleeker than the pre-war frigates and cruisers the human navies had used to picket systems and escort the giant fleet carriers, but her dark hull was studded with weapons and sensor blisters. She looked almost like a flattened arrowhead, he recalled, her dark armour providing protection against everything short of heavy plasma cannons or laser warheads. Or a direct nuclear hit. The heavy plasma cannon at her prow seemed to glow with deadly light.

"I can fly you around her, if you wish," the pilot said.

"I've already seen her," John said, a little wistfully. No matter how many times he was shuttled to *Warspite,* he would never see his command for the first time again. "Take us to the airlock."

The pilot nodded, then cut speed as the cruiser grew and grew until she dominated the horizon. John braced himself, half-expecting a collision, but there was only a dull thud running through the craft as the shuttle latched on to the airlock. He smiled to himself as he felt the gravity wobble, then rose to his feet as the airlock hissed open. It was impossible to escape the sense that he was coming home. He picked up his duffle bag, slung it over one shoulder and stepped through the airlock, back onto his ship.

"Captain," Commander Howard greeted him. "Welcome back."

"Thank you, Commander," John said. "And I congratulate you on your well-deserved promotion."

"Thank you, sir," Howard said.

John allowed himself another smile as they walked towards the bridge. He hadn't expected to be able to keep Philip Richards after they returned to Earth, not when his appointment as XO had only ever been temporary. But he had no doubts about Howard's competence - or, for that matter, of his ability to handle the crew. If nothing else, Juliet Watson should have been disqualified for her inability to discipline her subordinates.

"There's a full briefing for you in your terminal, sir," Howard said, "but basically we're at full fighting readiness. Armed and dangerous, ready for a scrap."

"We may need to be," John said. He'd spent two days reading intelligence reports and they'd all agreed that *everyone* was setting course for Vesy. Three British warships and a troop carrier wouldn't be enough to control the chaos, even if they held undisputed rights to the system. "And the new tactical officer?"

"I knew her from *Sidney Smith* as the assistant tactical officer, sir," Howard said. "She'll fit in well, I think. So far, her work on simulations has been perfect."

As long as she doesn't freeze up when she faces actual combat, John thought. He pushed the thought aside. He knew *Sidney Smith's* commanding officer and he wouldn't have allowed an incompetent onto his command deck. *She should do fine.*

"Weapons loads are complete, sir; one hundred percent," Howard continued. "The bureaucrats don't seem to have got in our way for once."

"Glad to hear it," John said. He sat down in his command chair and hastily reviewed his two private monitors, then looked up. "I relieve you."

"I stand relieved," Howard said.

He didn't look too happy, John noted. Being promoted alone had been a heady responsibility, but he'd been in effective command of *Warspite* for the last month. John wouldn't have blamed him for feeling a little resentment, not now someone else had come in and taken over command. But then, Howard *had* known that John was the ship's formal commanding officer. He'd just have to deal with it.

"We'll meet in my office for a proper chat in an hour," John said, after a moment. He'd need time to review the files to determine what, if anything, should be discussed. "Until then, is there anything that requires my urgent attention?"

"No, sir," Howard said. "Chief Engineer Johnston has gone to Nelson Base, but he's due back this evening. The remainder of the senior crew are currently embarked; I've provisionally scheduled a dinner meeting for tomorrow evening at 1800. We *are* currently lacking ten crewmen after they were hastily recalled to fill billets on *Theodore Smith*, but the Admiralty promised me that replacements would be found before our scheduled departure date."

John groaned. The war had left too many promising young officers and crewmen dead. It would take years to replace the dead; even now, five years after the war, the Royal Navy was still short on trained personnel. And getting newcomers just before they left could cause its own problems. It wasn't unknown for commanding officers to offload problem cases rather than do the paperwork to arrange for a court martial or dishonourable discharge. By the time *Warspite's* officers discovered the problem, they might be light years from Earth and unable to do anything about it.

"Make sure I see their files before they're transferred," he said, reaching for one of his personal displays. "Any problem children can be left behind, I think."

"Yes, sir," Howard said. He cleared his throat. "Midshipwoman Powell has requested a transfer to another ship, but so far no one has been willing to take her."

"We're too short of crew," John said. He didn't blame the poor Midshipwoman for wanting to leave. She'd been forced to serve as a steward, to all intents and purposes, which had slowed her career down considerably. And, even in this day and age, being unable to reach *Lieutenant* by twenty-five tended to suggest, very strongly, that the midshipman or woman was impossible to promote. "Suggestions?"

Howard nodded. "We have seven midshipmen, sir," he said. "Powell can be taken off the rota entirely, but the other six can handle the duties of a steward between them. Unless, of course, we can get a couple of dedicated stewards. We have to host the Ambassador and her party, after all."

"That's true," John agreed. "We should be able to take a pair of stewards with us, particularly if they're cross-trained in something useful. Put in a request at the Admiralty and see what you get."

"Yes, sir," Howard said. "This may cause problems in the bunks, of course."

"Tell them to suck it up," John ordered. He'd never been a Midshipman, but he'd had to deal with starfighter pilots being his equals one day and his superiors the next. It wasn't an uncommon problem. "They will be able to handle it, I am sure."

"Yes, sir," Howard said.

"And if they don't, point out that Midshipwoman Powell did *all* the work on our last cruise," John added. He looked down at the deck. "Speaking of which, find her something that will give her a chance at early promotion, should she do well."

"Yes, sir," Howard said, again. He hesitated, noticeably. "The only other issue is that Doctor Stewart has…issued a formal warning note that you haven't attended for your physical in the last seven months. He's insisting that you attend within the week or he will be forced to file a complaint with the Naval Medical Board."

John fought down the urge to grit his teeth. "You *have* pointed out to him that I was on Nelson Base for the last six months and I had a *full* physical when I returned to Earth?"

"Yes, sir," Howard said. "We all had the full physical."

He shuddered. John didn't blame him. It seemed impossible for anything dangerous to spread from the Vesy to humanity - and vice versa - but the Naval Medical Board hadn't been inclined to take chances. The entire crew had been checked and rechecked until the Board was satisfied that there was little risk of cross-species infection. Having a routine physical check seemed pointless, compared to an extensive session of being poked and prodded by the best doctors in the business. But it was also naval bureaucracy at its finest. Someone would notice that the ship's commander had no physical exam on file and demand explanations.

"I will see the doctor tomorrow, unless something comes up," John promised. He didn't have the time for a long battle with the Medical Board. "I'll let him know personally."

"Thank you, sir," Howard said. He paused. "With your permission, I have to review the latest tactical simulations..."

"I'll see you in an hour," John promised.

He settled back in his command chair and brought up the latest reports. Howard had done a good job of keeping everything in order, even though he'd probably been snowed under with work. Juliet Watson had been a poor record-keeper and Richards simply hadn't had the time to attend to paperwork. But Howard had done well for himself...John smiled coldly, then brought up the personnel reports and started to read. Everything looked as well as could be expected when half the crew was on leave at any one time.

As long as they stay active when we leave the system, he thought, opening the file containing his orders. Unusually, there were a distressing number of weasel words, rather than the curt sentences he was used to seeing. *Anyone could interpret these in any number of different ways.*

He sighed, then started to read carefully. It wasn't easy to follow the different lines of logic; the First Space Lord, if anything, had understated the problem facing him. He was to ensure that Britain secured a controlling interest in Vesy - or that the local system remained neutral, allowing free passage - but at the same time he was to prevent cultural contamination by anyone. And yet, he *also* had orders not to irritate the other human powers - or the Tadpoles, should they show interest in a third intelligent race. He checked through the intelligence reports, but found nothing to suggest the Tadpoles might be coming too.

They will know about the Vesy, he thought. The treaty that had ended the First Interstellar War bound both parties to share information on any other intelligent races that might be discovered. A note in the file stated that formal notification - and copies of the original reports from Vesy - had been sent six months ago, just after *Warspite* had returned home. *But will they want to do anything about them?*

He shook his head, then looked up as the hatch hissed open, revealing a short woman with red hair cropped close to her scalp. She blinked in surprise as she saw him, then hastily snapped to attention and saluted. John rose to his feet and returned the salute, taking a moment to study the officer closely. The uniform she wore marked her as a tactical officer, Howard's replacement.

"Captain," she said. "Lieutenant-Commander Tara Rosenberg, reporting for duty."

"Welcome onboard," John said. It *would* be her turn on watch, wouldn't it? *Warspite* might be operating with minimal crew while she waited in orbit around Earth, but Howard had clearly insisted that the senior crew still rotate watches. Good for him. "I'm Captain Naiser."

"I've heard a lot about you, sir," Tara said. She looked embarrassed, but pressed ahead anyway. "Is it true you actually went down to a planet and convinced a bunch of rebels to give up their hostages?"

John had to smile. "Something like that," he said. It was true enough, but the rebels had realised they'd backed themselves into a corner first. "We'll have a chance to talk properly later, Commander. You have the bridge."

Tara nodded and saluted, again. "Thank you, sir," she said. "I relieve you."

"I stand relieved," John said.

He stepped through the hatch and walked down to his cabin, located only five metres from the bridge. It had been left untouched since his departure - the air smelt faintly musty when he stepped inside - but it definitely felt like home. He glanced at an old picture of Colin he'd placed on the desk, then checked his appearance in the mirror and sat down at the desk. It was almost time for Howard to arrive, so he read through a handful of additional files before the XO tapped on the hatch.

"Come," John said.

Howard stepped into the cabin, looking amused. "I just received an update from Engineer Johnston," he said. "Apparently, he won't be back until tomorrow morning."

"I'm glad to hear it," John said. Howard sent him an odd look - clearly, he hadn't realised that Mike Johnston was attempting to court Juliet Watson - then schooled his face back into bland inoffensiveness. John concealed his own amusement and waved a hand at the sofa. "Please, take a seat."

"Thank you, sir," Howard said, as he sat down. "I understand you met Lieutenant-Commander Rosenberg?"

"She seems competent, judging by her record," John said. "But she only saw service towards the end of the war?"

"Yes, sir," Howard said. "There aren't that many experienced junior officers at the moment."

"Too true," John mused. "We really should work on bringing more mustangs into the ranks."

He sighed, inwardly. He wasn't *precisely* a mustang, but he knew that mustangs faced considerable hardships as they made the jump from being an enlisted crewman to an officer's billet. They were often more experienced than their fellows, who were normally quite a few years younger, yet they rarely fitted in socially. The Old Boy's Network that cast a long shadow over promotions boards didn't normally boost the careers of mustang officers. It was often considered preferable to assist a junior officer with the right connections.

"She did handle herself well, sir," Howard said.

"I know," John said.

He cleared his throat. "You seem to have done an excellent job," he added, "so thank you."

"Thank you, sir," Howard said.

"I also expect you to speak your mind," John added, after a moment. He tapped the datapad meaningfully. "I know that what gets written down isn't always the precise truth, but really...I do need your uncensored impressions of everything from the crew to our orders. It won't be held against you."

"Yes, sir," Howard said.

John met his eyes. "So tell me," he ordered. "Are there any problems I should know about that aren't in the reports?"

Howard looked back at him, evenly. "The only real problem I have, sir, is that the crew have grown alarmingly used to inconsistent first officers," he said. His voice was very flat. "Commander Watson largely left matters in the hands of department heads, who often didn't have the authority to deal with various problems; Commander Richards...ah, Senior Chief Richards...was a hands-on XO, but he often let himself get preoccupied with the small things, rather than the bigger picture. I therefore found myself dealing with officers who thought they had to handle problems themselves and crewmen who thought they could come to me with anything."

"Ouch," John said. He'd been an XO himself, but his predecessor had been a good man and a reliable officer. "How have you been coping with this problem, which - I note - has never been mentioned in the files?"

"I held a long meeting with the department heads shortly after our return to Earth and outlined what I expected them to do and what I expected them to forward to me," Howard said. "There was some dispute - they'd grown used to the extra authority - but I managed to handle it. I also spoke with the Senior Chief and worked with him to both maintain my distance and support crewmen who needed advice and a helping hand."

"Very good," John said. He'd discuss the matter with Richards later, he knew, but it *sounded* good. "What problems have the crew had?"

"The usual, sir," Howard assured him. "A couple of outbreaks of drunkenness, after alcohol was smuggled up from Sin City. A nasty little fight between two crewmen that put one of them in sickbay and the other in the brig; I've had them both handed over to the redcaps for long-term investigation and punishment. And one incident of a crewwoman using a hacked pleasure implant and nearly killing herself."

John winced. "How did you handle the drunkenness?"

"Both crewmen were put on punishment duty," Howard said. "I didn't feel they deserved to be busted, but they needed to feel some punishment for nearly killing themselves. The crewwoman has been remanded to Luna City for psychotic observation and evaluation. I don't think she will ever be able to return to active duty."

"Probably not," John agreed. He'd have to read the notes, but if someone was stupid enough to hack a pleasure implant it was quite likely they'd accidentally kill themselves. The crewwoman had been lucky, for a given value of luck. She might spend the rest of her life hopelessly addicted to the sensation of having her pleasure centres triggered, time and time again. "But keep an eye on it anyway."

"Yes, sir," Howard said. He paused. "Is this normal? I mean…all these problems…"

"They tend to get worse when we spend months at anchor, doing bugger all," John told him, flatly. "Crewmen are at their best when there's something to do; they're at their worst when they're stuck in the ship, while the pleasures of Sin City are only a shuttle flight away. It's why we try hard to keep them busy."

He shrugged, then glanced at the datapad. "I'm transmitting our orders to you," he added, after a moment. "We'll discuss the problems we will face later, once you've had a chance to read them. It won't be an easy mission."

"Yes, sir," Howard said. "I understand we will be transporting ambassadors."

"One ambassador and her staff," John said. "And we're going back to Vesy."

"Hopefully, no Russians this time," Howard said.

John snorted. "Maybe not," he said. He'd glanced at the orbital monitors while he'd been on Nelson Base. A number of ships had filed flight plans for Vesy - and several others had filed plans that were so vague that he suspected they too were heading to the newly-discovered alien homeworld. "But everyone else is coming instead."

CHAPTER
FIVE

As a child, Corporal Percy Schneider rather suspected he would have loved Fort Knight. It looked rather like a Wild West fort, complete with wooden outer walls, a handful of buildings just beyond the doors and a large Union Jack flying in the strange-smelling breeze. But, as an adult, he was grimly aware that Fort Knight wasn't particularly defensible against anything more dangerous than Braves on horseback. The ten Royal Marines - and thirty former Russian prisoners - wouldn't be able to put up much of a fight if the base came under attack.

But at least we could hold long enough to get the civilians out, he thought, although he knew the civilians wouldn't be able to stay away for long. Vesy was an *alien* world, without any safe places for runaway humans. *And we would make them pay for attacking us.*

He sighed, then walked towards the office they'd put together from prefabricated components borrowed from Pegasus. The Vesy themselves admired the prefabricated buildings, but they'd been happy to take a few trinkets in exchange for building wooden cabins and barracks for the human settlers. Percy had a feeling that the base would be expanded rapidly, once Earth heard about the existence of a second alien race; besides, paying the Vesy to help expand the facilities kept them sweet. He was all-too-aware that there would be no help from any other human faction if the base came under attack.

"Corporal," Platoon Sergeant Danny Peerce said, as Percy stepped up to the metal doorway leading into the office. "The miscreants are inside."

"Thank you, Sergeant," Percy said. "I'll chew them out personally."

"Just remember there aren't any replacements," Peerce warned. "You can't have anyone beached permanently - or dumped in the brig."

Percy nodded. They had an odd relationship; he might have been given command of the section, a ten-man team of Royal Marines, but Peerce outranked him - and had much more experience, to boot. And yet, the Sergeant seemed content to treat Percy as a promising young officer who needed mentoring, rather than an outright subordinate. Percy wasn't sure if his family name was working in his favour, or someone had seen promise in him he hadn't seen for himself, but it led to some awkward conversations. It would have been harder if he hadn't had a sneaking suspicion that Peerce was actually *enjoying* himself.

It must be nice to mentor an officer you can relieve if necessary, Percy thought, as he stepped through the hatch. *Normally, it wouldn't be so easy to get rid of an over-promoted upper-class twit.*

"Gentlemen," he said, as Peerce followed him into the office and closed the hatch behind him. "I trust you have an explanation for this?"

Private John Hardesty and Private William Oakley exchanged looks. "We thought we wanted to spice things up a little," Hardesty said, finally. "They wanted to learn what we were doing..."

"So you decided to teach the Vesy how to play Poker," Percy said. He had no idea if it was against regulations to teach aliens how to gamble, but he had a feeling it was probably covered by the non-interference edict. Except, of course, for the simple fact that the non-interference edict had already been smashed to pieces by the Russians. "And now the game is spreading through their society?"

"Yes, sir," Hardesty said.

Percy fought down the urge to rub his forehead in frustration. The hell of it was that there was very little to do on Vesy, besides standing guard and talking to the aliens. He couldn't spare the manpower to do building work, let alone exercises that might work off some of the growing boredom. And there certainly weren't any available women - or men - to chase. The former hostages were off-limits, even if they'd been interested. He didn't really blame the two for looking for something else to do.

"Do you know," he asked, "what this will do to them?"

"No, sir," Oakley said.

"Me neither," Percy said. "It could cause a great deal of damage - and not just to them!"

He groaned, inwardly. It was easy to see the Vesy getting into debt to a pair of humans - and trading gold or silver to pay off the debt. He'd heard tales of men stationed in the Middle East who'd wound up in real trouble after taking bribes from the locals. But it was also easy to see his men being corrupted and then manipulated into secretly passing information or technology on to the Vesy. What would a Marine do when he owed the aliens more than he could reasonably pay…and knew he would be in deep shit if his superiors ever found out?

"We are guests on their world," he added, sharply. "When you were gambling, what were you gambling for?"

"Chips," Oakley said. He sounded rather offended. "We weren't gambling for money, sir."

"And how long," Percy asked him, "would it have stayed that way?"

It hadn't been *that* long since he'd been a mere private himself. He still remembered gambling with his fellows on deployment…and how easy it had been to wind up in debt, once they moved from gambling with matchsticks to playing for real money. He'd learnt a sharp lesson after his first real game, when he'd been taken for a ride by an older and more experienced player. It could easily have ended badly, with him owing most of his salary to the cardsharp. There was one in every unit.

But eventually gambling for matchsticks loses its thrill, he thought, ruefully. *Because really, what's the point of playing for matchsticks?*

He pushed the thought aside and glowered at the pair of them. Peerce had been right, as always; there wasn't much he *could* do to them. They weren't on Earth, where they could be reassigned, or a starship where there was no shortage of miserable tasks to do for punishment duty. He needed them both on the walls, just in case the shit *did* hit the fan.

"You will *not* talk to the aliens, at least until I am relieved by superior authority," he ordered, coolly. "You will remain in Fort Knight. In addition, you will forfeit one week's pay as a reminder not to gamble with big green men. Do you accept my judgement?"

Hardesty opened his mouth. "Sir, I…"

Oakley elbowed him sharply, cutting off his friend's response. Percy silently blessed him; if the case had been heard by someone higher up the food chain, it was unlikely they would have gotten off so lightly. They *could* request an appeal to a superior officer, if they wished, but it would probably have gone against them. A superior might not be so inclined to understand the unique pressures of living on Vesy, surrounded by hordes of aliens who could turn nasty at any moment.

"We accept," Oakley said, quickly. "We won't have any further contact with the aliens."

"Glad to hear it," Percy said. He relaxed, slightly. "You *do* realise that we almost lost the Russian base when the aliens attacked? And that Fort Knight is *flimsy* in comparison?"

He waited for his words to sink in. None of them had any illusions about just how long they could hold out, even with modern weapons. They'd kill hundreds of aliens for every Marine, Percy knew, but they couldn't hope to replace the bullets they fired, while the aliens had almost unlimited weapons and manpower. The Vesy would just keep soaking up the bullets and pressing forward until they stormed the walls and over-whelmed the fort.

Or dig a tunnel underneath the base, he thought, sourly. *Or come up with a devious way of using our weapons against us.*

"We cannot take the risk of provoking them into attacking us," he added. "A fight over gambling debts could easily have gotten out of hand, leading to an outright battle we could only lose. Do you understand me?"

"Yes, sir," Oakley said.

"Yes, sir," Hardesty echoed, a little sullenly. "I understand."

"Then go," Percy ordered, nodding to the hatch. "I…"

There was a sharp tap at the hatch. Peerce opened it. "Mr. Fanwood?"

"I was hoping to speak to the CO," Fanwood said. He was a tall bald man, wearing a pair of trousers and little else. He'd been hastily assigned to Vesy from Pegasus, which had caused no end of problems as the engineers had been kitted out for sub-zero temperatures, not sweltering tropical heat. "I have a final report for him."

"Come in," Percy said. He glanced at Hardesty and Oakley. "Dismissed, gentlemen."

"Come with me," Peerce ordered. "Now."

Percy watched him lead the two miscreants out of the office, then turned to Fanwood. "What can I do for you?"

"We've got the generator and the last of the prefabricated buildings installed," Fanwood informed him, cheerfully. "Most of the crap we brought wasn't suited for an Earth-like planet, Corporal, but we managed to adapt it without problems. In addition, there's enough battery power and supplies to keep us going for at least two weeks."

Percy frowned. "I thought the idea was to keep us going for three."

"Rubbish," Fanwood said, in his best impression of Major Bloodnok. "Whoever heard of a Fort Knight lasting three weeks?"

"When I get my hands on the person who insisted that the *Goon Show* made suitable entertainment in the mess," Percy said, "I'm going to strangle him."

Fanwood snickered. "It's a terrible pun," he agreed. "More practically, however, there are limits to what we could bring from Pegasus. We may wind up dependent on food from the locals."

Percy groaned. The Vesy biochemistry wasn't entirely compatible with humanity's, something that really shouldn't have surprised him. Most of their food was safe to eat, but some tasted disgusting to humans and some was outright poison. It wasn't something he wanted to rely on, if it could be avoided, yet there were limits to how much could be recycled in the base. They might wind up buying food from the Vesy after all.

And if we do buy food from them, he asked himself, *what will they want in return?*

He was no diplomat. No one on the base was a diplomat, because no one had anticipated running into an uncontacted alien race. All he could do, when the aliens sent delegations to the base, was tell them that proper diplomats were on their way and that they would all be free to talk to them, when they finally arrived. But with different alien factions having different ideas about how to deal with humanity, it was going to be one hell of a mess by the time the diplomats arrived. Until then...

We don't have much we can trade to them, he added, mentally. *And anything we give them might wind up being used against us.*

Fanwood cleared his throat. "We might be able to start planting crops from Earth in the local soil, using the remains of the Russian farms, but it would probably have an impact on the local ecology," he said. "I'd prefer not to risk it here."

"I understand," Percy said. No one would shed any tears for a weak planetary biosphere, consumed and ruined by an influx of plants from Earth, but Vesy was another matter. Quite apart from the fact that crops from Earth might not take root properly, the ecological disaster they might cause would do untold harm to the Vesy themselves. "Didn't the Russians do any impact work?"

"I rather doubt they cared enough to bother, even if they had the ability to try," Fanwood said, darkly. "There's certainly nothing in their records to suggest they considered the impact on the local biosphere before scattering seeds into the fields."

"Probably not," Percy agreed.

He shook his head. "Is there anything else we can beg from Pegasus?"

"I doubt it," Fanwood admitted. "The base was intended to grow gradually, Corporal. They weren't given a surplus of supplies before the original founding mission departed Earth. It's risky even passing as much as they have to Vesy; no matter what else happens, the colony program has stalled until they get replacements. There's little else they can spare without risking their own lives."

"I understand," Percy said. "Their margin for error is growing alarmingly thin."

"Too thin," Fanwood agreed. "And Pegasus is even less habitable than Vesy."

Percy cleared his throat. "Thank you," he said. "You and your men will probably be uplifted when the freighter returns, but until then…"

"We were looking at ways to improve the local building industry," Fanwood said, cutting him off. "It wouldn't be hard to teach the Vesy how to make bricks and mortar, or even cement. We have quite a body of outdated knowledge in our files that they would treat as manna from heaven."

"I don't think that's a good idea," Percy said.

"You must admit they need it," Fanwood countered. "You've *seen* their living spaces!"

Percy nodded. He'd seen a hidden village, buried in the forest, and the interior of a giant city that reminded him of ancient ruins in Mexico. They'd both been filthy by human standards; the streets coated in layers of bodily wastes, despite the risks of disease, the Vesy themselves hardly bothering to wash when it wasn't raining heavily. The medics suggested their immune systems were stronger than the average human immune system, something they needed desperately. Their cities were breeding grounds for disease.

"It wouldn't be hard to show them how to build sewers," Fanwood continued. "Hell, the Romans had sewers! Or even just to build gutters and wash the shit out of their cities for good. Or…"

"That problem may take care of itself," Percy pointed out. "They know how to produce gunpowder now."

He held up a hand before Fanwood could say a word. "I understand your feelings on the matter, sir, and I will pass your suggestions to the diplomats when they arrive, but right now we are not meant to interfere in their affairs."

"We have already interfered," Fanwood snapped. "Our mere presence *here* is interference in their affairs!"

He was right, Percy knew. The buildings just outside Fort Knight didn't belong to a single city-state; they belonged to representatives from every city-state for a thousand miles and traders who had come to see what the humans had to trade. He'd told the Vesy they'd contacted first, months ago, not to interfere with the gathering of representatives, but he had a feeling it hadn't gone down very well. The factions who had aided the human race clearly believed they had first right to any rewards.

And if we weren't here, he thought, grimly, *they would be trying to kill each other by now.*

It wasn't a pleasant thought. Before the Russians had arrived, the Vesy had largely been grouped in city-states, not unlike Ancient Greece or Rome. The Russians, by arming a particular faction, had introduced the Vesy to the concept of *empire*…and, even after their defeat, several Vesy factions were trying to build their own empires. It was impossible to monitor the locals to any great degree - Percy didn't have the tools to keep an eye on them - but satellite observation revealed that a number of city-states were waging increasingly brutal wars against one another. The influx of tools, gunpowder and a handful of human weapons had only made the slaughter worse.

"I would suggest you make your representations to the diplomats," he said, curtly. "This isn't the time to do anything that might upset one of the factions."

"The factions might become upset because we haven't paid them for their services," Fanwood offered. "How do you plan to cope with that?"

Percy shrugged. The Vesy would have to be insane if they attacked Fort Knight...assuming, of course, that they comprehended the sheer scale of the Human Sphere. There was literally nothing they could do against a single destroyer raining rocks from high overhead, as *Warspite* had proven in the final moments of the first Human-Vesy engagement. But would they understand the danger? The further away the city-states were from the battle, the more their inhabitants would believe the reports to be exaggerated. They might not take the threat of retaliation from the stars seriously.

"There has to be something we can offer now, something that will keep them tranquil," Fanwood insisted. "Corporal..."

"The decisions involved are well above my pay grade," Percy said. He was surprised he'd been left on Vesy at all, rather than his immediate superior. And his orders were really nothing more than defend Fort Knight, look after the former hostages and wait for the diplomats - and reinforcements. "I have no intention of making a bad situation worse before the diplomats arrive."

"It's been six months," Fanwood said. "How long do you intend to stay here?"

Percy snorted. "I suppose we could always *walk* home," he said, sarcastically. "You could always invent surface-to-surface wormholes if you have nothing else to do."

He shook his head. "I knew we would be trapped here for months," he added. "We didn't really have a choice."

"Hah," Fanwood said.

He nodded to Percy, then turned and walked out of the hatch, closing it firmly behind him. Percy sighed, then looked back at his datapad, resting on the desk. He had reports to write, even though there was little to say. And, no matter what he said to Fanwood, there were times when he wondered if they'd been abandoned on Vesy. It shouldn't have taken more than a couple of months for a ship to arrive from Earth.

They're probably still bickering about what to do, he thought, as he picked up the datapad and started to type in his next report. *A whole new alien race…they have to see opportunities here. And while they're arguing, we're quartered safe out here.*

He shook his head. Whatever else could be said about Fanwood, the man was right about at least one thing. Vesy might not remain safe for very long.

CHAPTER
SIX

"Rather cramped, isn't it?"

Ambassador Joelle Richardson did her best to ignore Grace Scott's comment as she followed the young midshipman into the Officer's Mess. HMS *Warspite* was small, compared to the fleet carrier she'd travelled on during a brief visit to Tadpole-Prime, and her quarters were correspondingly tiny. Joelle didn't particularly care - she'd slept in worse places - but some of her staff had been moaning and groaning ever since they'd seen the small compartments they were expected to share.

The Officer's Mess didn't look any larger than her office on Earth, although it was a great deal more barren. Each of the bulkheads was painted white - one held a painting of *Warspite* that, she assumed, had been done by one of the crew - and the table was plain metal, covered in white paint. The idea of hosting a diplomatic discussion in such surroundings was laughable, although she had a feeling that it would help the diplomats to come to a quicker resolution. Or, the more cynical part of her mind suggested, start them issuing declarations of war.

"Ambassador Richardson," a voice said. She looked up to see the Captain rising from his chair and walking around the table to greet her. "I'm sorry I didn't get a chance to meet you earlier."

"That's quite all right," Joelle assured him, taking his hand and shaking it briskly. Her staff had complained, loudly, but she knew from prior experience that starship crews had a great deal of work to do before their ships could depart. "It's easier to get settled in before we meet formally."

She studied the Captain with some interest as she let go of his hand. He was tall, his dark hair cropped close to his scalp, his face lined in a manner that reminded her of far too many other combat veterans. His piercing blue eyes would have been attractive, she suspected, if she hadn't sensed a single-minded purposefulness surrounding him. The dark uniform he wore showed off his muscular body to best advantage.

And he went down to a planet to confront rebels in person, she thought. The media had made much of it, even though a number of talking heads had condemned Captain Naiser for leaving his ship in an emergency situation. *This is a brave man.*

"Please, be seated," the Captain said, indicating a row of chairs. "We took the liberty of having food shipped up from Earth."

"Thank you," Joelle said. She sat, facing a dark-skinned officer who regarded her with curious eyes. "It's been far too long since I was on a starship."

She indicated her party as the Captain returned to his chair at the head of the table. "Grace Scott, my assistant; Colonel John Mortimer, Security Expert; Professor Scott Nordstrom of Edinburgh University, Xenospecialist; Penny Schneider, embedded reporter."

The Captain's eyes narrowed at Penny's name, but he said nothing. Joelle puzzled over it for a long moment, then remembered Penny telling her that her brother had been assigned to *Warspite* and then left behind on Vesy, in charge of the garrison there. Later, Joelle had looked it up and confirmed that the Schneider children, born to a war hero and then adopted by another war hero with excellent aristocratic connections, were destined for a glittering future. It was probably why Penny had won the coveted post of embedded reporter, despite her youth.

"I read your paper on the implications of contact with the Vesy," Captain Naiser said to Professor Nordstrom, once he'd introduced his crew. "It was quite provocative."

"Thank you, Captain," the Professor said. "Unfortunately, I was not permitted to interview you before writing my paper."

"There's little to add that didn't go in the reports," the Captain said. "They're not human, really, and that's the important issue."

Joelle nodded. "We have some experience with non-human minds already, Captain," she said. "The dangers have been noted and logged."

"And we have more space for mistakes," Colonel Mortimer added. "The Vesy, quite simply, do not pose a threat to us."

"Not physically," Professor Nordstrom said. "However, it cannot be denied that contact with them may do us considerable social and political damage."

Joelle smiled, rather ruefully. "Captain, can I suggest we eat first? We'll be here all night if he starts to discourse on the dangers."

"Of course," the Captain said. He signalled a steward, who came forward pushing a large trolley of soup bowls. "We can stay here all night afterwards, if you wish."

The soup tasted faintly of carrot and coriander, Joelle discovered, as she sipped it thoughtfully and studied the crew. Commander Howard - she'd taken the precaution of skimming through the personnel files during the flight to *Warspite* - looked calm and composed, while - beside him - Lieutenant-Commander Rosenberg appeared to be bored, although she was doing a good job of hiding it. Joelle couldn't help a flicker of sympathy; she'd always hated ceremonial dinners as a junior representative, when she'd been too junior to be allowed to talk, but too senior to be left in her quarters. Beyond her, the Chief Engineer had finished his soup and was muttering quietly to an officer she didn't recognise. The stewards removed the soup bowls as soon as they were finished, then started to bring out the next set of dishes. They might have lacked the polish of the Foreign Office's catering staff, she noted absently, but they were efficient.

"That tasted better than I expected," Grace muttered.

"Remind me to discuss the definition of diplomacy with you later," Joelle muttered back. It had been a long time since she'd tasted military food, but she didn't remember it with any fondness. "They brought this up from Earth for us."

Grace looked embarrassed, which faded quickly as she dug into her roast beef and Yorkshire pudding. It wasn't something the average person on Earth would enjoy very often, not now; Joelle couldn't help a twinge of guilt as she recalled that rationing was still in place over large tracts of Britain. Hell, one of the reasons more and more people were emigrating to Britannia or Nova Scotia was that there was no rationing there, as well as more room to breathe. It probably wouldn't last indefinitely, she was sure, but there were definite advantages to getting in on the ground floor.

"This is very good," she said, addressing the Captain. "Your crew are excellent cooks."

"Thank you, Ambassador," the Captain said. "Turning military rations into something edible requires an above-average cook."

Joelle had to smile as she finished her dinner, then allowed the stewards to take it away and bring a large pot of tea. There would be no coffee tonight, not if she wanted to sleep. The sooner she got used to sleeping on the cruiser, the better. It was something she'd learned from her mentor, back when they'd travelled to Tadpole-Prime.

"I don't see how contact with the Vesy could cause political damage to us," Commander Howard said, once the dishes were cleared away. "Professor?"

Professor Nordstrom cleared his throat. "If you will pardon a slight digression," he said, "all human affairs are governed by strength. A stronger...ah, *person* could have his way with a weaker person, no matter how his victim felt about it. Internationally, a stronger nation can get what it wants from a weaker nation, as they have the strength to impose their will."

He took a breath, then leaned forward. "There was a period in human history where we preferred to pretend that wasn't true," he continued. "We tried to convince ourselves that it was immoral for strong countries to pick on weaker countries...and then that the strong country was *always* in the wrong. The Age of Unrest was a direct result of our failure to ensure that weaker countries knew, if you will pardon the expression, their place. They believed themselves immune to punishment because the strong chose to bind themselves with their own decency."

"The strong picking on the weak is called bullying," Commander Howard said, dryly.

"Yes, but only if the victim doesn't deserve it," Professor Nordstrom said. "If a weaker country is hosting a terrorist camp that poses a threat to a stronger country, is it bullying for the stronger country to destroy the terrorist camp, no matter where it is located?"

He shrugged. "It is important to note," he warned, "that the Vesy are primitive compared to us. There will be a very strong temptation to use force to get what we want from them."

Joelle couldn't disagree. She'd worked in both gunboat diplomacy - practiced against countries that were too weak to pose a threat - and actual diplomacy with the Great Powers, where outright conflict would probably result in mutual annihilation. There was no patience for negotiating with weaker countries, countries inhabited by people too stupid to realise the true cause of their problems. If they caused trouble, they got walloped. It had been the way of things since the Age of Unrest had swept aside a great many illusions.

"This leads to a second point," Professor Nordstrom added. "There is a tendency amongst a certain kind of people to believe that the wiser folks should act as parents to the unwise folks - and you should have no doubt in which category they place themselves. They see themselves as the parents and everyone else as the children - and, in doing so, assert the right to dictate how people live their lives. Indeed, before the Age of Unrest, there were entire organisations and charities that, with the best of intentions, set out to inflict their so-called wisdom on so-called primitive societies. The results were rarely pleasant."

He met Howard's eyes. "The weaker societies were often devastated by the influx of bad wisdom," he said. "But the stronger societies lost the wisdom to *question* the rightness of their actions. Being charitable was seen as a good thing in itself; there was no awareness that charity had to be tailored to local requirements or that the ultimate intention needed to be weaning the weaker societies off charity. There was no feedback system that allowed them to actually measure the success of their acts. Nor did they have any real understanding of the societies they were trying to improve. Their...*idealised* view of the locals prevented them from actually understanding them.

"In short, they acted like bad parents, alternatively scolding the child and preventing him from having to face the consequences of his mistakes."

"They believed in the concept of the noble savage," the Captain said, slowly.

"Precisely," Professor Nordstrom said.

He looked down at his cup of tea, then back at the Captain. "We could teach the Vesy so many things, Captain," he said. "But they would grow into cheap copies of us, at best, with all the virtues of their society destroyed. And we would see that as a good result, so we would not hesitate to do the same to another alien race, should we encounter one."

Grace snorted. "But why should we leave them in squalor?"

Joelle smiled, inwardly. She'd picked her staff for their differing ideas in the hopes it would give her multiple different viewpoints...and, it seemed, she'd succeeded magnificently.

"They can always get themselves out of squalor," Professor Nordstrom pointed out, dryly.

"They can't," Grace said. She took a breath. "If the reports are accurate, life on Vesy is nasty, brutish and short. We could make their lives so much better simply by introducing a few ideas and concepts to them. Don't we have a moral duty to assist those less fortunate than ourselves?"

"But how long would it be," the Professor asked, "before you started telling yourself that you always knew better than them? That you knew what was good for them and anyone who disagreed was merely being short-sighted?"

Grace glowered at him. "If I see a child living in squalor, it would be my duty to help," she said, flatly. "Does that change when the child isn't human?"

"You might be taking a child away from loving parents," the Professor pointed out. "Or you might be committing yourself to look after the child for the rest of your life."

He paused. "I understand your argument," he admitted. "There is a certain emotional impulse to help the less fortunate. But, at the same time, we have to be careful what we teach them to do. Simple measures against disease, as you suggest, would cause a population boom, which in turn would put a strain on their ability to feed their people."

"And an expanding population might start waging war on its neighbours for living space," the Captain said, quietly. "Your decision to cure diseases for them might kill more people, in the long run, than the diseases."

"It happened," Professor Nordstrom said. "There were other problems caused by meddling in purely *human* affairs. One problem that repeated itself, time and time again, were attempts to feed the hungry by shipping in food from more productive countries. Would you like to guess what happened?"

He went on before anyone could answer. "In some cases, the food was seized and used to feed armies," he answered his own question. "But in others, it completely destroyed the profit motive for producing food *locally*. And so, when the outsiders lost interest in supplying food, there was no one there to take up the strain and the entire population plummeted sharply."

"But we have to *try*," Grace insisted. "You're saying it's immoral to interfere, while I'm saying it's immoral *not* to interfere."

"We would need to let their society adapt to each new introduction," Professor Nordstrom said, bluntly. "However, it wouldn't be too long before we were trying to steer their society ourselves, without regard for what *they* wanted. And that leads to another problem."

Joelle had to smile. "Another problem?"

"A more serious problem," Professor Nordstrom told her. "When you were a child, your parents looked after you, helped you through your problems and disciplined you when you were naughty. They cooked for you, cleaned for you and ensured you never had to face any *real* long-term consequences for bouts of random naughtiness. Being a child isn't really like being an adult.

"Now tell me; would you *enjoy* having someone treat you as a child, now, or would you resent it bitterly?"

He was right, Joelle knew. It had been a long time since she'd fled the nest, and she still loved and honoured her parents, but she wouldn't want them running her adult life. The thought of being told what to do and what not to do at thirty years old was thoroughly unpleasant. If her parents *had* been able to control her life, she knew she would have resented their meddling bitterly. Hell, she'd resented them telling her what to do at *thirteen*.

"The Vesy may be primitive, but they are not children," Professor Nordstrom continued. "I've said that time and time again, to everyone who will listen; they are not stupid and they will resent us trying to steer their development into something we would consider civilised. It doesn't matter what intentions we have, it doesn't matter how much we know that they don't; they will hate and resent us for everything we do for them. And that hatred may eventually find expression."

He looked around the compartment, warningly. "And how long will it be until we start regarding them as children? One does not *hate* children. One does not subject children to adult punishment. But one does not consider children mature and responsible either."

"And so they will rise up against us," Captain Naiser said.

"They need time for their society to adapt to meet ours on a more equal basis," Professor Nordstrom said. "I don't think they're going to get that time, not when so many other parties heading to Vesy."

"Their society might improve," Grace said. "We could warn them of the dangers…"

"There were a number of countries in Africa that were granted access to sex-selection pills for their children," Professor Nordstrom said. "Those countries were inhabited by people who were culturally inclined to favour male children. They knew the dangers, but they used the pills anyway… and, thirty years later, fought a series of brutal civil wars over access to women. We could wind up giving the Vesy comparable problems."

"Then we do our best to come to terms with the other nations," Joelle said. "We may be able to place limits on what can be shared with the Vesy."

"It won't work if one party refuses to uphold the limits," Professor Nordstrom said. "Smugglers were quite happy to ship pills to Africa after the international charities were formally banned from supplying them."

"We can prevent smugglers from shipping anything to Vesy," Joelle said, flatly. She gave the Captain a long look. "We need to discuss the matter later, if you don't mind."

The Captain nodded. "I will be happy to meet with you when I'm not on duty," he said. "Leave a note in my inbox and I will get back to you."

Joelle nodded. She had a private suspicion that the Captain would set the meeting time to suit himself, but it hardly mattered. It was hard to blame him for resenting her and her staff for clogging up his ship.

She finished her mug of tea, then rose. "With your permission, I will seek my bunk," she added. By custom, once she was gone the others could leave too, if they wished. She had a feeling that the Professor would stay and chat with the officers, while Grace would probably seek out her own bunk. God alone knew what Penny would do. "I'll speak to you once we're underway."

"Of course, Ambassador," the Captain said. He rose, too. "And thank you for your company tonight."

See if you still like me after we start working together, Joelle thought, ruefully. *It won't be easy.*

CHAPTER
SEVEN

"Miss Schneider would like an interview," Howard said, as John came onto the bridge and took command. "She actually sent three messages, each one with the same request."

John had to smile. It would be quite awkward when her brother found out she was on the ship, let alone what she'd been doing. "What did you tell her?"

"That you were too busy making preparations for departure," Howard said. "I think she will probably start bombarding you with requests, again, once we leave."

John sat down in the command chair and checked the status display. *Dashing* and *Daring* had taken up position on each side of the freighters, while *Tootal* was holding position just in front of them. She wasn't exactly a warship, John reminded himself, but she could give any pirate ship a nasty surprise if one dared to attack her. But then, even the *thought* of piracy had seemed absurd until recently. How could anyone afford to keep a pirate ship running while raiding worlds and ships on the edge of explored space?

The Russians did it, he thought, sourly. *But their ships were breaking down well before we caught them.*

"Tell her that I will make time for an interview once we pass through Terra Nova," he said, finally. "I've really been interviewed too many times in the last six months."

"Yes, sir," Howard said.

John settled down in the command chair, then inspected the list of updates from Nelson Base. The small squadron was cleared to depart, on schedule, with a hint that if they could leave earlier the Admiralty would be pleased. They were fully provisioned, ready to take the quick route to Vesy, while a handful of other ships would take the longer route. It was irritating that the handful of interstellar liners couldn't use alien-grade tramlines - it meant he had to endure having the Ambassador and her staff on his ship - but there was no way around it. Nothing smaller than a fleet carrier could jump a liner through a tramline…

He pushed the thought aside and glanced at the crew readiness reports. "The replacements arrived onboard?"

"Yes, sir," Howard said. "They seem to be fitting in well, based on one day of active service."

"Keep an eye on them," John ordered. He cleared his throat, then looked at the communications console. "Lieutenant Forbes, transmit a Prepare to Depart signal to the convoy, with a baseline tag of ten minutes."

"Aye, sir," Lieutenant Gillian Forbes said. "Signal sent."

John nodded in acknowledgement. Lieutenant Forbes had spent the last five months grappling with the Vesy language database the Russians had amassed and, while no human could speak the language properly, she was sure she could understand Vesy-One. No one, not even the Russians, were sure if there were other languages on the planet or not, although John was inclined to suspect there were. The Roman world had been far smaller than an entire planet and they'd spoken dozens of different languages. But they'd also had Latin as a common language…

He shook his head. No doubt they'd find out when the small army of researchers went to work on Vesy.

And it lets us keep control, he thought, with some amusement. *We can deactivate automatic translators and voders if necessary.*

"They've acknowledged," Lieutenant Forbes informed him. "They're powering up their drives now."

John nodded, feeling a spark of genuine excitement. It wasn't quite the same as taking *Warspite* into the unknown - he couldn't help feeling a twinge of guilt at not having completed the survey of local stars and tramlines around Pegasus - but there was definitely *something* about taking his small squadron away from Earth. He, not the Admiralty, not the Prime Minister, not even the King himself, would be in command, master of his squadron. It was a heady responsibility, but one he enjoyed. There was nothing quite like it as a starfighter pilot.

But you had other entertainments, he reminded himself. *You could spend your time off-duty shacked up with Colin and no one gave a damn.*

The thought caused him a flicker of pain. It had been five years since the war, five years since Colin had been blown to bits by the Tadpoles... and his loss still hurt. It sometimes made him wonder if there was something wrong with him, when most starfighter pilots moved from love interest to love interest with nary a qualm. Or maybe it had just been love...hell, they'd talked about finding a home together when the war came to an end. Not, in the end, that it had mattered. Colin had died and John had been unable to even *think* of staying on as a starfighter pilot. It felt too much like a betrayal.

He cleared his throat. "Mr. Howard," he said. "Ship's status?"

"All systems are nominal, Captain," Howard said. "We are ready to depart on your command."

"Lieutenant Forbes, send a signal to Nelson Base," John ordered. "Inform them that we are departing on schedule."

"Aye, sir," Gillian said.

John sucked in his breath, feeling a dull thrumming echoing through the hull as the main drives came online. This time, there would be no problems; this time, everything had been checked and rechecked twice by different officers. If there was another criminal gang operating within the bowels of his ship, it would have been forced to pull in its horns or be mercilessly exposed to the cold light of day. This time, he would not suffer the humiliation of having his starship drifting helplessly through space, an easy target for anyone who wanted to pick off a cruiser without risk.

And the pirates taught us that there are still threats out there, he thought, bitterly. *And the Tadpoles may restart the war if they feel we are still a threat to them.*

It wasn't a comforting thought. The Russians hadn't been particularly forthcoming on the question of just how many ships might have gone rogue and it was quite possible there were more deserters out there. There were a number of Russian ships unaccounted for, according to MI6, but the chaos of the Battle of New Russia had probably concealed their destruction from prying eyes. And the Russians were not the only ones who had lost ships. John had been told, in confidence, that a review of the available records suggested that upwards of seventeen ships from other interstellar powers remained unaccounted for.

We should have asked the Tadpoles for their records of the battle, he thought. *But no one really wanted to open that particular can of worms.*

"Course laid in, sir," Lieutenant Carlos Armstrong reported. "We're on a least-time course to Vesy."

John leaned back in his command chair. "Lieutenant Forbes," he said, "order the other ships to follow us."

"Aye, sir," Gillian said.

"Helm, take us out," John added.

Another dull quiver ran through the ship as she came to life, slowly heading out of orbit and into the open space beyond. John watched the holographic display carefully, silently counting the number of starships leaving Earth. The swarm of giant colonist-carriers he recalled from *Warspite's* first departure hadn't slowed at all; indeed, it had only grown more frantic. Hundreds of thousands of people were leaving the planet each month, hoping to set up a home somewhere well away from Earth. The human race would no longer have most of its eggs in one basket.

And if we'd lost Earth, we would have lost the war, John thought, grimly. *Most of our population and industrial base would be gone.*

He caught sight of one icon and frowned. The Indians had refused to join the British Commonwealth, when it had reasserted itself during the Age of Unrest, and they'd been held back by their determination to make their own way into space, but they were catching up now. INS *Viraat* was large enough to pass for an American fleet carrier, although her commissioning had been delayed when the Indians had obtained the formula for heavy ablative armour and coated her hull for additional protection. Not that John particularly blamed them, he had to admit. The Battle of New Russia had taught the human race that lightly-armoured carriers were nothing more than easy targets for the Tadpoles, who had casually wiped out seven such ships in the battle.

She could almost pass for Theodore Smith, he thought, recalling the first of the post-war British carriers. She'd entered service only the previous year and was still working up, along with her two sisters. *All she would need is more armour and more heavy weapons.*

He sighed, inwardly. Beyond her, there were hundreds of other warships, belonging to twenty different human powers. No one would take the risk of leaving Earth undefended, not after the bombardment; no one, not even the powers that refused to cooperate with their neighbours outside the Solar System, would ignore the Solar Treaty. If someone tried to challenge humanity over its homeworld, every spacefaring power would react...

And if we do have a clash with someone outside the Sol System, he thought, *it won't be allowed to spread here.*

"Captain," Howard said. "All systems are functioning at acceptable levels."

"Good," John said. He wouldn't be *entirely* happy until they'd jumped through the first alien-grade tramline - that had been when disaster had struck, months ago - but it was a relief to know that everything seemed to be working properly. Some problems only showed themselves when the ship was actually underway. "And the squadron?"

"They don't seem to be having any difficulty keeping up with us," Howard said.

Armstrong coughed. "We could move faster, sir."

John shook his head, even though he knew Armstrong couldn't see him. "I think we need to stick with them," he said, dryly. "Keep an eye on the convoy and inform me if there are any problems."

"Yes, sir," Howard said.

"And remind the crew that we are approaching the Last Line," John added. "If they want to send any messages home, they won't have another chance for a few weeks."

"Yes, sir," Howard said, again.

John glanced at his display, then shrugged. There wasn't anyone on Earth he cared to send a message to, not now. His parents had always disapproved of his career choice, while his sister had swallowed the wrong line of propaganda and assumed that John was responsible for killing hundreds of aliens. Given that they'd been trying to kill his men at the time - and killed or enslaved hundreds of thousands of their own kind - it wasn't something that would keep him up at night.

Instead, he looked at the final set of intelligence reports from MI6. Hundreds of starships were on their way to Vesy, although - as most of them were incapable of using alien-grade tramlines - it was quite possible the squadron would beat most of them to the planet. At that point...he cursed under his breath as he recalled his orders. He'd asked the First Space Lord for clarification, but the Admiral hadn't been able to give him any. There was too much risk of being unable to maintain the balance between the two political factions in the Royal Navy.

Life was so much easier when we were fighting the war, John thought, morbidly. *At least we knew who the enemy was, back then.*

"Captain," Armstrong said. "We will make transit in ten minutes."

"Inform our guests," John ordered. It was rare for a Royal Naval crewman, at least one on active service, to have a bad reaction to the transit through the tramline, but sometimes a vulnerable civilian wouldn't be noticed until they made the jump. "And tell the doctor to stand by, just in case."

He groaned, inwardly. As always, the ship's doctor had been distressingly thorough when he'd poked and prodded at John, even though his sensors could have told him most of what he'd picked up by touch. John knew he wasn't the only crewman to dread physical exams - it seemed to be common throughout the Royal Navy - but there was no point in complaining. It was laid down in regulations and no one, not even the ship's commander, was spared.

"Aye, sir," Howard said.

The Ambassador has been out-system before, John thought. *So has Professor Nordstrom - he was one of the researchers who went to Heinlein, where humans and Tadpoles are trying to live in harmony. But what about the others?*

He cursed under his breath. There simply hadn't been time to review *all* of the files.

"Tramline in five minutes," Armstrong reported.

"Lieutenant Forbes, transmit all final messages in the buffer," John ordered. Any other messages would be stored, at least until *Warspite* encountered a homeward-bound starship on her cruise. "Attach our final status report, then close communications."

"Aye, sir," Gillian said.

John forced himself to relax. It always felt nerve-wracking approaching a tramline, even one as well-known as the link between Earth and Terra Nova. He knew, intellectually, that there was no real chance of a collision, or a hostile force waiting on the far side, but emotionally it was hard to believe. He'd earned his wings just after the war began, after all, and both sides had tried to ambush the other as they'd jumped through the tramlines.

"Tramline in one minute," Armstrong said. A timer appeared on the display, counting down the seconds. "Transit in five...four...three... two...one..."

John braced himself. The universe dimmed, just for a second, then returned to normal. But the display had blanked out and was hastily reformatting itself as the ship's sensors sucked in data from all over the Terra Nova system. Hundreds of icons flickered into existence, marked with warning messages that indicated that they might have changed position before the emissions from their drives reached *Warspite*. It might have been just his imagination, but it looked as though Terra Nova was seeing *less* organised activity these days. The miners might have decided to head to the newer colony worlds to try their luck there.

It would be hard to blame them, he thought, coldly. Terra Nova had been a mistake from the start, when so many different groups were settled in close proximity and expected to get along; their feuding factions had only recently been taking their dispute into open space, as if they wanted to convince the interstellar powers to intervene. *This isn't a safe place to live.*

"Transit complete," Armstrong reported.

I noticed, John thought. He didn't say it out loud. Regulations insisted that Armstrong had to make his report, even if it was easy to tell if the jump had completed or not. *And nothing went wrong, this time.*

He keyed his console. "Engineering?"

"Puller Drive is powering down, Captain," Mike Johnston reported. He'd sounded more cheerful over the last two days. It had been so obvious that John had a quiet suspicion he'd gotten lucky on Nelson Base. "All power curves are nominal."

"Good," John said.

"I'd like to run a handful of additional tests, just to be sure," Johnston added. "Do you mind...?"

"Not at all," John said. After what had happened the last time they'd left Earth, he would happily have underwritten any number of tests while they were still in an inhabited star system. "We will make our next transit in" - he glanced at the display, running through the calculation in his head - "nine hours."

"Plenty of time," Johnston said. "Engineering out."

John nodded, then looked at Howard. "Start running tracking exercises," he ordered, flatly. "I want to know everything we can about everyone in the system by the time we leave."

"Aye, sir," Howard said. It would be good practice for when they arrived at Vesy, they both knew. They'd have to watch for smugglers entering through the tramlines, as well as rogue miners and others who might try to stake a claim to the system. A human population within the Vesy System would cause no end of legal problems. "I'll get the tactical crew right on it."

John nodded, then checked his inbox. They should have received an update from the Royal Navy's guardship, but it was really too early to expect one. It would probably be at least four hours before one was transmitted, assuming the guardship even saw *Warspite* and her convoy arriving. Instead, he rose to his feet. There was no shortage of paperwork he had to do in his office, now they were on their way.

"Commander Howard, you have the bridge," he said. "Inform me once the guardship sends us the intelligence packet."

"Aye, Captain," Howard said.

John stepped through the hatch into his office, then shrugged off his jacket and sat down at the metal desk. He was mildly surprised he hadn't been urged to give up his cabin to the ambassador, even though it wasn't really much bigger than the VIP quarters, but it would have been inconvenient. The office might have been *his*, yet his XO and several other crewmen were expected to use it from time to time. *Warspite* simply didn't have the hull volume to give *everyone* an office.

And I wouldn't trade you for a full-sized fleet carrier, he thought, rubbing the bulkhead affectionately. Not that he'd *get* a fleet carrier, unless he was *very* lucky. It had been sheer luck - and a certain amount of expendability - that had earned him *Warspite*. *You're far more nimble than any wallowing pig of a carrier.*

He tapped his terminal, snorted in annoyance as he realised there were several *more* requests for an interview from Penny Schneider, and then a message from the Ambassador. *She* wanted a meeting too, over dinner. John couldn't decide if she thought that food would make the ideas flow better, or if she reasoned she'd have a better chance of catching him if she asked him to dinner. She had to know he wouldn't have much free time.

Sighing, he keyed out a reply to both women and then went to work.

CHAPTER
EIGHT

"Tell me something," Grace Scott said, as John stepped into the ambassador's cabin. "Are your quarters any larger than this?"

"Only by a couple of square meters," John said, dryly. He'd met too many people like Grace Scott before, men and women who thought it was their job to be offended on their principal's behalf. "*Warspite* is a cruiser, not a fleet carrier."

Grace looked unconvinced. "Then why didn't you assign the largest cabin to Ambassador Richardson?"

John met her eyes and held them. "Because my cabin is right next to the bridge, where I need to be if there's an emergency," he said. "The VIP cabins are towards the rear of Officer Country because they aren't required to do anything if we run into trouble."

"It's quite all right," Joelle Richardson said, as she emerged from the sleeping compartment. "I really have been in worse places, Captain."

"And you could be bedded down with the midshipmen," John said, as she held out her hand for him to shake. "They have to sleep doubled-up because of your party."

Grace frowned. "Aren't they used to it?"

"No," John said, flatly.

He gazed around the cabin. It *was* small, yet there were three compartments and just enough room to swing a cat. John was pretty sure his midshipmen would have been delighted to have such a cabin to themselves, particularly if they didn't get the duties that normally came with a private compartment. The bulkheads were bare, but there was no reason why the ambassador couldn't hang pictures on the metal or cover them with cloth or mirrors to give the impression that the cabin was larger than it seemed. Compared to the cabin he'd shared at the Academy, it was paradise incarnate.

You could bring a person to your bunk and have fun, he thought, wryly. *There would certainly be no need to negotiate with your bunkmates for some privacy.*

"I've taken the liberty of ordering food for the three of us, Captain," the ambassador said, as John sat at the small folding table. "And please call me Joelle."

"Call me John," John said.

Joelle smiled. "I read your service record," she said, as Grace glanced into the next room and then sat down next to John. "I understand you saw service in the war?"

"Yes, Ambassador...*Joelle*," John said. That was hardly a secret. The media had done endless profiles on him, ever since he'd returned from Vesy with the news of a second alien race. It was amusing to note just how much they'd gotten wrong...and how much they'd deliberately misinterpreted in hopes of writing a better story. "I flew starfighters against the Tadpoles."

Grace coughed. "Do you have to call them *Tadpoles*?" She asked. "It isn't the nicest thing to say. And it implies inferiority to humanity."

"Their name for themselves is unpronounceable," John reminded her. "There's no point in trying to call them by their proper name. They don't seem to care."

"It's still a bad attitude," Grace said.

John shrugged. He had the feeling he was being tested. Nothing in Joelle's file had suggested she had problems calling her subordinates to heel, if she felt it necessary. If she was tolerating Grace acting like a spoilt teenager, she presumably had a reason for allowing her aide to embarrass herself. But what?

"We understand that they are powerful, and that the last thing either side wants is to resume the war," he said, flatly. "That is all we really need to understand."

He cleared his throat. "I flew starfighters until I transferred to capital ships and made my way up through the ranks," he added. "It has been an interesting career."

"You encountered a whole new alien race," Joelle said. "What are your...*impressions* of them?"

"Primitive, by our standards, but bursting with potential," John said. An alien observer might have said the same of humanity, if he'd peered down at Earth five hundred years ago. "Also quite barbaric, by our standards. The purges of the God-King's supporters made the Spanish Inquisition look inefficient."

"It's unfair to judge them by our standards," Grace pointed out. "They're not human."

John smirked, remembering Colin's verbal games. "But isn't it more insulting *not* to judge them by our standards? To treat them as children who cannot be expected to understand the seriousness of their crimes?"

"They are, to some extent," Joelle said. "Five years ago, they had no idea that they weren't the only intelligent life in the universe."

"Five years ago, *we* had no idea we weren't the only intelligent life in the universe," John countered. "And then we ran into the Tadpoles."

He shuddered at the thought. Humanity had been in shock, ever since the first attack on Vera Cruz, and it hadn't been until the end of the war that the philosophical implications had begun to sink in. The human race was no longer alone...and, if the Tadpoles weren't *that* far from human space, just how much of the galaxy was already taken? And, if the Tadpoles had been more advanced than humanity when the war had begun, might there be other more advanced races out there, some potentially hostile? Might humanity run into a race armed with weapons that made nukes look like firecrackers?

"They didn't even have the *concept* of alien life," Joelle pointed out. "We did, even if we didn't believe they truly existed."

"True," John agreed.

The hatch opened, revealing a steward carrying a large tray of food. John leaned to one side as the three plates were placed in front of them, then the steward retreated as silently as he'd arrived. At least they'd managed to get a pair of *real* stewards, he reminded himself, as he lifted the lid to reveal beef stew, mashed potatoes and greens. There was no need to waste a midshipman's time serving as a steward, in addition to his or her regular duties.

"We are going to need to work together," Joelle said, when she had eaten enough to satisfy the first hunger pangs. "I understand that I am cleared to talk to diplomats from other human powers, but you're expected to talk to military officers."

"If they are cleared to talk to me," John said. "Military officers are not normally expected to set diplomatic policy."

"Their superiors will have to clear it," Joelle said. "But could you work with them, if they were cleared to work with you?"

"It shouldn't be a problem, as long as we agreed on the ground rules," John said. "We managed to work together fairly well during the war."

Joelle frowned. "But managing the aftermath was tricky," she said. "The Japanese believe that at least one of their carriers was sacrificed without due cause, while the French think their interests were unheeded and the Russians...well, the less said about the Russians the better."

"Really?" John asked. "Why?"

"Diplomatic disaster," Joelle said, shortly. She didn't seem inclined to address the subject any further. "Suffice it to say that the Russians feel boxed in and unwilling to cooperate too openly with the other powers."

John winced. The Russians had reclaimed their personnel - and, even though they faced charges ranging from desertion to breaking the non-interference edict, their mere existence gave the Russians something to bargain with. They knew more about Vesy than anyone else, save perhaps for the Marines John had left on the alien world. It was quite possible that there was already a Russian ship or two heading to Vesy, intent on picking up where the renegades had left off. Or maybe they would sell what they knew to the highest bidder.

Should never have let them out of Geneva, he thought. He'd done his best to follow the politics closely, but precisely *why* the Russians had been allowed to return home was beyond him. Someone must have done a considerable amount of horse-trading behind the scenes. *It was unlikely the Russians would simply put them in front of a wall, as soon as they returned home, and have them shot.*

"It does raise questions concerning jurisdiction," John said. "If all of the interstellar powers cooperate, we can limit access to Vesy. But if one or more powers refuse to cooperate, it will be impossible to legally blockade the entire world. It isn't the Britannic System, where we own everything."

"Do the best you can, I think," Joelle said. "In the long run, if we are unable to secure a joint agreement, our objective is to convince as many Vesy factions as possible to sign up with us."

"Then trade weapons," John said, flatly. "That will get you all the factions you could possibly want."

Grace coughed. "Are you seriously suggesting that we *encourage* the locals to fight?"

John gave her a long considering look. "You want them to sign up with us," he said, somehow managing to keep his voice level. "If so, you have to give them something they want in exchange - and what they want, most of all, are human weapons. Weapons that will give them a decisive advantage against any city-state that *doesn't* have access to human weapons...and weapons that will even the odds against any city-state that *does*."

"We could offer them medicine," Grace said. "Or...there are all sorts of little ideas we could give them."

"None of which will help them worth a damn if they are crushed by their neighbours," John said. "The God-King created an empire, Miss Short. It might not have lasted, but it introduced the concept to them. City-states with human weapons will seek to impose themselves on their neighbours; city-states without them will do whatever it takes to *get* them. And if that means signing up with the Russians, instead of us, they will do it."

He scowled down at the table. "You're trying to outbid other human states," he added, darkly. "Even if *we* have qualms about offering weapons, the Russians or Chinese or even the French won't have any hesitation. The states that sign up with us will defect or get crushed, once their neighbours are armed to the teeth. And any medical ideas we give our friends will be taken by force."

"You're treating them as if they're human," Grace said. "They may not react like us!"

"They were struggling for supremacy for centuries before the Russians arrived," John said. It was tempting to blame everything on the Russians, but there was no evidence that the Vesy had been peaceful at any point in their history. Their city-states were ringed with solid walls, suggesting they had good reason to fear attack. "I judge them by what we saw - and what we saw was barbaric savagery."

"By human rules," Grace insisted. "Their rules might be different."

John shrugged. "If you gave Napoleon nukes," he said, "would he have hesitated to use them, judging by the standards of the time? If you gave Philip of Spain machine guns, would he have paused before unleashing carnage on a scale no one of that time could envisage? If you gave the Romans television, would they delay long before installing one in every household so the entire population could enjoy its bread and circuses?"

Grace scowled. "What's your point?"

"Human civilisation developed slowly, adapting to new technology as it came along," John said. "No, I don't think Napoleon would have hesitated before unleashing nukes; his society simply wasn't advanced enough to understand the implications of using them. Even television...one could make a case that television retarded the development of human civilisation. The Vesy are nowhere near advanced enough to be able to handle our technology without inflicting major damage on their society."

"And yet you're still judging them by human rules," Grace insisted.

"And yet *their* rules don't see anything wrong with mass slaughter," John countered. "Nor did Napoleon see anything wrong with sacking cities, George Washington see anything wrong with sending the Indians smallpox-infested blankets, Philip of Spain see anything wrong with slaughtering thousands of people because their noblemen had embraced one sect of Christianity over another. We have to accept that they don't play by our rules."

"Captain," Grace said. "That's..."

"That will do," Joelle said. She tapped her fork against her plate meaningfully. "I apologise, Captain. Some of my staff put their idealism ahead of their common sense."

John glanced at Grace. She was blushing. "I was surprised you didn't invite Professor Nordstrom," he said. "I'm sure he could have countered her points more openly."

"I wanted to talk with you alone," Joelle said. She glanced at Grace. "I'll speak to you later, if you don't mind."

It was clearly a dismissal. Grace nodded, then rose to her feet and stalked through the hatch to the sleeping compartment. John wondered, inanely, if the ambassador and her aide were sleeping together, instead of just sharing a cabin, then dismissed the thought. Even if it were true, and he rather doubted it, they weren't covered by navy regulations against fraternisation.

"It's always interesting to have multiple different viewpoints on a given topic," Joelle said, once the hatch had closed. "But, at the same time, it also causes problems when the arguments start overriding everything else. Do you have that problem in the military?"

"Sometimes," John said, thinking of Admiral Fitzwilliam and Admiral Soskice. "But we are trained to pull together, when necessary."

"You may be right," Joelle admitted. "Selling weapons is perhaps the only way we can get large numbers of Vesy on our side. But, at the same time, it will not go down well on Earth."

"Politics," John said, making the word a curse.

"And public relations," Joelle added. "You probably know just how many factions there are that want to help the Vesy, while others just want to quarantine their system or even commit genocide, on the theory the Vesy *might* be a threat one day."

"I know," John said.

"We have to patch together several different agreements, John," Joelle said. She stood and paced over to the drinks machine, then pushed a switch. Two plastic cups of coffee dropped down into the dispenser. "We need agreements with the Vesy to give us access to the system, but we also need agreements with other human powers to limit just what we pass on to the Vesy. And that will get people like Grace" - she nodded towards the hatch - "het up about us treating the Vesy as children."

"Which may be the best thing to do," John observed.

"But Professor Nordstrom is right," Joelle added. She picked up one of the cups and passed it to John, then took the other for herself. "The Vesy will resent it hugely if we hold them back - or if we are *seen* to be holding them back. And yet, if we set up schools and teach them how to be...well, *human*, that will shatter their society beyond repair."

John took a sip of his coffee. "Does their society deserve to be saved?"

Joelle looked back at him, evenly. "Do you believe we should destroy it?"

"They are savages, by our standards," John said, flatly. "In some ways, they are more repressive than many human societies. One might rightly question if such a society deserves to exist."

"We answered that one during the Age of Unrest," Joelle pointed out. "The idea of reshaping foreign societies was abandoned. Instead, we chose to merely seal them off from civilised lands."

"Which condemned millions of people to a life of suffering," John said, "which was made all the worse by educated youngsters leaving in droves."

Joelle shrugged. "We couldn't fix their problems when we had access to the boundless resources of space and all the time in the world," she said. "Now, with most of our resources tied up in rebuilding after the war, we couldn't spare anything for the Third World. They can solve their own problems, if they wish."

She sat down again, facing him. "I will need your support, Captain, and your advice," she said. "This won't be easy."

"You will have as much support as I can give you," John promised. "But I don't expect everyone to fall into line. Control over Vesy will grant control over the system - and there are seven tramlines here. The system is a prize worth fighting for."

Joelle gave him a sharp look. "You expect one of the interstellar powers to try to seize the system by force? Invade Vesy itself?"

"It's a possibility," John warned. "The Vesy couldn't put up any real resistance to a single destroyer; hell, a freighter could smash any opposition from orbit with the right weapons kit bolted to the hull. Come up with an excuse to invade, take the planet by force, make agreements at gunpoint with the surviving city-states, then announce the system closed to everyone else and declare victory. There's no reason why it couldn't work."

Joelle looked disturbed. "Unless we got the majority of the interstellar powers to agree that invading Vesy is off the table," she said. "It isn't as if it's a human world - and the last war ended with a return to the *status quo.*"

"That would compromise their ability - and ours - to launch punitive strikes," John pointed out. The Tadpoles could have prolonged the fighting if humanity had demanded compensation for the death and devastation caused by the war. "I don't think they would go for a flat ban on invasion. What if some of their people come under attack?"

"You have a nasty imagination," Joelle said. She reached for a datapad and made a note, then looked back at him. "What else do you have in mind?"

"Too much," John said. "For example, what happens if smugglers start shipping in tech manuals as well as weapons and pieces of technology? Something dating back to 1800 would be useless to us, but very informative to them."

Joelle groaned. "It's going to be a mess, isn't it?"

"That's why they pay us the big bucks," John said. "But don't count on this being sorted out in a hurry."

CHAPTER
NINE

It hadn't been easy to provide a *precise* translation of any of the titles used by Vesy rulers, not when it was impossible to define how they were selected or even what they were supposed to do. Some of the city-states seemed to have a limited democracy - with very restricted franchises - while others were ruled by powerful citizens or religious factions. Ivan, who appeared to be an elected king, seemed to fall somewhere in the middle. Percy had long since given up trying to work out how the system worked. It was something he would cheerfully leave to the xenospecialists when they finally arrived from Earth.

He bowed, keeping one hand on his pistol in line with local traditions, as Ivan stepped into the meeting room. The Vesy was very definitely inhuman; tall, taller than the average human, with scaly green skin, dark and beady eyes and a flattened nose. He wore a long dark cloak that passed for formal wear, among the aliens, and metal chains that ran down from his neck to vanish somewhere in the enshrouding folds of his cloak. The sword hilt poking out from the robes was a clear warning that Ivan was armed, a freeman of his city-state as well as its ruler. He'd been the ruler before, Percy knew, but now he was something different. But then, his former city-state was something else too.

"I greet you," Ivan said, in careful English. The Vesy seemed to have a natural gift for languages; by now, English was spreading as fast as Russian. Percy would have been impressed if he hadn't known that

Russian-speaking slaves commanded high prices in the slave markets. "I thank you for meeting me."

"I welcome you," Percy said. As always, listening to the Vesy reminded him of how he'd spoken as a child, before his mother had started to scold him for talking with his mouth full. It wasn't *easy* to make out the words, but it could be done. "I am honoured to have you at my door."

The Vesy smiled, human-style. "There is much to discuss," he said. "We shall be blunt."

Percy nodded, unsure if Ivan was using the Royal 'We' or speaking about both of them. The aliens might speak English, but attempts to translate from Vesy-One to English tended to cause problems, particularly when Russian was also involved. Percy had heard that it had been worse, trying to talk to the Tadpoles, yet he found it somewhat hard to believe. Besides, the Tadpoles had been helped by communications officers who'd had plenty of time to prepare for an encounter with alien life. *He* had a handful of Russians and their former hostages.

"There are several powerful coalitions forming against us," Ivan said. "We require your support."

He paused. "One of them has support from a rogue human."

Percy winced. He had always suspected that some of the Russians had been on detached duty when the Russian base had been overrun, then vanished into the countryside when the God-King and his forces were crushed. None of the Vesy factions had openly *admitted* to keeping a Russian or two prisoner, but Percy wouldn't have expected them to give up such a potential advantage. A trained Russian soldier could teach his captors everything from human military tactics to gunpowder weapons and other basic firearms. Given just how many ideas had washed across the planet in the wake of the God-King's defeat, it would be hard to be sure if one or more had been sown by a Russian advisor.

And we never found all the bodies, he thought, sourly. *Too many were simply lost in the final bloody hours of fighting.*

"I understand," he said.

He cursed under his breath. There was no way he had the authority to enter into a long-term agreement with Ivan, even if he'd had the force to back it up. But not entering an agreement could be just as disastrous. He'd come to realise, in the months since he'd first met the alien, that Ivan was willing to do whatever it took to protect his own people. And, if he didn't, he would be removed. His people might respect him, as one of the aristocrats who had forged a link between themselves and the British base, but they wouldn't tolerate failure.

"We require your support," Ivan said, again. "We cannot risk being caught by superior force."

Percy gritted his teeth. Trying to put together a political map of Vesy had been a nightmare, even for the Russians; his best guess was that city-states from outside the God-King's reign of terror were pressing against Ivan and the other survivors of that war. They had intact armies and, presumably, gunpowder weapons of their own. God knew the Russians had been lax about preventing the spread of knowledge about muskets and rifles - or cannon. The Vesy might have been primitive, but they weren't stupid. Duplicating Russian-designed weapons wouldn't take long.

And the God-King's empire wasn't held together by anything stronger than naked force, he thought. *There's nothing holding it together now.*

He thought, rapidly. The hell of it was that he had next to nothing *to* offer and he knew it all too well. Ten Royal Marines, armed with modern weapons, could dominate the battlefield...until they ran out of ammunition. He didn't even have an orbital bombardment system he could call upon, if the shit hit the fan. And none of the tactics he might have used, on Earth, to win time would be workable on Vesy. There was certainly no way he could slip an assassin into an enemy city and shoot their leadership dead...

"There are some ideas we could give you," he said. One of the Marines had dug up the plans for primitive hot air balloons, similar to the observation balloons that had been used in the late 19th century, but he wasn't sure if they would be any use to the Vesy. More advanced weapons would take years to make. "But I don't have the resources to offer you more."

Ivan didn't move - the Vesy stayed inhumanly still, when not moving deliberately - but he didn't seem pleased. "We have supplied you with workers, with materials, with food," the alien said. "And yet you will not assist us in our time of need?"

"There will be assistance when the ship returns," Percy said, although he had no idea if that was actually true. It was quite possible that the

World Court would agree to quarantine Vesy permanently, at least until the Vesy reached into space on their own. "However, I have only limited supplies…"

He stopped as his radio bleeped. "Corporal, report to HQ," Peerce said. There was an urgency in his voice that Percy had never heard before, even when the shit was hitting the fan. "I say again, report to HQ at once."

"Excuse me," Percy said. "I need to run."

Ivan nodded, mimicking the human expression. The meeting room was not only outside the walls, it was designed to make both races as comfortable as possible. Ivan would be able to relax until Percy returned, if he wished, or return to his city-state and resume the discussion later. Percy nodded back, then hurried out the door and down towards the gateway leading into the fort. Nothing seemed to have changed, he noted as he passed the guests and entered the large prefabricated building, but Peerce's voice had sounded urgent. Had a starship finally returned to Vesy?

"Corporal," Peerce said, as Percy entered the compartment. "The orbital satellites have picked up a number of ships heading to the planet."

Percy nodded. "Human ships?"

It would have been a stupid question, once. It wasn't any longer.

"IFFs suggest they're a mixture of American, French and Indian ships, with a handful that aren't broadcasting IFFs" Peerce said. "There may be more; the orbital network isn't designed to track ships beyond a couple of AUs. The Indians seem to have the largest contingent; there are nine freighters, five warships and a starship of indeterminate design and function. She might be a troop transporter."

"Shit," Percy said, as he checked the holographic display. None of the ships were British, as far as he could tell, and he had a feeling they'd resent being told what to do by a mere corporal…particularly one who had nothing to back up his orders. If the newcomers wanted to land on the other side of the planet, there was nothing Percy could do to stop them. "Send them the pre-planned greeting, then an invitation to land at Fort Knight."

"We might find it hard to handle them all," Peerce said. "We don't have the barracks or warehouses to cope with more than a small influx."

"At least they'd have access to translators here," Percy said, although he knew Peerce was right. He couldn't help feeling more than a little out of his depth. Would it really have been so hard for a starship to be dispatched back to Vesy at once? "We can offer to introduce them to the locals."

There was a long pause. "Picking up a signal from the Americans," the operator said, after a moment. "It's relayed through the satellite network."

Percy nodded. "Let's hear it."

A dark-skinned man appeared in the display. "This is Captain Samuel Johnston of USS *Rhode Island*," he said. "Thank you for your invitation to land at Fort Knight. It will be our pleasure to join you on the surface as soon as possible."

"Thank you," Percy said. "Welcome to Vesy."

The American's image vanished from the display. Percy let out a sigh of relief; it looked as though the Americans, at least, were going to be reasonable. But then, the Americans might not have access to the files from either *Warspite* or the Russian deserters. They might feel it was better to make their first contacts with the Vesy through Fort Knight. The next starship might not be so cooperative.

"Picking up another signal," the operator said. "It's from one of the ships without an IFF."

"Greetings," a voice said. There was no visual image. "We represent the Society of Interstellar Brotherhood. It is our intention to land on Vesy and assist our new brothers to reach for the stars."

Percy groaned. The Society of Interstellar Brotherhood had picketed Redford Barracks on Earth, back when he'd been stationed there. He honestly hadn't been able to understand why *anyone* would consider aliens to be brothers of men, not when the sole known alien race - at the time - had started a war and slaughtered millions of humans. And then they'd started insisting that humanity intervene and save the Tadpoles from themselves or something along those lines. Percy really hadn't paid too much attention. The idea of humanity trying to do more than maintain the peace was laughable.

"Welcome to Vesy," he said, carefully. "I must inform you that all contacts with the Vesy are handled through Fort Knight, so please take a slot in orbit and await landing permission."

"We have no intention of waiting before we make contact," the voice said. "You have no authority to deny us permission to land."

Percy wondered, briefly, if he could ask the Americans to intervene. But it would be something well about his pay grade…and it could easily explode in his face, if it led to a diplomatic incident. Instead, he thought fast. There had to be an argument he could use to convince them to see sense.

"You will need translators to *talk* to the Vesy," he said, after a moment. "The only way to get them is to work through Fort Knight. Of course, you *could* land elsewhere, but you would have to relearn their language for yourself and they might misinterpret your actions…"

There was a long pause. "We will work through Fort Knight, if we can land within a day," the voice said, finally. "Our ship isn't chartered indefinitely."

Percy glanced at the data download - someone on the ship had had the sense to send their details, *finally* - and groaned. They'd chartered an Israeli ship - and the Israelis were notoriously stubborn about defending their rights. His half-formulated plan to take their shuttle, then seize their starship and hold the Brothers in orbit until more ships arrived from Earth would have to be abandoned. It would cause a major diplomatic incident for nothing.

Peerce reached over and tapped the mute button. "Bring them down here," he advised, softly. "We can hold them at Fort Knight if necessary."

"Understood," Percy said. He untapped the button and cleared his throat. "We will arrange living space for you at Fort Knight. You should be able to land within a day, as you request."

He sighed inwardly as the connection broke. Fort Knight was large, but not large enough to host *everyone*. They'd need to expand, which would make defending the fort even more of a nightmare. God alone knew how many groundpounders the Americans had brought, but he couldn't simply hand the fort over to them…

"Picking up a message from the Indians," the operator said. "They want to talk to whoever is in charge."

Percy nodded. Moments later, an Indian face appeared in the display.

"This is General Anjeet Patel," he said. His voice was curt, too curt. "Fetch your commanding officer at once, boy."

"I am in command," Percy said, fighting down a flash of anger. He hadn't been addressed in such tones of contempt since he'd started his early training. "My superiors have yet to relieve me or send reinforcements."

"How convenient for them," Patel sneered. "They can blame any diplomatic mistakes on an officer so young he has yet to learn how to shave."

Percy forced his voice to remain calm. "Welcome to Vesy," he said. Perhaps the best response to the Indian's unpleasantness was to ignore it. "Do you require living space at Fort Knight?"

The Indian puffed up. "It is the official position of my government that the Vesy and no one else are masters of their homeworld," he said. "We do not recognise your claim to control orbital space, nor do we believe you have either the right or the ability to prevent us from forging alliances with alien factions. Or do you wish to dispute this?"

"No," Percy said, carefully. The Indian was right; Percy simply didn't have the ability to prevent anyone from landing wherever they chose. "However, in line with Provision Seven of the Outer Space Treaty, please keep us informed of your movements."

The Indian didn't seem inclined to argue *that* point. Percy wasn't too surprised. Provision Seven insisted that all spacefaring powers should notify the others of their movements, at least when moving through crowded orbital space. Earth's early days of expansion into space had been marred by the Cold War, where a rocket launch could easily be mistaken for the first strike in a nuclear war. Since then, all powers had kept the other powers updated, even when the Outer Space Treaty had been largely superseded by the Solar Treaty.

And they won't want to set any precedents that could be used against them later, Percy thought. Britain wasn't the only power that had an interest in Vesy. *Or we might retaliate elsewhere.*

"We will land at once," Patel said. "Goodbye."

His image vanished from the display. Percy cursed under his breath, wondering just what the Indians were planning, then looked at Peerce. The Sergeant seemed just as mystified as Percy himself.

"If Ivan wanted you to help him," Peerce said finally, "the Indians might make him a better offer."

Percy nodded. Nine freighters was a significant investment…and, judging from their ponderous movements as they settled into orbit, they were loaded to the gunwales. God alone knew how long it would take the Indians to make contact and learn to speak the alien tongue - although it was quite likely they would find aliens who could speak either English or Russian - but once they did, they would definitely have something to trade. Somehow, judging by Patel's attitude, he had a feeling the Indians wouldn't hesitate to trade weapons in exchange for political influence.

"Picking up a shuttle launch," the operator said.

"Track them," Percy ordered. The satellite net was pathetic, compared to the networks orbiting Earth, but they should be able to keep an eye on the Indians. "Let me know where they're going."

It was nearly ten minutes before he had an answer. "They're heading to City #34," the operator said. "We don't have any contact with them, as far as I know."

Percy glanced at the map, then nodded. City #34 was five hundred miles from Fort Knight, just past the edge of the God-King's empire. If that was a coincidence, he would eat his dress uniform cap.

"They learned something from the Russians," Peerce commented, putting Percy's thoughts into words. "That *cannot* be a coincidence."

"It looks that way," Percy agreed. The Indians would be making contact with city-states that had heard of off-worlders, but hadn't had any real contact with them or access to advanced weapons. They'd be hungry for tech and the Indians would be happy to supply. "It's going to be a right mess."

He sighed, then looked at the next wave of starships approaching the planet. American, French, Chinese…a hundred NGOs, corporations and media outlets…and not a single British warship. He'd lose control very quickly, if he'd even had it in the first place. The Indians had probably broken the ice, simply by refusing to acknowledge his authority…

"Keep in touch with as many of the newcomers as possible," he ordered. It wouldn't be long before Fort Knight gained a few thousand new citizens. "And try to convince them to land here."

But he knew, as he looked at the map, that it wasn't going to happen.

CHAPTER
TEN

Penny Schneider had never really seen the value of a military career. Her biological father had been called back to the colours at short notice, leaving his family alone, while her adopted father spent most of his time away from Earth. She had considered a military career, when her brother had joined the Royal Marines, but it had never really appealed to her. The idea of being a reporter was much more attractive.

It hadn't been easy. Jobs were in short supply on Earth and she had a feeling that the only thing that had saved her from the labour pool was her name and family connections. Even so, getting a post as a reporter had required a great deal of luck - and snaring the assignment to HMS *Warspite* as an embedded reporter had probably relied on her family connections, no matter how embarrassing she found them. But then, with a brother who was already on Vesy and an adoptive father who might become First Space Lord one day, she was better-placed to gain a scoop than most of the other reporters.

She sighed to herself as she checked her equipment, then tapped the buzzer outside the Captain's cabin. She'd been given nearly unrestricted access to *Warspite,* but interviewing crewmen had seemed rather pointless after the first couple of interviews turned up nothing of great interest. The crewmen and marines seemed more interested in flirting with her than giving her a scoop, although she had to admit it was unlikely they had anything new to offer after endless interviews on Earth. It was hard to find a crewman from the first cruise who hadn't been plastered across the datanets, their names and faces public knowledge. In hindsight, she couldn't help wondering if she'd been tricked.

But nothing has really happened yet, she thought.

She shook her head as the hatch slid open, dismissing the thought. *Warspite* had made three jumps, progressing up the tramline chain towards Vesy; nothing could reasonably be expected to happen until they actually reached their destination. Then, she hoped and prayed, her attachment to the ambassador would pay off. A solid story from Vesy would make her career, putting her beyond the charge of using connections to force her way onto the staff; hell, if she acquired a reputation for working on Vesy, she would be the go-to girl for future assignments. It was definitely something worth aiming for.

And won't Percy be surprised to see me, she thought, as she stepped through the hatch. *His little sister all grown up.*

The thought made her smile. Percy had been annoying, in the way of older brothers to younger sisters since time immemorial, right up until the moment their lives had been turned upside down by tidal waves. Their mother had been lost, somewhere in the chaos - it hadn't been until much later that Penny had realised that their so-perfect mother had been having an affair - while they'd had to struggle to survive. And Percy, annoying Percy, had become terribly over-protective. Not that Penny really blamed him, not after their parents had died; they'd only ever had each other. But it had grown more and more wearying as she'd grown older and finally found a place for herself.

"Miss Schneider," the Captain said, breaking into her thoughts. "I believe you requested an interview?"

"Yes, thank you," Penny said.

She stepped forward, the hatch closing behind her, and looked around the Captain's cabin. It was larger than the compartment she was sharing with a midshipwoman, but not by much. The bulkheads were bare, save for one that was covered in medals, commissioning papers and a large photograph of Captain Naiser with another man. He'd been quite handsome as a young man, Penny decided, before the war had overwhelmed him. Now, there was something in his blue eyes that suggested he wasn't quite the same.

"Please, take a seat," the Captain said. "I do hope you recall the rules concerning media interviews?"

"Of course," Penny said, nettled. She'd paid close attention to the briefings, after all; the briefing officers had been trying to tell her how to stay alive in space. "The recordings will be run past the censors first, before being released on Earth, even though we're not at war."

"Good," the Captain said. He sat on a comfortable armchair, watching her through cold blue eyes as she set up her recorder. "You never know what will prove important to enemy intelligence agents until it does."

Penny scowled. "Off the record," she said, "why is it that everyone treats reporters as enemy spies?"

The Captain snorted. "Off the record? Reporters, as a general rule, are more concerned with snatching the latest scoop than thinking about the consequences of releasing their scoop. It doesn't take much imagination to realise that they might tell the enemy something useful, then hide behind claims of freedom of the press."

"I wouldn't do that," Penny insisted. "My brother is at risk! And my adopted father."

"Reporters are often incapable of judging what is and what isn't sensitive material," the Captain pointed out. "I could tell you a hundred facts about *Warspite*, but would you be able to tell which of them are classified?"

Penny scowled, again. "Point taken."

She finished setting up her recorder, then tapped a switch. "Preliminary background interview with Captain John Naiser, 23rd March 2207 at 1745," she said, for the record. It was a habit she'd never managed to lose, even though the recorder would attach date and time metadata to the recording. "Subject: alien contact."

The recorder clicked once, in acknowledgement. It was larger than it needed to be, she knew, but reporters had discovered over the years that using a device that was clearly visible tended to work better than something so microscopic that it couldn't be seen with the naked eye. Besides, there had been quite a few lawsuits when people had been recorded without their permission, some of which had resulted in massive payouts.

"Captain," she said. "How much can you tell me about your early life?"

"Nothing that hasn't already been said a thousand times," the Captain said. "My life was thoroughly dissected on the datanet after we returned from Vesy."

Penny groaned, inwardly. She should have expected that reaction. It was hard, very hard, to move through modern life without leaving an electronic trail, although the bombardment had erased quite a few records from existence. The Captain might not have been Prince Henry or Princess Janelle, but it wouldn't have been hard for the reporters to uncover his early life and expose it to the world. It helped that he'd been one of the heroes of the war who hadn't gone down with *Ark Royal*.

She gave him a pleading smile. "You can't tell me something no one else knows?"

"I don't think so," the Captain said. He seemed to be enjoying her discomfort. "I was a perfectly ordinary child, then a perfectly ordinary starfighter pilot, then a war hero..."

Penny seized on that, quickly. "Do you feel you deserved to be feted?"

"I wasn't the only hero of the war," the Captain said. "I did my duty and that was all there was to it."

"I understand," Penny said. Her father - *both* of her fathers - had rarely talked about their service, but she knew they'd both had nightmares. "What do you believe we should do about the Vesy?"

The Captain didn't seem thrown by the sudden change in subject. "My personal opinion is that we should quarantine their world and leave them to develop on their own," he said, flatly. "Nothing good can come of us meddling in their affairs. Let them develop on their own until they build starships, then they can meet us on even terms."

"But by then our starships will be even more advanced," Penny pointed out. "I'm sure *Warspite* could smash the first starships to jump through the tramlines with ease."

"Yes, she could," the Captain agreed. "But the crews of those ships knew much - much - more about the universe than the Vesy. The difference between their vessels and *Warspite* isn't really that great, nor is anything we have truly beyond their comprehension. For the Vesy, the gulf between us and them is so great as to be unimaginable. It will take them centuries to develop all the theories we have discovered and then progress past them to join us on an equal level."

"They need to make the theories to make the theories," Penny said. She paused. "If that makes any kind of sense."

"It does," the Captain assured her.

Penny considered it, slowly. The Captain seemed content to wait for the next question, rather than volunteer information or ask her to hurry up. In truth, she wasn't sure what to say, let alone ask. The Captain wouldn't be impressed if she asked for more information that was already in the public domain. A more experienced reporter, she was sure, would have found better questions to ask.

"My brother is still on Vesy," she said, slowly. "Did you intend to leave him there for so long?"

The Captain looked irked. "No," he said. "I had hoped a ship would be dispatched earlier, perhaps before other nations launched their own ships. Six months on an alien world would be pushing their endurance to the limit."

Penny blinked in alarm. She might have found Percy irritating, at times, but she didn't want him *dead*. The thought of something killing her brother was unthinkable...and he might be dead now, only they would never know. How could they know when no ship had visited Vesy since *Warspite* had left?

"I'm sure he's fine," the Captain said, reading her expression. "The Royal Marines are tough."

"I couldn't help noticing that 3 Para has been dispatched to Vesy," Penny said, fighting to keep her voice under control. "Do you expect trouble?"

"It is normally a good idea to prepare for trouble, even if you don't expect it," the Captain said, flatly. "Having forces on the ground might be necessary if something goes badly wrong."

Penny frowned. "The Vesy might rise up against us?"

"Or someone might provoke them into attacking a smaller human group," the Captain countered. "I really don't like the idea of missionaries going out among the Vesy. They are unlikely to be welcomed, particularly when they're not offering anything beyond the word of god."

"I see," Penny said. She took a breath. "When we get there, Captain, what do you intend to do?"

"It depends on what we find when we get there," the Captain said. "If we're the first to arrive, we will set up on the surface and make contact with the Vesy factions; if we're not, we will proceed as we think best. A great deal depends on just how the other nations react to the Vesy."

Penny let out a breath, then made a show of clicking the recorder off. "And myself?"

The Captain shrugged. "I believe you are, technically, embedded with the ambassador, rather than my ship," he said. "If you want to go down to the surface, you may go with her - or, if you wish, go on tour if the Vesy are willing to show you around."

"Thank you, Captain," Penny said. She clicked the recorder back on. "Now, do you feel that *Warspite* represents a whole new model of warfare...?"

———

"We have four days until we reach Vesy," Colonel John Mortimer said, once the ambassadorial staff had gathered in the compartment. "It is as good a time as any to go over the mission-specific protective details, all the more so as we lack a Foreign Office close-protection detail. They have chosen to pass those responsibilities to the Paras."

Joelle frowned, inwardly. It hadn't been her choice, and she'd argued against it, but the Foreign Office had been insistent. The dedicated close-protection teams, who had watched over British diplomats for years, were to be replaced with heavily-armed Paras from the Parachute Regiment. Perhaps it was a good idea - she'd seen the videos of the final battle on Vesy - but the Paras weren't trained in keeping a low profile. Their mere presence could be considered provocative.

"You may not approve of that decision," Mortimer continued, as if he'd read her thoughts. "I advise you, however, to accept it. The Paras are highly-trained soldiers who may be precisely what you need to get out of trouble, should you get into it. However, the person who is principally responsible for taking care of yourself is yourself."

He leaned forward, cutting off any debate. "You will each be given a tracking implant before you leave the ship," he said. "We should be able to find you wherever you are, as there will be nothing on the planet capable of blocking the signal; however, I strongly advise you never to leave Fort Knight without informing us and taking a security detail. Do *not* leave the base without permission, no matter what you're told. Troops have been lured away before and they have not always returned alive."

Joelle winced. She'd been involved with negotiations after a pair of soldiers had been lured away from a garrison in North Africa. It had ended very badly, with one of the soldiers dead and the other mutilated so badly that it had taken months to put him back together. The insurgents had paid - their base camps had been flattened from orbit, along with a pair of local villages that had supported them - but it should never have been necessary. They'd been very careless to leave the base and walk straight into a trap.

At least the Vesy won't be showing hot girls to horny and isolated men, she thought, wryly. It was very hard to tell the difference between male and female Vesy - and no one, at least no one human, would find either sex attractive. *But they could probably come up with a very attractive bribe, if they wished.*

"Those of you who are cleared to carry weapons may do so, at will," Mortimer added. "Bear in mind that all such weapons and ammunition have to be accounted for, at all times. The Vesy, if they feel like stealing from us, will consider such weapons to be prime targets; *don't* let go of them and, if you do lose one, report it at once. You will be in shit, but trust me; you will be in *deeper* shit if one of those weapons winds up being used against us, catching us unaware. If you're not cleared to use a weapon, you may borrow the shooting range 3 Para intends to set up and take a brief proficiency course."

He held up his hand. "Yes, you're diplomats, and you try to settle things through talking rather than shooting," he warned. "But you may need to shoot your way out of trouble if all hell breaks loose."

Joelle nodded when several heads turned to look at her. She'd never been caught in a trap, but she had been shot at twice, an experience she would have gladly foregone. It had been years since she'd carried a pistol outside the Foreign Office's shooting range, but she made a mental note to draw one for herself and practice when she had a moment. The Vesy had no reason to comprehend just how much firepower could and would be brought to bear against anyone who threatened a British Ambassador. It had been a long time since any state had just swallowed an offense to the flag.

She looked back at Mortimer, who had moved on to a different subject.

"They may attempt to open private negotiations with you," Mortimer said. "Either to purchase technology or weapons off you, or to try to learn more about our negotiating stance and society. Report all such contacts to Ambassador Richardson *at once*. Do not take any payment from them without permission, as they may intend to blackmail you later; it's happened before, on Earth, and it may happen here. There is no shortage of horror stories in the files if you care to look at them.

"In addition, do not tell them anything about our society, no matter how harmless you feel it may be. There is no way to know what they may be able to use against us."

Grace put up her hand. "Isn't that rude?"

Mortimer gave her a sharp look. "Explain."

"They may try to talk about comparing our lives," Grace said. "It would be rude for us not to talk about life on Earth."

"But you won't, because you might tell them something important without realising it," Mortimer told her, flatly. "We will be telling them more about ourselves, but not in a piecemeal fashion."

"But how could it be used against us?" Grace asked. "They can't *get* to Earth!"

Joelle spoke before Mortimer could formulate a response. "You might accidentally tell them that we have a rivalry with the other Great Powers," she said. "Or tell them something that allows them to *think* we have a rivalry. They would then try to play us off against the other Great Powers, which would allow them to get better terms."

"Or you could tell them about the war," Mortimer said. "They might start thinking they could talk to the Tadpoles instead."

He cleared his throat. "Take recorders with you whenever you leave the fort, but do not mention them to our hosts," he added. "All recordings are to be handed over to the researchers at Fort Knight for long-term study. Do *not* turn off the recorders, even when you go to the toilet. I assure you that the researchers have better things to do than watch you shit."

Joelle smiled at her staff's horrified reactions. "If worst comes to worst," she said, "you can just hold it in until you get home."

"Indeed," Mortimer agreed. "Your piss might be a state secret."

He chuckled, then resumed his lecture. Joelle settled back and forced herself to relax, despite the growing excitement in her chest. Four days… and then she would set foot on an alien world, speak to alien minds…

One hell of a challenge, she thought. *And I'd better be ready.*

CHAPTER

ELEVEN

General Anjeet Patel watched, feeling a surge of sudden anticipation, as the shuttle flew over the Vesy city, then proceeded towards the LZ they'd identified in the fields, a mile from the alien settlement. He had to admit the city was a remarkable sight, given the technological limitations the builders faced; towering stone buildings, some covered in patches of green grass-like plants, surrounded by a wall that would be practically invulnerable, faced with Stone Age weapons technology. India had plenty of old buildings of its own, but there was something about the vibrant *realness* of the alien city that called to him and repelled him in the same breath. Perhaps it was the sense that it was subtly wrong, somehow, or perhaps it was the awareness that the minds that had designed the city were very far from human.

"Take us down," he ordered, as they hovered over the designated LZ. "And deploy the troops as soon as we land."

The shuttle touched down with nary a bump; the hatches opened a moment later, disgorging a dozen heavily-armed soldiers who fanned out around the shuttle, watching for potential threats. Anjeet rose to his feet and strode out of the hatch himself, taking a deep breath as he stepped onto alien soil. The air was hot and wet, smelling of something he couldn't even begin to identify, something very definitely *alien*. He took another breath, willing himself to suppress his reaction, then forced himself to relax. It wouldn't be long before diplomacy began.

They won't have any difficulty seeing where we landed, he thought. He hadn't trusted the Russian files completely - and the British base was sitting far too close to where the Russians had lived and worked - but it hardly mattered. The local aliens could hardly avoid coming to see what the humans were doing, ensuring he had a chance to make contact with a whole new alien faction. *All we have to do is wait.*

He smiled as he caught sight of an odd bird-like creature fluttering its way through the air, flying towards a grove of strange-looking trees. Another followed, keeping a wary distance from the humans; he couldn't help wondering if they knew to be afraid of human weapons or if they were merely concerned about the strangers. The Vesy were humanoid too, after all, and the bird-like creatures might not be intelligent enough to tell the difference. Or maybe they were just naturally frightened of creatures that were larger than themselves.

His radio buzzed. "General, we have a line of aliens leaving the city," the orbital observer said. "They're heading right towards the LZ."

"Keep tracking them," Anjeet ordered, calmly. "Do they appear to be armed?"

"Only with swords, spears and bows," the observer said. "However, they are wearing long cloaks and may be concealing more modern weapons."

Anjeet smiled. In his experience, people liked to show their strength before starting negotiations, if only to prove they simply couldn't be pushed too far. If that held true for the Vesy too, and nothing in the Russian files suggested otherwise, they would have carried modern weapons if they'd had them. That was good, he told himself. Their new allies would be hungry for human weapons and technology, which would make them *very* willing to do whatever it took to get their hands on them. India would have a very strong bargaining position indeed.

"Keep tracking them," he repeated. "ETA?"

"At current rate of progress, twenty minutes," the observer said. "They're moving at quite a clip."

Don't want us to leave before they have a chance to speak to us, Anjeet thought. The one downside of his refusal to coordinate with the British - let alone everyone else who had arrived - was that there was no way to know just who the British had talked to during their six months in sole control of the planet. He rather doubted the British had had a chance to do much, but it would have been nice to know. *They must be desperate after the God-King showed them that empire was possible.*

He waited, feeling sweat trickling down his back, until the aliens finally came into view, standing at the edge of the field. He'd thought himself prepared for their appearance, knowing that they were far closer to humanity than the Tadpoles, yet he couldn't help feeling a shiver as they stood there. Somehow, looking at the Tadpoles was far easier, despite the complete lack of real common ground. The Vesy were just close enough to humanity to make him feel uncomfortable, as if his mind insisted on seeing them as human even though they unquestionably weren't. It was, he hoped, a reaction he would overcome very quickly.

The Vesy stopped, then made a show of laying down their weapons on the grass-like ground before resuming their advance, holding their hands in the air to show they were unarmed. It made Anjeet wonder if the Russians had taught them how to approach human ships, or - more likely - if it was something they'd developed for themselves. Humanity had evolved ways to signify a lack of weapons long before they'd reached for the stars.

He frowned as he studied the group. There were six of them in all, five wearing coloured robes with their heads uncovered, the sixth wearing a long hooded cloak that hid his face from view. Was there a reason for that? He had no idea; maybe it was a woman, hiding her face from the infidels, or maybe it was the person who was actually in command. Anjeet reminded himself, sharply, that it was dangerous to jump to conclusions, not when aliens were involved. Their culture was so different from humanity's that something as simple as shaking his head might be interpreted as a major insult that could only be washed away by blood.

The lead Vesy stepped forward. "I greet you," he said, in halting Russian. "I am" - he said something that sounded like a rock falling into a muddy patch - "and I rule the city of" - something else, equally unpronounceable - "as its master under the gods. I bid welcome to honoured guests from the stars."

"I thank you, in the name of India," Anjeet said, also in Russian. Thankfully, he'd taken the time to brush up during the voyage. Russian wasn't common outside Russia itself - Eastern Europe and Central Asia still preferred English - but the Russian renegades had taught the Vesy how to speak their language. "It is our hope to arrange a mutually beneficial trade with you."

There was a long pause. Anjeet found himself wishing he knew how to interpret their body language. Two of the five stood still, the others twitched their arms in a manner that could signify anything from excitement to a maddening itch. The sixth showed no reaction at all.

"We would welcome trade with our illustrious guests from the stars," the lead alien said, finally. "What do we have to offer you in return?"

Anjeet allowed himself a smile, knowing the aliens would probably understand the expression. "Land," he said, simply. "We require territory to set up a base. We would be happy to trade goods for land."

There was another pause. The aliens conferred briefly amongst themselves, then turned back to face the Indians. "What are you prepared to offer in exchange for land?"

I never claimed to be a haggling wife, Anjeet thought. It was clear the aliens were fishing for information, perhaps even making use of the language barriers to extract *more* insight into the human mind, and yet... they couldn't be blind to the literally priceless goods he could offer. Did they want him to spell out what he could offer them? Or were they testing him to see if he would offer them the equivalent of beads and rattles?

He looked right at the alien's beady eyes. "What do you want?"

The alien's hands twitched. "The other humans have traded weapons," he said. "We will trade you land for weapons of our own."

Anjeet kept the smile off his face. "It will be our pleasure to trade weapons," he said. "We can offer you a demonstration of their power right now, if you wish."

He wasn't surprised the talk had moved so quickly to weapons, not after the God-King had started to build a genuine empire. Human weapons had tipped the balance of power so decisively in his favour that any state without access to such weapons, even primitive muskets and cannons, was doomed. Anjeet was quite happy, in line with his orders, to supply as many human-designed weapons as his new friends could possibly want. They would be enough to ensure their allies became much more powerful, even to the point of building an empire of their own.

His lips twitched. Furthermore, any human-designed weapon would require human-designed ammunition. He could practically give the weapons away, in exchange for land, and then drive a hard bargain over each bullet. And, as the weapons had been designed in India, they would have problems obtaining compatible ammunition from other human powers.

The aliens held another brief conference. Their words would be recorded and fed through the translator, Anjeet knew, although the translations were very far from perfect. This time, one of the aliens leaned up to the veiled alien and muttered to him, so quietly that Anjeet couldn't hear a single word. The answer, if one came, was completely inaudible.

"We would be happy to see a demonstration," the lead alien said, finally.

Anjeet nodded to one of the soldiers, who had already been carefully briefed. The young man unslung his carbine, then pointed it into the air, tracking one of the bird-like creatures as it swooped over the field. He pulled the trigger - the Vesy jumped at the sound, hands reaching for weapons they were no longer carrying - and the bird-like creature disintegrated into a mass of feathers and bloody chunks of meat. The Vesy seemed shocked, even though they had seen - or at least heard about - human weapons in action. Perhaps it was the staggering accuracy of the weapons. Everything Anjeet had heard about longbows suggested that accuracy wasn't one of their prime attributes.

Although a skilled man might be able to shoot a bird out of the air, he thought, as the aliens conferred once again. *It would still take years of training for them to learn how to use a bow so effectively.*

His eyes narrowed as he looked, once again, at the veiled figure. He had shown no reaction at all; it might have been concealed by his robes, but Anjeet was starting to have a suspicion that the figure was quite familiar with the sound of guns. Indeed, the more he looked at him, the more he wondered if he was staring at a human, rather than another alien. No human could hope to walk like one of the aliens, not without breaking multiple bones, but the robes would conceal anything strange about his movements.

"We will talk," the alien leader said, finally.

"We will," Anjeet agreed. He motioned towards his shuttle. "Would you care to join us in the shade?"

He had been curious to see what the Vesy made of the shuttle, but it didn't look as though they were particularly impressed. To them, he realised dully, the inner cabin looked like a soulless metal room. Indeed, it was the sheer preponderance of metal that seemed to impress them the most. Their world didn't lack for metal, according to the Russians, but gathering so much together in one place would be a remarkable feat, for them. The shuttle would be literally priceless even if it was completely grounded, unable to return to the skies.

"We require five square kilometres of land," he said, once the Vesy had explored the shuttle and squatted oddly on seats designed for human posteriors. "For this, we are prepared to trade…"

The Vesy might have been aliens, but they knew how to drive a hard bargain. It took nearly two hours before they had agreed to sign over the land, in exchange for three thousand human rifles, machine guns and various other weapons, as well as 10'000 rounds of ammunition and free human passage through their territory. The whole concept of an *exclusive* agreement seemed foreign to them - Anjeet had the feeling they would probably try to play other human factions off against the Indians, once other human factions arrived - but for the moment the Indians were the only humans who had made contact, save for the British. And it didn't seem as through the British were interested in selling weapons.

Assuming they have them to sell, Anjeet thought. Fort Knight had looked tiny, when he'd peered down at the base from orbit, and had a mere Corporal in command. *They didn't come here expecting to run into aliens, so they didn't bring anything they might have wanted to trade.*

"We will move the shuttles to the land as soon as possible," Anjeet said, when the discussions were complete. "And start ferrying down your payment immediately afterwards."

It would be more than that, he knew. His freighters held enough pre-fabricated components to put a small fortress together on alien soil. If things went sour, they would be able to hold out indefinitely against the best the aliens could do…or shelter while they called in KEW strikes from orbit to obliterate the imprudent aliens.

He looked at the veiled alien, once again, then took a gamble. "Who are you?"

There was a long pause, then the alien pulled back his hood to reveal a pale human face. It wasn't familiar - the Russians had refused to provide lists of potential deserters on Vesy - but that hardly mattered. All that mattered was that the Russian had spent the last six months trapped among the Vesy, learning more about them than anyone else.

"I am surprised the Indian Government was the first to send ships," the Russian said, in poor English. "The British should have been able to take the lead."

"There were too many political battles on Earth," Anjeet explained. "And to whom do I have the pleasure of talking?"

The Russian clammed up. Anjeet felt his patience start to fray.

"Your comrades have been shot for desertion and various other crimes, chief amongst them embarrassing their government," Anjeet lied smoothly. In truth, the surviving Russians were being milked of everything they knew about the Vesy. "However, I need someone with experience of talking to the aliens on their terms. Come work for me and I will ensure you leave with a new identity and a small fortune."

The Russian eyed him, darkly. "How do I know you're telling the truth?"

"You don't," Anjeet said, wondering if the Russian had cracked. Six months without seeing another human face, six months surrounded by aliens who might easily turn on him at any moment…it was enough to drive anyone insane. "But do you really want to spend the rest of your life here?"

He watched the Russian closely, wondering just which way the man would jump. It would be easy enough to trade additional weapons or ammunition for the Russian, if he demanded to stay with the Vesy, and the Russian had to know it. Or, even if the Indians showed no further interest in him, his own government would want his head. Embarrassing the Russian Government carried a death sentence, particularly now. Anjeet had no idea *just* why the other Great Powers had practically sent the Russians to Coventry, without supplying any of the aid they'd promised as part of the peace deal, but the Russians were clearly furious about it.

"My name is Nikolai Petrovich Zaprudnyi," the Russian said, finally. "I was an advisor to the Vesy when…when the base was captured by the British. The Vesy I was with were captured by another city-state, who took me and sold me onwards."

Anjeet nodded. He didn't blame the Russian for not trying to escape his captors. Where would he go? The British would be supremely unwelcoming and there were no other human bases on the planet, at least as far as he knew. Now…absently, he made a note to ensure that Zaprudnyi was properly debriefed. He could tell the Indians more about local politics than they could hope to find out for themselves.

"We'll buy him off you," he said, to the Vesy. Slavery was legal on Vesy, after all, and they'd bought Zaprudnyi from his former captors. "I can offer an extra 1000 rounds of ammunition for him…"

Another long haggling session followed. The Vesy had relied on Zaprudnyi to tell them about humanity, it seemed, and they weren't keen to let go of him. Anjeet didn't really blame them, but he needed the Russian himself. In the end, Zaprudnyi was sold to the Indians for 3000 rounds of ammunition and a handful of radios. Faster communication between the city-state - which Zaprudnyi insisted was called something that translated as Flowering Spring - and its armies would only help their expansion. It would probably also lead to micromanagement, Anjeet considered, but it was something he would leave them to find out on their own.

"Thank you," Zaprudnyi said, when the aliens were shown out the hatch. "I…I thank you for saving my life. They would have killed me eventually."

"You're welcome," Anjeet said. "My intelligence officers will debrief you, *thoroughly*. Tell them everything they want to know; indeed, help them as much as possible."

He paused. "Why did they bring you with them?"

"They wanted my impressions of the shuttle and your offers," Zaprudnyi said. "I told them to take what they could get."

"Excellent advice," Anjeet said, dryly. The shuttle rocked as the pilot prepared to move to the land he'd purchased at such high cost. "And I'm sure you will be very helpful in the future."

CHAPTER

TWELVE

"Transit complete, Captain," Armstrong said.

John nodded in relief. The passage through Pegasus had been slower than he'd expected, as they'd needed to hold a long-range conversation with Governor Brown and his team of experts. Unsurprisingly, Brown had complained - hugely - about diverting so much material from his supplies to Vesy, while Captain Minion had been forced to remain at Pegasus, rather than spread his ships between the two systems. It had boded ill for the future.

"Send a standard IFF pulse to the satellite network," he ordered, shortly. "And then take us towards the planet, best possible formation speed."

"Captain," Lieutenant Gillian Forbes said. "I'm picking up multiple IFF signals orbiting Vesy, sir, and several more in the out-system."

John swore, mentally. "How many?"

"At least thirty orbiting the planet itself," Gillian said. She worked her console for a long moment. "I'm picking up Indian, American, French, Israeli and Turkish signals, sir."

We were beaten here, John thought, bitterly. It wasn't entirely unexpected, given how badly the political debate had broken down, but he'd hoped to get to the planet before anyone else could arrive and complicate matters. *God alone knows what's happening on the surface.*

He frowned, thinking hard. It was a minimum of seven hours to Vesy at their current speed, as the freighters couldn't hope to match *Warspite's* acceleration. He could shave that in half by leaving the destroyers with the freighters - and the troop transport - but that would make him look frantic. And he *would* be frantic. It didn't *look* as through the various newcomers had started a fight, either with Fort Knight or each other, and he had no legal right to deny them access to Vesy. God alone knew who would win *that* debate in the World Court.

Because if we follow the standard rules, he thought, *either the Vesy hold the legal right to tell us all to fuck off...or the Russians own the system. Neither one will please the Admiralty.*

"Send them all a standard greeting," he ordered, finally. "And then send a message to Fort Knight, requesting a complete update."

"Aye, sir," Gillian said.

John tapped his console, sending Ambassador Richardson a brief update, then scrutinised the display as it started to fill with more and more icons. The Indians seemed to be the largest presence - they had sixteen ships orbiting the planet, five of them warships and one of them a heavy troop transport that had only just entered service. It was possible, John had to admit, that they'd scooped up a small army of researchers and stowed them onboard the transport, but it didn't seem likely. He had a feeling the Indians had brought a considerable number of troops to show that they had no intention of allowing anyone else to dictate to them. Beyond them, there were three American ships, one French ship and a number of others that had been chartered by various NGOs, religious organisations and the media.

And there are several survey ships operating in the system, he thought, grimly. *Looking for asteroids to mine, setting up a cloudscoop...or what?*

His console chirped. Moments later, Joelle Richardson's face appeared in the display.

"Captain," she said. "It appears we were beaten to the planet."

"That would appear to be the case," John agreed. They were too far out to tell if the newcomers were sending shuttles to the surface or not, but he wouldn't have bet against it, not when whoever made a deal with the Vesy first would have an edge against everyone else. "There are at least three governments represented here, as well as a number of other interested parties."

"So I see," the Ambassador said. "Can we get to Fort Knight without being intercepted?"

John blinked. "I don't believe that any of the powers represented here will try to keep us away from the planet," he said. "But, at the same time, we cannot police the entire system and keep *them* from landing, if they haven't done so already."

"I understand," the Ambassador said. She paused, thinking hard. "With your permission, Captain, I would like to send signals to the other nationalities, requesting a conference to discuss a joint approach to Vesy."

"Granted," John said. He had no grounds to deny the request, even if he'd wished to. "I should warn you, however, that our ability to enforce our position is very limited. Some of the nations represented here are our allies."

The Ambassador frowned, then cut the connection. Her face vanished from the display, which blinked back to showing the squadron following *Warspite* like ducks following their mother. John's lips twitched at the mental image, then he looked at his first officer. Howard was looking as concerned as John felt. They'd sketched out contingency plans for discovering they weren't the first to return to Vesy, but it had been impossible to guess at just which way things would go. The presence of so many Indian ships was a nasty surprise.

The Indians have always had a chip on their shoulder, John thought. He'd served with Indians, during the final months of the war, and they'd struck him as having something to prove. *And they do have a colony in the same general direction. But what do they want from Vesy?*

"Inform Captain Hadfield and Lieutenant-Colonel Boone that the situation isn't what we hoped for," he ordered, quietly. "We have yet to receive any updates from the surface."

"Aye, sir," Howard said.

John frowned, inwardly. The original plans would definitely have to be scrapped. He'd hoped to deploy 3 Para to Fort Knight, then allow the diplomats to make contact with the aliens in a single location where they could be protected. But now, with other governments, NGOs and religious factions running around, it would be impossible. If nothing else, they'd have to coordinate long enough to prevent accidental clashes between the different groups.

"Captain," Gillian said. "I just received a secure datapacket from Fort Knight."

"Transfer it to my console," John ordered. He knew he should probably get some rest - it would be at least five hours before anything happened - but he couldn't bring himself to leave the bridge. "And then copy it to the Ambassador and Captain Hadfield."

He tapped his console, opening the datapacket. Percy Schneider had been in command of Fort Knight for far too long, given his extremely low rank, but at least he'd managed to get his motley crew through the wait unharmed. Fort Knight wasn't quite where he'd expected it to be, but as he read on, he saw why. The handful of engineers and prefabricated equipment the marines had been able to obtain from Pegasus hadn't been sufficient to transfer everything to the planned location.

We muddled through, he thought, sourly. If they'd known they were going to be encountering aliens, he rather suspected the Admiralty would have doubled the supplies sent to Pegasus; instead, they'd had to strip one system of vital resources to maintain a base in another system. It had been sheer luck that the consequences hadn't been much worse. *But the long-term effects might be unpleasant.*

The diplomatic section of the report pulled no punches. Thankfully, the Americans and French - and most of the NGOs - had agreed to operate from Fort Knight, but the Indians and a handful of NGOs had flatly refused to have anything to do with the British. Percy Schneider had monitored the Indian activities as best as he could, noting that they'd clearly started to establish a base four hundred kilometres from Fort Knight and, he assumed, make contact with the local aliens. But he knew nothing else about their plans.

Shit, John thought. He cursed the diplomats under his breath. Would it really have been so politically incorrect to dispatch another warship or two to Vesy as soon as *Warspite* returned to Earth? *We won't be able to convince them to change their posture now.*

"Keep us on our current course," he ordered, as he started to skim through the more detailed sections of the report. There was no point in trying to increase speed and get there sooner, not when there were so many problems. "Once we're in orbit, the first teams can head down to Fort Knight."

He glanced at the timestamp on the report and frowned. Five days. Five days between the arrival of the Indians - and the others - and *Warspite* and her squadron. Five days. And if they'd left even a week earlier, they would have beaten everyone else easily.

Captain Hadfield - he'd been promoted after *Warspite's* return to Earth - popped up in John's display. "Captain," he said. "The situation is not optimal, but Wilson and I believe we can proceed with the planned landing."

"Understood," John said. "However, it will need to be coordinated to avoid running into the other powers. I believe most of them will have brought their own guards too."

"Yes, sir," Hadfield said. "We do have practice operating with the Americans and French."

"And the Indians have landed well away from Fort Knight," John agreed. "Very well; prepare your troops for deployment once we enter orbit."

He sighed as the connection closed. Five hours to orbit and then...? He had a feeling, somehow, that the ambassador and her staff were going to be earning their pay.

"That's the shuttle inbound, sir," the operator said.

"Thank you," Percy said. "I'll meet them at the shuttlepad."

He took one last look at the office he'd made for himself, then walked out the door and down towards the gates. He'd been relieved beyond measure when the next group of arrivals had proved to be a British squadron, then terrified when he'd been sent a private message informing him that *Captain* Hadfield and Lieutenant-Colonel Wilson Boone of 3 Para were on their way - and that the first order of business was a long chat with Percy about his conduct during the six months he'd been cut off from Earth. Somehow, Percy expected that it wouldn't be a pleasant conversation.

But there will be mail, he reminded himself. It was a consolation, of sorts. *Maybe not physical mail, but definitely recorded messages.*

The shuttlepad had been built by the Vesy to Percy's specifications, he recalled, as he watched the shuttle land neatly in front of him. A line of Paras jumped out, weapons in hand, and surveyed the scene for possible threats. Percy couldn't help noticing that some of them stared at the Vesy labourers, watching from a safe distance, as if they'd never quite believed in them, no matter how many visual images they'd seen. Five years after the war, it was still hard for some people to grasp the existence of one alien race, let alone a second. Percy and his men had grown used to the sight through long experience, but it would be a while before the Paras were truly used to the Vesy. He just hoped there weren't any unfortunate incidents before they learned how to survive on the alien world.

Behind them, Captain Hadfield emerged from the shuttle, wearing light armour and carrying a rifle slung over his shoulder. His face was expressionless, but Percy couldn't help suspecting that he was privately annoyed as he examined the buildings just outside the walls. If *Percy* could see them as a problem, the far more experienced Hadfield would have no difficulty in doing the same. And Lieutenant-Colonel Boone had more experience than Percy's entire section put together.

And the Paras have always picked fights with us, he thought, feeling his heart sinking. *Boone will happily remind the Captain about my failures for the rest of the deployment.*

"Corporal," Hadfield said, as Percy saluted them both. "Show us the office."

"This way, sir," Percy said.

He led them through the gates, then into the small office. It looked cramped to them, he was sure; a single metal table, a pair of metal chairs and a small terminal perched on the table. But then, he hadn't spent much time in it; he'd needed to do too many things to allow himself to become shut away in the room. Maybe Boone would want a bigger office. The diplomats certainly would.

"Corporal," Hadfield said, once the door was closed. "Perhaps you would care to explain why you allowed the aliens to build their habitations so close to the walls?"

Percy took a breath, placing firm controls on his temper. "I did not feel that attempting to convince them to build elsewhere would be workable, sir," he said. "The last thing I wanted was to give offense to our hosts."

"Hosts who could turn nasty at any moment," Hadfield pointed out, coldly. "Having their buildings so close to the wall would have allowed them to storm the fort before you could react."

"I had contingency plans, sir," Percy said. "Mortars would have reduced the buildings to sawdust within seconds, if necessary."

Hadfield glowered at him. "You still took a dangerous risk."

"And why," Boone said, speaking for the first time, "did you not establish a permanent settlement on an island, as per your orders? And why did you allow so many representatives from other nationalities to land at Fort Knight?"

Percy controlled himself with an effort. "Permission to speak freely, sir?"

"Granted," Hadfield said.

"I had ten marines, a handful of former Russian prisoners, and a small number of engineers from Pegasus," Percy said, flatly. "It was literally impossible to avoid enlisting alien help to build the fort, which required us to build it on the mainland, near our alien allies. I simply did not have the force to deal with them if they decided to attack us, perhaps because we insulted them in some way. The best I could have done, before your ships arrived, was die bravely. We would have made them pay a price for attacking us, sir, but the outcome would have been inevitable."

Boone smiled. "And so you decided to rewrite your orders?"

"My orders called for me to set up a base and maintain friendly relations with the local aliens until the diplomats arrived, sir," Percy said. "Setting up the base on an island, as planned, would have made it harder to maintain friendly relations. So too would have discouraging them from coming to visit us, or trying to hawk goods and supplies to the base. I believe I did the best I could, given the resources I had on hand."

He took a breath. "Furthermore, I did not have the resources to threaten the Indians or anyone else who wanted to land on Vesy," he added. "I invited them to work through Fort Knight so we could keep an eye on what they were doing. Had I refused, they would simply have copied the Indians and landed somewhere away from the base. I would therefore have been unable to monitor their activities."

"I see, *Corporal*," Boone said. "You feel you did the best you could, with the forces you had on hand."

"Yes, sir," Percy said.

Boone looked at Hadfield, who nodded.

"I am inclined to agree," Hadfield said. "But I'm afraid I have good news and bad news."

Percy had to fight down the urge to groan. He'd always hated the good news/bad news game, if only because his mother had been fond of it. The good news was never good, while the bad news was always horrific. Or so it had seemed at the time. As a mature adult, it struck him that he'd been a little brat more than a few times.

"The good news is that you're promoted, effective immediately, to Second Lieutenant," Hadfield said. "It's actually backdated six months, as you might expect, so you were paid the full wages. Not that it matters at the moment."

Percy nodded. There was literally nothing to spend his money on, either onboard ship or on Vesy. The money would remain in the bank on Earth until he returned home or died, in which case it would be forwarded to Penny. He didn't have any other biological relations left, as far as he knew. They'd certainly never found his mother's body.

And he'd been promoted! Someone must have approved of him...

"The bad news is that you will no longer be the commander of Fort Knight," Hadfield continued, remorselessly. "Lieutenant-Colonel Boone will be replacing you, I'm afraid."

"Yes, sir," Percy said. He'd expected as much. "Will we be returning to the ship?"

"No, *Lieutenant*," Boone said. "You and your men have been placed on the list of people to be sent home for leave, when the next ship departs Vesy, but for the moment your section will serve as a Quick Reaction Force. The experience you have garnered of operating on Vesy is too important to waste."

And we'll be teaching the Paras what we know, Percy thought. *They'll need to learn fast.*

"It will be a welcome change, sir," he said, instead. "However, I should warn you that the aliens are getting impatient. They want what they know we can give them - and they want it soon."

"Or they'll go somewhere else," Boone said. "I believe Ambassador Richardson will open communications with them as soon as she arrives, once we get some proper security set up here."

"And the spooks will want you to be debriefed," Hadfield added. "You're going to be rather busy, Lieutenant."

"Yes, sir," Percy said. He *would* be busy…but at least he wouldn't be out on a branch, feeling as though some bastard was planning to cut him off with a saw. "I look forward to it."

Hadfield gave him a look of pure mischievous evil. "And you should also send your sister a message," he said. "I believe she's planning to interview you."

Percy blinked. "How…?"

It struck him a moment later. "She's on the ship?"

"Embedded reporter," Hadfield confirmed. "And really quite depressingly enthusiastic."

"Oh," Percy said. The thought of Penny on Vesy…he'd *tried* to be protective, but she'd stuck her head into the lion's den anyway. "I'll send her a message as soon as possible."

CHAPTER
THIRTEEN

Joelle stepped through the hatch and closed her eyes, taking a long deep breath as she took her first step onto an alien world. Or *another* alien world, she reminded herself. Part of the reason she'd won the assignment was because she'd already visited an alien homeworld. She tasted pollen in the air, along with a warm humidity that startled her, and a scent that was oddly flavourful, like warm perfume. The wind shifted, blowing warm air against her bare face, then faded away again. It felt rather like a tropical day in the Maldives.

Where diplomats meet to talk, then have fun, she recalled. The Maldives had been effectively depopulated during the Age of Unrest, when the capital city had been torn apart by rioting and then evacuated. *I wonder how many of my fellows will make the same connection?*

She opened her eyes and stared at Fort Knight. It looked crude, like far too many military bases, and yet there was a certain charm to it that caught her attention. Perhaps it was the strange mixture of human and alien architecture, or perhaps it was because it was the sole major human settlement on the planet. Around it, beyond the walls, were dozens of other buildings, not all of them alien. The Americans and French had already started to occupy the barracks the Vesy had put together for them.

"Ambassador?" Grace asked, from behind her. "Are you alright?"

"I'm just admiring the scenery," Joelle said, without looking around. There had been health warnings included in the briefing, one of which had covered the potential danger of pollen on human health. The medics were watching for the first signs of anything akin to hay fever or allergic reactions, although - so far - no one had shown any signs of more than mild sneezing when breathing the alien air. "It's a very strange city."

"It's a very primitive settlement," Grace said, as she walked forward. Joelle sensed, rather than saw, her wrinkling her nose. "It's covered in mud."

"I think this isn't meant to be a permanent settlement," Joelle said. The Vesy knew how to work stone, after all; she'd seen images of their giant stone cities. "They just wanted to build a settlement as quickly as possible, so they built it out of wood. It isn't as if there is a shortage of wood on the surface."

Grace sniffed. "We could show them something better," she said. "Couldn't we?"

"Probably," Joelle said.

She turned her head and blinked in shock. The Vesy were *staring* at her, staring with an intensity that chilled her to the bone. It was such a penetrating stare that she felt naked, even though she'd worn a light suit that covered everything, save for her hands and face. She'd even donned a hat to keep the sun off her head. The Vesy might be primitive, she reminded herself savagely, but they'd seen humans die. They knew humans weren't gods.

And that will make them more dangerous across the negotiating table, she thought, as she saw a uniformed officer emerging from the gates of Fort Knight. *They will drive a hard bargain.*

"Ambassador," the officer said. "I'm...ah, *Lieutenant* Schneider, Royal Marines. I have been charged with showing you the fort and escorting you to meet with Ivan, the local alien ruler."

Grace stepped forward. "Do you have to use the Russian names for them?"

"Their names are unpronounceable," Schneider said. He didn't quite say that such details had been included in the briefing notes, but Joelle was sure he *wanted* to say it. "We decided to stick with the Russian names until we obtained better translations."

"You wrote most of the reports," Joelle said, as she allowed Schneider to lead them towards the fort. "I read them with great interest."

"Thank you, Ambassador," Schneider said.

They stepped through the gates and into the fort itself. It was larger than Joelle had realised, with a number of low barracks and a handful of prefabricated buildings from Earth, all patrolled by men in jungle camouflage uniforms. The Union Jack flew over the main building, but the Stars and Stripes dominated another and the French Tricolour flew over a third.

"We gave one barrack hall to the Americans and one to the French," Schneider explained, as they walked past the barracks. "The smaller groups have been allocated space in a communal building and told to behave themselves, basically. We've been running language and alien culture lessons for them in the hopes of avoiding problems."

Grace coughed. "Do you know enough to avoid cultural misunderstandings?"

"Not enough," Schneider said. "They're egg-layers; anything connected to their eggs and hatching is pretty much a berserk button for them. The concept of bastardry seems completely alien to them - I think it's because they recognise family members by scent - but we've been warned not to even *suggest* that someone did something to the eggs before they hatched. Other than that...they do have religions, which they're reluctant to discuss, so I would advise you not to raise the subject with them."

"That doesn't seem very specific," Grace pointed out.

"As far as we can tell, we have contact with twelve or thirteen city-states, some of which were badly mangled by the God-King," Percy said. "That's a tiny percentage of the planet's population, all from an area smaller than England. It's quite possible that there are cultures on the other side of the world that are very different; we just don't know about it, yet. It will take years to properly survey the entire world."

He shrugged. "For us, giving someone the thumbs up is a good thing," he added. "In the Middle East, it's insulting. What's taboo in this part of the world may be enthusiastically practiced in a different part of the world."

Joelle nodded in understanding. Dealing with cultural differences hadn't been considered a priority since the Age of Unrest - few people cared to honour customs they regarded as brutal, barbaric and inhuman - but it could be important during talks with Japan, China or even Russia. A Japanese negotiating team might be led by someone who never said a word, even during high-level discussions, while the Chinese were quite happy to have the talks stretch out over weeks if necessary. And the Russians could be quite reasonable as long as they believed that no one was going to give them an inch, let alone a mile.

The rest of the tour proceeded quickly. Joelle was impressed, all the more so when she saw hundreds of Vesy working on the next set of barracks on the far side of the fort. The walls would have to be expanded to provide cover, she suspected, but Fort Knight was already taking on the characteristics of a minor town. It wouldn't be long before more prefabricated buildings were brought down from orbit and used to expand the facilities still further.

"Tell me something," she said. "How secure is the base?"

Schneider hesitated. "We have rules against allowing the aliens into the base without an escort, all the more so now as we have the firepower to back it up," he said. "However, if they attacked in force, we would probably be overwhelmed without orbital firepower to even the odds."

He paused, again. "We haven't been able to run coordinated bug sweeps yet, however," he added. "I imagine that various intelligence parties are already trying to pick up what they can from us."

Joelle nodded. "The conference rooms will need to be swept regularly," she said. "For what time did you organise the meeting with the alien ambassador?"

Schneider glanced at his wristcom. "It is due to take place in two hours," he said. "Do you want to freshen up first?"

"Yes, please," Joelle said. Sweat was already running down her back. "Show me to my quarters, if you please. I can sort through the briefing notes and update my plans."

Grace gave Schneider a long look. "What do you make of them? The aliens, I mean, when you talked to them?"

"Don't expect them to have any patience with evasive speech," Schneider said, after a moment. "They are plain blunt men, as far as I can tell. They won't tolerate anyone trying to string them along."

Joelle nodded. It was something to bear in mind.

She hadn't expected much from the quarters and she wasn't disappointed. Her suite was nothing more than a pair of rooms, a makeshift shower and a couple of pieces of alien designed and built furniture. Grace grumbled when she saw the shower, which made Joelle smile; her aide had never lived or worked away from civilisation for a day, let alone a long-term assignment to another country. Poor showers weren't *bad*, not compared to howling mobs intent on looting, raping and murdering western ambassadors. She washed herself quickly under the lukewarm water, then hastily reread the briefing notes while Grace took a shower herself. There was nothing new there, save for a warning that the Indians might be making all sorts of deals with the Vesy and no one had any idea what they might be.

And that is the question, Joelle thought, as she changed into new clothes. *What are the Indians offering that we will have to match?*

Schneider returned, when the time came, and led her towards the conference building outside the walls. Joelle considered arranging to have something lighter than a heavy suit in future - it was unlikely the Vesy would care if she wore shorts and a t-shirt instead of the suit - and then pushed the thought aside as Schneider escorted her into the conference room. An alien, a real live alien, was standing in front of a table, peering at her. Joelle heard Grace gasp behind her, even though they'd seen aliens before when the shuttle landed. Up close, the alien smelled faintly odd, a scent that reminded her of a heady perfume. It made her think of weekends in the countryside when she'd been a little girl, down on the farm with her relatives and their small collection of animals.

And you hated it when you realised that Harry Pooper had been slaughtered, then turned into the pork roast you had for dinner, she thought, as she bowed to the alien. The memory was so strong it almost overpowered her. *How long did it take you to go back to the farm after you discovered the truth?*

"I greet you," she said, in English. She could speak Russian, if necessary, but she would prefer to use English. "I am Ambassador Joelle Richardson. I speak for my people."

"I am Ivan," the alien replied, also in English. There was definitely an accent, but he spoke English better than she'd expected. "I speak for my people."

Joelle hesitated, then sat facing him. Grace stood behind her; Schneider, after exchanging a wave with the alien, left the room. The alien didn't sit; the briefing notes had made it clear that they preferred to stand, even where a human would have seen someone looming over them as a threat. Their body language was still largely a mystery...Joelle forced herself to remember, again, that she wasn't dealing with a human wearing a funny suit. The Vesy might look closer to human than the Tadpoles, but they were still alien.

"I must be curt," the alien said. There were faint intonations in his flat voice, but it was impossible to tell what, if anything, they meant. "I speak with authority to make agreements on behalf of my people. Do you speak with the same authority?"

"Within certain limits, yes," Joelle said.

"That is unacceptable," Ivan said. "Do you or do you not have authority to speak on behalf of your people?"

Joelle took a moment to compose an answer. "I have authority to make agreements with you, within certain limits," she said. "As long as those limits are not infringed, I can make binding agreements on their behalf."

She frowned inwardly, mind racing. The aliens had accepted then-Corporal Schneider's status as the man in charge, but they'd also understood that he had no power to make long-term agreements with anyone. Now, with a genuine Ambassador on the spot, they clearly expected substantial discussions. And with the Indians up to something, only a few hundred miles away, they had good reason to want to move fast.

Perhaps it would have been better, she thought, *not to discuss the possibility of limits at all.*

"I will accept that, for the moment," Ivan said. The beady eyes winked at her. "I have been given to understand that your race is unfailingly polite, when discussing matters between two separate" - he paused for a long moment - "nations. Is that correct?"

"Largely so," Joelle said. The Vesy didn't really have a concept of *nations*, or anything greater than the city-states. That would probably change soon, with or without human intervention. "We believe it helps prevent disagreements that become wars."

"That is not our way," Ivan said. "We believe that it is better for requests and demands to be stated clearly, without room for misunderstandings. Our" - he used a word in his own language - "speak bluntly."

While carrying a big stick, Joelle guessed. Really, it shouldn't have been a surprise, even without Schneider's warnings. The Romans and Greeks hadn't been big fans of diplomacy either, at least not when they held the upper hand. *The word he used must mean something akin to a diplomat.*

"That would be acceptable," Joelle said. She'd been called all sorts of nasty things at diplomatic meetings and never lost her cool. It helped that she'd known she was backed by one of the largest sticks in the known universe. "You may speak bluntly."

"We have seen what your...*technology* can do," Ivan said. "We have seen you, and the Russians, deploy weapons that dominate the battlefield. We have seen your medics heal wounds and repair damage that should have killed the victim. We have seen that you have so much we want. We want it."

Joelle hesitated, then nodded. "What do you want, precisely?"

"Weapons, medicine and tools," Ivan said.

His beady eyes met hers. "We allied with your people when they first arrived on the planet," he added. "However, the existence of other human...*nations* has changed the balance of power. We must obtain technology from you or seek it from others."

And that, Joelle knew, was a very blunt statement. She understood Ivan's dilemma; if they stayed loyal to the British, city-states that signed up with other nations might start considering them potential targets...and if they failed to obtain any modern weapons, they would be slaughtered by their opponents. It had been a long time since she'd studied the complexities of North American diplomacy, in the days before the American Revolution, but she suspected her current situation had more in common with the early colonial settlements than she cared to admit. If she didn't keep the aliens on her side, through bribes and gifts, they would go to the other human powers.

But the Professor is right, she thought. *Introducing new technology will disrupt their society beyond repair.*

"We can provide you with technology," she said, slowly. She did have considerable room to manoeuvre over precisely *what* she sent to them. "However, I should warn you that you might find that introducing something new may do serious damage to your society."

"So will being crushed by another city-state armed with your weapons," Ivan pointed out. It was hard to be sure, but she had the feeling the alien was laughing at her. "It would *destroy* our society."

He was right, she knew. She'd seen the images from *Warspite's* first visit to Vesy, when the God-King's rapid expansion had shattered into ruin. He'd enslaved entire populations, including Ivan's home city; now, it was sheer luck that enough of the slaves had survived to start a new city. Conquest didn't mean a few hundred dead, not now; it meant death or slavery for hundreds of thousands of aliens. Ivan's new city might die as easily as the old.

Ivan cleared his throat. "There is no longer any choice for us," he said. "Supply us with weapons and technology or we must go elsewhere. Our spies report that your rivals have already begun arming their new allies, giving them weapons we cannot match. Help us or lose us."

Joelle heard Grace cough behind her. She knew what was going through the idealist's head; there was no reason, no matter the situation, to add human weapons to an already poisonous stew. But cold practicality worked against them. She could not afford to gain a reputation for abandoning her allies, not on a planet where they *needed* alien allies. God knew a reputation for being a flaky ally had plagued the United States throughout the Age of Unrest, when it had needed allies more than ever before.

"We will supply you with weapons, if you wish," she said, finally. She knew she needed to confer with her diplomatic staff as well as Captain Naiser and Lieutenant-Colonel Boone, but she had a feeling that the Vesy would not accept any more delays. Time was not on their side. "However, we will want some other concessions in exchange."

Ivan rocked back, slightly. "Name your price," he said.

Joelle smiled to herself, despite her growing concern, and then started to negotiate. There was a wish list, after all; permission to explore alien territory, permission to learn about the alien culture, detailed intelligence reports on the neighbouring city-states…the list went on and on, covering all kinds of topics. It might be interesting, she thought, to see just how much Ivan was prepared to concede.

But when he conceded almost everything by the time the meeting reached its end, she realised that the alien wasn't just nervous, he was *desperate*. And that, she was sure, spelt trouble.

CHAPTER
FOURTEEN

"They refused to consider an exclusive agreement," Ambassador Joelle Richardson said, through the communications link. "Other than that… they agreed to whatever we wanted."

John frowned. "Everything?"

"Yes, Captain," Joelle said. "We now have a whole series of rights. Our people can visit their city-state, if we like; we can speak to their people and carry out research into their culture and society. But it all comes at the price of fuelling the local arms race."

"I'm not surprised," John said. He remembered meeting Ivan, after the attack on the Russian base. The alien had struck him as ruthlessly pragmatic - and quick-thinking, willing to ally with the British newcomers to fight the Russians. "They don't have much choice."

Joelle's eyes narrowed. "Do you agree with them, Captain?"

John took a moment to consider his answer. "There are times when the niceties must be thrown out of the airlock," he said. "For us, and I imagine for them, survival comes first, always. They need our weapons to survive. If they don't get their hands on them, Ambassador, they will be overwhelmed by those who do."

"And if we refuse to supply them, they will turn to other powers," Joelle said, slowly. "It doesn't seem right, somehow."

"Professor Nordstrom believes that our involvement will destroy their culture," John said. "Your aide believes that we have a moral right to assist them in *improving* their culture. But the aliens don't have time to worry about the long-term, not now. They need to worry about staying alive and relatively free."

He shrugged. "Does it really make any difference who supplies the weapons?"

"It might to the Prime Minister," Joelle said. "What happens when the media picks up on a massacre and blames it on British weapons? The Opposition will make hay out of it in the Houses of Parliament."

"Politicians," John said. It wouldn't be the first time that idealism - and an understandable urge to avoid controversy - had led to a diplomatic disaster. "If you don't give the aliens weapons, you lose them to other powers; if you do give them weapons, you can be charged with aiding and abetting a war between alien factions. It doesn't seem like a situation wherein you can actually *win*."

"We could offer a security blanket ourselves," Joelle said. "We did it a couple of times on Earth."

"And both times eventually ended with the blanket being withdrawn," John pointed out. It had been much worse in the Age of Unrest, when old certainties had been falling everywhere and once-trusted alliances became nothing more than ink on paper. "The Vesy would be fools to trust us to look after their interests."

"We mean them well," Joelle said, stung.

"They would be fools to take that on trust," John said. "What happens if there is a General Election and the next Prime Minister decides to cancel our commitment to Vesy? Their only viable course of action is to get their hands on human weapons, either from us or some other nation."

"You sound as if you approve," Joelle said, darkly.

"I understand Ivan's position," John said. "He really doesn't have a choice."

"Because of the Indians," Joelle muttered. She cleared her throat. "Are they really giving weapons to their allies?"

"We have orbital recordings of aliens training with human weapons," John said. He swung his terminal around and tapped a switch, reviewing the images. "The Indians had to have supplied them, Ambassador. There's nothing too heavy, no long-range artillery or anti-aircraft weapons, but enough to give their allies a decisive advantage, assuming we don't supply weapons ourselves. They might expand more rapidly than the God-King and overwhelm Ivan and his people before they can learn to defend themselves."

"And if that happens," Joelle said, "who do we talk to?"

John nodded in understanding. It had been an old problem on Earth, during the Age of Unrest; the people the Western Governments preferred to talk to were rarely the people in power. If Ivan was killed and his city-state crushed, should the British recognise the facts on the ground...or what? Intervene in a war between two different alien factions, a war that might drag in human powers? It seemed absurd to think that a war on an alien world could lead to a general human war, but if the assassination of a single man could lead to the First World War...

But the world was ripe for a major war, he thought. *There might well have been a war anyway, even if the spark happened to be something different. The alliances would still have come into play and all hell would have broken loose.*

He shook his head. It wasn't likely to happen. The Great Powers knew, beyond a shadow of a doubt, that they weren't alone in the universe. A major war between human powers might end with the Tadpoles taking advantage of humanity's sudden weakness to invade human space and put an end to the potential threat, once and for all. John wasn't sure he'd blame them; if the situation was reversed, he would have seriously considered doing the same.

"We have no choice, but to start supplying weapons," John said, flatly. He glanced down at his terminal, then frowned. "I believe the first crates will be shipped down to the planet tomorrow."

"That's fast," Joelle said.

"All part of the service," John said. He grinned. "3 Para is down and deployed, so we can assure ourselves that the weapons will remain safe, for the moment."

He paused. "I'd like you to refrain from mentioning weapons that can be used against shuttles," he said. "And if they ask for MANPADs, tell them we don't have any."

Joelle gave him a puzzled look. "Don't you think they'd have the intelligence to work out that they exist?"

"I'd prefer not to give them ideas," John said. He rather suspected the Vesy *would* be able to deduce their existence, but he had no intention of supplying any such weapons to *any* alien faction. And the Indians, if they had any common sense, would do the same. "I understand that you are to meet with the other ambassadors and representatives in a couple of days?"

"I am," Joelle confirmed.

"I would ask you to suggest - strongly - that we place a blanket ban on supplying heavy weapons," John said. "Not small arms, not rifles; weapons that can be used against us. It could lead to real problems."

"I'll bring it up," Joelle said. She winced. "It isn't going to be an easy meeting, Captain."

"I know," John said. "I've spoken to my American and French counterparts, but they've both been somewhat non-committal. It may require a more formal agreement before they cooperate..."

He paused as his terminal started to bleep. When he looked at it, he saw a new wave of starships had entered the system, led by a Turkish destroyer and a pair of pre-war Brazilian frigates. The frigates were tougher than they looked, he knew all too well; several of them had served with honour in the war, despite being slower and far less manoeuvrable than the more modern ships. Behind them, there were nine freighters and a passenger liner, one of the few in commission. Only the very rich could afford to sail between the stars in comfort.

"We have newcomers," he said, dryly. "If you'll excuse me, I need to get to the bridge."

"Understood, Captain," Joelle said. "Good luck."

Her image vanished from the display. John took a moment to gather himself - life had been so much simpler when he'd been plotting how best to dislodge the Russians from Vesy - and then rose, walking through the hatch to the bridge. There was work to be done.

———

"I must say I've been in nicer prisons," Penny said, as she peered around the tiny room. "It has a definite lack of charm."

"And when," Percy asked as he closed the door behind them, "were you in prison?"

"I was ordered to do a feature on the renovation of Dartmoor Prison," she said, as she turned to face her brother. "It was definitely not the nicest place in the world, but it was nicer than *this*."

She waved a hand at the wooden walls. The tiny room wasn't large enough to swing a cat, there was a faint smell of something unpleasant drifting through the air and the washroom facilities reminded her of the refugee camp she'd endured in the days following the bombardment. And the only source of illumination was a lantern someone had hung from the rooftop, which cast an eerie light over the entire scene.

"But it's on an alien world," Percy said, as he sat down on the bunk. "That must count for something, mustn't it?"

Penny nodded, ruefully, and leaned against the wall. It *was* an alien world…and she had to admit she'd already recorded enough footage to please her bosses, back home on Earth. She sighed, then studied her brother thoughtfully. Percy had always been muscular, even before he'd started training in earnest, but now he looked older, more mature. It was hard, sometimes, to reconcile the older brother who'd put worms in her hair as a child with the grown man sitting in front of her. And yet, after the bombardment, they'd both had to grow up in a tearing hurry. They couldn't be children any longer.

"I see you got promoted," she said. She smiled, teasing him lightly. "You're actually quite famous on Earth, you know. They're already planning to do a movie about your life, with Thomas Morse in the lead role…"

"Shut up," Percy said, crossly. "I really hope that's a joke."

"Well, it's Lawrence Newman instead of Thomas Morse," Penny said. She broke off at his glare and changed the subject. "You're right, Percy. This *is* an alien world."

Percy sighed. "Why did you come here?"

"My bosses thought I'd be good at it," Penny said. She wasn't surprised that Percy objected, not really. He'd been terrifyingly over-protective since the bombardment, even though she was only two years younger than him. "And it was definitely a chance to make my name."

"Perhaps as someone who died on Vesy," Percy said. "This isn't a safe place, Pen-Pen."

Penny felt her cheeks flush at the childish nickname. "Call me that in public and I'll tell your manly friends about the time you got stuck in the mud, when we were in Skye."

"Point taken," Percy said. The old Percy would probably have shouted an insult…but that Percy had died with their parents. "But Penny, it really isn't safe here."

"You don't make a reputation for covering safe places," Penny pointed out, crossly. "Or did you earn your medals for standing on guard outside Buckingham Palace?"

"That's a different regiment," Percy said, automatically. "And they *earned* their medals when terrorists tried to storm Buckingham Palace."

"You know what I mean," Penny said, resisting a childish urge to stamp her foot. What was it about being with her brother that brought out the worst in her? She was a mature adult with a career of her own, not the fourteen-year-old brat who'd amused herself by scaring away Percy's girlfriends. "I need to do something spectacular to earn a reputation."

Percy laughed. "Well, you *do* realise that there are quite a few other reporters on the planet?"

"I have embedded myself with the ambassador's party," Penny countered. She knew there would be meetings that excluded the press, but she'd have near-complete access otherwise. "I should at least get a clean shot at a scoop or two."

"Embed yourself with the planned visits to alien cities," Percy suggested, sarcastically. "You might learn things you didn't want to learn."

He took a breath. "How *is* your career?"

Penny winced. She was a very junior reporter and, despite the protection of her name, she wasn't entirely immune to pressure from senior reporters and editors. There were so few jobs available at any one time these days, after the bombardment, that few people were prepared to say no if their boss started putting unreasonable demands on them. She had had a sneaking suspicion that she hadn't been promoted earlier because of her name, although she *had* received the coveted posting to Vesy. But then, she had both aristocratic connections and a brother already stationed on the planet.

Percy reached out and took her hand. "Who do I have to kill?"

"It isn't that bad," Penny assured him, hastily. "It's just hard to make any headway when the older reporters guard their posts like…"

"Dogs in the manger?" Percy guessed.

"More like hyenas gnawing at carrion," Penny muttered. She glowered down at the wooden floor. "If an assignment is offered that promises fame, expect all of the older reporters to pull strings to get it for themselves. There's no real sense of comradeship among the bastards when they are really chasing name recognition, not a tradition of long service. The ones that reach the very highest levels are practically regarded as little tin gods. They can get away with practically anything as long as they keep delivering the goods."

She sighed. "There's this bitch who looks like a doll," she added. "She keeps saying she was actually assigned to *Ark Royal*, but I don't believe her. And yet she keeps getting all the good assignments because she's got real name recognition. I don't have that yet…"

"Our name is known across the country, if not the world," Percy pointed out.

"Just for who our father was," Penny snapped back. "I'm not known for *myself*."

She pulled her hand free, then glowered at her brother. "I'm going to use this assignment to make my name," she said, firmly. "And you are not going to get in my way."

"Just don't ask me to be interviewed," Percy said, tiredly. "And please, watch your back."

"I always do," Penny said. She had picked up the habit at the refugee camp and never really lost it. "I still shoot every weekend for practice."

"Make sure you spend some time at the shooting range here," Percy said. He sighed. "Do you have a registered firearm?"

"Not from here," Penny said. It hadn't been easy to get the gun permit, even though the government had been practically handing them out like candy after the bombardment. There just hadn't been enough policemen or soldiers to maintain order over large parts of the country. "I brought the pistol I got in Newcastle."

"Get the weapon registered at the shooting range or draw yourself a new one from the armoury," Percy said. "No one wants to lose a weapon to the locals - but if we do, we want to know what we lost. There's a colossal fine if you lose one and don't actually report it."

"I thought there was a colossal fine if you lost the weapon anyway," Penny said. She'd been required to place a bond for the pistol before she'd been allowed to buy it. "Or is it different here."

Percy smirked. "You would be astonished just how much equipment is marked down as having being lost during a war," he said. "It provides a convenient excuse for…losing something that actually got lost on exercise, or was shipped elsewhere owing to bureaucratic stupidity."

"Oh," Penny said. She looked her brother in the eye. "Is it really a problem?"

"We've lost quite a few small trinkets," Percy said. "I believe they were stolen by some of the local workers while they were building the fort. Even something minor to us" - he looked around, then nodded at the lantern - "is worth its weight in gold to them. I think that several datapads crammed with books and movies have gone missing over the last six months."

Penny blinked. "You *think*?"

"I know they went missing," Percy said. "But I don't know where they *went*."

"Well," Penny said, after a moment. "I'm sure the Vesy will be *very* interested to see the sort of movies you used to hide on your datapad."

"You might have a point," Percy said. He didn't look as embarrassed as he'd done when their mother had caught him watching porn, Penny noted. "It would teach them a great deal about human biology. And some of the books might teach them something about how the human race is governed."

Penny shook her head. "The fantasy shit you used to read won't teach them anything," she disagreed. "All those wizards and goblins and things that go bump in the night…"

"Thrillers will," Percy said. "One of the missing datapads had a complete set of books by Brett Mole, the former naval officer who used to write military thrillers about a general war between America and China. Someone could put together a great deal about the two different systems of government, merely by reading the books."

"And a great deal about pre-war weapons and tactics," Penny said. Brett Mole had retired from the navy and gone into writing well before First Contact. "But it will be all magic to them, won't it?"

"I don't know," Percy said. "No amount of reading *Wizards of Wisdom* will teach someone how to use magic, not when the rituals are all nonsensical and there's no such thing as magic. But they know our technology works…and they may make reasoned deductions from what they read. It could turn into a major problem."

His eyes narrowed suddenly. "And they have been fighting each other regularly," he added, sharply. "So, again, watch your back. And keep an eye on your possessions."

"I will," Penny promised. She'd make sure she kept her recorder and communicator with her at all times. "Now, why don't you tell me more about the planet and its population?"

"Because there are some things you really have to experience for yourself," Percy said. "And I would hate to spoil the surprise."

CHAPTER
FIFTEEN

The conference room was as good as Grace and a handful of aides from other human powers could make it, Joelle knew, as she stepped into the room. But she knew it didn't remotely live up to the standards of conference rooms on Earth. A large pair of fans blew cold air over the table, which was made from wood and polished until she could practically see her own face reflected in it, while a single smaller table was covered with glasses and large jugs of boiled water. They'd been warned, more than once, to keep all liquids covered, at least outside of the air-conditioned buildings. It didn't normally take more than a few minutes for insects to descend on anything uncovered and start devouring it for themselves.

But that isn't a bad thing, she told herself, as the other diplomats started to file into the room, a handful carrying bug detectors so they could do their own private sweeps. *It should focus a few minds on where we are, rather than the comforts of Geneva.*

She concealed her amusement with an effort at their appearance. The black suits and ties were gone, replaced by shorts, slacks and shirts. None of them looked particularly diplomatic; they looked more like middle-aged men and women going to a holiday resort for the first time in their lives, trying to be hip and yet not having the slightest idea how to pull it off. Joelle couldn't help thinking, as she took her seat around the round table - carefully designed so that no one appeared to be in charge, or more important than anyone else - that maybe they would actually get something *done*. Time was not exactly on their side.

"Thank you for coming," she said, once the last bug sweep had been carried out and everyone had taken a seat, along with a glass of water. "I apologise for the informality of these rooms, but right now we don't have better living spaces for humans."

"There is no need to apologise," Sam Schultz said. The American leaned forward, one hand stroking his flaming red beard. "We quite understand."

Joelle nodded in relief. Whatever else they'd done, every interstellar power that had expressed an interest in Vesy had sent a grown-up diplomat, rather than someone who would quite happily delay matters by raising issues with the tables, the food, the staff or anything apart from the issue in question. Such adult children had played a major role in *delaying* the second mission to Vesy, leading to the chaotic scene in orbit. But then, she reflected morbidly, it might be precisely what they'd wanted all along.

She took a moment to survey the table. The Americans and French were allies, although the Americans had an election campaign underway and the French tended to look for their own advantage, first and foremost. Every other interstellar power did the same, of course, but the French were refreshingly honest about it. The Indian representative, a dark-skinned woman wearing a pair of white trousers and a tight shirt, might be an opponent, if handled badly; beside her, the Turks and Chinese both looked inscrutable. Joelle had a feeling the Turks and Indians had conferred previously - British Intelligence was sure that the two minor powers had been quietly collaborating for years - while the Chinese could jump either way. And who knew just what the Brazilians, Germans and Japanese had in mind? They'd only sent a single warship apiece.

"I will come right to the point," she said, mentally throwing the standard diplomatic rulebook out of the airlock. "There's no point in trying to quarantine Vesy, not any longer. Quite apart from the damage the Russians caused, by introducing gunpowder to alien warfare, our own people will not let us. I have in my hand" - she held up a datapad, waving it in front of them - "a series of requests from hundreds of private interests, ranging from charities to corporations that believe Vesy is an untapped paradise. It will be impossible to keep them from landing on the planet."

"Not least because you set up a base yourself, six months ago," Louis Barouche pointed out, dryly. The French Ambassador smiled, rather coolly. "It would seem absurd for you to argue for quarantining Vesy now."

Translation; you want a share for yourself, Joelle thought.

She kept her face impassive. As far as she could tell, Vesy had nothing to offer apart from raw knowledge, but knowledge could be quite useful when an enterprising company found a way to use it to make money. It wasn't as if there was any point in strip-mining the entire planet. What could the planet offer that couldn't be extracted, without so many ethical, legal and practical barriers, from the asteroids drifting in orbit around the star?

"We need to devise a framework for handling such requests in the future, one we can all support," she continued. "The current situation is unsustainable."

"My government's position is that the Vesy, and the Vesy alone, are masters of their world," Rani Begum said. "While we recognise that Russia was the first human state to encounter the Vesy, we do not accept that gives them any claim to the planet or the star system. The Vesy got there first."

"Now hold on, wait a minute," the American snapped. "The Russians in question were deserters, not representatives of the Russian Government!"

Joelle winced. Something had happened between Russia and the other Great Powers, something bad, something that had practically led to Russia's exclusion from the rest of the world. And yet, she had no idea *what*. Someone had kept the information so tightly restricted that nothing, not even a peep, had leaked out to the media. She hated to admit it, but that scared her. What could convince so many people, from so many different countries, to keep their mouths firmly closed?

And, she thought, *to hate the Russians at the same time?*

"The point is immaterial," Barouche said. "We can all agree, I think, that none of us have a pressing claim to own the system."

"My government upholds that point," Rani said.

"My government would agree," Joelle said. The public would probably not react well to any attempt to claim Vesy for Britain, not when it was already inhabited by a native non-human race. "However, the fact remains that the Vesy are simply incapable of preventing human factions from meddling on their world. Furthermore" - she held up a hand - "they are already badly contaminated. I do not believe we can prevent it from spreading all over their world."

"You make it sound as though they have caught a disease," the American grumbled.

"On the face of it, my government would not object to setting up a framework for contacting the Vesy," Rani said. "However, we insist on maintaining our own contacts with the aliens."

"I would tend to agree," Barouche said.

"You mean you wish to gain influence over the system," the German said. "You have already landed a considerable amount of supplies at your base."

"That is correct," Rani said, simply. "How many of you" - her dark eyes swept the room - "really do *not* intend to gain influence over the aliens?"

None of us, Joelle thought, ruefully. *She's right.*

"Then let us be careful what we introduce," Barouche said. "They are simply not mature enough, as a society, to accept what we give them."

"They're not children," Schultz snapped. The American leaned forward, resting his elbows on the table. "I believe we shouldn't be *treating* them as children."

"Tell me," Barouche said. "How many of our problems last century came from giving advanced technology to people who were culturally unable to handle the implications?"

Joelle had to smile. "It wasn't just the Middle East that had problems because of technology's rapid advancement," she pointed out. "The rest of the world had problems too."

"But everyone else was able to understand and embrace change," the Frenchman countered. "The Middle East could not...and eventually, when we found a way to live without them, we cut them out of the global network."

"That's an old argument," Joelle said. She'd heard it before from Professor Nordstrom and Grace, who'd fought and refought it time and time again. "The problem here is that we are not dealing with humans."

"They test out as roughly equal to us," Schultz said. "They're not *inherently* less intelligent than ourselves."

"That doesn't mean they have the social experience to cope with new technology," Barouche snapped. "You might as well give growth hormones to a baby and expect a mature adult at the end!"

"I believe we are getting away from the point," Rani said. Her cool voice cut through the air in a manner Joelle could only admire. "I assume there is a proposal in mind for a working framework?"

Joelle nodded. "First, I believe we should place limits on what sort of weapons we supply to the Vesy," she said. She glanced briefly at Rani. "It may be too late to keep from supplying *some* weapons to the locals, but we need to make sure they don't present a threat to us. In particular, we would like to ban antiaircraft weapons, long-range missiles, tanks and other systems they do not know - yet - exist."

"They will," Schultz pointed out. "I believe 3 Para has a number of LAVs."

Light Armoured Vehicles, Joelle translated, inwardly. They were thin-skinned, compared to heavy Wellington tanks, but by local standards they were effectively unstoppable. *And he has a point.*

"It will be far easier to keep the arms race from getting out of control if we *all* agree not to sell tanks," she said, instead. "And there is a certain risk inherent in providing weapons to forces that may not be entirely under our control. It could lead to a diplomatic nightmare."

She watched their faces as the implications sank in. Small arms could come from anywhere, everyone knew it. But heavier systems, even simple antiaircraft weapons, could be traced back to their producer. And who knew what would happen then, if one such system was used to shoot down a shuttle? The Indians could get the blame if one of the factions they backed shot down a British shuttle. It could lead to a major diplomatic crisis, perhaps even a war.

"We will certainly consider the list of banned systems," Rani said, finally.

There were nods from around the table. They were experienced enough, after all, to understand the dangers in providing advanced weapons systems to unreliable aliens. Better to work together, at least to some extent, rather than cause a major headache for their superiors back home. Besides, it wouldn't really work against any of them.

"Second, I believe there should be a flat ban on NGOs supplying weapons to the Vesy," Joelle continued. "I also think there should be strict limits on what they can and cannot do on the surface. Trying to win Vesy converts to their religions might lead to real trouble."

"I don't think the President would approve a ban on missionaries," Schultz said. The American looked irked at the mere suggestion. "There is such a thing as religious freedom..."

"And what will you do," Rani asked dryly, "if one of your missionaries gets killed and eaten by the locals, merely for daring to question their religion?"

Joelle frowned. She knew little about the Vesy religions - the marines hadn't really had a chance to do any proper research - but she did know they worshipped multiple gods. It struck her, suddenly, that the Hindus might have an unfair advantage when it came to talking about religion to the aliens. *They* shared the concept of multiple gods.

"Good question," Schultz said. "I wish I had an answer."

"You will need one soon," Rani said. She looked at Joelle. "I for one would agree to a ban on weapons, but not on anything else."

"Then we would need to agree to search ships as they approach Vesy," Joelle said. She'd talked it through with Captain Naiser and Colonel Mortimer beforehand and they'd both agreed that the only way to make it work was to search any incoming ships...which would only be possible if *all* of the powers agreed. "Inform any newcomers that weapons shipments will not be permitted and search the ships to make sure they're complying?"

There was a brief argument between several ambassadors. Joelle listened, understanding their concerns. No one would be particularly happy to allow any of the other powers to search their ships, not when no one really *owned* Vesy. But, on the other hand, they all agreed that the last thing they needed was independent groups and NGOs adding *more* weapons to the arms race. By the time they hammered out a rough agreement, Joelle felt tired, headachy and desperately in need of a bed.

"The President may disagree," Schultz said. "There are several groups that believe we should just give the Vesy everything, in hopes of putting them on the same level as ourselves. If that happens, the agreement will have to be cancelled."

"And corporations will be complaining loudly to their representatives, the ones they bribed," the Chinese Ambassador sniped. "You might find yourself pushed into doing something actively harmful to American interests."

Joelle sighed, inwardly. The Chinese Government was a bizarre mix of fascism, communism and capitalism that made no sense to anyone outside China. In some ways, China was the most repressive state amongst the Great Powers…while, at the same time, it was also the freest. What could one make of a nation that alternatively crushed protest ruthlessly and encouraged its population to take part in government? But then, it was hard to argue that *Britain* didn't have its own issues too. None of the states that survived the Age of Unrest were quite what they'd been before all hell broke loose.

"It hardly matters, I suppose," Schultz sniped back, "when the corporations and the government are practically the same thing."

"The NGOs can continue to work through Fort Knight, for the moment," Joelle said. "It will be our pleasure to allow them to use the facilities."

"That raises a different issue," Barouche said. "Who is in charge of security at Fort Knight?"

"Us, for the moment," Joelle said. It wasn't a point she could budge on, not really. "Should you wish to land troops of your own, we can consider sharing command. Until then, we will remain in control of the outer layers of security."

The Frenchman nodded, but didn't argue further. Joelle suspected that his government was planning to set up its own base as quickly as possible, even though they hadn't sent more than a warship and a freighter to Vesy. They'd be more interested in laying the groundwork for crafting long-term influence on the planet than securing Fort Knight.

But we may have to make concessions later, she thought. *Not all NGOs will want to operate through Fort Knight when other nations have their own bases.*

"This leads to yet another issue," Schultz said. "Who takes action when our people come under threat?"

"The Indian Government has authorised General Patel to take whatever steps he deems necessary to handle any threats to Indian property or personnel," Rani said, quickly. "It will be our pleasure to extend that protection to other nationalities as well, should they wish it."

"And what," Schultz asked, "will you want in exchange?"

Joelle cursed under her breath. "3 Para will attempt to rescue anyone who gets into trouble," she said, after a moment to gather herself. "However, our forces are very limited."

"I believe my government is reluctant to assign ground forces," Barouche said. "But the marines on our ships will be happy to assist, if necessary."

Problematic, Joelle thought. Mortimer had pointed out that it might take far too long to get forces from orbit down to the ground, leaving them dependent on 3 Para. *What happens if we wind up dealing with multiple threats at the same time?*

Rani cleared her throat. "I believe we should not allow the Vesy to get the impression they can hurt humans at will," she said. "If humans come under attack and we can respond, we will. There will be no price for this service."

And if you believe that, Joelle added silently, *I have a lovely palace in the centre of London to sell you.*

She scowled as the argument raged backwards and forwards. The Indians might not demand a price, up front, for saving people at risk, but there would definitely be a cost. Perhaps they'd demand political support, later on, or perhaps...she shrugged. There were too many possibilities, none of them good. She would need to talk privately to some of the other ambassadors and plan out a response.

"We have at least a working framework," she said, when the argument finally died away. "It will need to be tested, of course, when the next wave of NGOs appear, but we can work on it."

"Of course," Schultz said. "But again, it will need to be confirmed by my government."

Joelle nodded, then watched as the other ambassadors rose to their feet and headed out the door. Some of them would take shuttles back to orbit, others would stay at Fort Knight and continue their attempts to make contact with various alien factions. Judging by some of the shuttle flights they'd tracked from orbit, all of the nations were making their own bids for influence.

And how long will it be, she asked herself silently, *before they start landing all over the planet?*

She sighed, then rose herself. A shower, even a weak one, seemed an excellent idea, after which she could write up a report for the Prime Minister and then climb into bed. And then…

See what tomorrow brings, she thought. *It's a whole new world out here.*

CHAPTER

SIXTEEN

"Do we really have to walk to the city?"

"I think we do," Penny said, ruthlessly pushing down the impulse to slap Grace Scott as hard as she could. "There aren't any roads or railways out here."

She glowered at the older woman, then kept walking down the muddy path towards the alien city. Sweat trickled down her back, leaving her feeling hot and sticky; her limbs ached, despite all the marching she'd done when she'd been pushed into joining the Combined Cadet Corps. But then, she hadn't really done much work since the refugee camp, even as a young reporter. And there was nowhere in Britain as hot as Vesy.

Percy must be having a hard time, she thought, as she looked at the marines. It was impossible to separate Percy from the other soldiers, not when they were all wearing the same armour, helmets and jungle camouflage. They had to be sweating even worse than herself, she was sure, but none of them complained. *Listening to her is quite bad enough.*

She gritted her teeth as a swarm of chattering insects passed over the small group, then faded away into the undergrowth as the path opened up, revealing the alien city gleaming in the sunlight, dead ahead of them. Penny stopped in awe, hastily checking her recorder to make sure she was filming everything. The city looked old and new at the same time, human and inhuman…and the walls were lined with hundreds of aliens, staring at the humans as if they'd never seen such strange creatures before. Penny heard Grace let out an expression of admiration, then mutter a curse as they started walking again. The city was surrounded by a handful of fields, each one worked by a small army of aliens. None of them raised their heads to watch as the humans went by.

They're shackled, Penny thought, as she saw the chains attached to metal cuffs around their ankles. She couldn't help remembering her visit to Dartmoor, where some of the worst criminals in Britain had been held before they were marched up to the gallows and hung in front of a jeering crowd. *They're slaves.*

Grace coughed. "Why are they shackled?"

"They're slaves," Penny answered, dryly. Percy had told her that the Vesy still had chattel slavery, but she hadn't really believed it. Chattel slavery was so inefficient, at least when compared to technology, that humanity had abandoned it long ago. But the Vesy still faced the same problems daunting humanity's ancestors. "I think it's to keep them from running away."

"That's...that's so uncivilised," Grace burst out. "We don't keep slaves."

"We do keep sex slaves," Penny pointed out, snidely. She'd heard stories of sex slave rings sweeping up young and pretty refugees, or bringing in women from the Middle East to Britain and forcing them to work as prostitutes. "As long as someone can make a profit from selling the labour of someone else, there will be slavery."

Grace gave her a nasty look, then turned her gaze away from the slaves. Penny recorded them for a long moment, her recorder catching several minutes of footage of a Vesy who was clearly an overseer, as she followed the marines down to the city. Up close, it was even more impressive; the walls appeared to be made of solid stone, instead of brick or something else that might have been put together piece by piece. Indeed, if it had been made by humans, she would have unerringly suggested the wall was made of concrete. It might well have been, she told herself. She had no idea how concrete was actually produced, but she didn't think it required advanced technology.

"Remember the rules," Percy said quietly, as the small column came to a halt outside the gates. "Don't go wandering off, don't discuss certain matters with the aliens and don't go where you're not welcome."

Penny nodded in understanding as the gates slowly opened to reveal a small band of aliens, all wearing gold cloaks. Gold seemed to be a status symbol amongst the Vesy, she'd gleaned from the files, for much the same reason as it had been among humans. Some of the Vesy wore fancy masks that were practically works of art, in their own way; others were completely naked, save for loincloths. She took a long breath and winced as she realised the city smelt appallingly bad. Even the Reclamation Zone near Cornwall, where hundreds of thousands had died when the tidal waves hit, didn't smell so bad.

"They don't have a proper sewage system," Professor Nordstrom said, quietly. He seemed to have coped with the walk fairly well, although his shirt was stained badly from sweat. "I think they probably don't even have cesspits to get rid of their waste, even though they now have a reason to use it - gunpowder. New York had a similar problem with animal dung once upon a time."

He was right, Penny saw, as they walked through the gates and into the city. A handful of animals that looked rather like scaly horses were pulling carts through the streets or being ridden by aliens who were clearly *very* high in status. The streets looked to have been paved with stone, but it was hard to tell; they were covered in mud and animal wastes. Combined with the frequent rainfalls - it had rained several times on Vesy since her arrival at Fort Knight - she had a feeling the roads, stone or not, rapidly turned to sludge. It wouldn't be easy for them to clean the roads regularly, no matter what they did.

"This place must be a breeding ground for disease," Grace gasped. "Is it safe?"

Penny shrugged. Percy had told her that cross-species infection was unlikely...and, just to be sure, they'd all been given extensive booster shots. It might be quite some time before the first Vesy was allowed to set foot on Earth - the medics were still trying to unravel the mysteries of the alien genome - but they should be safe. Or so she hoped. There was no shortage of movies that started with some idiot bringing an infectious disease home from another world.

"The odds of a disease jumping from the Vesy to you are lower than the odds of you managing to have children with a cow," Professor Nordstrom said. "Not that we shouldn't take precautions, just in case."

"They have to learn to keep their streets clean," Grace protested. "Can't we warn them?"

"Perhaps they've learned there isn't any point in trying," Professor Nordstrom said. "Or they may find it comfortable. There's no way to know."

Penny nodded, then watched as the marines and the aliens spoke briefly, exchanging short choppy sentences in English and Russian. Percy looked at ease, speaking to the aliens, even though he was no diplomat. But then, from what she'd heard, a classically-trained diplomat would be useless on Vesy. Behind him, the line of visitors - unfortunately *not* including the ambassadors - shifted uncomfortably in the heat, waiting for permission to walk into the city and explore. Thankfully, it only took ten minutes before the aliens motioned for the humans to enter.

"Stay together," Percy warned them, yet again. "Do *not* go wandering off."

Yes, brother, Penny thought, as she started to film the interior of the city. *We hear and obey.*

She pushed the thought aside as she studied the city. It looked strange to her eyes, a confusing mixture of a dozen styles, as if her brain was having problems trying to interpret what it was seeing. Parts of it reminded her of videos of cities from the ancient world, while other parts looked suspiciously like Victorian London, complete with aliens hurling the contents of chamber pots out into the streets. Beside her, Professor Nordstrom chatted enthusiastically about social pressures and just what they did to the aliens, while Grace maintained an undignified silence until a pair of alien children ran into the road and stared at the humans.

"They're sweet," Grace said.

"Better not go any closer," Professor Nordstrom said, as Penny filmed them. "You don't know how the aliens will react."

Her legs started to ache as they were shown building blocks, larger than she would have believed possible without technology, and temples to a dozen different gods. She filmed the temples with particular interest, admiring the statues of the gods and wondering precisely how they'd been made. They looked far too perfect to have been made with stone-age technology. One of them was definitely made of gold, or at least covered in gold; oddly, it looked the least like the Vesy themselves, even though the other gods resembled giant aliens.

Grace frowned as they were moved on, yet again. "I don't see any women..."

"You probably have," Professor Nordstrom said. "The only real difference between the males and females is that women have wider hips, I believe. Both sexes have retractable genitals."

"If that's true," Grace said, "how do they tell each other apart?"

"By scent," Penny reminded her. That had been covered during one of the innumerable briefings. Clearly, Grace hadn't been paying attention. "And when a female enters her season, all hell breaks loose."

A dull gong ran through the city as they reached a large open park. In the centre, there was a giant cooking fire, with aliens turning meat on spits as they prepared to greet their guests. A handful of chairs, clearly designed for humans, were placed nearby, really too close to the fire for comfort. It took Penny a moment to work out that the aliens were trying to be hospitable, as they preferred to stand. They'd still produced chairs for their human guests.

"Now that is interesting," Professor Nordstrom said. "Is that a way to welcome us or a subtle insult?"

"It is kind of them to provide chairs, surely," Grace said. "My legs are sore after walking for so long."

"Maybe," Professor Nordstrom said. "But, at the same time, sitting down may be a sign of submission in their culture, given that they clearly prefer to stand. They may see it as us going down on our knees in front of them."

Penny frowned. "Do you think we should stand?"

"I don't know," Professor Nordstrom said. "If we have problems untangling social cues in other human societies, and we do, what sort of problems will we have dealing with aliens?"

Percy came back to greet them before Penny could formulate a response. "The meat they have cooked for us is edible," he said, flatly. "However, there is no guarantee you will actually *like* it. If you don't, leave it on your plate. We have ration bars for those who genuinely can't stomach the alien meat."

He sounds as though he doesn't know me, Penny thought. Was he trying to pretend that they weren't actually related…or was he trying to help Penny's career by denying any connection between them? *I'd have to take him out of the recording in any case.*

She watched the aliens as they were served meat by the cooks and then tore into it with teeth and hands. They didn't seem to have heard of the concept of cutlery either, she noted; they just ate with their hands, regardless of the temperature. The marines were served after the alien dignitaries, although not all of them touched the food. It seemed rude until she realised that the aliens might have poisoned the food, even though it would be suicidal. The thought made her want to decline the plate that was finally offered to her, containing a handful of pieces of meat that looked to have been thoroughly overcooked. She'd had redder pieces of meat at steak houses when she'd ordered *well done.*

"Take it," Professor Nordstrom urged. "It might be rude *not* to take it."

Penny sighed, then took the plate and tried a piece of meat. It felt hot to the touch, but tasted surprisingly good. She nibbled it thoughtfully, then found herself wolfing down the next two pieces without demur. It was definitely something that could be sold on Earth, she told herself, and perhaps something that would win credit for the Vesy. There was always a demand for new styles of cooking in London…or there had been, before the war. It would be a long time before Londoners started eating out so often again.

After the dinner was finished, the Vesy put on a show. Penny watched and recorded a set of strange dances, all of which were greeted with a hooting sound that was probably their version of applause. Some of the dances involved weapons, the aliens waving swords around in a manner she *hoped* was choreographed, others seemed to be completely unplanned, the aliens jumping up and down at random. It reminded her of some of the stranger dances she'd seen on Earth as people tried to amuse themselves at the refugee camps, but she had a feeling there was a pattern, she just couldn't see it. Finally, a line of aliens wearing masks appeared and performed what seemed to be a play. It would probably have made more sense, she told herself, if she'd been able to understand the words.

"It may be a ritual recreation of a religious story," Professor Nordstrom commented, as the actors walked back out of sight. "Something along the same lines as a Christmas Play."

"They wouldn't have the same myths, though," Grace said.

"Probably not," Professor Nordstrom agreed. He smiled, suddenly. "But what if they *did*?"

Penny remembered interviewing a priest shortly before her assignment to *Warspite*. He'd been quite determined to prove that humanity was God's favourite creation, which he'd done by pointing out that Jesus had been sent to die to save humanity from itself. The Tadpoles had no such story, he'd said; indeed, the Tadpoles didn't seem to have anything resembling a religion, at least as humans understood the concept. He'd been convinced that it proved that humanity was special.

But what if they have stories, she asked herself, *that match the stories of the Norse Gods? Or the Hindu Gods? Or the Roman Gods?*

She pushed the thought aside as a single alien stepped up to where the dancers had stood, wearing a set of gold robes.

"Our friends," he said, in curiously-accented English. "It is our honour to welcome you to our city after it has been restored. You have come to us to restore the balance, sent by the gods to redeem us when we had fallen. The forces of the false god have been shattered, the demons he sent have been destroyed. To you we offer our thanks."

Penny's eyes narrowed. Was he calling the human race *gods*?

It may not be a very good translation, she reminded herself. Percy had told her that talking to the aliens wasn't easy, no matter how simple the subject. There were just too many ways something innocent could be misunderstood. *They may be talking about something else entirely.*

"But we also offer our thanks to the gods," the alien continued. "To them, we offer our lives and souls."

He stopped. Another alien appeared, wearing nothing. Penny couldn't help herself; she glanced between his legs, only to see a mass of scarring. Beside her, she heard Grace retch in horror as the alien advanced and stopped in front of the first alien. There was a long pause, than he fell to his knees.

The professor was right, Penny thought. *Sitting down* is *a form of submission for them.*

The first alien pulled back his cloak to reveal a loincloth and a sword, which he drew and held in the air. It glittered in the sunlight as Penny realised, to her horror, just what was about to happen. Grace gasped again, then cried out as the alien slashed down with the sword and smote the prisoner's head off with a single blow. The body crashed to the ground; moments later, the head landed next to it. Grace vomited in shock; Penny had to swallow, hard, to keep herself from throwing up too. She'd seen horrors in the refugee camps, and later as a reporter, but she hadn't seen a man beheaded right in front of her.

"We offer this fallen one to the gods," the alien said. He didn't seem to notice that at least half of his human audience was in shock. "His blood will nourish the Earth and return to us what was stolen."

"That can't have happened," Grace said. "It was a trick. It has to have been a trick."

Penny rolled her eyes. "It happened," she said. Didn't Grace understand that the Vesy weren't human? And that they couldn't be judged by human standards? "Professor, what *was* that?"

Professor Nordstrom looked pale. "Human sacrifice was often seen as giving life to the gods or to the land," he said. He sounded oddly perturbed by what he'd seen. "They may believe that they were actually doing the prisoner a favour..."

Or not, Penny thought, as the Vesy hooted so loudly that it drowned out the Professor's voice. *If that video gets home...it will turn the whole world upside down.*

It was a bitter thought. Humans had their own long history of barbarism, but that was in the past...except it wasn't, not entirely. The bombardment had brought out both the best and worst of humanity, creating a world where strangers had helped one another and, at the same time, gangs had roamed the land, searching for food, drink and women. But anyone who expected the Vesy to be anything other than savages would be badly shocked when they saw the recording. They would be utterly horrified.

She considered, briefly, deleting it, but she knew there was no point. There were other recorders in the field. All she could do was write a covering note and hope the editors at home didn't decide to portray the Vesy as monsters. Because if they did...

They might insist we abandon them altogether, she thought, *or try to fix their society for them.*

CHAPTER
SEVENTEEN

"They're barbarians," Grace burst out.

Joelle raised an eyebrow. Grace had a naive view of the world, but she had never done anything, as far as she knew, to threaten British interests. For her, someone who had insisted that the Vesy should be helped as much as possible, to change her mind…something unpleasant must have happened. Maybe she should have gone to Ivan's city after all.

"Are they?" She said, studying her aide. "What happened?"

"They killed him," Grace said. "There was this…mutilated alien and they *killed* him, right in front of us. They sacrificed him to the gods!"

"I see," Joelle said. She'd seen quite a few foreign traditions that struck her as barbaric, but public executions weren't one of them…provided, of course, that the criminal deserved to die. It would have been hypocritical in the extreme to file protests when Britain did the same, although normally with more due process. "And that surprised you?"

Grace stared at her wildly. "They're *monsters*! We're allied with monsters!"

"They're not human," Joelle said, evenly. "And most *humans* don't agree on a common standard of morality. What do you expect?"

She sighed, inwardly. It hadn't been easy for her to accept that the Tadpoles accepted an infant mortality rate that would have horrified humanity, if the positions had been reversed. In the past, maybe, child mortality had been terrifyingly high, but modern medicine had ensured that children almost always survived long enough to reach adulthood.

The Tadpoles, on the other hand, could have saved their children, they just didn't care to try. It had led to some uncomfortable discussions before the whole subject had been declared *verboten*.

Grace sat down on the uncomfortable chair. "We shouldn't be giving them any more help until they abandon the idea of human sacrifice," she said. "Or killing people, or keeping slaves..."

Joelle met her eyes. "Do you want to drive them to another interstellar power?"

"We can't encourage them to kill their own people," Grace protested.

"I was unaware they needed encouragement," Joelle said. She allowed her voice to soften, slightly. "They will change, given time and technology. Slavery will no longer be economical when their technology reaches the point where it can replace the slaves."

"They're holding *billions* in bondage," Grace flared, "and you're talking about economics?"

"I rather doubt they're holding *billions* in bondage," Joelle said, coolly. The most optimistic assessment of the planet's population was just below a billion, although the researchers had hastened to clarify that it was largely guesswork. Some parts of the planet seemed less developed than others, less capable of supporting large populations. "And yes, that's the way they work."

She sighed, feeling a flicker of sympathy for her aide. Grace had been born in an era where Britain and the other Great Powers had no need to coddle the smaller nations, not when there was nothing the Great Powers wanted or needed from them. There was no need to pay lip service to human rights on one hand and turn a blind eye to gross abuses on the other. To her, having to compromise her principles to get what she wanted was something of purely academic interest. Joelle, who'd spent time negotiating with the Tadpoles, knew she needed a more pragmatic view of the universe.

"Tell me something," she said. "Where were you during the bombardment?"

"The University of Britannia," Grace said, puzzled. "Why?"

Joelle nodded. That made sense. Britannia had never been attacked during the war, despite housing one of the largest shipbuilding complexes outside Sol itself. Grace would not have known real danger, or the long-term chaos inflicted by the bombardment. She would never have had to fight to survive, or crouch in a refugee camp and pray the guards didn't decide to turn nasty. It had given her a decidedly naive view of the world.

"There's nothing we can do," she said, flatly. "We need to work with the aliens, the ones who have allied with us, to maintain a presence on the surface. And if that means tolerating their...*barbarities*, it means tolerating their barbarities."

Grace shook her head. "The public wouldn't stand for it."

"The public has stood for a great deal in the past," Joelle said, darkly. "I don't think there were ever protests when we hammered some little state in the Middle East for daring to raid our shipping. Nor did anyone complain when refugee boats were sunk in the channel after the bombardment, or when we had to send military units to Ireland to assist what remained of the Irish Government."

"But this is different," Grace insisted. "These aren't *humans*."

"I doubt it will matter," Joelle said. She had a suspicion the media would make a great deal of hay out of it, but no one would really care. "There's very little we can do about it without fatally compromising our position here."

Grace looked stubborn. "I want to file a Memorandum of Disagreement," she said. "This isn't going to reflect well on us."

Joelle lifted her eyebrows. "Do you know," she asked lightly, "what that could do to your career?"

"Yes," Grace said.

"You would have disagreed, publically, with your superior," Joelle said, anyway. "There would be questions, when we got home, and if they disagreed with you your career would be at an end. And most of the Mandarins in the Foreign Office are ruthlessly pragmatic. I can guarantee they *would* disagree with you."

She paused. "I can forget I ever heard that, if you like," she added. "You wouldn't need to mention it again."

"I have to," Grace said. "This is *wrong*."

Joelle silently gave her points for idealism, then deducted them for naivety. Grace's career would not survive a Memorandum of Disagreement, not unless there were strong reasons for their mutual superiors to back Grace over Joelle. The hell of it was that Joelle could even admire Grace's willingness to gamble with her career, but she knew, all too well, that there was nothing they could do. Perhaps, she wondered privately, some of her predecessors from before the Age of Unrest had felt the same, as they were forced to watch helplessly while their hosts made a joke of human rights.

We need to keep our alien allies, she thought, grimly. *And that means we cannot reprimand them like children.*

"If you are insistent on filing a Memorandum of Disagreement, you may do so and it will be carried home on the next ship to leave Vesy," Joelle said. She wouldn't check to see if Grace had actually done so, she told herself. It would give Grace a chance for second thoughts. "I won't try to stop you."

"Thank you, Ambassador," Grace said.

Joelle held up a hand. "Don't thank me yet," she said. She allowed her voice to darken as she held Grace's gaze. "*However*, I will not tolerate you attempting to disrupt our relationship with our alien friends. You are not to lecture them, you are not to step away from the official script and you are not to do *anything* that might suggest we will make poor allies. If you do anything of the sort, you will spend the rest of the deployment in *Warspite's* brig and face a Board of Inquiry when you get back home. Do you understand me?"

Grace swallowed. "Yes, Ambassador."

"Good," Joelle said. "I would prefer not to put you in a position where your duty conflicts with your principles, but I'm afraid it's already too late. There's no point in offering your resignation now as you'd only remain stuck on Vesy…"

"With the bill for the trip home awaiting me," Grace interrupted.

"Quite," Joelle agreed.

She gave Grace a considering look. "Take the rest of the day off and get some sleep," she added, then paused. "Get something from the dispensary to help you sleep without nightmares. You'll probably need it. Tomorrow…there's a whole backlog of NGO ships to inspect before they're allowed to land on the planet. You'll probably be needed to help smooth ruffled feathers."

"Thank you, Ambassador," Grace said. She frowned. "Is it always like this?"

Joelle smiled. "Like how?"

"Like…having to watch something awful when you're on a diplomatic assignment," Grace said. "Or…"

Joelle had to smile. "The French will seek whatever advantage they can for themselves," she said. "If you give them an inch, they'll take a mile. The Russians will take you to dinner, then stuff you until you feel you're going to burst, hoping to put you in the right frame of mind to give them whatever they want. You won't be in any state to argue. The Chinese will happily spend weeks talking about nothing before finally getting to the point…

"In short, yes; you will have to learn to roll with the punches and handle the unpleasant surprises they throw at you," she concluded. "An alien being executed in front of you? If you stay in the service, you'll probably see a great deal worse before you're done."

She watched Grace leave the room, then opened a new file and hastily jotted down her recollections of the meeting. It was hard to blame Grace for being horrified, but it wasn't an attitude she could tolerate, not now. There was no room for being squeamish when working for the Foreign Office. Enemy diplomats might not come at you with guns and bombs, but they would skilfully isolate any hint of weakness and use it to achieve their aims. If Grace had accidentally caused a diplomatic rift between the British and their allies, Joelle had no doubt that the Indians would happily take advantage of it.

And that would give them control over more of the surface, she thought, sourly. *They might wind up with a decent claim to the entire system.*

Putting the file aside, she went back to work.

———

"Lieutenant," Lieutenant-Colonel Wilson Boone said, once Percy had entered his office and saluted. "What happened?"

Percy didn't allow himself to relax. "The aliens sacrificed one of their prisoners from the war to their gods," he said. "It was not a pleasant sight."

Boone snorted. "Any more or less pleasant than seeing one's comrades ripped apart by plasma guns?"

"No, sir," Percy said. He'd taken a moment to look up Boone's service record and discovered that the officer had served on Target One, back during the war. "The civilians didn't take it very well, however. Some of them were publicly sick."

"That must have surprised the Vesy," Boone said. "What did you tell them?"

"That the food didn't quite agree with human stomachs," Percy said. "It did happen before with some of their meats, sir, so I thought it an acceptable excuse."

"Good thinking," Boone said. He gave Percy a sharp look. "Did they buy it?"

"I think so, sir," Percy said. "They do know we can't eat everything of theirs, sir; some meats are poisonous, others are definitely an acquired taste."

"Which is worrying, because it gives them a chance to poison us," Boone said. "Or would you say that wasn't a problem?"

"I don't think they could poison *all* of us," Percy said. "Only a couple of my Bootnecks ate the meat they offered, sir. Even if they did…they wouldn't be able to do anything about the rest of Fort Knight, or the ships overhead."

"Good to know," Boone grunted. "Do you think they're telepathic?"

Percy blinked, thrown by the sudden twist. "Sir?"

"It's on the list of possibilities," Boone said, tapping a sheet of paper. "The contingency planners went a little mad, Lieutenant. We have plans here to cope with them being able to read minds, or control minds, or infect us with tailored diseases that would spread back to the Human Sphere before going active and slaughtering us all."

"A little mad," Percy repeated. "Sir, with all due respect, there isn't a shred of evidence that they can read their own minds, let alone ours."

"There isn't a shred of real evidence that humans have any psychic powers at all," Boone pointed out, "but that doesn't stop people from believing in them. The Tadpoles don't have any psychic powers either. And I'm required to sign off a list of potential threats."

He sighed. "There was a story I read as a child," he said. "I've forgotten the title; a human starship meets an alien starship, several hundred light years from Earth. The aliens are reasonably friendly, but neither side dares to go home for fear the other will follow them and locate their homeworld. They even come up with elaborate plans to seize the other ship, only to discover that the other side had the same idea. In the end, they swap ships…because it's the only way to be sure they can get home without letting the other follow them."

Percy considered it. "I don't think we're facing the same situation here, sir," he said. "The Vesy may be alien, but they're primitive. They don't have the ability to threaten us, either directly or indirectly."

"I still need to verify it," Boone said. He shrugged, then leaned forward. "How are your men coping with the current deployment?"

"Better for being able to get out of the fort," Percy said. "We've been learning much more about the surrounding area, now we've been able to roam further afield."

"Good, good," Boone said. "There will be another wave of landings in a week, if the updates are to be believed; I'm going to want you to escort the NGOs as they make contact with more alien cities and communities. There will probably be additional media visits to their cities too, which will also require escorts."

"Yes, sir," Percy said. Penny would probably *love* it. "Do I still have authority to sit on them, if necessary?"

"I'm afraid so," Boone said. "Try not to hurt their feelings *too* much, Lieutenant."

Percy groaned, inwardly. His men were no longer completely alone on an alien world, but they still had strict orders to refrain from doing anything that might provoke the Vesy to attack - or, more practically, switch sides. If a reporter asking dumb questions could provoke a human into a furious rage, with a burning desire to bury his fist in the reporter's jaw, who knew what it would do to the aliens? Would one of them try to behead a reporter?

And that would be an amusing thought, he told himself, *if Penny wasn't one of those reporters.*

She'd coped well, he had to admit, with watching the sacrifice. But then, she'd seen horror; the waves, the rising floodwaters, the desperate bid for safety…and then, sleeping in the refugee camp while her brother had been dispatched to one of the work gangs fighting to build defences before the waters rose again. Percy didn't know *precisely* what had happened to her there, but his imagination provided too many possibilities. Perhaps his baby sister was tougher than she looked.

Boone cleared his throat. "On other matters, you may be assigned to watch the Indians," he added. "Could you and your men move overland to their base?"

Percy considered it. The Royal Marines had been known to march for hundreds of miles, if necessary, but there were four hundred miles of largely unfamiliar country between Fort Knight and the Indian base. They had plenty of experience at sneaking through jungle terrain - Percy had fond memories of training cycles in Latin America - yet he rather doubted their ability to move undetected. Humans would stick out like sore thumbs if they showed themselves to prying satellites, high overhead. And besides, the Vesy were alarmingly good at sneaking through the undergrowth.

"Not without being detected," he said, finally. "We could call it a long-range patrol, without trying to make a secret out of it, but the aliens would flock to see us."

"So I've been told," Boone said. "They're not scared of us, are they?"

"This isn't Earth," Percy said. "There's no datanet, just...rumours. Aliens who live a mere hundred miles from the God-King's empire may not really believe in his existence, let alone the Russians. A thousand miles away? The battle here, the battle that ended when *Warspite* hammered the aliens from orbit? It's going to sound like a myth to them. The gods dropped fire from the sky and obliterated whole armies. They probably won't believe it, not really."

He shrugged. "To them, sir, we look strange...but not fearsome."

"Or so we are told," Boone said. "Humans tend to have a more xenophobic response."

"The Vesy have their gods," Percy said. "Some of them are...well, big Vesy-like creatures in the sky. Others look like they would give Lovecraft nightmares. Hell, sir; they still believe in entities hiding in the jungle and fairies at the bottom of the garden. I think they're a little more familiar with the concept of intelligent life that doesn't look like them than we tend to believe."

"Good thinking," Boone said. He frowned, contemplating his finger-nails. "Have you mentioned that to the Professor?"

"I haven't had a chance to talk to the Professor, sir," Percy said. He recalled the man, but he hadn't had any real contact with him before the trip to the alien city. "He seemed to have a better understanding of what we were seeing."

"Tell him your theory," Boone said. "He may make something of it."

"Yes, sir," Percy said.

"And write up a complete report about the visit too," Boone added. "I may need something to show my superiors, once the report gets home. Human sacrifice...the Vesy aren't cute and cuddly, are they?"

"No, sir," Percy said. His lips twitched with amusement at the thought. "But if they looked like teddy-bears, would we actually take them seriously?"

"I dare say a few more people will take them seriously from now on," Boone said. "Dismissed, Lieutenant."

Percy saluted, then left the room.

CHAPTER

EIGHTEEN

"Captain," Lieutenant-Commander Tara Rosenberg said. "I have another freighter heading towards the planet. The IFF identifies her as a chartered vessel."

John nodded shortly as he glanced at the display. There were quite a few chartered ships in orbit now, some sending shuttles and supplies down to Fort Knight. Thankfully, the agreement to search all such ships was holding up, although John rather doubted it would last indefinitely. There were two new governments involved now and neither one had signed the agreement.

And the folks back home might just cancel it anyway, he thought. *Not everyone will approve of searching chartered vessels.*

"Mr. Armstrong, put us on an intercept course," he ordered.

"Aye, sir," Armstrong said.

"Contact the ship," John added, glancing at Lieutenant Forbes. "Send them a copy of the agreement and order them to prepare to be boarded."

"Aye, sir," Gillian said.

John settled back in his command chair as *Warspite* picked up speed, heading towards her target. The freighter looked to be a modified *Liberty*-class ship, an American design that had been produced in large numbers and then sold to a dozen other spacefaring powers. There was nothing particularly special about them, which had been a large part of the design's appeal. The owners didn't have to keep purchasing spare parts from the United States.

"Her IFF identifies her as a Ceres-registered ship," Gillian said. "She's apparently called the *Makeweight*."

"I see," John said.

He cursed under his breath. The Ceres Association was the largest independent asteroid community in the Sol System, recognised as a nation in its own right. It might not have been considered one of the Great Powers - it barely operated a handful of small warships - but it was economically formidable and had thousands of allies scattered throughout the asteroid belt. And they were quite happy to register starships, rather than go through the more complex registration procedures demanded by the Great Powers. It had created a whole series of headaches in the past, before the war.

So what are we looking at here? He asked himself. *An independent freighter flagged to Ceres or an official diplomatic mission?*

The latter seemed unlikely, he had to admit. Ceres didn't have many diplomats, not least because it didn't have much of a government. Indeed, political pundits had been predicting the imminent collapse of the Association for the last seventy years. Besides, they would have identified themselves as such when they arrived. It was far more likely that someone had chartered the freighter and set off to Vesy.

"Picking up a response, sir," Gillian said. "They're demanding free passage to Vesy in line with the Outer Space Convention of 2190."

John shook his head. "Inform them that they have a choice between being searched or returning to more settled space," he said, flatly. This was going to cause at least one diplomatic incident, he was sure. *Ceres* hadn't signed the agreement, and given that no one owned Vesy, there were scant legal grounds for denying the ship passage to orbit. "We cannot risk making the situation on the ground worse."

There was a long pause. "No response, sir," Gillian said.

"They're accelerating," Tara reported.

They're mad, John thought. *Warspite* could catch the freighter with two fusion cores down, even if the freighter had a head start. In this case, they were actually accelerating towards *Warspite*, as if they were playing a demented game of chicken. *They have to be out of their minds.*

"Light them up," he ordered, tartly. At this range, it was unlikely they could actually *miss*, but targeting the freighter so blatantly would be enough to make anyone reasonably sane sit up and pay attention. "And repeat the demand that they cut their drives and prepare to be boarded."

There was a long pause. "Picking up a visual signal," Gillian said.

"Patch it through," John ordered. A face appeared in the display. "This is Captain John Naiser of HMS *Warspite*…"

"This is an absolute outrage," the face snapped. "You have no right to bar our passage!"

John kept his temper under firm control. "To whom am I speaking, if I may enquire?"

"I am Senior Brother Kent Thompson," the face sneered. "I represent the Society of Interstellar Brotherhood. You did not attempt to search our first ship, so we do not concede we have a legal obligation to allow you to search the second."

"Tell me," John said. "Are you the commanding officer of *Makeweight*?"

"No," a different voice said. Thompson scowled as a new face appeared in the display, an older man with the hairless scalp of an asteroid dweller. "I am Captain Samsun."

John hesitated. He couldn't help thinking that Captain Samsun looked harassed. Maybe he'd come to regret allowing the Brothers to hire his ship. *John* would not have cared to share a ship with Kent Thompson, if that was the attitude the Brother showed to everyone. But it wasn't something he could do anything about, not now.

"Captain, it has been decided, *pro tem*, that shipments of weapons and certain other prohibited goods to the Vesy is banned," he said, trying to ignore Thompson. "I have a legal right to search your ship for any such goods and hold them until such time as you depart this star system. The governments back home may overturn this at some later date, but for the moment I have to enforce it."

"To the best of my knowledge," Samsun said, "Ceres has not agreed to abide by any such agreement."

"*Exactly*," Thompson said. "You have no right to stop us!"

"That is debatable," John said. He couldn't help noticing the flicker of irritation that passed over Samsun's face. "What is *not* debatable is that I have the *ability* to stop you. Cut your drives and prepare to be boarded or turn about and leave this system."

Thompson sneered. "Or what?"

"Or I will cripple your ship," John said.

"A bluff," Thompson snapped.

"Which will not be called," Samsun said. He raised his voice. "Cut engines, then unlock the airlocks."

"*Captain*," Thompson protested. "I…"

"Your ship will be boarded in five minutes," John said, as *Makeweight* cut her drives. "I strongly advise you to cooperate."

Thompson scowled at him, then vanished from the display as the link was cut. John wondered, absently, if Samsun would like the Marines to remove Thompson and his cronies from the ship, then dismissed the thought and tapped commands to his men. Captain Hadfield would search the ship thoroughly, with some help from Richards and his crew, and then report back to him. And then they could make a decision on allowing *Makeweight* to pass.

It was nearly two hours before the Marines returned to *Warspite*, bringing Thompson and Samsun with them. John took a moment to survey the manifest before they were escorted into his office, shaking his head at just how much had been removed from Earth. The farming equipment was under an embargo, if he recalled correctly, given just how hard it had become to feed Earth's teeming population. And then there were the weapons…how the hell had the Brotherhood managed to obtain so many weapons? And what did they plan to do with them?

"I must lodge a formal protest, with your government and mine," Samsun said, as they were shown into the office. "Your crewmen poked their way into everything."

"That is their job," John said. Richards was an old hand at hiding things around a ship and knew precisely where to look, when working for the other side. "Still, for the moment, we are only concerned with weapons."

He looked at Thompson, who seemed a little more subdued in the presence of armed marines, and met his eyes.

"Why did you bring so many weapons on a *peaceful* mission?"

Thompson glowered at him. "The Vesy need human weapons to survive," he snapped. "We will give them weapons without a price tag!"

"They must have cost you a pretty penny," John observed. It would be hard to purchase so many weapons in Britain, not without valid End User certificates. "Where did they come from?"

"Our chapter in America purchased them for us," Thompson said, finally. "They're all tested and guaranteed."

"I'm glad to hear it," John said, dryly. "However, they will not be going down to the surface."

He ignored Thompson's splutter. "Next question," he said. "How did you obtain the farming equipment?"

Thompson's face hardened. "Is this an interrogation?"

"It might be," John said. "There isn't a country on Earth that would willingly sell farming equipment, not now. They need it to feed themselves. That means you either bought it illegally or..."

"It was produced in Ceres," Thompson said, quickly. "They were trying to sell to Earth, but not *exclusively* to Earth."

"I see," John said. "And the medical equipment?"

"Ditto," Thompson said. He smirked. "As you can see, we broke no laws."

"I would ask why you brought so many books on political theory and philosophy," John said, "but I'm honestly afraid of the answer."

"The Vesy need assistance in moving up the ladder of civilisation," Thompson said. "The books we bought can help them to reshape their society."

"Into what?" John asked. "No, never mind; I don't want to know."

He met Thompson's eyes and held them. "The weapons you bought will be confiscated," he said, "as will the educational programs and terminals. There *is* a blanket ban on selling them to aliens, I might add."

"We were not planning to *sell* them," Thompson insisted.

"I would dearly like to see you try that argument in front of a judge," John said. "The letter of the law may ban *selling* the items, but the *spirit* of the law certainly bans *giving* them as well."

"It is an unjust law," Thompson insisted.

"That's as maybe," John said. "But there are chances we are not going to take, not now."

He took a breath. "If the weapons and other confiscated items are useful, you will be paid a fair price for them," he continued. "If not, you may reclaim them when you leave the system."

"Daylight robbery," Thompson snapped.

John ignored him. "You will be assigned an orbital slot and a time for shipping the rest of your wares down to Vesy," he said. "I would advise you to make sure you read the briefing notes and study the presentations before you land. Contact with the Vesy will take place under supervision, at least until we're sure you can speak to them without causing additional problems or discussing issues that are considered forbidden. If this is unacceptable, turn around and leave the system."

"The Brothers have friends everywhere," Thompson said. "Your career will be blighted..."

"My career is not at stake here," John said, although he knew that wasn't true. Admiral Soskice probably held a grudge after John had relieved Commander Watson of duty and might take the opportunity to drive a stake through John's career. "What *is* at stake is preventing a social and political disaster on the planet below. If you cause problems, I will not hesitate to have you unceremoniously removed from the planet."

"Very well," Thompson said, grudgingly. "In the interests of saving the Vesy from selfish human interests."

"Thank you," John said. "Major Hadfield? Escort him out and hold him in the shuttlebay until I have finished speaking to Captain Samsun."

He watched Thompson leave, escorted by two burly Marines, and then looked at Samsun. "Long trip?"

"The longest," Samsun said. He looked tired and worn. "If I'd realised just how much of a problem they would be, I would have let the damned bankers take my ship. No *wonder* hardly anyone else wanted them."

"I'm sorry to hear that," John said, sincerely. "And I'm sorry I may have caused you problems with your government."

"They will probably lodge a protest," Samsun said. He smiled, rather wanly. "And if I had more energy, I would be screaming the place down."

"I wouldn't blame you," John assured him. "What do they *want*?"

"They see themselves as being on a religious mission, only without god," Samsun said. "If I never hear another lecture on the duties and obligations of the human race to our alien brothers, I will be happy. I think they're in for a nasty shock."

"Quite probably," John agreed.

He smiled, rather tiredly. The sacrifice had been the first major glimpse into the Vesy society, the first sign that the Vesy played by very different rules to modern humanity, but it hadn't been the last. One reporter had recorded a long ceremony where the slaves were formally declared enemies of the state, something that had reminded John of Sparta and the Helots. After they'd completed the ceremony, each of the slaves - bound in iron chains - had been whipped, then put back to work. Some of the reporters had even started to file stories suggesting that the only true solution was for the human race to take over completely.

And that won't go down well at home, John thought. *God knows we have enough problems without trying to invade an alien world.*

"Tell me something," Samsun said. "Can I just abandon them here?"

"I don't know," John said, after a moment. Was that a joke...or was he serious? "What does your contract say?"

"It's a little vague," Samsun admitted. "I was merely hired to take them to Vesy."

"Then you can, it would seem," John said. "I'd make sure they have somewhere to stay first, though. You probably don't want to be hit with a lawsuit implying that you abandoned them to the wolves."

"Or to the Vesy," Samsun agreed. He lowered his voice. "Captain, between you and me, they were talking about doing more end runs around any governmental presence on the surface. I think they may have brought Apocalypse Files too."

John blinked in surprise. Apocalypse Files had been common during the Age of Unrest, even though they'd never been necessary. They were nothing more than instructions for rebuilding civilisation from scratch, assuming a nuclear war or a biological plague that exterminated much of the human race, but they were fantastically detailed. John had seen copies in the British Library, back when he'd been a student. Now, they were rewritten and dispatched to colony worlds, just in case something happened to Earth. It would have seemed pointless if the human race hadn't run into the Tadpoles.

"Good thinking on their part," John said. It wasn't as if Apocalypse Files were hard to find, let alone copy. Most of them were firmly in the public domain. "They could build on what the Russians introduced, even without further interference from outside powers."

And they will have to be confiscated, if they exist, he thought, inwardly. He made a mental note to order Fort Knight to check everything when the Brothers landed. *They'd put too much information in alien hands.*

He sighed, then rose. "I'm sorry you had to endure their presence," he added, "but you *did* take their money. Where do you think it came from, by the way?"

"I have no idea," Samsun said, as he rose too. "The Bank of Ceres confirmed they had the cash to pay, up front, for a trip to Vesy, so I didn't much care."

John nodded. Ceres had a banking sector that made Switzerland or the Cayman Islands look transparent, a legacy of the trouble the asteroids had had breaking free of their founder corporations. The Brothers could have got their money from anywhere and then funnelled it through Ceres, if they wanted to obscure the source. A few rich idiots, a pound or two apiece from millions of people…there was no way to know.

Perhaps we should find out, John thought. *That freighter-load of goods must have cost well over a million pounds.*

"Drop them off at Vesy, then go home," John advised. Under the circumstances, it would be hard to blame Samsun for not sticking around. Lurking in orbit wouldn't shift cargo, unless there were some goods to go home. "The Marines will escort you back to your ship."

"Thank you, Captain," Samsun said.

John watched him go, then sat down at the desk. The Brothers had chartered two ships, one from Israel and one from Ceres; the former, at least, known for responding badly whenever someone interfered with their shipping. Ceres was unlikely to be pleased either, even though Captain Samsun might not press the issue. It was the principle of the thing. Britain - and the other powers - might wind up having to pay compensation for searching the ship and confiscating some of the goods. But that led back to the original question. Where, just where, did the money come from?

Maybe I'm just being paranoid, he thought. It wasn't as if the Society of Interstellar Brotherhood was a small organisation. If every one of the millions of members they claimed to have donated a pound, they'd have millions of pounds. *Or maybe something sinister is going on.*

He hastily wrote out a short update for Ambassador Richardson, warning her of the incoming ship and potential problems, and then fired off a message to Captain Samuel Johnston. The American might not know just what weapons the Brothers had bought, but he could certainly send a request back home for the information. Who knew *what* it might turn up?

His intercom bleeped. "Captain," Howard said. "The shuttle has reached *Makeweight*."

"Good," John said. "Once she's back, take us towards the planet and transmit a full update to System Command."

"Aye, sir," Howard said. "Any other issues?"

"Inform Chief Richards that I wish to speak with him at his earliest convenience," John said, flatly. It meant *now*. "And keep an eye on *Makeweight*. I want to know if he does anything stupid."

"Yes, sir," Howard said. He sounded puzzled, but didn't question the order. "We'll keep a close eye on him."

CHAPTER
NINETEEN

"Are you a religious man, my son?"

Percy took a moment to consider his answer. Father Brennan was a tall thin man, wearing a black outfit with a wooden cross hanging around his neck. He wasn't a bad man - and, unlike some of the others, he hadn't complained loudly at the thought of having to walk to an alien city - but Percy couldn't help feeling suspicious. Religious disputes were likely to lead to far more clashes between humans and aliens.

"There are no atheists in foxholes, father," he said, carefully. "Are you looking for converts here?"

"We believe in issuing the call to all," Father Brennan said. "The call may not be heeded, the call may even be mocked, but all that matters is that the call is issued. Those who do not choose to heed the call will have to live with the consequences of not doing so."

"I know very little about your sect," Percy admitted. "But as long as you don't try to compel worshippers, you shouldn't have any problems."

"We believe that the rightness of our position will shine through the clouds of ignorance on Vesy," Father Brennan said. "By definition, a polytheistic religion cannot be correct because it really consists of worshipping incredibly powerful beings. They may as well worship *us*. But God, the One True God, is literally everything, the be-all and end-all of our multiverse. He is truly worthy of worship."

Percy considered it for a moment. "The Vesy may not take kindly to you telling them otherwise," he said, warningly. "You need to be aware of the dangers."

"If it is God's will that I die issuing the call," Father Brennan said, "I will accept it."

He paused. "You would be welcome at one of our prayer meetings, my son," he added. "All are welcome."

"I'm not particularly religious," Percy said. He'd seen too much of what religion could do to people, people who might otherwise have been good and decent. "And I have grave doubts about allowing anyone, no matter what he calls himself, to serve as an intermediary between myself and God."

He glanced back at the rest of the column. The handful of reporters looked used to marching by now, although sweat was pouring down their faces and soaking their clothes. Behind them, a handful of NGO experts were grumbling along, clearly resentful that the ban on ground transport applied to them too. Percy wasn't feeling too sorry for them; in the week since they'd landed, they'd made themselves pains in the arse wandering around Fort Knight and demanding to be allowed to talk to the Vesy, or alternatively holding interviews with the media where they'd pledged to bring the Vesy into the modern age. But now they were finally going to meet an alien face to face.

The city came into view, looking smaller than Ivan's city-state. Percy couldn't help noticing that the walls had been badly damaged at some point in the recent past, probably through cannonballs, and that hundreds of aliens were swarming over them, trying to repair the stone barriers as quickly as possible. It was hard to be sure, but most of the aliens looked to be free, rather than slaves. The city might have been liberated, in the wake of the God-King's death, yet it had taken months for the population to return.

They probably took in a lot of stragglers too, Percy thought. *Vesy who had nowhere to go.*

He nodded to his men as they walked up to the gate and passed through, entering a giant clearing with a handful of alien dignitaries waiting for them. By now, he was starting to separate out the different castes of aliens; some were rulers, although how they gained power was a mystery, others were priests or scribes. The real problems came when a single alien shared two or more roles.

"I greet you," he said, as the alien leader approached. "As promised, I bring wise men to speak with you."

"I welcome them," the alien answered. His beady eyes flicked from face to face, clearly wondering which of the 'wise men' would be most useful. "We understand that you do not wish to give offense, but you also do not wish to eat with us?"

It took Percy a moment to realise it was a question. The Vesy shared food with their visitors, a sign of peace and friendship...or at least of a localised truce. *Not* taking the food they were offered was a sign of something other than peace, he knew all too well. But the aliens, at least, had realised that humans had problems eating their food.

"We have brought food of our own," Percy said. "We will eat with you, if you will allow us?"

"Interesting," Father Brennan muttered, as he took a ration bar. The Vesy ate something that looked like cold bread and meat, cooked in a foul-smelling oil. "They understand our problem?"

"They know we have problems with their food," Percy muttered back. He had problems with the ration bar too, which might have been edible but simply wasn't very tasty. "I think they find it something of a relief. They rarely have a surplus of food, Father. The idea of hosting guests who don't need to be fed is quite welcome to them."

He shrugged. "They also understand that we don't think of it as an insult," he added. "There may be some problems, as we extend our visits well beyond the original landing zone, but we will overcome them."

Thompson stamped over to them, looking irked. "Can we hire alien porters next week?"

"You could, I suppose," Percy said. The issue hadn't come up yet, which was surprising, but it was a rational solution to the problem. "Can't you carry everything yourself?"

"No," Thompson said. "The farming gear alone is far too heavy."

Percy concealed his amusement. Captain Naiser had not only ordered the weapons confiscated, he'd also ordered the men on the ground to make a careful search of everything else the Brothers had sent down to the planet. Percy had led the crew and he'd uncovered a surprising amount of material that skimmed far too close to the banned list. In the end, the Brothers had been left with the farming gear, a handful of technological trinkets and a surprising amount of medical supplies.

They probably expected to be allowed to land their shuttle right next to the alien city, he thought. *We forbade them to land anywhere but Fort Knight.*

"Check when we get back to the Fort," he said. Thompson was sweating like a pig, despite wearing shorts, a shirt and a pith helmet. "There should be no shortage of labourers willing to porter for you. Just make sure you pay them well."

"Of course," Thompson said.

He marched off, looking thoroughly pissed. Percy shook his head after him - he had the feeling that Thompson was in for a nasty surprise - then turned to watch as the alien leader gave a long speech of welcome, half in English and half in Vesy-One. It would be recorded for later translation, Percy knew, but he had a good idea what it said. The Vesy welcomed their honoured guests with odd table manners and poor tastes in food.

"Tell me," Father Brennan said, elbowing Percy. "How do you tell the difference between the priests and everyone else?"

"The priests are the ones who wear the masks," Percy said. The masks were truly beautiful, he had to admit, combinations of gold leaf and silver feathers that glimmered brightly in the sun. "When they have them around their necks, they're in mortal form; when they actually have them on their faces, they speak for the god. Indeed, in some ways, they *become* the god."

"Ah," Father Brennan said. He gave the aliens a long considering look. "We have nothing like it, of course."

The aliens came forward, the priests seeking out their human counterparts. Percy kept an eye on Father Brennan and his fellows, including people from four different religions, but they seemed to be talking peacefully in broken English. Maybe it was harder to offend each other, he considered, if they couldn't really *understand* each other. Or maybe they were both being really polite.

Thompson seemed to have having worse luck. "Marine," he bawled. "Some help, please!"

Percy signed inwardly, then walked towards the small group. Thompson and his assistant, a young woman no older than Penny, were surrounded by a handful of Vesy rulers, all wearing golden robes. The discussion seemed to have become heated, although no punches were being thrown. It wasn't a consolation, Percy feared, when it looked like that would change at any moment.

"I'm here," he said, quietly. When had *he* become a diplomat? He was trained to fight on behalf of the United Kingdom, not negotiate with aliens. "What seems to be the problem?"

One of the aliens spoke rapidly in his own language, so fast that Percy doubted he could have followed the words even if he *had* a basic understanding of the speech. Another answered in the same tongue, casting what looked like a reproving look towards Thompson. The overweight man started to splutter, then looked at Percy.

"They are insisting that we provide them with weapons," he said. "And when I said we couldn't supply weapons, they wanted to leave."

"Then you might want to respect their wishes," Percy said.

"But we have so much else to offer them," Thompson protested.

"Come with me," Percy ordered. Thompson gave him a nasty look, but followed him to a place where they should be out of earshot. "You're offering them something that isn't any practical use to them."

Thompson stared at him in disbelief. "How can they *not* want to farm?"

Percy stared back at him, feeling much the same way. How could someone have organised such a large freighter-load of supplies and, at the same time, be completely blind to some of the implications? *Percy* had known…although, to be fair, Percy had spent six months camped out on Vesy, chatting with the locals and gaining a feel for their society. And he'd put it all in his reports which, as far as he knew, were freely available to everyone at Fort Knight.

"The only thing they care about, right here, right now, is survival," Percy said, flatly. It was why the first demand Ivan had made, and repeated every week for six months, was for weapons. There was no point in being wealthy if they couldn't defend themselves. "You…"

"I'm giving them the tools they need to survive," Thompson insisted.

"No, you're not," Percy said. He cleared his throat. "Suppose, for the sake of argument, you manage to teach them how to double the amount of food they produce in a year. Let's suppose you manage to do that, adapting the farming tools you brought to local conditions without problems. What happens then?"

Thompson blinked at him. "They eat more?"

Percy sighed. "No," he said. "The Vesy in the nearest city with access to human weapons, be they weapons we gave them or weapons they copied from the Russians, will attack and take the food, as well as the city. You will simply make them a better target, a more tempting target, to hostile city-states. They're not stupid, Mr. Thompson. You're offering to make them victims of their own success."

"I can't believe it works that way," Thompson said, stubbornly.

"You would make them both rich and weak," Percy said. "How many human states were rich and weak - and how many of them lasted long enough to reform?"

"We can offer medicine as well as farming tools," Thompson said.

"Which will, again, make them a bigger target," Percy said. He shook his head. "You can't offer them weapons, sir, so they have no interest in talking to you."

"I will lodge an official protest with the British Ambassador," Thompson said. He sounded as though he expected the mere threat of a protest to sway Percy, although Percy had no idea quite what he could do. "We came to help our brothers..."

"That is your right, sir," Percy said. He kept his voice calm with an effort. "However, right now, you are offering them nothing they actually *want*. You need to bear that in mind when you approach the Vesy."

Thompson sighed, then peered towards where his small audience had been. They'd left, leaving him looking embarrassed. Percy concealed his amusement at the sheepish look on the face of Thompson's aide, who clearly hadn't been able to keep the aliens from losing interest. But, to them, Thompson had to seem like a fool...or an asshole. Neither one would encourage them to talk to him.

"Stay back," Percy advised. "Take a moment to gather yourself before you return to the fray."

Thompson glowered at him. "Is that what they told you in Boot Camp?"

"No," Percy said. He couldn't help feeling a flicker of sympathy for Thompson's aide. The poor man might be brimming with love for the Vesy, but he didn't have any for his own assistants. "It's just common sense."

He shook his head, then turned his attention to the other NGO representatives. Most of them didn't seem to be doing well, although one woman did seem to have captured the interest of her listeners. Percy made a mental note to check on what she was offering them, then glanced over at Father Brennan. He was chatting to one of the priests, while the others seemed to have split up to talk one-on-one. The Marines looked relaxed, but their hands never went far from their weapons. They knew, all too well, just how quickly a situation could move from seeming calm to outright chaos in the blink of an eye.

"She has ideas about helping the alien women," Thompson muttered, nodding to the woman and her audience. "I think she has the idea that blanking their...*scent* at the right time would remove the mating instinct."

Percy frowned. The Vesy females went into mating season, on average, every third month or thereabouts. He'd already spoken quite sharply to a couple of Marines who'd joked about the Vesy going into heat, as if they were dogs. When a female entered mating season, her scent proved irresistible to anyone who wasn't closely related to her; males would quite happily fight one another merely for the chance to mate with a female when they could be reasonably sure of siring a clutch of eggs. It made it harder for them to leave their homes during mating season, or even when they were on the verge of going into season. Their lives, consequently, tended to be alarmingly restrictive.

"It might," he agreed, slowly.

Part of his mind, the part that was an emotional human, was appalled at the whole system. It just didn't seem right. God knew he'd been in parts of the world where women were treated worse than slaves and it had horrified him. But, at the same time, he feared what would happen if they meddled with the system. It might have terrifying unexpected consequences.

Something to raise with my superiors, he thought. He was no longer - thank god - in command of the sole detachment on the planet. He could kick it up the ladder to someone else. *Let them worry about it for a change.*

He glanced at his wristcom, then nodded to his men. The guests were rapidly rounded up and a final set of goodbyes were said to the aliens, then they hastened out the gate and back down towards the road leading to the former Russian base. It didn't look as though anyone had been working on the roads, since the God-King's fall, but Percy wasn't too surprised. The Russian commander had clearly studied Rome and knew the importance of the famed Roman Roads in allowing the Romans to move their troops around their territory. And then he'd introduced the idea to the God-King.

Father Brennan slipped up beside him as they set a slow pace, purely for the benefit of Thompson and his ilk. "It was an interesting conversation," he said. "But I'm not sure I fully understood what I was being told."

Percy smiled. "Did *they* understand what *they* were being told?"

"They thought Jesus was a minor god," Father Brennan said. He sounded oddly amused by the suggestion. "I don't think they understood the importance of the crucifixion to us. They thought the story of Jesus and the Resurrection to be laughable. One of them even claimed to be *descended* from a god."

"So did Julius Caesar," Percy said. It had been a long time since he'd studied Caesar in school, but it had been one of his favourite classes. He'd even wanted to be Caesar before it had dawned on him that the Roman Empire was no more. "It wasn't an uncommon claim before the evolution of monotheistic religions."

"They did invite me back," Father Brennan said. "I will definitely go, if I can."

Percy shrugged. The decision wasn't in his hands any longer. Besides, he had no idea just *what* the aliens would do with human religions. Add God, Yahweh and Allah to their pantheon or embrace them wholly, calculating that it would bring more help and weapons from the human settlers? Or would they agree with Father Brennan and decide that a single god made more sense than a hundred minor gods?

He made a mental note to raise the possibilities in his report, then turned his attention to the march. If they kept going at their current pace, they'd be back at Fort Knight within two hours, by which time Thompson would be too tired to do anything but sleep. Percy would have a chance to file his report first and then…

He shrugged, again. That too was no longer his decision.

CHAPTER
TWENTY

"So tell me," Anjeet said. "What do you make of the rumours?"

Nikolai Petrovich Zaprudnyi looked thoughtful. He'd changed, in the two months since the Indians had picked him up, after the medics had taken a long look at him and insisted that he eat a proper diet laced with nutritional supplements. Anjeet rather approved of the Russian's willingness to do whatever it took to get a new identity and enough money to live the rest of his life somewhere comfortable. It ensured he would remain loyal as long as necessary.

"They seem to be taking them seriously," Zaprudnyi said, carefully. "But it may be a long time before trouble bubbles into the open."

Anjeet smiled. Stories grew in the telling - particularly when they were repeated with someone with an axe to grind. It hadn't been too hard to suggest that India, which was a majority-Hindu country, was more inclined to be friendly to Vesy religions than anyone else; indeed, a couple of the priests he'd brought with him had found common ground with their Vesy counterparts. Monotheism, in all its manifestations, was strikingly different to anything the Vesy had developed for themselves. And suggesting that the missionaries who'd come to tend to the Vesy would soon move on to compulsion hadn't been difficult at all.

The Vesy themselves, as far as he had been able to tell, had no real hesitation over adopting gods from different cities. It was generally acknowledged, among them, that all gods were real, even if they were not *worshipped*. A Christian, a Muslim or a Jew would hesitate to pray in another's style, even when visiting a city run by a different faith, but the Vesy would see nothing wrong with praying to a different god in a different place. It was just *polite* to pay homage to the gods of other cities. But the Russian-backed God-King had upset the rules and now the Vesy were worried.

"Oh, I doubt that," he said, mischievously. "The priests won't like the idea of alien religions spreading through their lands."

It was a galling thought, but he had to admit that the first Muslim missionaries to enter India had had an unfair advantage. The caste system had been stronger in those days, much stronger, and it had offered little to those born at the bottom. Islam, on the other hand, had proclaimed itself a religion of equality, at least to those who submitted to Allah. It was no wonder, he had forced himself to consider, that Islam had spread so rapidly into India. The Vesy faced much the same problem, with the added disadvantage that the missionaries were backed by stunningly powerful force. It hadn't been hard to suggest that, sooner or later, the monotheists would attempt to force their religion on the Vesy by force.

"They're not stupid," Zaprudnyi disagreed. "They wouldn't challenge vastly superior force."

Anjeet shrugged. The Vesy had real problems comprehending the power at human fingertips…which wasn't too surprising, as they'd only recently discovered that their world was a sphere orbiting a star. But if they should happen to come to believe that they had a choice between fighting or accepting terminal decline, they might well decide to fight. Who knew? Their gods might help them to win? And they might even have Indian allies…

He smiled at the thought. Agreeing to ban NGOs from bringing in weapons had been the sole accomplishment of the ambassadors on Vesy. Thanks to the constant arrival of newcomers and skilled delaying tactics, nothing *else* had been agreed. There was no universally accepted commanding officer, no one in command of the various troops on the surface; if all hell broke loose, everyone would be fighting on their own, rather than as a coordinated force. Anjeet wasn't worried about the dangers - he had five thousand soldiers defending his growing base - but he knew some of the other powers *were*. They were terrifyingly exposed on the surface, against hordes of potential enemies.

And when they get into real trouble, he thought silently, *we will be there to help them. For a price.*

"We will see," he said, out loud. "Tell me; how are they coping with their new weapons?"

"Very well, once they get the idea," Zaprudnyi said. "There were some...*incidents*...when they didn't understand what they were being given, but we smoothed them out piece by piece and continued training. They didn't seem to care about the deaths. Right now, they're evolving tactics of their own to make use of their new weapons."

Anjeet nodded. The Vesy hadn't had any real concept of firearms until the Russians had arrived, but they were learning. "And are they likely to be a danger to *us*?"

"The training officers have carefully not mentioned anything that might pose a real threat," Zaprudnyi assured him. "The heaviest thing they possess is a mortar; they have no antitank weapons, no antiaircraft weapons, no plasma cannons. They shouldn't be able to threaten this base or Fort Knight, now the British are there in force."

"Unfortunate, that," Anjeet said. If something were to happen to Fort Knight, it would knock the other powers back a pace or two. They'd waste a lot of time making sure it couldn't happen again. "But they can hurt smaller detachments?"

"As long as they're prepared to soak up casualties," Zaprudnyi said.

Anjeet nodded. The British - and everyone else - didn't realise it, but they were sitting on a powder keg. Allowing the missionaries to land on Vesy had been a mistake, one that would send tremors through the alien society. And it hadn't been the only one. The aliens were starting to wonder if the NGOs really took them seriously, simply because they hadn't provided weapons and the aliens *needed* weapons. It had been simple enough to use that as a selling point, when it came to expanding *Indian* influence.

Idealism, he thought, with a flicker of contempt. *What can it do?*

"We continue, then," he said, shortly.

He looked up at the map; nine city-states had joined the Indian-backed alliance, while two more were wavering. Given time, they should have control - directly or indirectly - over a large area, locking out influence from other human powers. The fact that the concept had largely been borrowed from the British Raj in India would amuse no one, he rather suspected, apart from himself. It wasn't likely the British would appreciate the irony.

Control is simple enough, he thought. They'd distributed weapons like seeds on the land, giving them to any alien faction who showed even the faintest sign of willingness to join the alliance. *Let them become dependent on us - and then make sure they pay for what they need.*

———

"Things seem to have settled down a bit," Joelle said, as she poured tea. "Or isn't that your impression?"

John took a moment to consider his answer. He hadn't *wanted* to visit the planet, but Joelle had invited him and he knew he couldn't have reasonably declined the request. His instincts told him, though, that taking too much time off his command deck could be disastrous. The Vesy might be primitive, but that didn't keep them from posing a danger to the human visitors. And besides, new ships were arriving all the time.

"For the moment, things seem to be under control," he said, carefully.

He took his mug of tea, emblazoned with the logo of the Royal Engineers, then glanced around the office. It had been improved considerably, with new air conditioning and secure data terminals, but it might just create a misleading impression. There was no point in putting a new coat of paint over a damaged bulkhead.

"A very diplomatic answer," Joelle said. She sat down facing him, holding her mug of tea in one hand. "Have you ever considered a career in the Foreign Office?"

"God forbid," John said, before he realised he was being teased. "We'd probably wind up at war with the entire world at the end of my first day in office."

"It isn't normally *that* bad," Joelle assured him. "You normally just end up a lame duck ambassador if you don't get told to take yourself and your aides out of the country by the end of the day."

John lifted his eyebrows. "A lame duck ambassador?"

"No one pays any attention to you," Joelle said. "It happens, quite a bit; someone will always try to contact the PM if they think you're not being generous enough. The PM will then take it out on you, for allowing some foreign leader to get the impression that you don't actually speak for the country. He will not be pleased."

"I see," John said. He sipped his tea, thoughtfully. "This is good tea."

"First thing you learn in the Foreign Office," Joelle said. "How to make tea. They call it a secret test of character."

"How to make tea," John repeated.

"Oh, yes," Joelle said. "As you progress up the ladder, you will get people asking you for a little more than a cup of tea. Learning how to give them what they want without showing any irritation at the request - or how to turn it down - is an essential lesson to learn. That, or my mentor couldn't be bothered hiring a proper steward and gave me the job."

"Sounds reasonable," John said. He cleared his throat. "For the moment, Ambassador, we seem to have the situation under control. All NGOs, whatever their...cause, are being landed at Fort Knight and briefed before being allowed to go out under supervision. There are so many of them that Colonel Boone doesn't have the troops to escort them all. The national detachments have started to set up their own bases, but for the moment Fort Knight remains the centre of activity, save for the Indian base."

He frowned. "I'm afraid the reports from there aren't good."

"Ambassador Begum keeps stalling me," Joelle said. She sniffed, disdainfully. "As if I would be taken in by such tactics."

"I imagine she doesn't want any further agreements," John said. "We have proof, if you want it, that the Indians are doing a great deal more than merely supplying weapons. They're supplying training as well. It will make any city that allies with them more deadly in future.

"Worse" - he leaned forward before she could say a word - "they're setting up factories as well. We don't know for sure what they're designed to produce, but my intelligence staff believe they're intended to produce ammunition."

Joelle's eyes narrowed. "Ammunition?"

John nodded. "You can't fire a weapon without ammunition," he said. "I suspect the Indians have been practically giving away weapons to the Vesy, then driving a hard bargain over each ammunition clip. The Vesy can't produce ammunition for themselves, so they really have no choice but to do whatever the Indians want. If the Indians cut them off..."

"They'd be wiped out as soon as they ran out of ammunition," Joelle said, darkly.

"The God-King's followers were slaughtered," John agreed. "Or held for sacrifice."

"Yeah," Joelle said. "That was something of a problem."

John nodded, ruefully. One month since the sacrifice had been long enough for the media reports to be sent to Earth and a reply to get back. It hadn't gone down well, with questions being asked in the Houses of Parliament about just why Britain was sending *any* aid at all to the Vesy. The NGOs hadn't helped; the farm equipment they'd shipped to Vesy could have been used on Earth, or so various politicians were insisting. It hadn't made anyone look good.

"So far, we haven't received any orders to keep the Vesy from killing their own people," Joelle added. "But that might change."

"I hope not," John said. "How would we even *begin*?"

He looked down at the mug of tea, cursing the politicians and reporters under his breath. It was generally agreed, on Earth, that a nation could do whatever it liked within its borders, as long as it didn't threaten foreign nationals or the rest of the world. No one had any real stomach for interfering on humanitarian grounds, not now. If the inhabitants of a country wanted change, they could change themselves.

But the Vesy were different, at least in some eyes. They weren't human - and they were primitive. John had no doubt that a single destroyer could smash any overt resistance from orbit, but a long grinding insurgency would be a nightmare that would drain human resources beyond belief. If human politicians had no stomach for trying to impose a peace on Terra Nova, why would they have felt differently about the Vesy?

The Vesy aren't human, John reminded himself. *Perhaps that makes a difference.*

"That's the problem," Joelle said. John brought himself back to the conversation with a start. "I don't think we *could* stop them, unless we offered fairly considerable bribes."

"They might not take them," John said. "Are *you* a religious person?"

"I was raised Presbyterian," Joelle said. "I can't say I ever really followed the faith."

John shrugged. "One of my old boyfriends was a Reformed Buddhist," he said, smiling fondly. It hadn't lasted, but they'd shared some good times. "He would never eat meat, you see; I used to tease him about it when I was young and immature. I don't think I could have convinced him to try a bacon sandwich, no matter what bribes I offered."

"He took it seriously, I suppose," Joelle said.

"He did," John agreed. "Point is, Ambassador, would they change even if we offered them everything?"

He placed the empty mug on the table, then smiled. "We live in an age of profound scepticism," he continued. "The Age of Unrest left us with a permanent fear of religious mania and a ruthless determination to prune down any group that started planning a holy war, even if it meant civilians getting caught in the crossfire. We know so much about the universe, including the existence of two other intelligent races, that we don't really take religion that seriously any longer."

"If that was true," Joelle pointed out, "there wouldn't be any missionaries landing on Vesy."

"Point," John agreed. "But *my* point is that we don't see religion as something to become emotional about, not now."

"I don't think that's true for everyone," Joelle said.

"We have an unspoken agreement to mind our own business when it comes to religion," John conceded. It was true enough; a person could worship whatever they liked, as long as they kept it to themselves. "We no longer tolerate people trying to impose religious norms on an entire population. However, the *Vesy* do not share our view of the universe."

"There are lots of humans who do not share *that* view of the universe," Joelle objected. She held up a hand before he could say anything else. "I take your point, Captain, but not everyone will."

"Precisely," John said. "So you need to tell your superiors that meddling in alien religions is likely to end in disaster. They take their religions *seriously*."

"I'll try to bring it to their attention," Joelle said.

John nodded. "The other concern may be a little more immediate," he added. "A couple of Indian ships have been exploring the other tramlines, taking notes about where they actually lead."

Joelle frowned. "And where *do* they lead?"

"Good question," John said. "They're not talking. There's been no attempt to claim any of the systems as yet, apart from our claim to Pegasus, but that may not last."

"Because the Outer Space Treaty grants transit rights to anyone with a colony at the end of a tramline chain," Joelle finished. "If they registered a claim to one of the other systems, they'd have a legal right to pass through the Vesy System whenever they pleased."

"Quite," John agreed. "I'd like to detach one of the destroyers to do some basic survey work, but we're desperately short of ships. Can you ask the Admiralty for reinforcements?"

Joelle blinked. "Can't you?"

"I've tried," John said. There was a good prospect that the commander of any other warship that arrived would be senior to him, but he wouldn't have cared. "The Navy is stretched a little thin at the moment, Ambassador. They may not take the request seriously unless you countersign it."

He sighed. "A few more American or even French warships would be equally welcome," he admitted. "I don't trust the Indians or the Chinese. It's impossible to prove anything, but I have a feeling they're not searching ships as thoroughly as they should."

"Shit," Joelle said. "There's no way to prove it?"

"Not without rigging a freighter ahead of time with visual sensors and recording everything," John said. "We'd need someone else to collaborate, too; we have an agreement that each nation is responsible for searching its own ships. The Indians have brought in another dozen freighters in the last week alone."

Joelle's eyes narrowed. "Bringing what?"

"I wish I knew," John said. "Weapons? Factories? Farming gear? Pornography?"

"I don't *think* the Vesy would be interested in our porn," Joelle said, dryly. "Mind you, they *did* let a couple of researchers watch the sex act. Only they wanted a demonstration of *our* sexual activity in return."

"Oh, dear," John said. He shook his head in amused disbelief. Colin and he had made a game out of having sex in odd places, but they'd never even considered doing it while being watched by a bunch of aliens. And the aliens might feel cheated if they did. "Did they try the Ivanova Defence?"

"I believe they played it straight," Joelle said, deadpan. "A male and female researcher volunteered - *for science*! The video has already been sealed."

"Good," John said. "Someone is probably going to go down in history for *that* one."

"Probably," Joelle said. She ran her hand through her hair. "But compared to everything else they've asked us, that one is relatively minor."

John had his doubts, but kept them to himself.

CHAPTER
TWENTY ONE

Penny was reluctant to admit it, but she was becoming bored.

It wasn't something she would ever have told Percy - he would only have laughed at her, or told her not to upset Murphy - yet it was true. The Ambassador seemed to do nothing other than hold secret meetings with either the other ambassadors or the aliens, while she was running out of other important people to interview. She'd been able to record hundreds of interviews with other visitors to Vesy, but most of them had been unable to say much that was actually newsworthy. Indeed, the NGOs had expressed a great deal of self-congratulation while the missionaries had expressed their disbelief at certain alien practices.

She scowled at the thought, then peered towards Great Thinker Kun, a missionary from the Eminent Rationalists, standing on a platform and addressing a group of aliens. Even *calling* him a missionary was a stretch - he'd insisted on being referred to as a Great Thinker in their brief interview - but Penny honestly found it hard to call him anything else. He clung to his idea of a rational universe, of one that bent to human will, as strongly as any of the religious visitors clung to their god. And he'd hit on her, as soon as the interview was over. Penny still got the giggles when she thought about the chat-up lines he'd tried to use.

As if there was any universe where it would be rational and logical for me to have sex with him, she thought, dryly. *I'd have to keep my eyes closed as I opened my legs.*

She smirked in droll amusement. Kun - she rather doubted that was his original name - was completely bald; he'd admitted, during the pre-interview talk, that he'd had his entire body permanently depilated. His eyes had been replaced by implants that allowed him to see better - or so he claimed - at the cost of pushing his face firmly into the uncanny valley. He looked alarmingly like a pre-space depiction of an alien; indeed, with the formfitting suit he wore, he looked more alien in some ways than either of the two *actual* alien races mankind had encountered. The Vesy didn't seem to find him strange or sinister, as far as she could tell, but they didn't seem very impressed either.

And there isn't anything rational about sex either, she added in the privacy of her own mind. *A rational woman would use an exowomb rather than carry a child for nine months, particularly if she doesn't want to develop feelings for the brat.*

"And I say to you, there is nothing that we cannot understand, given time," Kun bellowed, in oddly-accented English. Penny had never been able to determine where he'd been born, although she had a feeling it was one of the asteroid settlements. They tended to be more accepting of rational and objectivist views of the universe. "Once, we knew nothing of what caused thunder and lightning and so we imagined the existence of gods. Now, we understand the process that causes the sky to flash and rain to fall from the clouds. There are no gods."

The aliens shifted, their beady eyes flickering with...*something*. Penny had watched a dozen missionaries try to talk to the aliens, but none of them had ever outright denied the existence of the alien gods. She honestly wasn't sure if the aliens came to listen because they were curious or because they were ordered to attend, yet...cold ice tingled down her back as she realised that Kun might have gotten them into trouble.

"Once, we could not understand how to sail the seas in stormy weather," Kun continued, although he had to know that the aliens wouldn't understand the reference. Their planet's surface was eighty-five percent land, not water; their seas were tiny, the largest being smaller than Australia. "Now, we have solved the problem of sailing through even the strongest of storms, without prayers to gods to save us from their wrath. Once, we saw asteroid impacts as the wrath of the gods; now, we have starships that can intercept falling rocks before they hit the ground. There are no big men in the sky protecting us in exchange for prayers. Just a universe that is there for us to bend to our will."

Shit, Penny thought. It was hard to read the expressions on alien faces - she had an idea their faces were largely immobile save when they were trying to mimic human expressions - but they didn't seem pleased. Several aliens in purple robes were muttering angrily to the aliens surrounding them…it took her a moment to recall that purple generally meant priest. Kun had insulted the alien religion - all of their religions - right in front of the aliens who were charged with upholding them. *What has he done?*

She glanced at the Paras, who seemed equally unsure what to do. There was no overt threat, nothing they could respond to with force, yet they were aware that the situation was on the verge of turning nasty. One of them was yammering into a mouthpiece, clearly calling in and asking for orders; the others were grasping their weapons, ready to fight to defend themselves. Penny wished, suddenly, that Percy was there.

No, you want him to live, she thought, as the first stone flew through the air and cracked hard against the alien building behind Kun. The alien who'd thrown it was either a rotten shot or was trying to scare Kun, rather than cause a mass slaughter. *Shit…*

"Get back, you fool," she shouted, as several more stones flew at Kun. "Get back!"

"This is irrational," Kun shouted, using an amplifier to boost his words so they echoed over the square. "There are no gods and…"

He staggered backwards as a stone struck him in the chest, then fell off the edge of the platform and plummeted towards the ground, hitting it with a dull thud. The crowd stamped their feet, then moved forward as one of the Paras grabbed Kun, threw him over his shoulder and hastily moved backwards. The sound of chanting from the aliens was growing louder as they advanced forward, moving their feet in a complex dance. Penny's mind grappled with the problem as she backed away herself, fighting down the urge to draw her pistol from her belt. The aliens could run faster, so why weren't they…

It's a ritual, she thought, suddenly. The aliens were picking up speed as their chant echoed over the city, a single repetitive sound that was repeated from every temple in the vicinity. *They want to scare us as well as bless their gods.*

A new hail of stones flew towards the handful of humans. One struck a Para on the head, although he was wearing his helmet and it did no harm. Another nearly struck Penny as she turned and ran, two more smashing down around her feet as she passed the Paras, unsure if she should try to carry Kun or not. She knew she was nowhere near as strong as one of the soldiers, but they were the ones with the weapons to defend themselves. But then another crowd of angry aliens appeared, in front of them. They were trapped.

"This way," a Para snapped. He kicked open a door, then led the way into a large building and slammed the door closed. Inside, it was decorated in an ornate manner that reminded Penny of Admiral Fitzwilliam's family home. Her adopted father's family would probably have been impressed. "Get that door closed and barricaded!"

"There's nothing here to use as a barricade," another Para said. It struck Penny, suddenly, that she'd never learned their names. "Get everyone through the next door."

Penny nodded, then followed two of the Paras into the next room. Behind her, she heard the sound of fists beating on the door and one of the Paras swearing in a manner that would have shocked Percy, if he'd heard it. Or maybe not, she reminded herself, as they ran through the second room. It was just as alien as the first, but the floor was made of earth rather than stone. She puzzled over it for a moment, then checked her recorder was still functioning, uploading everything to the growing planetary communications network. Whatever happened to her - and she had heard quite a few horror stories about reporters who had come to gristly ends - the story would get out.

She heard a crashing sound from behind her, followed by gunfire. The Paras had strict orders not to open fire unless there no other choice, not when it could seriously upset the aliens. If they'd held fire earlier, despite the stones, they wouldn't have panicked now. The aliens had to be presenting an overwhelming threat. She heard screams torn from alien throats, then the sound of chanting grew louder, overwhelming the screams. It was almost hypnotic.

A hand slapped her back, shocking her. "Get up the stairs," the Para snapped. "Hurry."

Penny nodded, then obeyed. The stairwell felt oddly slippery as she ran up it, then stopped dead as she ran into another wooden door. She twisted the knob and practically fell into the next room as an explosion shook the building. There was another burst of firing behind her, then the remaining Paras ran up the stairs and slammed the door behind her.

"Rigged up a Rupert Bear downstairs," one of them snapped to the Para carrying Kun. "They're a little more careful now."

"Let's hope it lasts," the other Para said. "Ammo check?"

Penny tuned him out and looked around the strange chamber. It smelt weird to her, like the landscape in Britain after the tidal waves had washed over the country. Watery, moist…and earthy, in a way she'd never smelled since a visit to a farm as a young girl. The floor was covered with a layer of dirt, while the walls were decorated with carvings of aliens holding hands and prancing around like idiots. It made no sense to her at all.

"Hey," a voice said. She almost jumped out of her skin. "Ammo check?"

"Pardon?"

"Ammo check," the Para repeated. It seemed to have gone quiet downstairs. "How many clips do you have for your pistol?"

"Three," Penny said. She pulled it out of the holster and held it out to him. "Do you want it?"

"Keep it," the Para advised. "If they overwhelm us, make sure you use the last bullet for yourself."

Penny shivered. "Is it going to come to that?"

"I don't know," the Para admitted. "We don't have any way of looking outside, but…it's quite likely we're trapped here until help arrives."

"Oh," Penny said. "And what if help *doesn't* arrive?"

"We die," the Para said, simply. "Or we get taken for sacrifice, which is worse."

"Thank you," Penny said. She swallowed, hard. The darkened chamber was getting to her, more than she cared to admit. It was the creepiest place she'd ever been in, even worse than picking her way through flood-damaged houses in the hopes of finding something to eat, or a place to hide from rioting gangs. "What's your name?"

"Hamish," the Para said. He paused, then smiled. "Buy you a drink after this?"

Penny surprised herself by laughing. "Maybe," she said. "If we get out of here without losing everything..."

Another explosion shook the building. "That was the Rupert Bear," the Para said, turning back to his comrades. The sound of chanting started to grow louder again. "They're coming."

"Shit," Penny said.

——

"Captain," Howard said, as John surfaced from an uncomfortable sleep. "We have a situation on the surface."

"Shit," John muttered. He tossed the covers aside and stood, silently grateful he had a habit of sleeping in his underclothes. "What's happening?"

"A party - one of our parties - that visited City Seven has come under attack," Howard said. "The Paras escorting them report that they're currently trapped in an alien building and are requesting help as fast as possible."

John gritted his teeth as he sat down in front of the terminal and pulled up the map. City Seven - it had been deemed easier to number the cities, rather than rely on imprecise translations or transliterations of alien names - was a good seventy miles from Fort Knight, far enough from the base that few of the NGOs wanted to visit it without some form of motor transport. Getting there would be a pain unless they used the helicopters...

And we don't really have a choice, he thought, grimly. *Colonel Boone will probably see the same thing.*

"Contact Colonel Boone and tell him to proceed as he sees fit," he ordered. Boone *was* the commander on the ground, even though John - as the Royal Navy's senior officer - was in command of the overall mission. "And offer to provide fire support if necessary."

"Aye, Captain," Howard said.

"And then send a flash message to the Ambassador," John added. It was unlikely she hadn't already been notified, but it wouldn't be the first time something slipped through the cracks in the system. "And send a duplicate to every other military formation in the system."

"Aye, Captain," Howard said.

John nodded, then rose and grabbed his uniform jacket. There was nothing he could do, unless Boone called for fire support, but he was damned if he was staying in his quarters when the shit was hitting the fan. Besides, it wasn't impossible that some other powers would have forces on alert, ready to intervene. Some fast talking might be necessary.

Damn the Indians, he thought. *We need a centralised ground command and we needed it yesterday.*

———

"Mail call," Percy carolled, as he stepped into the makeshift barracks. "Get your mail here!"

His section sat up with varying degrees of eagerness. It was a Royal Marine tradition that the senior officer distributed the mail when on detached service, if only to allow the officer a chance to gauge the morale of his men before they went back into action. Personally, Percy rather wished they'd stolen the American tradition of serving breakfast to the men on the day before deployment instead, but it wasn't something he could change.

He dug into the bag and removed a handful of physical letters and parcels. There had been hundreds of electronic messages for them on *Warspite*, including a 'Dear John' letter that really should have been held back until the section returned to Earth, but there was nothing quite like receiving a real letter. He held out the first letter, made a show of being unable to read the recipient's name on the top, then passed it to its owner and handed out the others.

"Got two letters for you, Sergeant," he said to Peerce. "They both look important."

"Dear Dan," Peerce said, as he took the letters. "Your account is now overdrawn. Pay up or we will send Fred and George around to break your kneecaps."

"I hope not," Percy said. He frowned; his crash-course in being an officer had included a sharp warning that he needed to set a good example to his men, including not getting into debt or purchasing something he didn't need. He'd never really thought about it, but he knew it could be a problem. "*Is* that likely?"

Peerce shrugged. "One's from my aunt," he said, "and one from my brother-in-law. Never liked the bastard."

Percy allowed himself a moment of relief, then glanced at his letters. One was clearly from Penny, probably dating back to before the moment she'd been assigned to the mission as an embedded reporter, the second was from Admiral Fitzwilliam and the third was definitely from Canella, judging from the perfume. He opened it up and a small datachip dropped out, followed by a handwritten letter. Percy put the chip in his pocket for later viewing - he had a feeling he'd need privacy to see it - and then opened the letter. Canella chatted about nothing in particular, merely telling him that her boss had stopped harassing her after realising just who she was dating. Percy made a mental note to have a few words with the asshole when he returned to Edinburgh, then considered heading to the private booth. There was time, he was sure, to view the chip…

His bleeper buzzed, urgently.

"Grab your gear," he snapped, as half-read letters were hastily dropped into pockets or locked drawers. An urgent alert meant they might have to deploy anywhere on Vesy, given that they were supposed to be the QRF. Luckily, all they really needed to do was don their helmets and grab their rifles. "Move it!"

His earpiece buzzed as he pulled his helmet over his head. "Lieutenant, there's a small party trapped in City Seven," Colonel Boone said. "We're looking for a diplomatic solution now, but you may have to get them out. You are authorised to use the copters; I say again, you are authorised to use the copters."

Percy swore under his breath - ten men weren't much against an entire city - then double-timed it out of the barracks and over to the helipad. The two helicopters were already swinging their rotors, ready to leave as soon as the marines were onboard. Thankfully, they'd practiced deploying in a hurry; Peerce took four men to one helicopter, while Percy led the rest to the other. There shouldn't be any real threat to the aircraft, he'd been assured, but…

We might be about to find out the hard way that we're wrong, he thought, as a nasty thought struck him. Penny had said she'd be heading to City Seven, hadn't she? *What if they do have something that can shoot us down? The Russians might have left something behind.*

He pushed the thought to the back of his mind as the helicopter lurched into the air. There was no choice. If the diplomats failed, they couldn't let humans be killed.

Of course not, he thought, crudely. *It would set a very bad example.*

CHAPTER
TWENTY TWO

"I haven't been able to contact anyone from City Seven," Grace said, as Joelle hurried into the communications centre. "They're not answering our calls."

Joelle swore. Giving radio to the Vesy - or at least a handful of radio sets linked to the planetary communications net - had been a gamble. The upside of being able to talk to the city's leadership as quickly as possible was balanced by the grim awareness that other human powers would be able to radio to the Vesy themselves. But the radios had clearly failed in their overall function, at least if they couldn't raise anyone in the city. Maybe the aliens had suspected them of being rigged, in some unimaginable manner, to spy on them.

Which we considered before deciding it would come back to haunt us, she thought. In hindsight, that might have been a mistake. It wasn't as if the Vesy had any way to locate a bug that happened to be far too small for anyone to see with the naked eye. *We might have a better idea of what was going on if we spied on them.*

She shook her head. "What is the current situation?"

"The team have made their way into an alien building and are trying to stay ahead of the mob," Mortimer said. He tapped the scene in front of him, showing the live feed from the orbiting recon satellites. "The Royal Marines are inbound; ETA nineteen minutes, but they have orders to hold off unless a diplomatic solution cannot be worked out."

Joelle bit her lip. "It looks as though we cannot talk to anyone," she said, grimly. The display was showing an angry mob clustered around the building, some carrying out dead bodies. They all seemed to be Vesy, so far. "Can the Royal Marines get them out?"

"I'm not sure," Mortimer admitted. "The current plan seems to be to simply pick the team off the roof, then get back into the air. But they may have something that can impede the helicopters as they approach."

"Shit," Joelle said. They had an agreement...which was, in the end, nothing more than ink on paper. Besides, the Russians might have let some heavy weapons slip into alien hands before their base was over-whelmed. "We can't hold off, can we?"

Mortimer never took his eyes off the display. "No, Ambassador," he said. "The longer we delay, the greater the chance they will run out of ammunition and be overwhelmed. They *may* be held as hostages...or they may simply be killed on sight."

Joelle groaned. "What caused this?"

"Unknown," Mortimer said. "The crowd simply went mad."

"We'll figure it out later," Joelle said. It was a catch-22 situation. If the British public had been shocked to hear about the live sacrifice, they'd be horrified to learn that British citizens had been torn apart by alien mobs... or that British troops, in the hopes of escaping the mob, had killed dozens of aliens. "Tell Colonel Boone that we have been unable to make contact with the local leadership" - *which might be lying low until the shit stops flying around*, she thought darkly - "and that he is to do whatever he feels necessary to get our people out of there."

She sat down, knowing she might well have destroyed her career. There would be detailed media reports whining about human and alien casualties, questions in parliament and threats of inquiries in Geneva. The PM held a majority, but he wasn't invulnerable. Throwing Joelle under the bus might seem the best solution to a short-term problem. It was tempting to equivocate until the matter was taken out of her hands, yet she knew better. The buck stopped with her.

Grace stared at her. "There will be...be people killed."

"Yes," Joelle said. "I know."

———

"You are cleared to intervene," Colonel Boone said. "Weapons free; I say again, weapons free."

"Thank you, sir," Percy said.

He contemplated the tactical situation, checking the constant stream of updates from the orbital network. There was no point in trying to land and fight their way through the city, not when it would have been needlessly costly. The simplest solution was the one that had occurred to him as soon as he'd taken his first look; land on the roof, pick up the trapped humans and then beat a hasty retreat. It held risk - the aliens might have something that could bring down the helicopters - but less so than trying to batter their way through the city.

"I have two platoons getting kitted out now with full combat armour," Boone added. "They'll be on their way shortly."

"Understood, sir," Percy said. The QRF hadn't been wearing more than light armour, if only because no one would have been able to endure heavy armour for long. An oversight, clearly. "Can they be held in reserve?"

There was a pause. "I'll order them to hold at Point Delta," Boone said. "But you may need them sooner."

Percy nodded, wordlessly. The Paras were tough - he ought to know; they'd spent the last month training with them, when they hadn't been on patrol - but they would take far too long to get ready to move. Besides, having a couple of extra helicopters wouldn't make much difference. As much as he hated to admit it, it was better to risk a handful of marines immediately than bring in a small army within the hour.

"Thank you, sir," Percy said. "We're moving now."

The connection broke. Percy keyed a switch, then hastily outlined his plan. There were no objections, merely a handful of suggestions. Percy took note of them, updated the plan and finally muttered a series of orders to the pilots. They were both experienced men, having flown missions for the Paras and SAS in the past. They'd carry out the mission or die trying.

The Vesy don't think in three dimensions, he reminded himself. It had taken *him* time, on Salisbury Plain, to learn to appreciate the danger posed by aircraft...or drones so stealthy that it was impossible to see or hear them, before they dropped a missile on an unwary soldier's head. *They won't be expecting us to drop out of the sky.*

"Sergeant, cover us as we go in," he ordered. City Seven - the name translated to something along the lines of 'Home of the Flowery Heart' - was coming into view, a towering mass of stone buildings surrounded by fields and a solid wall. "We are weapons free; I say again, we are weapons free."

And that lets us shoot at any threats we see, without restraint, he thought, grimly. One way or another, they were about to go down in the history books. *God help us.*

He gritted his teeth, then glanced at his men. They looked quietly confident, like the professionals they were.

"Take us in," he ordered.

———

"Get up the next flight of stairs," Hamish ordered, as he carried Kun away from the previous stairwell. "Hurry!"

Penny nodded, then ran up the stairs. The aliens had put a lot of effort into the building, she was sure, but she couldn't figure out what it was *for*. All, but one of the rooms had earthen floors...which was understandable on the ground floor, yet perplexing on the upper levels. It was almost as if the aliens had wanted to grow something inside, but there was hardly any light. What came through the slatted windows was barely enough to satisfy mustard and cress.

Hamish followed her up, holding Kun effortlessly with one hand and carrying a small pistol in the other. No threats materialised at the top, so he relaxed slightly and looked around, concerned. Penny saw the worry on his face and understood; hell, she shared it. The whole complex simply didn't make any sense.

Or maybe we're just missing the key to unlock the mystery, she thought, as she sagged against the stone wall. If the Vesy had been human, she would have unhesitatingly said that the carvings were intended to be erotic. Maybe they *were* and she was looking at the alien version of the *Kama Sutra*. Or...she shook her head, wishing that Professor Nordstrom had accompanied them. *He* might have understood what they were seeing.

The remainder of the Paras rushed up the stairs, one of them unhooking a grenade from his belt and tossing it down towards the aliens. There was another explosion, oddly muffled, followed by howls and screams. Penny gritted her teeth, unwilling to look down and see what the blast had done to the aliens. Really, it was strange just how hesitant the aliens were about simply running up the stairs. Maybe their mobs were more rational than their human counterparts, or maybe there was something about the building that made them reluctant to charge in and to hell with however many were killed. She looked around again, feeling an unwelcome suspicion blossoming through her mind. The earthen floors looked patted down, but there were places where she could imagine someone had dug...

She glanced at the Paras, holding position near the stairwell, then knelt down and started to dig into the ground. Hamish gave her an odd look, but said nothing as she plunged her fingers into the earth. She hadn't realised just how *deep* the earth was, even though they'd run up the stairs; she mentally kicked herself, then kept digging. The earth was changing constituency with remarkable speed...

And then she touched something that felt hard and yet slimy.

Hastily, she pulled back the dirt, feeling her eyes go wide with horror as she realised what she was seeing. It was an egg, only far - far - larger than any of the eggs she'd eaten as a child; indeed, it was roughly the size of a newborn child. She touched it gingerly and realised that, although the shell was really quite hard, it was trembling slightly, like the beating of a tiny heart.

"This is a birthing centre," she said, in awe. She'd known the aliens were egg-layers, but she'd never considered the implications. "This is where they bring their eggs to hatch."

"Shit," Hamish said.

It took Penny a moment to understand the implications. God alone knew how the aliens regarded children - the Tadpoles might not have cared if humans had fished their young out of the water, then eaten them with chips and mushy peas - but *humans* wouldn't have warm feelings towards *anyone* who decided to turn a nursery into a battlefield. The aliens had held back because they'd been scared of harming the eggs, just as humans might hesitate if children were under threat. Quickly, she returned the egg to the soil and covered it up, then looked at the ground. There could be hundreds of eggs, buried just below the soil.

"We just got word from the head sheds," another Para said. "We have to get up to the roof."

"Understood," Hamish said. He glowered at Kun's stunned head, then nodded once to Penny. "Follow me up to the top."

Penny nodded and did as she was told. Behind her, she heard several gunshots as the aliens started pushing back up the stairs. Now they knew what they knew, it was clear the aliens were *definitely* holding back. She fought down the urge to run faster as they reached another floor, then another. Their walls, too, were dotted in the same elaborate carvings. No matter how many times she looked at them, she couldn't escape the impression that they were designed to instruct Vesy in how to have sex.

But sex cannot be a learned behaviour, she thought, puzzling over the question to keep from fretting over the very near future. *How would we have survived if we had to be taught how to have sex?*

The warm air struck her as soon as she reached the rooftop, warm and moist and promising a thunderstorm. Down below, she could hear chanting as more and more aliens joined the mob outside the building, while others were climbing up other buildings, carrying bows and spears as they moved. She had barely a moment to realise that one of the aliens was actually taking *aim* at her before a spear flashed past her and fell over the other side of the building.

"Keep your head down," Hamish snapped. Kun moaned, uncomfortably. "Keep your head down and wait."

Penny nodded, feeling her body start to shake. She'd held herself together when they'd been running up the stairs, but now? They were trapped, unable to hold out forever, and when they were captured…she grasped the pistol and held it, tightly. Perhaps Hamish was right, after all, and she should save one final round for herself…

…And then she heard the chatter of helicopter blades.

———

"There she blows, sir," the pilot said.

Percy nodded, grimly, as the alien buildings came into view. It was easy, thanks to the transponders, to tell which one held the humans, but the surrounding buildings were lined with aliens, all carrying primitive weapons. A handful even carried *human* weapons, although he couldn't tell if they were British, Russian or Indian. They seemed to be staring at the chopper in disbelief, as if their minds refused to accept that something like it could actually fly. But that would change...

He cursed as he saw the aliens scrambling up the walls of the target building. He'd been taught how to climb seemingly-impassable surfaces in basic training; the aliens, it seemed, had much the same training themselves. Judging from the reports, all they'd need to do was get onto the roof to take the humans from the rear. It couldn't be allowed.

"Warn them off," he ordered. He had the legal authority to engage the climbers, but he would prefer to avoid additional casualties. "As loud as you can."

The pilot keyed the mike. "WE ARE TAKING OUR PEOPLE," he said. The racket was so deafeningly loud that several of the climbing aliens lost their grip and fell towards the ground, far below. "LET US DEPART IN PEACE AND NO ONE WILL BE HARMED..."

An arrow hit the side of the helicopter and splintered. Moments later, alarms sounded as bullets started pinging off the aircraft's armour. Percy wasn't too worried - the helicopter had been designed with tougher enemies in mind - but the prospect of a lucky hit grew more and more acute with every second. He pushed his concerns aside as the helicopter moved closer, bullets still slamming into the hull. It wasn't going to end well when they opened the hatches...

"Target the gunmen and return fire," he ordered. "Take them out."

"Yes, sir," the pilot said. He tapped a switch and the helicopter's machine guns opened fire, vaporising their targets. Some of the aliens scattered; others, more disciplined, held their positions and kept firing until they too were picked off. The weight of incoming fire slacked noticeably. "Targets destroyed."

"Take us down," Percy ordered. He keyed his radio. "Sergeant, provide covering fire."

His heartbeat started to race as the helicopter plunged towards the rooftop, creating a whole new problem. Could the building take the weight? He had no way of knowing. The pilot held the craft just above the roof, then fired two more bursts towards a set of aliens who had been scrambling back into firing position. Moments later, the hatch slammed open.

"Go, go, go," Percy snapped, leading the way out of the craft. The roof hatch was just in front of him, according to the reports. "Move it!"

He reached the hatch and peered down into the darkness. A Para - carrying a man slung over his shoulder - peered up at him, then practically jumped up onto the roof. Behind him, Penny followed, looking completely terrified and yet grimly determined. Percy thought, suddenly, of their mother, then caught her arm and shoved her towards the helicopter. There was another hail of gunfire from the aliens and Penny dropped to the ground. For a horrified moment, Percy thought she'd been hit, then realised she'd dropped down when she'd heard the firing. He scooped her up, practically threw her into the helicopter, then waved up the remaining Paras. They tossed grenades back down the stairs to cover their retreat as they reached the rooftop.

"Get into the helicopter," Percy snapped. "Hurry."

Two aliens appeared on a nearby rooftop, carrying something that looked alarmingly like a small rocket launcher. Percy didn't hesitate; he unslung his rifle and fired two rounds towards them, forcing the aliens to duck. He didn't expect to hit anything, not without taking proper aim, but it should teach them to be more careful. One of them dropped the launcher and it exploded, blowing both aliens off the roof.

The last of the Paras passed him as explosions shook the building. Percy cursed again as he realised the helicopter was cramped, then motioned for three of his men to get inside. He slammed the hatch closed as soon as they were in the craft, then jumped onto the skids and held onto the handles for dear life. The pilot yanked the craft into the air as Percy secured himself to the hull with one hand, heading up and away from the city. Percy forced himself to look down as the city fell away beneath him, a handful of rounds passing the craft before they were safely out of range. He'd ridden on the outer hull before, in training exercises, but it had always given him the willies.

Next time, bring a bigger helicopter, he told himself. He would have laughed, if he hadn't been clinging to the side of the aircraft. They hadn't had any time for proper planning and preparation. Given how little warning they'd had, they'd done remarkably well to get in, complete the mission and get out before it was too late. *Or maybe I should have brought fewer men.*

He snickered at the thought, then sobered. They'd had their first major clash with the aliens since the fall of the God-King…and who knew, really, what would happen next?

And where, he added to himself, *did that rocket-launcher thingy come from*?

CHAPTER
TWENTY THREE

"You seem to be intact," the doctor said. "I recommend a change of clothes, but other than that…"

Penny barely heard him. Her entire body was shaking with fear and remembered horror. It seemed as though she'd been far too close to death. Somewhere along the line, she'd lost control of her bladder and wet herself…and she hadn't even noticed. It hadn't been until the doctor had started to examine her that she'd realised her crotch was soaking wet.

And to think I was bored, she thought, bitterly.

"It's natural to be a little shaken after being in danger," the doctor continued. "Take the rest of the day off, if you like."

"I don't think much of your bedside manner," Penny muttered. She wrapped her arms around her chest in the hope it would stop the shaking. "No words of false comfort? No sweet nothings? No pills?"

"I'm a military doctor," the doctor pointed out, dryly. "Soldiers don't normally want words of false comfort and would probably try to hit me if I uttered sweet nothings."

Penny had to smile, despite her nerves. "What about the others?"

"Kun is currently in a drug-induced coma," the doctor said. "Two of the Paras got hit with stones, but their body armour coped admirably. They have some bruises, which they will probably show off if you ask nicely, and not much else. I believe they're being debriefed now."

"Oh," Penny said. She would have to see Hamish and his comrades again, if only to thank him for saving her life. "Will I be debriefed too?"

"Probably," the doctor said, "but I insisted on getting you and Kun some medical treatment before anything else happened."

"It was his fault," Penny recalled. "Kun's, I mean. He straight up told them that their gods don't exist."

"Not the brightest thing to do," the doctor agreed. "Make that clear to the intelligence crew, when you speak to them. They may already have preconceptions of just what happened."

Penny nodded, then rubbed her shoulder. Her recorder was gone, but she'd definitely had it in the helicopter; someone had probably taken it while she was in shock and handed it over to the intelligence crews. It was quite likely her superiors would make a fuss, yet she found it hard to care. The evidence needed to convict Kun of gross stupidity was on the recorder, after all.

There was a knock at the door. "Come in," the doctor said, after a brief glance at Penny. "But this had better be important."

The door opened and Percy stepped through, looking worried. "Is she alright?"

"*She* can speak for herself," Penny snapped, before the doctor could say a word. "And she's fine."

"Just make sure you stay with someone else for the rest of the day, if you're still shaking," the doctor advised. Penny glowered at him. She knew who would want to spend the rest of the day with her. "But physically, you're fine. I can prescribe sleeping tablets if you need them."

"No, thank you," Penny said. She'd used them once or twice and they'd always left her feeling rather thick-headed the following morning. She had the very definite impression that she would require all her wits around her when she was debriefed. "I'm fine, really."

She slipped off the table and down to the ground. Her legs felt unsteady, for a moment, then she forced herself to stand upright properly. Percy watched her, concerned, but she refused to show any sign of weakness in front of him. The doctor nodded once, then turned back to his terminal and started to tap notes into the machine. Penny was tempted to watch - she knew doctors often added things to their notes they never said out loud - but she didn't have the time. Instead, she allowed Percy to lead her out of the room and into a small corridor.

"I'm glad you're alive," Percy said, once they were alone. "I'm…I was desperately worried about you."

"So was I," Penny admitted. The shakes were fading away, replaced by a warm awareness that she'd survived her first brush with real combat. "Can we go back to my room so I can have a shower?"

Percy glanced at her, then nodded. Thankfully, the corridors were largely empty; they barely saw anyone before they entered the new living block. Penny allowed herself a moment of relief, then hurried into the communal shower and turned the water on. It was, as always, lukewarm. She'd hoped for a proper shower, but reporters were classed as somewhere below alien porters and biological threats.

"Go to my room," she said, as she started to close the door. "Get my robe from behind the door and bring it back here."

She took a long moment to wash her body, rubbing her skin clean, then dried herself with one of the communal towels and took the robe Percy offered her. It felt surprisingly warm against her bare skin, but she told herself it was just another effect of staying alive. Percy smiled tiredly at her as she came out of the shower compartment, then led her back to her room.

"I don't think you should be alone right now," he said, flatly.

Penny scowled. "Don't you have somewhere to be, *Royal Marine*?"

"I've got my bleeper," Percy said. He tapped his belt, then leaned forward. "And I - my entire section - have been told, in no uncertain terms, to remain here so we can be debriefed by the head sheds. We're not exactly withdrawn from the front lines, but it will be a long time before we're called up again."

"Oh," Penny said.

"We're still defending you," Percy added, mischievously. "But we're pretty much the last line of defence right now."

Penny nodded, then led the way into her room. It wasn't much; a cramped bed, a tiny washbasin and a set of drawers, but it was home as long as she stayed on Vesy. A faint rattling sound could be heard as the air conditioner fought to keep the temperature at a reasonable level, losing the battle one step at a time. She sat down on the bed, then shook her head in droll amusement. Where the hell was Percy supposed to sit?

He solved that problem by sitting on the floor, then crossing his legs and peering up at the picture Penny had hung on the wall. It had been taken seven years ago, before the war; their father and mother stood together, with their children between them. Percy didn't look anything like as muscular as he did now, she had to admit, while she looked disgustingly cute. Their mother had been fond of dressing Penny up whenever they went out together.

"They still haven't found the body," she said, following his gaze. "No one really knows what happened to her."

Percy looked irked. "I still haven't been able to uncover the mystery of just what happened to our father, either," he admitted. "I thought you were going to crack the puzzle all by yourself."

"The whole affair is cut and dried, as far as my editor is concerned," Penny said. "And the other person who might be able to tell us that we know, outside our work, is the same person who flatly refused to talk about it."

"Admiral Fitzwilliam," Percy said.

Penny nodded, slowly. Admiral Fitzwilliam had always treated them well, even though they weren't his biological children, but there were some things he had refused to talk about, even to them. If there was anyone who had a *right* to know what had happened on *Ark Royal's* final flight, it was Percy and Penny...unsurprisingly, that argument hadn't managed to unlock the Admiral's lips. He'd simply refused to discuss the matter at all.

"We'll find out one day," Percy said. He looked up at her. "I don't suppose I can convince you to go back to the media ship and stay there?"

"No," Penny said, flatly. She smirked, then said the next words with malice aforethought. "I owe Hamish a drink."

Percy frowned. "You're going on a *date* with a Para?"

"It isn't a date," Penny protested. "It's a drink."

"Not that there's much else to do here," Percy muttered. "Look, I know how this is meant to go. I'm meant to object hugely, which will encourage you to go on the date anyway, despite my misgivings. So I won't do anything of the sort. In fact, I will tell you that Hamish is a wonderful man."

"Thank you," Penny said. "So you won't object to me going for a drink with him?"

Percy sighed as she started to giggle. "Just make sure you don't go until you're feeling a bit more stable," he warned. "You're not in a good state for making decisions right now."

"Tell me something," Penny said. "Would this explain some of your girlfriends?"

"Probably," Percy muttered. He pointed to the pillow, meaningfully. "Get some sleep, Pen-Pen. You need it."

"I know," Penny said. She glanced at her watch, then frowned. 1445; it felt later, much later. "You can go see to your men, if you like. I won't go anywhere until morning."

———

"I'm not looking for recriminations," Joelle said, as she glared around the office. Grace, Colonel Boone, Mortimer and Professor Nordstrom looked back at her, while Captain Naiser was attending electronically. "What I want to know is what happened and why."

"The why is simple," Mortimer said. "We studied the records from Miss Schneider's personal media device. Kun, who clearly wasn't a great thinker, told the aliens, outright, that their gods did not exist. They didn't take it too kindly."

"Damn it," Joelle snapped. "What was he *thinking*?"

"Probably that it was his duty to bring the cold light of rationality to the comforting darkness of ignorance," Professor Nordstrom said. "Or so he claimed, on his Social Blog. The Eminent Rationalists believe that religion held humanity back for years, wasting effort on crusades and jihads and wasting resources building temples to God we could have been using to develop ourselves. They presumably feel that the Vesy suffer from the same problem."

"And the Vesy got pissed," Mortimer said.

"It's worse than that," Boone offered. The Para leaned forward, grimly. "They had to take refuge in what we assume was a birthing chamber. Our xenospecialists believe that they lay the eggs, then leave them in the ground to ripen. The battle will almost certainly have killed dozens of unborn children. They won't take that very kindly either."

He paused, then nodded to Professor Nordstrom.

"It's impossible to be sure until we hear from them," the Professor said, "but there's a very strong possibility that children of aristocrats, religious personalities and other people of importance were killed. It would make sense, we think, for most Vesy to lay their eggs at home, rather than place them in a birthing chamber."

"We do have maternity wards," Joelle pointed out.

"I don't think it's the same," Professor Nordstrom said. "Our children are completely helpless when they come out of the womb. Their children are already quite tough when they break out of the egg and fight their way to the surface."

Joelle shivered, feeling a moment of pity for the infant aliens. The idea of being buried alive was one of humanity's worst nightmares, but the Vesy were practically born in the soil. Maybe they liked the idea of having them all born in one place, or maybe it was designed to allow the children to impress on one another, to become familiar with their scent before their parents arrived to collect them. Scent was important to the Vesy; indeed, it was quite possible that one city's population would smell quite different to another city's population.

They may have problems understanding us because we don't smell right, she thought, morbidly. *Or they may never be able to create proper nation-states because the larger the group, the less communal the smell.*

She shuddered, then pushed the thought aside. "So we have a major crisis on our hands," she said. "How do you propose we deal with it?"

"Give Kun to the Vesy," Mortimer said. "Let them do as they please with him."

"That would cause political problems back home," Joelle muttered. "We don't have an extradition treaty with the Vesy and, even if we did, we would need to try him in Britain first."

"The World Court may insist on hearing the case," Grace pointed out.

"Tell the Vesy he's dead," Captain Naiser offered. "They know he was carried out by one of the Paras, so tell them the rock actually inflicted internal injuries and that he died on the helicopter on the way back to Fort Knight."

"They'd want to see the body," Boone said.

"Tell them we cremated the body," Captain Naiser said. "They don't have any way of proving us liars."

"And what," Boone asked, "do we do with the *real* Kun?"

"Put him in the brig," Captain Naiser suggested. "We can send him back to Earth on the next ship, with enough evidence to put him in jail for a very long time. He's certainly guilty of ignoring the rules governing contact with the Vesy, if nothing else."

"His lawyer would probably point out that he didn't sign the rules," Grace said.

"Immaterial," Joelle said. "He caused a riot that resulted in the deaths of countless aliens, including unborn children, and nearly killed seven humans, including himself. I don't think we can afford to do anything else."

She looked at Mortimer. "Have him moved to orbit and dumped in the nearest brig before he gets out of his coma," she ordered. "His possessions can be seized, searched and then placed in the communal pool."

"Yes, Ambassador," Mortimer said.

"But we have two other problems," Boone said. "First, what are we going to say to the Vesy of City Seven, when their leaders finally come out of hiding? Second, where did that rocket launcher come from?"

"Shame your people couldn't capture it," Mortimer said.

Boone glowered at him. "It was destroyed," he said, "which suggests it wasn't a very well-made design. However, it wasn't the only human weapon involved in the skirmish. There were quite a few automatic rifles involved too."

Joelle tapped the table, sharply. "So where did *they* come from?"

"City Seven wasn't the recipient of any of *our* weapons," Mortimer said. "They could be Russian, but I rather doubt it. The Indians are the most likely suspects."

"They wouldn't have given the Vesy a rocket-launcher," Grace said. "Would they?"

"I wouldn't have thought so," Mortimer said. "But I could easily be wrong."

"It's something to raise at the next meeting," Joelle said. One had hastily been arranged for the following day, once word had spread to the other ambassadors. It wasn't a discussion she was looking forward to. "But whoever gave them the weapon has a strong motive to keep it to themselves."

"Because it's a weapon that could be used against us," Captain Naiser growled.

"Correct," Joelle agreed.

She sat backwards, feeling old. "So what are we going to tell the Vesy?"

"Tell them that Kun is dead and that we will pay compensation for the results of his stupidity," Captain Naiser said. "And then see what they want in exchange for burying the whole affair."

"Wait a minute," Boone growled. "It is a principle of our operations that we *don't* pay compensation."

"This is not a made-up claim," Captain Naiser snapped. "This isn't some backwards farmer trying to convince us that his elderly mother-in-law was accidentally killed by a rocket that missed its intended target by fifty miles, or that he had a hundred sheep in his backyard that were flash-fried by a plasma blast. There is no doubt that Kun provoked a riot, that upwards of a hundred Vesy were killed, that an unknown number of eggs were smashed…this is going to make us look very bad back home, if nothing else. What would *we* think if an outside force came into a nursery and killed a dozen children?"

"We'd want blood," Mortimer muttered.

"Exactly," Captain Naiser said. His image looked at Joelle. "Find out what they want in compensation, Ambassador, and pay it."

Joelle cursed under her breath. She must be getting old, because the media issue hadn't occurred to her even though a reporter had been caught up in the riot. By the time the news reached home, it would probably have mutated; the Paras would find themselves with a black mark on their record that made Bloody Sunday look like nothing. The simple fact that the Paras had acted in self-defence would be lost in the recriminations. By the time the government had finished its investigations, the truth would be completely buried under a mountain of shit.

"We've been trying to contact them," she said, "but so far there hasn't been a reply. When they do get in touch, we will offer what we can. But I don't know how we can give them a fair deal. They wouldn't understand the value of what we were offering."

"We can, but try," Boone said.

He sighed. "Other problems emerged, Ambassador," he said. "We still don't have a unified command structure for operations on the ground. I think we're going to need one if another group runs into trouble."

Joelle frowned. "I thought I gave orders for all away teams to be recalled."

"You did," Boone said. "Not all of the national groups obeyed, however; they are not, legally, under your command. I don't think the Vesy will really understand the difference between British and Americans, let alone Americans and Indians."

"They do have city-states," Grace pointed out.

"We must look alike to them," Boone countered. "It's quite possible that the Americans or the French will wind up being attacked for our sins."

"For *Kun's* sins," Joelle snapped.

"By the time the dust settles," Boone said, "that may no longer matter."

CHAPTER
TWENTY FOUR

Joelle rather wished she'd taken a sleeping tablet the previous night, even though she'd been warned, when she'd joined the Foreign Service, that nothing beat a good night of proper sleep. She'd stayed up late, fielding media demands for information and doing her best to put together a report for the Prime Minister, one that wouldn't lead to immediate political chaos back home. By the time she'd finally gone to bed, she'd been so tired that she'd barely closed her eyes before Grace had woken her with a mug of steaming black coffee and warned her that there were thousands of new messages in her inbox.

"Forget them," she'd growled, after a brief look. What sort of idiot believed that marking a routine request *urgent* would get him a quicker reply? All it did was bury genuinely urgent requests under a mountain of crap. "Get me something to eat, then we'll go to the conference room. There isn't time to worry about anything else."

Grace, mercifully, didn't question her as they strode down to the conference room, where a handful of security staff were carrying out yet another bug sweep. A steward was just preparing jugs of water and hot coffee; Joelle gratefully took a second mug, then sat down at the table as the other ambassadors started to file into the room. She was going to have the jitters later, she knew - too much coffee wasn't good for anyone - but for the moment she needed to be awake and reasonably aware. She'd just have to catch up on her sleep later.

"Go skim through the messages and forward anything urgent to my secondary account," she ordered Grace. "Anything else will have to be left until later."

"Yes, Ambassador," Grace said.

She left the room, looking pensive. Joelle watched her go, feeling an odd flicker of guilt at her aide's lost innocence. There were times when being an ambassador had far too much in common with being a prostitute. Idealism had to be sacrificed in the name of the greater national good. Grace would either learn to cope with it, burn out early or seek a transfer somewhere else. Joelle just hoped she wouldn't do either of the latter two until their time on Vesy was over.

"Thank you all for coming," she said, once the coffee had been poured and the remaining aides and security officers were out of the room. "As you will have heard, the situation on the surface has taken a turn for the worse."

"That's one way of putting it," Barouche sneered.

"Yes, it is," Joelle agreed. She ran through a brief outline of the riot and rescue mission. "So far, we have not been able to get in touch with anyone in authority at City Seven, but our orbital observations reveal that the city is in…well, a state of political foment. Several different factions appear to be fighting it out for superiority. In short, although we have already determined to pay compensation for the disaster, we have no one to pay it *to*."

She paused, inviting comment, then went on. "I have spoken to representatives from nearby cities," she added, "but none of them were able to offer help. Indeed, they were quite concerned with…rumours they'd heard from City Seven."

"You mean they thought you deliberately provoked the riot," Barouche said.

"Yes," Joelle said.

"Perhaps we should consider a different question," Schultz said. "Who allowed that fatheaded idiot to land on the surface anyway?"

Joelle winced, inwardly. "He was cleared by the spaceport crew, after reading the documents detailing the acceptable level of conduct and signing them," she said. "Might I point out that all attempts to ban religious representatives from the surface failed?"

"The President would not have tolerated it," Schultz admitted. He looked embarrassed. "I think that policy may have to be revised."

"That's one way of looking at it," Rani said. The Indian spoke softly, but Joelle couldn't escape the impression that she was amused. "However, such matters are really...what is the English expression? Locking the barn door after the horse has been stolen?"

"More or less," Joelle said.

She took a breath. "Word is already headed to Earth," she said. "There are courier boats at each tramline, ready to take messages through and relay them to the next courier boat. I give it a week - ten days at most - before Earth knows what has happened here. The media will have a field day."

"Which is bad news for the Eminent Rationalists," Schultz observed.

"Or perhaps not," Joelle said. "They could argue that the riot proves that they were actually *right* all along."

She shrugged. "I believe we have a good reason to ban religious representatives now," she said, instead. "We can do it *pro tem* and then reverse the policy if Earth refuses to endorse it."

"The President *will* refuse to endorse it," Schultz admitted. "Far too much of his support comes from religious factions who have stars in their eyes, almost literally, at being able to minister to an alien race. He cannot ban them from the surface without facing a backlash."

"Even at the risk of losing missionaries to alien attacks?" Barouche asked. "Or will he endorse punitive strikes when a missionary is actually killed?"

Joelle rubbed her temple, feeling a headache starting to pound under her skin. Ambassadors were political appointees, normally; Schultz couldn't go too overtly against his President's interests without risking his position. Hell, it wasn't as if she could openly defy the Prime Minister. But if one religious idiot had been enough to spark off a riot that had caused no end of problems for both sides, what would happen when the next religious idiot lit a match right next to a barrel of gunpowder?

"It wouldn't be the first time a missionary has been killed trying to minister to the souls of the unconverted," Schultz pointed out. "I certainly do not have authority to launch strikes to punish the Vesy for murdering them."

Barouche snorted. "Are you sure?"

"Perhaps we should introduce the Vesy to the concept of *persona non grata*," Rani offered, before the American could reply. "Tell them that they can kick out anyone they like and we'll take him away from their world, no questions asked."

"There isn't a united government here," Schultz pointed out. "One city-state might kick out someone, but another city-state might want him."

"There's another problem," Barouche added. "Your idea assumes a degree of rationality on their part. Their leaders may not have *time* to kick someone out before the riot begins."

Joelle suspected he had a point. She'd viewed the footage from the reporter's recorder and the sensors the Paras had carried and it had been clear, at least to her, that there had been no time to do anything before all hell had broken loose. Even with modern communications, she knew from bitter experience that matters could become a great deal worse before new orders arrived from further up the chain. The Vesy, lacking anything more advanced than mounted couriers, would have real problems reacting to a crisis before it blew up in their faces.

"Then we make it damn clear that they go in at risk of their lives," Schultz said. "Tell them there's no obligation to deploy troops to save them."

"I don't think your President would like that," Barouche said.

"And there would be spill-over problems in any case," Rani added.

Joelle shook her head. It was clear there wasn't going to be an agreement, even one that lasted long enough to get new orders from Earth.

"There is another issue," she said, as she tapped the terminal. Images recorded by the helicopters flickered into life in front of them. "You will note that the Vesy had a rocket launcher, one that exploded when it was dropped and hit the rooftop. Where did that weapon come from?"

"Not a very good weapon," Schultz said, after a moment. "It looks like a crude antitank weapon rather than something intended to deal with a helicopter."

"It would have destroyed the helicopter if it had hit its target," Joelle said, flatly. "Might I remind you, remind *all* of you, that we agreed to keep heavy weapons out of their hands?"

"I wouldn't argue that a single rocket launcher is a heavy weapon," Barouche said.

"My people were fired upon by aliens using human weapons," Joelle snapped. "It was sheer luck and excellent training that kept them alive - and if that rocket had been fired, we might be mourning a dozen dead humans instead of counting our blessings! I want to know where that god-damned rocket came from!"

She glared around the room. "Let's be brutally honest," she said, eying Rani. "We all want influence with the aliens, so we trade weapons because that's what the aliens *want*. There's no point, as you said, in locking the barn door after the horse has been stolen. But rocket launchers are an order of magnitude more dangerous than automatic rifles and gunpowder weapons. They can be turned against us!"

"The Russians might have left it here," Schultz pointed out. "It isn't as if we have a complete list of what they turned over to the God-King - or lost after their base was captured."

Joelle sighed. The hell of it was that Schultz had a point. It *was* quite possible the rocket launcher had been taken from the Russians...but somehow, she doubted it. A rocket launcher would have given its owner a great deal of local prestige, if it had been rarer than gold. The aliens would only have tried to fire the weapon if they thought they could get more... and that meant they had a source among the human powers currently involved on their world.

She looked from face to face. The Americans weren't too likely to supply rocket launchers, not when they had so many people exposed on the ground; the French, she suspected, would feel the same way. But the Indians had already started arming the aliens, with more weapons than Joelle cared to think about, and they might well decide to quietly ignore the agreement on not supplying heavy weapons. Anything that gave them an advantage on the surface would be considered acceptable. They already had a growing sphere of influence that was larger than anyone else's.

And they presumably want the whole world, she thought, coldly. *It would give them a claim to the entire system - and its tramlines.*

They weren't the only suspects, she had to admit. The Chinese or Turks might have slipped in the rocket launcher, perhaps just to cause trouble for the other powers. Or an NGO might have managed to get it through the military cordon, perhaps by dismantling it and hiding the pieces all over their ship. God knew they'd been complaining, loudly, about not being allowed to give weapons to the aliens. Or...

"We should try for an agreement not to sell any more weapons to the aliens," she said, "but that won't work, will it?"

No one disagreed.

"There is another issue," Schultz said. "We need a united command structure."

"My government would insist that *we* held command," Rani said. "We have the largest military commitment here."

That was true, Joelle knew. 3 Para and its supporting units consisted of little more than five hundred men, while the Indians had landed over five *thousand*. She silently totted up the numbers in her head and concluded that everyone else, if added together, *might* match the Indians, but the Indians wouldn't accept that as a valid reason to surrender command to anyone.

"But you don't have the largest commitment elsewhere," Schultz said. "India is still ranked sixth among the human powers."

Rani's eyes glittered with controlled rage. "The fact remains that we have the largest commitment *here*," she said, coolly. "Furthermore, we have two systems under our control within three jumps of *this* system. Cromwell, New Boston and Pegasus are small colonies by comparison. Should there be a sudden demand for additional troops, they will have to come from our territory."

She had a point, Joelle admitted silently. Britannia, New Washington and New Paris were all on the other side of Earth to Vesy; indeed, the local sector hadn't been properly surveyed until just before the First Interstellar War. New Delhi and Gandhi had been settled for over fifty years prior to the war, with ever-growing populations. They'd even kick-started the local infrastructure when it seemed likely that Earth would come under attack.

Not that they would have lasted long, if the Tadpoles had won the war, she thought. Earth had still been the centre of human industry, despite plans to move as much as possible out to the colonies. *They would have been wiped out before they could build up a real defence.*

"Then we compromise," Schultz said. "Fort Knight is still the centre of operations on the surface. Colonel Boone can hold overall command until Earth appoints an overall CO and assigns more troops."

"That would be acceptable to us," Barouche said. It was a surprising concession, which probably meant he intended to extract a price later. "My security officers speak well of him."

"But not acceptable to us," Rani said. "It is a precedent among the powers that whoever provides the most troops assumes command. Our troop levels are an order of magnitude higher than the British, who have the next highest contingent."

"Admiral Smith assumed command of Operation Nelson, despite having no less than *three* American carriers under his command," Schultz pointed out, smoothly.

"Arguably, he had three *British* carriers," Rani countered.

"Only one of which was a *fleet* carrier," Schultz snapped. "They couldn't carry more than a single squadron apiece."

"Admiral Smith was a special case," Rani said, changing tack. "He was the *sole* human officer to score any kind of victory against the Tadpoles, at least until the Battle of Earth. I believe just about every power on Earth gave him a medal, as well as an offer of honorary citizenship. He could reasonably claim to be the first true citizen of the entire world, if he had survived. Do we have any counterpart to him here? Really?"

Percy Schneider, Joelle thought. It wasn't worth mentioning. There was no way they could reasonably put a lieutenant in command of a multinational force. *And he didn't do more than remain in Fort Knight and stall the aliens until relief finally arrived.*

Rani rose. "I do not believe my government would accept anything less than command of the force, if we are to contribute the most troops," she said. "There will be no Indian participation without command... unless, of course, you bring in more troops of your own."

She stalked out of the room, closing the door behind her.

"Well, that's us told," Schultz observed.

Joelle thought fast. The Indian woman had been stalling, of that she was sure...but why? It was true enough that India - and many of the secondary human powers - bitterly resented not being treated as equals, yet it seemed odd to jeopardize everything over a dispute about who should assume command. Unless, of course, she was taking advantage of the opportunity to make a point. The Vesy might butcher everyone on the surface, if the worst came to worst, but it wouldn't change the balance of power on Earth one iota. *India* wouldn't be materially harmed by losing five thousand men.

They'd be embarrassed, she thought. *Or worse.*

"We can formulate a combined force without the Indians," Schultz said, flatly. "I nominate Colonel Boone for the post of CO."

"Agreed," Barouche said. "I dare say the Chinese will agree too."

Joelle had her doubts. The Chinese Ambassador hadn't attended the meeting, citing other concerns. Maybe it was a simple reluctance to commit China to anything, which was quite possible, or maybe it was a deliberate attempt to keep his options open as long as possible. It was hard to be sure where the Chinese were concerned.

"We will see," she said. She took a breath. "For what it's worth, I intend to propose to my government that we come to a joint agreement banning further weapon and ammunition sales to the Vesy."

"*That* won't please the Indians," Schultz observed.

"Or my government," Barouche added. "We are currently preparing to establish factories of our own on Vesy."

"Which will only make the situation worse," Joelle said. If the French followed the Indians, America and Britain would probably have to follow suit. God knew they couldn't tie freighters up indefinitely shipping ammunition to Vesy, not when there were so many other demands on their time. "This could end badly."

"It's already bad," Schultz said. He rose. "For what it's worth, I have reviewed the data from yesterday and I believe your men had no choice. I have communicated that to my government."

"Thank you," Joelle said. She knew it would be costly, even if there was no overt demand for payment, but for the moment she was grateful.

"We'll just have to see what happens when City Seven finally pulls itself back together."

"My people will speak to your people about the joint command," Schultz said. "They will have to try to work with the Indians, if only unofficially."

"Officially-unofficially," Joelle said, dryly. It wouldn't be the first time two nations, both of whom hated the other, had cooperated under the table. Rani might have to make her point, but she wasn't fool enough to totally disregard the possibility of working together. "We will see."

She watched them go, then sank back into her chair. Her body wanted sleep desperately, and perhaps a long soak in the bath, but there was no time. She had too much work to do.

"Grace," she ordered, keying her wristcom. "Inform Captain Naiser that I would like to speak to him onboard *Warspite* tomorrow, if that suits him."

"Yes, Ambassador," Grace said.

CHAPTER
TWENTY FIVE

"They are threatening our religions," Harkin said.

Anjeet nodded. He'd given the alien the name, drawing it from a book his sister had loved as a child, and the alien had accepted it without demur. But why not? They were just as eager to work with the Indians as the Indians were to work with him.

"That is what they always do," he said. "They believe in their one super-god and use him as an excuse to destroy those who believe in *other* gods. The God-King failed, so they are trying more subtle ways to break your will."

It was nonsense, of course, but it was flattering nonsense. And the aliens *wanted* to believe it, wanted to believe that they could stand against an overwhelmingly powerful foe, wanted to believe that they had allies who shared the same vision of the universe. Anjeet had no objection to providing them with all the weapons they wanted, although he had been careful not to mention some of the possibilities, and he hadn't attempted to enforce any standards of behaviour on them, save for upholding the growing Indian alliance network. The aliens hadn't raised any objections.

He smiled to himself as he looked around the room, decorated with strange alien woodcarvings. The British, Americans and French might insist on walking around with an armed escort, but the Indians had worked hard to show just how much they trusted the aliens by leaving the guards at the fort. It was a gamble, Anjeet knew, yet it had paid off. Every time he walked in and out of the city alone, with only a single pistol at his belt, it boosted his status in their eyes.

They don't need to know there's a team of armed and armoured men on permanent standby, in case of crisis, he thought, grimly. *Or that my uniform contains body armour and a hood...*

"They killed dozens of children," Harkin said. The Vesy didn't sound too upset - although it was hard to be certain - but he had to know it was a dangerous precedent. "Why?"

"They do not care about you, only for what they can do for themselves," Anjeet said. "Their lives come first, always."

He shrugged, inwardly. Judging from the reports, the British Paras had done very well to remain alive long enough to be rescued. Breaking into a birthing chamber was a stroke of luck, both good and bad; it had delayed the aliens for a while, but at the same time they'd ended up with egg on their face. Quite literally, he told himself, and concealed his amusement with an effort. He would have been very surprised if the aliens hadn't been quietly comparing notes with cities that had contacted other human powers.

"They even lied about Kun," he added. "They might have told you he was dead, but they only took him off your world."

The alien hissed in rage. He'd heard, of course, that Kun hadn't survived the riot, a message put out by the British from Fort Knight. Anjeet didn't blame them for trying to calm the aliens without giving them the idiot - it would have opened a whole can of worms - but he had no compunction about telling the aliens the truth. It would only keep them focused on the British as enemies.

"The city" - Harkin uttered a name that was completely unpronounceable - "is in disarray. It will be a long time before a new set of leaders are elected."

Anjeet nodded. It was hard for most humans to understand, but the Vesy had no barrier between Temple and State. A ruler would have both a religious career and a secular career, insofar as they diverged. Combined with something akin to a council populated by the various religious leaders, the aliens had a government system that was both democratic and religious. The contradiction between the two roles, he rather suspected, had caused City Seven to have real problems selecting new leaders.

Because one of their positions requires a willingness to work with humans, he thought, *and the other requires holy war. Their positions are contradictory.*

He nodded, thoughtfully. *No wonder the God-King was such a shock to their system. He didn't just preach one religion, he tried to eradicate all the others!*

"That is understandable," he said, turning his mind back to the original topic. The British might have been offering compensation - an unusual gesture in a world where the whole idea of offering compensation had been discredited long ago - but it would be hard for them to find someone willing to accept it. They'd smashed eggs and killed *children*. "What do *you* intend to do about it?"

"There can be no peace with those who would destroy religion," Harkin said. "Or deny the truth of the gods."

"Of course not," Anjeet agreed. "But you do realise that they have many advantages over you?"

The alien gave him a long considering look. They weren't stupid; they might believe the Hindu faith was compatible with their own, but they also understood that Anjeet would want something in exchange for his help. It was part of the reason, he knew, why they'd had so many problems grasping the concept of NGOs. The idea of *charity* was starkly alien - he smiled at the pun - to them. No Vesy gave something away when he could extract a price in return.

"We understand," he said. "But we have weapons."

"Not enough," Anjeet said. "Luckily, we have something that may tip the balance..."

———

"I spoke to two more alien cities," Ambassador Begum said, an hour later. "They're both willing to sign on with the alliance. It didn't take them long to work out that none of the cities allied with us had any visitors from the religious missionaries."

Anjeet nodded. He hadn't been sent any missionaries, but if he had he would have refused to allow them to land. There was no point in muddying the water; the aliens would be vastly insulted if *he* claimed his gods were real and theirs weren't, or even that they should switch to worshipping the Hindu gods on Vesy. It would be a different story on Earth, he was sure; he wondered, mischievously, what the media would make of the Vesy worshipping at human temples.

Probably claim we brainwashed them, he thought, sourly. It was hard to escape the impression that many westerners simply didn't take Hinduism seriously, regarding it as a throwback to a less-enlightened age. They'd certainly shown the same attitude to the Vesy religions, even though the Vesy were more tolerant than most humans. *But then, the Vesy believe in all gods, they just don't worship them all.*

"That's a good thing," he said, slowly. It hadn't been *that* hard to come up with a network of alien agents, not once they'd made it clear they were prepared to work with the aliens as equals. "And the propaganda?"

"At the moment, the general feeling is that the British deliberately smashed hundreds of eggs and killed the egg-matrons," Rani said. "We have been boosting this message as much as possible, of course."

"Of course," Anjeet agreed.

It was a stroke of luck, definitely. The egg-matrons were odd, even by Vesy standards; they were a religious group of eunuchs, male and female, who had the task of taking care of the eggs until they hatched. From what his people had been able to determine, they took no role in politics...but their persons were untouchable. They were protected by all of the gods, including the ones that remained unnamed. A Vesy who laid a finger on one of them, for whatever reason, risked being lynched. Even the God-King hadn't dared touch them when he'd captured more cities.

But the British had killed the ones guarding the birthing chamber in City Seven. It was an insult that was not to be borne.

Which means they will become more dependent on us than ever, he thought, darkly. *And eventually we will wind up in command of the whole planet.*

It helped, really, that there was no *need* to take direct control of their world. The British had worked through the Princely States, back in the days of the Raj; *he* would work through the allied city-states, giving them enough firepower to keep the rest under control. There was literally nothing, beyond formal control, that was worth the effort of taking from Vesy. Why invade when he could get nothing from it?

But we will have control of the tramlines and the outer system, he added, mentally. *And that is all that matters.*

He turned his attention back to the Ambassador. "Do you think the other ambassadors will surrender to your demands?"

"I doubt it," Rani said, tartly. "They do not trust us. I think they suspect the rocket launcher came from us."

Anjeet shrugged. "Lucky none of them got a close look at it," he said. The British must have wondered why it had been designed with a complete lack of concern for health and safety - the rocket could have been built *not* to explode when it was dropped - but it had helped to bury the evidence. "They will probably take it for a Russian design, something put together in a machine shop."

"One would hope," Rani said. She shook her head. "They won't give us command of a joint security force, General."

"I know," Anjeet said. It would have been useful if they *had*, but it might have made the next stage of the plan somewhat awkward. India would have been accused of deliberately fomenting trouble, then capitalising on it...and there would have been some very real proof, if anyone cared to look. "We'll stay out of the official arrangements, for the moment."

He shrugged, again. "Have you spoken to the NGOs?"

"Most of them are a little disillusioned with Fort Knight," Rani said. "I think a handful will be quite happy to move operations to here."

"Where they can teach our heavily-armed friends the advantages of improving their crop yield," Anjeet agreed. It was clear the NGOs had *some* influence in the West, at least in Britain and America; having them as allies might be useful and certainly couldn't hurt. "It should be workable."

"Of course, General," Rani smiled.

Anjeet nodded. "Can you keep stalling the other ambassadors?"

"For the moment," Rani said. "It depends on just how many other troops they're prepared to bring in - and what their public opinion makes of it."

"Nothing good," Anjeet said. "Our people back home will see to it."

———

"Hey," Hamish said.

Penny looked up and smiled as the Para sat down facing her. The refectory was almost empty so late at night, with only a handful of ration bars left in cupboards for anyone who fancied a late-night snack; they could easily talk without being heard. Hamish was wearing his uniform, but not the body armour she recalled from the riot. It had probably saved his life.

"Hey," she said, feeling suddenly shy. "Thank you for saving my life."

"You're welcome," Hamish said. "Did they debrief you too?"

"Yep," Penny said. After she'd fallen asleep, she'd been woken at 0900 with the news that Colonels Boone and Mortimer wanted to speak to her personally. The debriefing - more like an interrogation - had been horrendously detailed, going over the same questions time and time again until she'd finally told them she'd had enough. "They were... *thorough.*"

"They have to be," Hamish said. He looked uncomfortable, just for a moment. "They think we might have killed *children.*"

"We might well have done," Penny said. She had no idea just how well-protected the eggs were, under the earth, but the Paras had detonated several grenades. "It's something we may have to pay for, in the future."

Hamish scratched his shaved head. "We didn't have much choice," he said. "But we still feel like...ah, *crap.*"

"I have heard worse," Penny assured him. "My editor has a habit of bellowing obscenities at anyone who dares offer good excuses for not having an article ready for publishing."

"Not a friendly man then," Hamish said. "What are you going to write about the riot?"

"I've already written a short article and uploaded it to the next courier boat," Penny said. "I just told them the truth, blamed everything on Kun. Stupid bloody idiot should never have been allowed down to the surface."

"We'll probably get the blame," Hamish predicted, glumly. "We could have shot him in the back, they will say, or we should have shut him up by force."

"I made it clear that you weren't to blame," Penny said.

She sighed, inwardly. Her article hadn't been the first - and even though it was the only first-hand report, it probably wasn't sensational enough to attract a jaded public. If it bleeds it leads, her editor had said more than once, and nothing drew the eye like dead children. Her hands started to shake as she remembered the egg she'd held, wondering if the alien baby was dead or alive. The public would be revolted, she knew; they'd be torn between the impulse to swat any barbarians who thought they could lay hands on a British citizen and murder the Paras who had killed alien babies in the crossfire. And the politicians...

Some of them don't want to waste resources on Vesy, she thought. It wasn't as if Britain had much to spare. *They'd have an excellent excuse to pull our official presence off the surface and leave Vesy to the other powers, if they want it.*

"Thank you," Hamish said. "But would they listen?"

Penny snapped back to reality with a jolt, then hastily replayed their conversation in her head.

"I don't know," she confessed. She picked up her cup of water and took a swig. "I didn't know *this* was what you intended when you asked me out for a drink."

Hamish looked nonplussed for a moment, then laughed.

"I do have a bottle of...*something* I won at a poker match while we were on the transport," he said. "There isn't a ship in the Royal Navy that doesn't have an illicit still somewhere onboard. But the Sergeant would kick my ass if I dared drink alcohol here, even though I'm supposed to remain confined to base with the rest of the lads."

Penny frowned. "They're not letting you out the gates?"

"They're not letting *anyone* out the gates," Hamish said. "You know all the small groups that were out in the field? They've been called back and the gates have been sealed. Everyone is on alert, save for those of us involved in the balls-up. We've been told to stay here and wait."

"Fuck," Penny said.

"Yeah," Hamish agreed. "It's precisely the wrong message, if you ask me, but no one did."

"Maybe," Penny said. She cursed herself under her breath. If she'd been thinking straight, she would have checked the daily update as soon as she awoke. Instead, she'd written her article and felt sorry for herself. Percy would laugh at her if he ever found out. "Or it could be a way of showing we're sorry."

Hamish looked unconvinced. "From a military point of view," he said, "there's a certain advantage to *not* allowing anyone to push you around, even if you are to blame for whatever went wrong. Quite a few problematic situations in the regiment's long history started with politicians telling us not to slap back when we were provoked."

"Unless they're looking for an overreaction from you," Penny said.

"Could be," Hamish agreed.

He looked down at the table, then frowned. "I can take you for better drinks when we get home...?"

"I would be delighted," Penny said. She finished her water and put the cup to one side. "Tell me about yourself?"

Hamish looked at her for a long moment. "On or off the record?"

"Off," Penny said. She had done enough human interest interviews to last a lifetime, with the added problem that most of the people her editor *wanted* her to interview had flatly refused to talk to her. "I just want to talk."

"Not much to say, really," Hamish said. "Grew up in London, near the East End. Bit of a rough childhood, so I had a nasty time at school; eventually, one of the teachers told me I'd do well in the army, *if* I worked hard. He'd been a Sergeant, apparently; he worked with kids who were bigger and meaner than me and never batted an eyelid. Taming rough little brats was what he *did*. And then the waters came rolling over London and... well, to cut a long story short, I volunteered for service instead of being conscripted."

"Like Percy," Penny muttered. "What about your family?"

"Mum died when I was very young, dad never remarried," Hamish said. "He was turning to drink when the aliens hit us and London was drowned. I never saw him or my sister again."

"I'm sorry," Penny said.

"Don't be," Hamish said. "It wasn't your fault."

He shrugged. "The Paras took me out of Catterick and put me through hell before I qualified to join them," he added. "And then I spent two years on various deployments, including one on Mars. That was pretty cool, if weird. They say Mars will be habitable in another hundred years."

"So they say," Penny said. The Mars Project had begun before the tramlines had been discovered. "I've never been there."

"Go one day," Hamish urged. "It's spectacular."

He glanced at his watch. "And I'd better get back to the barracks," he added. "Knowing my luck, there will be an emergency call in the middle of the night."

Penny nodded, then leaned over the table and kissed his cheek. "Thank you, again," she said. "You still owe me that drink."

"I will, promise," he said. "If we ever get leave again, here, we can try to go somewhere together."

"We can try," Penny agreed. She gave him another kiss, then rose. "Goodnight."

Hamish smiled at her. "Don't let the bedbugs bite," he called. "Really."

Penny winced. They'd been warned about insects infesting the barracks as soon as they'd landed. As long as the rooms stayed cool, they weren't a problem…but they wouldn't stay cool forever. The air conditioning seemed permanently on the brink of breaking down.

"Goodnight," she said, again. "Bye!"

CHAPTER
TWENTY SIX

"Hell of a mess," John said. "There's still been no word from City Seven?"

Joelle shook her head from where she was sitting on his sofa, curled up against a cushion and holding a mug of tea in her hand. "Not a peep," she said. "The satellites tell us they're still fighting one another, but no new leader seems to have emerged."

"Pity we don't understand their politics that well," John said. He picked up his own mug of tea, then sat down facing her. Bringing her up to orbit was a risk, but he hadn't wanted to leave *Warspite* when the situation was in flux. "They might be going through a ritual contest of strength before choosing a new leader or they might be fighting a flat-out civil war."

He cursed under his breath. Joelle had ordered all British personnel to remain at Fort Knight - and strongly advised personnel from the other powers to do the same - and they were getting restless, while the Indians moved from strength to strength. It was hard to be sure, but it was starting to look like the Indians had no less than *thirteen* cities allied to them, thirteen cities that had already rejected visitors from the other powers before Kun decided to start a riot. He couldn't help thinking that it was merely the beginning. Kun, whatever he'd been thinking, had struck a blow at the underlying fabric of Vesy society. They'd reacted by turning away from the outsiders.

Save for the Indians, he thought. *And the Indians have an unfair advantage.*

"There's a second problem," Joelle added. "Ivan specifically requested a diplomatic visit - and named Lieutenant Schneider as the representative he wanted to see."

John looked down at the deck, puzzled. "They must understand he can't give them anything, surely?"

"I think so," Joelle agreed. "They certainly didn't ask for him or anyone else, once I arrived. And underhanded diplomatic manoeuvres aren't really their *thing*."

"As far as we can tell," John said. "I rather doubt any of them have had to deal with visitors from beyond the stars before."

"Maybe their gods are visitors from the stars," Joelle said. "Wasn't there an entire group on Earth that believed aliens were the source of our myths?"

John shrugged. If that were true, he would have expected a great deal more damage to Vesy society...but then, if it had taken place thousands of years ago, there might be nothing left but rumours and tales that had grown in the telling. He vaguely recalled a Hindu epic that might have been talking about a battle fought with modern weapons, if one squinted at it the right way. God knew there were no shortage of books dating back two centuries that had predicted the development of interstellar warfare... and thousands more that were laughably wrong.

"Maybe so," he said, finally. "How do you intend to proceed?"

Joelle took a sip of her tea. "We do have the basics of a unified command structure on the surface now, excepting the Indians," she said. "If nothing happens for a week, we might as well start extending our presence again. Give City Seven a wide berth and do our best to discourage religious lunatics from getting down to the surface. Tie them up in bureaucratic paperwork, perhaps."

"Might work," John said. "But it may take longer for any consequences to manifest."

Joelle gave him a sharp look. "Why do you say that?"

"Back during the War of 1812, there was a battle fought after peace was signed, because neither side could get word to their respective commanders before the attack went ahead," John said. "There was a working agreement, I believe, that anything along the same lines that took place after the peace wouldn't be regarded as a deliberate breach, as long as both sides returned to the *status quo* once word finally reached them. It hasn't actually happened in space, but it easily *could*, given the nature of the tramlines.

"The Vesy don't *have* instant communications," he added. "It could take weeks or months for word to spread over the local community; *years*, perhaps, for the entire planet to hear of it and by then the news will probably be badly distorted. Just because nothing has materialised immediately doesn't mean that it *won't*."

Joelle frowned. "Do you think it *will*?"

"I was never a religious man," John said. "Not really...but there are plenty of people on Earth who take religion seriously, even though we know enough about how the universe developed to see our existence as random chance. It had to happen somewhere, so why not Earth? And Tadpole Prime? And Vesy? Hell, Ambassador, the discovery of two other worlds that gave birth to intelligent races suggest that there *is* something truly random about the process. But a religious person will not see it that way.

"Kun struck at the heart of their religions - and, by now, the story will be growing more and more distorted as it spreads from city to city."

"Chinese whispers," Joelle said.

"Precisely," John agreed. He'd had the problem outlined to him while he'd been in the Academy; a message, repeated through dozens of mouths, might become something quite different by the time it reached its final destination. "God alone knows what they're thinking right now."

"Percy Schneider might be about to find out," Joelle said.

John nodded. He couldn't help thinking that that was a worrying sign. The aliens hadn't really shown any tendency towards double-dealing, as far as he'd been able to tell; they'd told the humans, up front, what they wanted and backed away when it was not forthcoming. There certainly hadn't been any attempt to stall the British while they held talks with other human powers. He had a feeling, indeed, that the Vesy would honour their side of the agreement as long as the humans honoured theirs. It was quite inhuman of them.

But if they had deliberately asked for someone they *knew* couldn't give them anything they might want...?

He sighed, bitterly. Kun was currently in the brig, complaining loudly about his injury, his imprisonment and the slop that passed for brig rations. He'd be sent home on the next warship to leave orbit, where he would be charged with...*something*. The legal team had already admitted that it would be hard to charge Kun with anything, given just how many precedents had already been set. Even *endangering lives* would be a hard charge to make stick in a suspicious court.

"Then we wait and see what he finds," John said. Could the aliens want to talk to a military leader? It wasn't clear how much they understood of human rank structures, but they had to know that Percy Schneider was greatly outranked by Colonel Boone or John himself. Or were they hoping to talk to someone they knew? "And then consider our response."

Joelle sighed. "No word from Earth yet, but I saw the stories going back," she said. "There will be riots on the street once they get onto the datanet."

"Look on the bright side," John said. "Maybe they'll send us reinforcements."

"I thought that wasn't likely," Joelle said.

John gritted his teeth. The vast majority of Britain's professional force - as opposed to the conscript force - was currently deployed in Britain itself, helping to deal with the problems caused by the bombardment. Getting 3 Para assigned to Vesy had been a stroke of luck; Boone had told him, during one of their first briefings, that 3 Para had been slated to go to Ireland before *Warspite* had returned to Earth. It was unlikely the Prime Minister would be able to dispatch any other units without risking a revolt among the backbenchers.

"It's not," John said. The French or Americans might have something to spare, but it seemed unlikely. It was even *less* likely that Russian forces would be accepted, if any of them happened to be sent. God alone knew what the Chinese would do. "I don't think they can even send us a few more warships."

He looked into his mug of tea, seeking answers. "Ambassador, I think we should seriously consider withdrawing our personnel and closing Fort Knight," he admitted. "The situation is too dangerous."

Joelle stared at him, shocked. "I have never heard a military officer advocate retreat before."

"We prefer to think of it as a tactical adjustment towards the rear," John said. He smiled humourlessly, then frowned. "If it was just military personnel on the ground, if we were fighting a war, I wouldn't advocate anything of the sort. Here, though, we have countless civilians on the surface, all exposed to alien attack. *And* said aliens have a very good reason to be pissed at us. If we pull out now, tempers will have a chance to cool."

"The Indians would not leave," Joelle reminded him. "Abandoning Fort Knight would surrender the planet to them."

"They would also take the brunt of alien...*displeasure* over Kun's stupidity," John pointed out. But he knew she was right. The British Government wouldn't want to create a situation where the aliens were largely aligned with the Indians, giving them a reasonable claim to the entire system. "Maybe you should convince the Prime Minister to push for a complete quarantine of the surface. Concede transit rights through the system in exchange for leaving the Vesy alone."

"They've already been contaminated, quite badly," Joelle said. "Their culture will never be the same again."

"I know," John said. It would be impossible to recover *everything* that might have been traded to the Vesy, if they'd been inclined to try. "But at least they'd have a chance to get used to the idea of alien life without us being so close to them."

"One would hope so," Joelle said. She shook her head. "The PM would need to horse-trade with just about everyone to get an agreement to ban further imports of weapons, let alone ban any further *contact*. Too many people would protest."

John sighed. If they'd stumbled across the Vesy before the Tadpoles, perhaps things would have been different. The five Great Powers could have come to a solution and imposed it on the rest of the Human Sphere, perhaps merely declaring the entire system off-limits save for researchers and xeno-specialists. There would have been no attempt to make contact, no attempt to uplift them to human levels...it would have been a better world. But history had had its little joke, ensuring that humanity encountered the Vesy when the Great Powers were in no condition to impose anything.

He frowned as a thought struck him. "Have the Tadpoles said anything?"

"Nothing at all," Joelle said. "We told them about the Vesy, as we were obliged to do under the terms of the peace treaty, but they never expressed any interest in sending researchers of their own. Maybe they just don't find the Vesy particularly interesting."

John shrugged. "It's possible," he agreed. "Or maybe they're just not interested in the past."

Joelle frowned. "This isn't the past," she said. "They made a mistake when they ran into us and ended up fighting a war that could have wiped out both races. Surely they'd be interested in more data on non-Tadpoles."

"You'd think, wouldn't you?" John said. "But who knows what *they're* thinking? They're not human, Ambassador, and they don't *think* like humans."

"They're not stupid either," Joelle countered. "If they were stupid, they wouldn't have pushed us to the brink of defeat."

And that, John knew, was true of the Vesy too.

─────

"So," Penny said, as she sat down facing Doctor Jill Pole. "You spoke about a breakthrough?"

"Indeed," Jill said. She was a short, rather dumpy woman wearing a long white coat and a pair of spectacles she almost certainly didn't need. "As you know, I've been studying a number of alien bodies since our arrival on Vesy."

Penny nodded, impatiently. The three days since the lockdown had been declared had been boring, apart from a second debriefing that was nearly as intense as the first and a chance to record interviews with the other Paras. No one was allowed outside the walls, not even the military; she'd even heard rumours that the entire fort was going to be shut down. By the time Doctor Pole had called her, Penny had been so bored that she'd been willing to go back to City Seven without an armed escort.

"It's really quite fascinating to study how their bodies develop," Jill continued. "In some ways, they're remarkably like us, even though their biology is completely different. But in others, they are…well…"

"Alien?" Penny asked.

"Of course," Jill said. "Do you realise, for example, that they have a *far* superior sense of smell to anything we possess? There's no point in trying to hide in the darkness from them, I think; they'd just be able to sniff you out. This may actually be why they don't seem to have any problems telling us apart, even though they all look alike to us. Each of us *smells* differently to them."

"That isn't exactly new," Penny said, tartly.

"It's important," Jill said, unabashed. "I think one of the reasons they are so brutally direct with one another is because they can't really *lie* to one another. A deliberate lie sets off changes in their scent that are easily detectable, at least to their fellows. They also can't hide their reactions, under certain situations. If a male should happen to find a female attractive, he won't be able to hide that fact - and vice versa."

"Sounds like they have it made," Penny said, who remembered her own adolescence with a kind of cringing horror. It had been hard to tell which boys were interested in her as a person and which boys had seen her as nothing more than an attractively-shaped piece of meat; hell, Percy had even confessed he had the same problem. How did one *tell* if a girl was interested or if she was just being polite? "They can have sex out of season, after all."

"Indeed," Jill said. She looked down at the table. "I think that one scent reinforces the other, although it's hard to be sure. A Vesy scenting the arousal of another Vesy will become aroused too. It doesn't seem to matter which party started it. All that matters is that you put a male and a female together and eventually sparks will fly."

Penny held up a hand. "None of this is particularly new," she said. "And I honestly have no interest in the details of alien sexual practices."

Jill frowned. "I'm getting to the point," she said. "When a female enters season, her scent changes and becomes overpowering. A male who isn't too close to her, genetically speaking, will chase her and try to mate with her. Put two or more males in close proximity and they will fight each other for the chance to sire her eggs. I think that's nature's way of ensuring that the father is strong because it's rare for a female not to get pregnant on the first attempt."

She paused. "Unfortunately, this means that females entering their season are confined to prevent them from mating with the wrong males," she added. "This restricts their lives in a manner that wouldn't be out of place in the Middle East."

"I know," Penny said, impatiently. "So what?"

"So *this*," Jill said. She tapped her terminal, then swung it around to face Penny, showing her an image of a chemical formula. "There are quite a few ways to block one's scent in combat, as you may be aware. This… is a modified scrubber. You put it in the alien and, when she enters her season, she won't actually emit the scent that draws males to her. She can live a normal life."

"By our standards," Penny said. "But what about by theirs?"

Jill stared at her. "Do you have any idea just how much time women used to waste, having children and raising them? Back in the bad old days, the woman would be completely dependent on the man to keep her fed and happy while she carried the children to term then raised them. Think of all the potential that was lost in wasted lives."

Penny frowned. She couldn't help thinking of Kun. "But if those lives had been spent…unlocking the mysteries of science," she said slowly, "there wouldn't be any children and the human race would die out."

"We have exowombs now," Jill said. "I wouldn't have to take years off my life to raise children."

"There was an asteroid settlement that practiced communal parenting," Penny said, thoughtfully. It had been quite a fad, back in the early days of expansion into space, to set up asteroids based on all sorts of ideas. "I think the children had all sorts of problems as they grew up."

"There was also an asteroid settlement that insisted that men and women had to be trained to the highest peak of perfection before they could have children," Jill snapped. "And what did *that* do to human development? Nothing. There were even stupider ideas that didn't even last a *year.*"

She tapped the terminal with one finger. "This will change their society," she insisted. "And their females *need* change."

Penny frowned. "But what will it do to them?"

Jill glowered at her. "Change their world?"

"There are implants that prevent women from getting pregnant," Penny said. "You get one inserted as soon as you have your first blood, unless you opt out. Like other birth control methods, they changed our world."

"Women no longer needed to be kept under control," Jill said.

"Yes," Penny agreed. "But what would happen if it suddenly became impossible to remove the implants? There would be no more children, not ever."

She rose. "And this will do a great deal of damage to the Vesy," she added. "You should destroy your notes and hope no one else stumbles over it."

"That won't happen," Jill said, tartly. "*Any* fool could do it."

CHAPTER
TWENTY SEVEN

Percy shifted uncomfortably as the section came to a halt, a kilometre from City One - Ivan's City. It had been a short march, but the body armour Colonel Boone had insisted he wear had made him sweat even more than usual in the muggy air. He'd hoped to wear full combat armour, when he'd heard about the alien request; the diplomats, still hoping for a peaceful solution, had flatly refused. Apparently, the Vesy would find powered armour intimidating.

He cursed under his breath, then unhooked the canteen from his belt and took a long swig of cool water. The restrictions on using armoured vehicles hadn't been lifted either, despite protests from NGOs who believed they were being used to hamper their activities on the planet. Boone had told him that two platoons of Paras and five armed helicopters were ready to back up the Royal Marines, if they were necessary, but Percy couldn't help feeling more than a little isolated, despite the dozens of satellites watching them from high overhead. It was easy to believe they were all alone on Vesy.

"Contact, sir," Peerce said, quietly.

Percy nodded, peering down the road towards the city as a handful of Vesy came into view. Nine of them wore nothing apart from loincloths, but they carried a small arsenal of human-designed weapons on their backs; the tenth wore golden robes edged with purple lining. It took Percy a moment to realise that the aliens knew their armour would be useless against human weapons, no matter how much they wore; they'd chosen to go almost naked instead to make it easier to dodge. He couldn't fault their logic, even though he disliked the idea of fighting nude. A well-constructed uniform could sometimes make the difference between life and death.

"Stay here," he ordered. "Keep your weapons at the ready; cover me if the shit hits the fan."

He took a breath, then marched forward. Ivan - it was clearly him in the lead - had designated the small hamlet as a meeting place, rather than his city. Percy wasn't sure if that was a good sign or not; a more public meeting would probably have given the aliens less manoeuvring room, if they wanted to be diplomatic. But, at the same time, he shouldn't have been called at all. The aliens *knew* he'd been replaced by someone who had actual power to negotiate.

Do they think they can pass a message to me, he asked himself, *or did they ask for me as a test, a test we may have failed?*

"I'm approaching the aliens now," he subvocalised. His superiors - Colonel Boone, Captain Naiser, Ambassador Richardson - were watching and listening through the sensors on his uniform, ready to offer advice and orders when necessary. "They're halting at the edge of the hamlet."

Ivan waved to him, then walked forward, leaving his guards behind. Percy watched him warily - he'd seen just how quickly the aliens moved - and waited for him to draw closer. The alien didn't seem to be armed, as far as he could tell, but *anything* could be hidden under his robes. Percy forced himself to relax as the alien closed, then stopped a bare meter from Percy's position. For beings that didn't seem to have a concept of personal space, at least amongst themselves, it was surprisingly polite.

They must find us sinister, he thought, dully. Humans had the same reaction when they looked at the Vesy, although most humans were already aware of the Tadpoles and hundreds of fictional aliens on their video screens. *We just don't smell right to them.*

"I greet you," he said, carefully. "I have come as you requested."

There was a long pause. Percy wondered, grimly, if he'd been right and the aliens had been testing humanity, a test they'd *definitely* failed. Maybe the Vesy had expected Ambassador Richardson to insist on going in person, rather than sending such a low-ranking representative. But the aliens had *asked* for that representative…

They're alien, he reminded himself. The Vesy might have made that request, secure in the belief it would be turned down. *They do not think like humans.*

"One of your people told ours that the gods do not exist," Ivan said, finally. "It is a concept we find…"

He said a word Percy didn't understand, but he guessed meant *blasphemous* or something along the same lines. The Vesy didn't worship *all* of their gods, yet they definitely *believed* in them. It wasn't something Percy understood, but he did understand - even without Penny's article, which she'd shared with him - why the Vesy had been so offended at the suggestion their gods didn't exist. Humans wouldn't have reacted kindly.

"There is currently a disagreement about how to proceed," Ivan continued. "The" - another word, which might have meant City Seven - "has yet to determine its response to the chaos."

"Tell him that we are prepared to pay compensation," Ambassador Richardson ordered.

Percy hesitated, then did as he was told.

Ivan's beady eyes looked angry. "Can your people bring the dead back to life?"

"No," Percy admitted. He'd known soldiers to survive injuries that would have had them declared legally dead a mere fifty years ago, but there was no way anyone could apply such techniques to the Vesy. The medics simply didn't understand the alien bodies well enough to try any revival techniques. "That is beyond our power."

"It has also caused problems in *my* city," Ivan continued, dismissing the matter as if it were pointless. He might well have been right. "I cannot guarantee that we will remain friendly to your people if you question the gods. We want the" - another untranslatable word - "handed over to us for punishment."

There was a pause. "Remind them that Kun is dead," Ambassador Richardson said. "And that his body has been destroyed."

Percy had his doubts. The head sheds would probably have asked more questions if someone had actually *died* on the mission, particularly the idiot who'd started the riot in the first place. It wasn't impossible that one of the soldiers would have shot him in the back, if everything seemed hopeless...

"Kun is dead," he said, flatly. "His body was destroyed..."

Ivan stared at him for a long moment. "Then we must have those aligned with him," he said, equally flatly. "Their crimes cannot be permitted to go unpunished."

And if it were up to me, you'd have them, Percy thought, as his superiors nattered in the background. *Those fucking idiots put Penny in danger!*

"There were no other members of his religion on the mission," Percy said, relaying Ambassador Richardson's words. It wasn't true, but he *had* heard that they'd been ordered back to orbit and dispatched through the nearest tramline. "All we can do is offer compensation for the deaths."

"Eggs that will never hatch," Ivan said. "They are gathered within the birthing chamber to hatch safely, free of all harm. And now they are dead."

Percy winced. He'd seen enough of the local wildlife to be sure that *some* of them, at least, would try to dig up Vesy eggs and eat them. There was nothing comparable on Earth, but human women carried their babies to term in the womb. Having a dedicated birthing chamber made a great deal of sense, particularly once the Vesy had learned to work stone and build their cities. They'd probably been designing forts against Mother Nature as well as their enemies since the day they'd put two and two together and got four.

"We will compensate the parents," Ambassador Richardson said, desperately.

"We don't know how they will react to that," Captain Naiser said. "Lieutenant...wait."

"It is not easy to remain aligned with you when our gods are called into question," Ivan said. "Nor is it easy to deal with fools who do not seem to understand our problems."

Percy said nothing. He merely waited. Ivan was trying to tell him something and, unfortunately, he thought he knew what it was. The alien's power base was largely focused around his ties to humanity - to Britain, specifically - rather than anything more solid. It wasn't really a surprise. His old city had been smashed by the God-King and the new city hadn't had time to really put down roots. But if his people were turning against the British, Ivan would lose influence and eventually his power. He would be replaced by someone who was less interested in working with Britain.

We could give them gifts, he thought. *But those gifts might not change the situation.*

It was a worrying thought. Right now, there were quite a few technological innovations humanity would give its collective soul to have. Force shields, teleportation, a way to avoid the tyranny of the tramlines... humanity wanted them. But would humanity accept them from advanced aliens should the aliens refuse to tell the human race how they worked... or would humanity convert to an alien religion if the aliens stated it as their price?

The Vesy must feel the same way, he told himself. *But they have the added disadvantage of knowing that they can't put forward a united front. One city-state that takes our weapons will have a decisive advantage over everyone else.*

"We must request no further discussions about religion," Ivan said.

It sounded a good idea, to Percy. The Vesy didn't need to have human religion shoved in their face, let alone be told that human gods were jealous gods. They could learn about human religion later, if they wished; they'd certainly meet humans on more even terms.

"We don't control all of the religious parties," Ambassador Richardson said. "But they could easily declare individuals or groups to be *persona non grata.*"

Percy nodded, then tried to explain the concept to the alien. Ivan didn't seem to understand, at least at first; the idea of missionaries was somewhat alien to him. Percy puzzled over that, then recalled that the aliens believed that certain gods resided in specific locations. They wouldn't *need* missionaries, not really. Those who happened to change cities would change the gods they worshipped too.

"We may not have the chance to tell them to leave," Ivan said. "Will they talk with the leaders first?"

"That will be a headache," Colonel Boone noted.

Percy groaned, inwardly, as his superiors started arguing again. Kun hadn't told *anyone* what he intended to say to the aliens; it was quite possible that missionaries would lie to the alien leaders, just to make sure they had a chance to preach to the alien population. And then there would be more riots and, worse, the aliens would see humans as inherently untrustworthy.

How do you know a human is lying? It would probably become an alien joke in a few years, if it wasn't already. *Their lips move.*

"Yes, they will," Ambassador Richardson said. "Indeed, if the alien leaders wish to have guards in place to arrest any speakers who go too far, that would be acceptable."

Percy relayed the message. There was another long pause.

"That will be suitable," Ivan said. "We must also request more weapons and training. The" - another set of words Percy didn't understand - "are growing more powerful. It isn't good for us."

"The Indian-backed cities, I suspect," Captain Naiser said. "They have been training more and more aliens to use human weapons."

"They also have been manufacturing cartridges on site," Colonel Boone said. "There are limits to how much ammunition we can pass to the aliens."

Percy winced. The Indians had definitely stolen a march on *everyone*. Guns were useless without ammunition and the Indians had a factory, producing thousands of cartridges a day. Colonel Boone wouldn't be able to risk handing his reserve stocks over to Ivan without courting disaster...

"We will provide more weapons and training," Ambassador Richardson said. "However, there are other things we can offer."

None of which will matter a damn if Ivan's people gets overrun by Indian-backed factions, Percy thought.

"We will consider the matter at our next meeting," Ivan said. He bowed. "I thank you for agreeing to our terms."

Alien sarcasm, Percy thought. He'd never seen it before, but he was certain he'd seen it now. *Just like our sarcasm.*

Ivan bowed again, then retreated back to his fellows. Percy watched him go, feeling oddly perplexed. Something was badly wrong, but what?

"Return to Fort Knight," Colonel Boone ordered. "You will be debriefed when you arrive."

"Understood, sir," Percy said, still puzzled. "We're on our way..."

It struck him as the aliens walked back to their city, leaving the humans alone. Ivan had *known* that Percy didn't have the authority to make anything more than local agreements, not when he'd been in sole command of Fort Knight. Indeed, he'd wondered over the demand for his presence, speculating that it was a test of some kind. Instead, the alien had listened to him without even questioning his authority, let alone his ability to make agreements. And that was strikingly out of character for them.

He tongued the implant in his mouth. "Colonel," he said slowly. "We may have a problem."

"Explain," Boone ordered.

"They never questioned my authority to make deals," he said. "Not at all."

"Interesting," Boone said. "They might assume you had the authority when we sent you out..."

"That's not what they do," Ambassador Richardson said. She sounded perturbed. "They were careful to question my credentials when I arrived."

"They don't assume anything," Percy said. "I think they would have checked my authority first, normally."

"I see," the Ambassador said. "Could they have overhead the radio? How good is their hearing?"

"It isn't much better than ours," Boone said. He cleared his throat. "Return to base, Lieutenant. I'll see you when you arrive."

"Yes, sir," Percy said.

———

"That's an odd development," Joelle said, once the link was broken. "What does it mean?"

"They may have adapted to our way of doing things," Grace suggested. "We sent the person they wanted, armed with the authority to make deals."

Joelle shook her head. "There was no suggestion he should check with me, no suggestion he wasn't anything but the one in charge," she said. The more she looked at it, the more it puzzled her. Schneider was right. Ivan had acted strikingly out of character. "They *knew* he didn't have the authority, on the face of it, to make deals."

Mortimer leaned forward. "It's possible their hearing is better than we thought," he said. "Or they may have deduced the presence of subvocal transmitters."

"Or been told," Captain Naiser added, from the communicator. "The Indians might have cheerfully warned them about implants and microscopic trackers."

Joelle frowned. Whatever the Indians were playing at, it would be unwise of them to reveal too many tricks to the aliens. If they hinted that Britain might be deploying nanotech spies into Vesy cities, it would suggest to even a mildly paranoid mind that the Indians could do the same. The more she thought about it, the more she suspected the Indians would have kept their mouths firmly closed. Why give up a potential advantage for nothing?

Unless they are trying to curry favour, she thought. *Or have an interest in proving us unfaithful.*

"They want us to provide them with more weapons and training," Mortimer said. "That leads to an interesting problem - we simply don't have that much on hand, now."

"And we will not be cutting our own supplies," Captain Naiser added. "That would risk leaving the base defenceless."

"We have orbital weapons," Grace said. "Don't we?"

"I'd hate to have to fire on troops attacking Fort Knight," Captain Naiser said. "They'd be too closely intermingled with our people."

"You did that when the God-King attacked the Russian base," Mortimer pointed out.

"And we were damn lucky to avoid a blue-on-blue," Captain Naiser said. "As it happened, we concentrated fire on the rear of the enemy columns. We would have probably hit our own people if we'd fired closer to the walls."

Joelle held up a hand. "I think we need to request more weapons from Earth," she said. "If we're in a bidding war..."

"We also need more ammunition," Mortimer said, firmly. "That may make the difference between success or failure."

The PM will love that, Joelle thought. It was bad enough that she was morbidly certain that she was already getting bad press at home. The media would go wild if they thought Britain was fuelling an arms race. *And we may need to set up factories of our own.*

She pushed the thought aside. "Debrief Lieutenant Schneider thoroughly, then consider assigning him to the alien training squads as an embedded observer," she ordered. "If that is acceptable to you, Colonel."

"I'd prefer to keep him attached to the QRF for the moment, if we're sending our people out again," Boone said. "The training crews have considerably more experience in teaching young people how to use guns."

"Understood," Joelle said.

Captain Naiser coughed. "Do you intend to release the lockdown?"

"I don't think we have a choice," Joelle said. She would have preferred to keep it in place for longer, but pressure was already growing. "The media already wants to get out there and start seeing what's going on, Captain, and the NGOs will not be far behind."

"Shit," Captain Naiser said. "And the missionaries?"

"They'll have the new agreement," Joelle said. "If they refuse to honour it, they can be kicked out - I'll make that clear to them."

"Allowing the aliens to arrest them will not please their governments," Boone noted, coolly.

"Better than dead missionaries," Joelle said. It would probably cause more problems, but at least the missionaries would be alive. "These are not the days when we would go to war to avenge the deaths of a few missionaries, particularly ones who knew the danger."

And, on that note, the meeting ended.

CHAPTER
TWENTY EIGHT

"Perhaps you would like to explain to me," John said, "*precisely* what you were thinking?"

Crewman Ryan Bjorklund and Crewman Francis Turner looked at each other, nervously. It was rare for crewmen to be called in to face the Captain; normally, disciplinary matters on the lower decks were handled by the Senior Chief. But Philip Richards had hauled them up to Officer Country as soon as they'd returned from the surface, without giving them a chance to agree on a story. He now stood behind them, glowering at their backs.

"Don't look at each other," John snapped. "I'm waiting for an explanation."

"Captain," Turner said. "I...we were down on the surface..."

John sighed, inwardly. He'd hoped to avoid shore leave problems - it wasn't as if there was much to do at Fort Knight, beyond walking around the perimeter and trying to chat up civilians - but he'd underestimated the ability of young men to get into trouble. Both Bjorklund and Turner had good records, yet they'd seemingly thrown away all common sense. It wasn't going to look good when they were considered for promotion.

Assuming it doesn't get them straight into a court martial, he thought. *That might be a very real possibility.*

"Let me read to you from the report," he said. "You went outside the walls and chatted to a number of Vesy. Somewhere along the line, you got into a gambling game with them. You won a couple of times, then you lost heavily. The Vesy you were playing with offered to forgive the debt in exchange for a couple of small items you happened to be carrying, correct?"

"Yes, sir," Turner said.

"You handed those items over to them," John continued. "They then offered to pay you for bringing more items out of the base, offering you small gold coins in exchange. You took those coins to the base, where they set off alarms and the Paras grabbed you. The missing items were noted during your search and they asked a number of pointed questions, correct?"

"Yes, sir," Turner said, again.

"So tell me," John ordered. "Just what were you thinking?"

"We allowed ourselves to be suckered, sir," Bjorklund said. "We haven't played a game since leaving Earth..."

"There isn't a day without a semi-legal game underway somewhere on the ship," Richards growled. "You play for sweets or leave-tokens or chores."

"They're not so exciting," Bjorklund confessed. "We gambled with the Vesy because we thought it would be different."

"And they took you for a ride," John said. The Paras had made it clear that the Marines had introduced poker to the Vesy, months ago. "They allowed you to believe you could clean them out, then wiped you out and demanded what you were carrying to pay the debt. What *were* you carrying?"

"A music player and a video player," Turner said. "They wanted the wristcoms as well, but we explained they weren't ours."

"You'd be staring down the barrels of a firing squad now if you'd handed *those* over," Richards said. "They really *don't* need our wristcoms."

John looked from one to the other. "And then they offered to pay you to bring them more," he added. "What did they want?"

"Anything," Turner confessed. "Anything, as long as it wasn't something we were passing to them already. They said they'd pay us in gold."

"I see," John said. "Just out of idle curiosity, how were you planning to explain the gold when you got home?"

Turner swallowed. It was clear he hadn't thought that far ahead.

"We could have traded it on the market," Bjorklund said. "We would probably have made a tidy profit on the deal…"

"And then been arrested, for selling something you shouldn't have had," John snapped. "I suppose one could say you've been very lucky. You might have infringed the rules on trading with the Vesy, but at least you didn't resort to outright theft."

He considered it for a long moment. Legally, he could throw them both in the brig - they could keep Kun company - until *Warspite* returned to Earth. But the Vesy would simply start looking for someone else who could be bribed into selling technology to them…and John had a feeling it wouldn't be long before harmless requests were replaced by demands for something dangerous. It might be better to use the two crewmen to keep the Vesy distracted, while they felt out which Vesy faction might be behind it. Or was it the Indians? Wristcoms would be useless to the Vesy, but the Indians could do some real mischief if they obtained the devices and used them against their owners.

"I will consult with Colonel Boone about your future," he said, finally. "You *may* have a chance to make up for your idiocy. Until then, the Senior Chief will find work for you to do…"

His intercom pinged. "Captain to the bridge," Howard said. "I say again, Captain to the bridge."

"Deal with them," John ordered Richards, who nodded and motioned for the two crewmen to follow him. There was no shortage of unpleasant jobs on a starship; they'd be kept busy and out of the way long enough to give John a chance to handle the situation. "I'll talk to you later."

He rose, then hurried through the hatch and onto the bridge. A new cloud of yellow icons had appeared on the display, heading away from the tramline and straight towards one of the few asteroid clusters in the system. Behind them, a second batch of ships was heading for Vesy.

"Captain," Howard said, rising from the command chair. "Group One came out of the tramline and headed directly for Asteroid Cluster B."

John sucked in his breath as he took his chair. It had been agreed, at least among the Great Powers, to leave the system's asteroids strictly alone. Vesy had been lucky in so many ways, but the system had relatively few rocky asteroids, barely enough to sustain a space-based industry. They belonged to the Vesy, the diplomats had ruled; now, *someone* was actively defying their judgement.

"Bring up our drives," John ordered. "Do we have an authenticated IFF yet?"

"Negative, sir," Gillian said. "They didn't transmit anything to either us or System Command."

"I see," John said. They weren't British, then; *Indian*? It was a possibility. "Helm, take us out of orbit on an intercept course."

"Aye, sir," Armstrong said.

John glanced at the tactical display, hastily calculating trajectories in his head as *Warspite* headed out of orbit. The newcomers, whoever they were, would definitely reach the asteroids first, unless he decided to push the drives to full power. But he had orders to try to conceal *Warspite's* top speed as long as possible…shaking his head, he silently calculated they'd reach the asteroid an hour after the newcomers. It would have to do.

He recorded a quick message to the Ambassador, then checked the other ships. One of them was British, thankfully; the others were mainly Indian or Italian. The Italians were relative newcomers to space - they'd been hit badly during the Age of Unrest - and he wasn't sure what they were doing on Vesy, but they were unlikely to pose a problem. Maybe their ships had been chartered by other powers. The Indians, on the other hand…

They keep bringing in more and more gear, he thought. Monitoring the Indians was absorbing more and more of his staff's resources; they just kept expanding, with little concern for Vesy society. John had the uneasy feeling that Britain would eventually drop out of the race, rather than try to keep pace. *But what do they want?*

"Captain," Gillian said. "The Ambassador sends an acknowledgement, but nothing else."

John nodded, unsurprised. There was nothing the Ambassador could say or do now, not when so much remained unknown. All she could do was wait and see what happened when *Warspite* reached the asteroids. Pushing the thought aside, he pulled up the latest readiness reports and skimmed through them. The crew really needed shore leave somewhere more congenial than Vesy.

Maybe head to Cromwell, he thought. Cromwell had almost no facilities for shore leave, but there was no shortage of lakes to turn into swim-
ming pools and mountains to climb; hell, merely being able to leave the
ship would be a good thing. *We'd be only a week or so from Vesy if all hell
broke loose...*

"Captain," Gillian said, two hours later. "I'm picking up a commercial
transponder signal from the newcomers. They're Turks."

John blinked. Turkish ships?

"Send back a standard challenge," he ordered. They were still too far
from the asteroids for a proper conversation, but at least they'd be able to
exchange messages. "Ask them to state their business here."

There was a long pause. Finally, a dark-skinned face appeared in the
display.

"Captain Naiser," he said, in accented English. "I am Director Nedim
Demir, Director of the Vesy System Mining Facility. I have claimed these
asteroids in the name of the Turkish Government."

The image froze, waiting for a second message. John cursed under his
breath, then keyed his console. The message would have to be recorded,
then transmitted.

"This is Captain Naiser of HMS *Warspite*," John said. "Your mining
facility is illegal, Director. It was decided by the World Court that the
asteroids and planets within this system belong to the native sentient race.
I must ask you to withdraw your ships."

He tapped a switch, sending the message. There was another pause
before the frozen image came back to life.

"Captain Naiser," the Turk said. "I must inform you that my government was not consulted about the decision, thus it is our considered
opinion that it does not apply to us. Furthermore, the decision stands
in conflict with other decisions regarding the Terra Nova System, all of
which ruled that a disunited planet could not exercise control over a star
system. The natives did not stake their claims in any meaningful manner,
ergo they have no claims."

John gritted his teeth as the image froze again. The hell of it was that
the Turks had a point -and probably thousands of allies, if the whole matter went to court. God alone knew how many corporations had stakes in

Terra Nova, stakes that would be at risk if the local government took control of the system. They'd back the Turks to the hilt, once the implications struck them. They wouldn't give a damn about the Vesy.

We cannot bar them from claiming the asteroids in a system that belongs to a native race, he thought bitterly, *because that would set a dangerous precedent elsewhere.*

He keyed his console. "Director, such matters should be discussed by the World Court," he said, flatly. He doubted it would get him anywhere. The World Court was no longer the power it had been, now that the Great Powers had been badly weakened. "I would *ask* you to stop your operation until the question of ownership has been decided."

There was another pause. "Legally, the asteroids belong to the person who first stakes a claim," the Turk said, once John's message reached him and he sent his reply. "That has been the *status quo* since the return to the moon. There is no unified government in this system, so there is no authority that can deny us the chance to exercise our rights. I cannot shut down my facility without instructions from my government to do so."

John glanced at his tactical officer. "Commander Rosenberg," he said. "Do you have a tactical analysis?"

"Yes, sir," Tara said. She keyed her console as she spoke. "There are twelve ships in all, five long-range miners, four standard freighters presumably carrying the mining crews and three destroyers, all pre-war ex-American Navy."

"Bugger," John muttered.

He thought desperately, trying to think of a way that didn't involve conceding the point. Force was still an option, but three destroyers - presumably heavily modified to take account of the lessons from the war - would be tough customers. It would probably end badly, even if he won. The Turks would be furious and would almost certainly try to find a way to strike back. Worse, if they had allies, it could lead to general war. Given how much was at stake, it was unlikely the Great Powers would unite against the Turks.

Because of money, he thought, bitterly.

He keyed his console. "Director, I concede you cannot be removed from the asteroids, for the moment," he said. A thought struck him and he smiled. "However, I should point out that your mining complex is uneconomical in the extreme. It is highly unlikely you will make anything from it, save more debts."

But that isn't what they want, he realised. He wasn't wrong - the Turks weren't likely to find customers for whatever they mined from the asteroid cluster - but that wasn't the point. The point was to establish a claim over part of the system. *They want to ensure that Vesy can never rule its own system.*

"Furthermore, the World Court may rule against Turkey, given the… special circumstances in this system," he added, cursing the bureaucrats. Would it really have been so hard to claim the system in the name of His Majesty's Government? Probably. "There may well be other complications caused by your stance."

He sent the message, then waited. "Such issues are not my concern," Director Demir replied, finally. "My orders are merely to establish this complex and defend it against all comers."

John didn't bother to reply. "Tactical, leave a passive sensor platform near the cluster to monitor their activities," he ordered. *Warspite* couldn't remain near the Turks, not without leaving the British forces near the planet dangerously weak. "Helm, reverse course and take us back to Vesy."

"Aye, sir," Armstrong said.

Howard shot John a concerned look. John had no difficulty understanding it. The Royal Navy never backed down, even when faced with overwhelmingly superior force. It was a tradition that had been shaped when Great Harry - Henry VIII - had created the Royal Navy and upheld against Napoleon, Hitler and the Tadpoles. And yet, arguably, John *had* just backed down against - technically - *inferior* force. It wouldn't look good on his service record.

And what, he asked himself mockingly, *was I supposed to do? Start a war?*

"Captain," Tara said. "An Indian starship has just broken orbit. She's heading for Asteroid Cluster A."

It took John a moment to realise what had happened. The Indians had either known what the Turks had in mind or they'd guessed it…which wouldn't be difficult, he reluctantly conceded. Why *else* would the Turks send a small fleet to an asteroid cluster unless they wished to set up a mining colony? And now the Indians intended to do the same, taking advantage of the old loophole in the law. All they really had to do to stake a claim was set up a transmitter on the surface and insist it was, as laid down by the law, an operating station. It wouldn't last longer than a year, but it would be long enough for them to get a proper facility set up…if they wanted one.

They might just see it as a bargaining chip, he thought. *What else might they do?*

He cursed under his breath as the implications struck him. If the World Court ruled against the Turks - and the Indians - their facilities would have to be removed, by force if necessary. But if the World Court upheld the precedent of Terra Nova and agreed the asteroid mining complex could stay, the two smaller powers would have a solid lock on the system's resources. The only thing he could do in response was to stake a claim to Asteroid Cluster C, which would undermine any attempt to throw the other miners out of the system. How could Britain bring charges against Turkey and India when she was unquestionably guilty of the same crime herself?

And the Vesy will be screwed out of the resources of their system, he considered. *But no one gives a damn about them on Earth. The tramlines are far more important.*

"Damned if I do," he muttered. "And damned if I don't."

Howard turned his head. "Sir?"

"Never mind," John said. He tapped his console. "Record to *Daring*, Priority-One," he said. "You are ordered to leave your station and proceed at once to Asteroid Cluster C, where you will establish small beacons as proof of British claims. Do not allow any other powers to impede your mission, if it can be avoided. I say again, do not allow any other powers to impede your mission, if it can be avoided."

He sealed the message, then looked at Gillian. "Encrypt the message, then transmit it directly to *Daring*," he ordered.

"Aye, sir," Gillian said.

John cursed under his breath. It was possible, quite possible, that he'd just fucked his own career. If the World Court ruled against mining facilities, someone would have to be thrown under the bus…and who better than the Captain who'd authorised a British ship to stake a claim to an asteroid cluster? But if it didn't…?

He looked down at his hands, then rose to his feet. "I'll be in my office," he said. He'd need to inform Ambassador Richardson, just so she knew a ton of shit was about to land on their heads. She would have good reason to blame everything on him. Indeed, it might be better for the country if he fell on his sword. "Mr. XO, you have the bridge."

"Aye, sir," Howard said.

"Inform me when we're within secure laser communications range of Fort Knight," he added. "I will need a secure link to the surface."

He nodded to his XO, then strode through the hatch, feeling the full weight of command settling around his shoulders.

CHAPTER
TWENTY NINE

"John," the First Space Lord's recorded image said. "At the risk of sounding rather melodramatic, and it is a risk, by the time you get this message the situation may have changed."

You can say that again, John thought, checking the data-stamp. The message was nearly two weeks out of date. *It* has *changed*.

"I probably don't need to tell you that the reports from Vesy are causing grave concern on Earth," the First Space Lord continued. "The media has turned a minor skirmish, caused by an idiot, into a deliberate mass slaughter of alien children. Questions have been asked in Parliament and, while the PM has been holding his own, it has come at the cost of losing a couple of backbenchers to the opposition. There have also been several major protests against any further involvement with the Vesy, either because we're contaminating their society or because it's a waste of resources; hell, some of them have framed the Vesy as barbarians who are unworthy of our assistance."

"Instead of considering them as *people* who come in all shapes and sizes," Joelle muttered.

"The PM has been attempting to put together a consensus in the World Court to formalise a complete ban on giving more weapons to the aliens," the First Space Lord said. "I believe the Americans and French are likely to sign on, after some horse-trading, but both the Chinese and Russians are non-committal. The Indians, in addition, have been loudly pushing the claim that the World Court doesn't speak for them - and they're backed by several other minor powers. It may take considerable horse-trading or a creditable threat of force to convince them *not* to meddle further on Vesy."

"He didn't know about the plan to start mining the local asteroids," John said. "The Turks must have kept it to themselves."

"MI6 believes there's a considerable amount of coordination going on between the minor powers," the First Space Lord added. "You are aware, of course, that they resent their position as minor powers; indeed, India, Brazil and Turkey have *never* truly accepted the World Court, let alone permanent subordination. They may see this crisis as an opportunity to even the playing field a little. I don't think they will push matters much further, but that could be just my optimism talking."

He smiled, rather thinly. "Unfortunately, both the media and our other commitments have made it impossible to send you any reinforcements. The media, in particular, have been urging a military pull-out from Vesy, leaving the aliens to the civilians. I don't think that will get any of us very far, but the media has never been known for their good grip on reality. There is very little point in trying to dissuade them when they get the bit between their teeth. The PM would prefer to ignore them, but our other commitments are a more serious problem. I don't think we can spare more than a handful of destroyers to support you and none are immediately available."

John cursed under his breath. He would have welcomed a small squadron or a fleet carrier, even if its commanding officer displaced him from overall command. As it was, three ships simply weren't enough to patrol the entire system, even with the assistance of the other Great Powers. And *they* would be staking their own claims to the asteroids, too. The Vesy were likely to look up one day and discover their system had been stolen before they truly grasped what flying through interplanetary space *meant*.

"I've attached a number of sealed orders to this message," the First Space Lord concluded, grimly. "If the shit hits the fan, you are authorised to open the orders that correspond to the situation and carry them out. You may also wish to start planning to evacuate our people on the ground, or move them to a safer location. Even orbit would probably be safer than anywhere on Vesy."

He paused. "Good luck, John," he added. "I'm sorry I don't have better news for you."

The image froze. John stared at it for a long bitter moment, then shook his head slowly.

"He didn't know what the Turks had in mind," Joelle said. "Did he?"

"I doubt it," John said. "He sent the message on a ship, rather than trusting it to the relay network, but even so the Turks would have left at least a week before it was recorded and dispatched. I doubt the Turks bothered to file a flight plan when they departed."

"Probably not," Joelle agreed. She shook her head. "I was speaking to the other ambassadors, John. They're *all* laying claim to asteroids now. There won't be any way to dislodge them short of war."

"Which would be unwinnable," John said. He doubted the British Parliament would tolerate a war for Vesy, particularly with public opinion torn in half. If the Vesy were considered barbarians, who in their right mind would want to send British boys and girls to fight and die in their defence? "And hypocritical, as we staked claims for ourselves."

"Perhaps a mistake," Joelle said. She didn't look angry, merely understanding. "But an action that will be used against us."

"Yes," John said. "But was there any other choice?"

The Ambassador shook her head. "What orders were you sent?"

John glanced at the header. "They're to be opened in case of a major conflict with the Vesy or a clash with another power," he said. "I can't open them now."

Joelle met his eyes. "But you can guess?"

"In the case of the former," John said, "I imagine it will be orders to evacuate everyone from the surface, as the First Space Lord said, and leave the planet alone. In the case of the latter...maybe fire off a few shots, for the honour of the flag, and then retreat, leaving the system occupied. No one really wants a war for Vesy."

"So it would seem," Joelle said. She sighed, bitterly. "The Vesy themselves would be forgotten as we started digging out old grudges and using them for propaganda."

John suspected she was right. Who had given a damn about some archduke who'd been shot in Serbia after hundreds of thousands of British, French and German soldiers had died on the western front? There had been uneasy rumblings that humanity's golden age of space exploration and settlement was drawing to a close, even before the Tadpoles showed up. It had been quite possible, in hindsight, that several human nations would go to war, eventually sucking in the other powers.

Because the Great Powers could only keep power by working together, he thought, remembering what he'd learned at school. *But their interests weren't always identical - hell, China and America nearly went to war twice. What would have happened if they'd destroyed one another?*

"It doesn't matter, right now," he said.

He looked up at the map showing the location of outposts on the planet's surface. Fort Knight was still the largest, but the Indians had a number of bases and the Americans and French had one each. And then there were the smaller outposts, staffed with researchers and NGO specialists that were dotting the land like measles. He knew that Fort Knight could be held, indefinitely, against anything the Vesy could bring to bear against the defences, but the smaller outposts were horrifyingly vulnerable. If all hell broke loose, a great many people were going to die.

"I need to talk to Colonel Boone," he added. "Can you speak to the other ambassadors?"

"I can try," Joelle said. "What do you want me to say?"

"That there won't be any reinforcements from Britain," John said. "And that it might be a good idea to pull their people into defensible positions before it's too late."

"I can try," Joelle said. "We need to try to come to *some* agreement about the asteroids, before it's too late."

"I think it's already too late," John said. "They're not going to give up their claims without a healthy dollop of compensation. And what can the Vesy offer in exchange?"

He shook his head. By human standards, Vesy was almost pathetically poor. There was nothing they had that humans *needed* and very little that humans *wanted*. They had no raw materials that couldn't be extracted from asteroids, no produce that couldn't be easily duplicated with human technology; they couldn't even sell themselves into slavery. John had heard stories about people being bought as slaves from parts of the Third World, but he couldn't see that happening to the Vesy. They were neither pretty nor unnoticeable.

"Maybe we should give up and just start a tech program," Joelle said. "Train Vesy to serve as asteroid miners..."

"And then what?" John asked. "What are they going to do with their wares?"

He groaned. It was rarely economical to ship raw materials from one system to another, not when it was a very rare system that didn't have a few hundred thousand asteroids floating around. By the time the raw material reached an industrialised system, somewhere deep within the Human Sphere, its price would have skyrocketed. It was very unlikely they would ever find a buyer.

The Turks might intend to merely stake a claim, then sell it, he thought. *Or they might have something else in mind. But what?*

Joelle frowned. "I take your point," she said. "Maybe we could invest in infrastructure here?"

"I doubt that would go down well with Parliament," John pointed out. "There isn't enough infrastructure at home, they will say; why is the government wasting time and money building factories for the Vesy? And then they will start wondering if the government plans to outsource industries to Vesy..."

"Shit," Joelle said.

John nodded. *Outsourcing* was practically a swear word, thanks to the Age of Unrest. It had played a major role in the economic crisis that had kicked the unrest into high gear and eventually sparked off a major conflict. Parliament would rise in a body and evict the Prime Minister from office if he proposed establishing major industries on Vesy. And anything less wouldn't be able to make use of asteroid materials.

Unless we try to tell them that we're saving the planet, he thought. But that wouldn't go down very well either. God knew people trying to save the Earth from humanity had caused all sorts of problems. *Or that we're trying to help them avoid our mistakes.*

"Talk to the Ambassadors," he said. He couldn't recall ever feeling so helpless, even when he'd laid eyes on the remains of HMS *Canopus*. "See what you can do."

Joelle looked doubtful. "I can try..."

———

Penny had seen Fort Knight from the air once or twice and she had to admit it had a certain charm, like the forts in the movies Percy had used to devour as a child. Indeed, she had wondered if Percy had allowed himself to be influenced by those movies when he'd designed the fort. But the Indian base was a brooding mass of solid metal, surrounded by high walls and bristling with weapons designed to repel attack from both the land and air. It squatted in the midst of what had once been farmland, the ground cleared to make it impossible to allow anyone to sneak up on it.

She sucked in her breath as the helicopter dropped down neatly towards the landing pad, a pair of heavy antiaircraft guns tracking the craft as it made its descent. Penny couldn't help feeling nervous, as if the guns could fire on their own accord and blow the helicopter out of the air. Maybe they would. She'd heard stories of journalists who'd died in war zones under suspicious circumstances, although she had a feeling they were exaggerated. Quite a few journalists, in pursuit of the one big story that would make their careers, had gone beyond the wire and been kidnapped or killed by insurgents or terrorists.

The helicopter touched down with nary a bump. "You're wanted out there," the pilot said, coldly. He'd barely said a word to her during the flight, even though she'd tried to make conversation with him. "I'll be here when you come back."

"Thank you," Penny said. Maybe he thought that all reporters were potential enemies...or maybe he thought she was dating Hamish and didn't want to steal a Para's girl. She rose, checked her recorder and handbag, then opened the hatch and peered out. "I'll be back soon."

"Miss Schneider," a female voice said, as she clambered out of the helicopter. A young dark-skinned woman, no older than Penny herself, was standing just past the safe line, smiling at her. "I'm Panda, Special Assistant to Ambassador Begum. If you'll come with me...?"

"Of course," Penny said. She couldn't help feeling a little dowdy as she eyed the Indian girl. Panda wore a long sari that both concealed her body and hinted at her curves. In many ways, it was more seductive than if she'd been naked. "I was wondering why I was invited here?"

"I believe Ambassador Begum likes your work," Panda said, as she turned and led the way towards the nearest building. "She chose you specifically."

Penny frowned, but - suspecting she wouldn't get any straighter answers - concentrated on looking around the Indian base. It wasn't just more military than Fort Knight - everyone she saw seemed to be wearing uniforms, save for Panda herself - it was completely free of any alien presence. There were no Vesy within the base, as far as she could see; no sign that it was anything, but a human compound. She could easily believe that the Vesy didn't exist, if she hadn't already met them. The base was a piece of India far from home.

The interior of the base was depressingly akin to British prefabricated buildings, without even a half-hearted attempt to make it liveable. Penny had lived in an apartment block put together from prefabricated components and it had been dull, even though some of the younger children had hung their drawings and paintings from the walls. Here, the Indians seemed not to care about decorating their base. Perhaps they intended to move on at some later date.

"We have a recorder for you, if you didn't bring one," Panda said, as they stepped into a large hall. "Did you?"

"I did," Penny said. "It should be fine, I think."

Just in case, she checked her recorder, perched on her shoulder. It was working fine, save for a message stating it couldn't establish a direct link with the orbital network or any nearby data processing nodes. Penny wasn't too surprised, even though it was worrying. Military bases tended to frown on anyone sending signals from within their defences and employed jammers to make it impossible. But the Indians, if she recorded something they didn't like, could easily confiscate and destroy her recorder before letting her go.

If they ever do, she thought. Kidnapping a reporter would cause problems for India, she was sure, but how many? Would the British Government really go to bat for a reporter? *I might stay in their jails for the rest of my life.*

She pushed the thought aside as a handful of Indians, led by Ambassador Rani Begum, stepped into the hall. Up close, it was clear that the Ambassador and Panda looked remarkably alike; indeed, they were close enough to be sisters. Or was the Ambassador Panda's mother? A wealthy woman in Britain could remain young, at least in appearance, right up until the day she died. There was no reason the Indians couldn't do the same.

"Take a seat," Panda urged. A couple of aliens followed the Indians, both wearing the gold and purple robes that designated them as religious and political leaders. "We're about to begin."

Penny shot her a sharp look, then sat as the diplomats mounted the stage. Someone moved behind her; she looked round to see a couple of Indian reporters, all wearing recorders of their own. She knew one of them by reputation - he was known for serving as a government shill - while the other was a stranger to her. There didn't seem to be any other reporters invited at all, save for Penny herself. It was an oddly worrying thought.

Rani stepped up to the podium and smiled, her gaze resting on Penny for a long chilling moment. No matter how young she looked, and she *could* easily have passed for Panda's sister, Penny was sure the Ambassador was a formidable woman. But then, as an ambassador and government representative, she would have to be.

"India has a long history with colonialism," Rani said. "Our country was invaded, our cultures were challenged and our resources were stripped from us. These experiences have given us a burning desire to prevent their repetition. India will not be turned into a colony again - and nor will anyone else. Today, we have signed an agreement with a cluster of Vesy city-states that have effectively become the most powerful state on the planet.

"This agreement is a mutual defence treaty against intrusions from those who would see the Vesy ripped apart, their unique culture turned into a pale copy of humanity. Should there be any direct involvement in Vesy affairs, by anyone, India is committed to use all necessary force to defend the Vesy against outsiders."

Penny stared at her. They'd done *what*?

She thought, rapidly. There was no way the Vesy could assist the Indians, if they came under attack from other human powers. That meant the Indians had committed themselves to defending the Vesy in exchange for...*nothing*. There was no point in a mutual defence treaty if one side couldn't uphold its obligations...

Or was there something else at stake?

"It is our duty, as a civilised nation, to take a stand against colonialism in all its forms," Rani continued. "We will not sit by and allow the Vesy to be exploited..."

CHAPTER
THIRTY

Joelle forced herself to remain calm as she stepped into the empty conference room and poured herself a mug of tea. Alcohol would have been better, considering the shock she'd had, but she didn't dare get drunk. At best, it would end her career; at worst, it would trigger off a major war. She sat down as soon as she could and focused her mind. The Indian gambit had turned everything upside down, once again. It was quite likely that the consensus she'd put together was about to come apart at the seams.

The American and French ambassadors entered, followed by a handful of minor representatives. Neither Italy nor Turkey had bothered to send formal ambassadors, but their representatives had insisted on being included in the meeting and Joelle hadn't been able to refuse. Everyone needed to attend. Hell, she hadn't been sure the *Indians* would be attending until Ambassador Begum's helicopter had landed at Fort Knight. She pasted a calm expression on her face as Rani Begum entered the room, then took her seat at the rear of the table. Joelle couldn't help noticing that the Turkish representative sat down next to her, while the Chinese ambassador sat in the middle.

He's doing a balancing act, she thought, grimly. What could India offer the Chinese in exchange for neutrality? They'd clearly found *something*. And *so the Big Five start to fray*.

"I believe we can dispense with the formalities," she said, once the door was closed. "Can I ask, Ambassador Begum, just what you were thinking?"

Rani met her eyes, evenly. "We have signed a mutual defence agreement with the Flowered Clan, as our Vesy allies wish to be called," she said. "We are committed to come to their defence, should they be attacked by a human power, and they are committed to come to *our* defence, should we be attacked by a Vesy power."

Joelle thought rapidly. That actually made a great deal of sense, assuming the Indians didn't want to send more troops to Vesy. They'd have additional forces they could call on, if necessary, while they could… discourage any human power from intervening with weapons the Vesy couldn't hope to match. Given how much firepower the Indians had in the system, they would probably win the first battle…but then, it would probably start a general - and thus unpredictable - war.

They're gambling that we wouldn't risk engaging their ships here and triggering a free-for-all, she thought. *And they might well be right, because that would leave humanity vulnerable to the Tadpoles.*

"Your governments have caused the Vesy considerable problems," Rani continued, with the air of a woman making a speech. "They are quite happy to work with us on even terms, but they resent, quite badly, humans treating them like children. Indeed, they were less than happy to be told that their gods don't exist. The long term implications of a single idiot telling them off for being what they are might well be disastrous.

"We, by contrast, have been treating them as equals from the start. We have understood their needs and wants, we have understood the problems facing them…and we have carefully refrained from doing something that might offend them. Please, tell me; just how happy would your people be if an alien race, armed with god-like power, told you that your religions were completely wrong?"

"That isn't the issue here," Schultz said. "The issue is that it was agreed that no power would sign any political agreements with the Vesy."

"And that was a mistake," Rani said. "You are aware, of course, that the Russians seriously destabilised their society. Their old balance of power is gone. The city-states that secure help from humanity will be the city-states that dominate the foreseeable future, at least on Vesy itself. They are not stupid children, Ambassador. I dare say they understand the realities of the universe far better than the American electorate."

Ouch, Joelle thought. But it wasn't true, not since the Age of Unrest. Western populations had had a rather nasty wake-up call. *We understood the realities of power much better at the end of the 21st century than we did at the start.*

"Furthermore," Rani continued, "India never signed any such agreements. The *Great* Powers assumed that they could decree a thing and it would be so. We did not sign such agreements, therefore we do not consider them binding."

She smiled at him, coldly. "You treat the Vesy as children," she pointed out. "Children, who can have adults run their lives; children, who cannot be trusted to make their own decisions; children, who can have their questions silenced with a simple assertion that their parents say so. We treated them as adults, right from the start, and we have reaped the rewards."

"There is no way your agreements with them are anything, but one-sided," Barouche pointed out. "They will be your slaves when they become wholly dependent on you for ammunition."

"They know it," Rani said. "Don't you understand? They are not a hypocritical species. They do not waste their time coming up with justifications for stealing something by naked force. They understand that we are trading openly, without trying to conceal what we're doing behind a fig leaf of respectability and they appreciate it. You...you keep talking to them like children who cannot be trusted to handle the truth."

And the British public wouldn't trust them to handle the truth, Joelle thought. She couldn't help feeling that Rani had a point. The aliens had made it clear, more than once, that they preferred blunt honesty to diplomacy. *But how do we explain anything else to the folks at home?*

Rani leaned forward. "The Indian Government has recognised the Flowered Clan as the effective government of Vesy," she continued. "They have a united force that no single city-state can match and, thanks to us, the training and equipment to crush resistance. With that in mind, we have signed a second treaty with them, granting us settlement rights on Vesy II and..."

"Out of the question," Schultz snapped. Joelle was equally shocked. "They do *not* hold the entire planet!"

"The British Government would agree," Joelle said, backing him up despite the chill running down her spine. The Indians, it seemed, had covered all the bases. If the Flowered Clan was the sole representative of the planet, their claim to Vesy II would stick; if not, they could set up a base on Vesy II anyway, relying on the Terra Nova precedent to make it stick. "There is no way we could grant total recognition to the Flowered Clan."

She frowned inwardly as the argument raged around the table. Barouche objected - the French wouldn't accept it either - but both the Chinese and Turkish representatives kept their mouths shut. That bothered her more than she cared to admit. The Chinese might be trying to remain neutral, which was understandable, but the Turks had just invested a considerable amount of money in snatching mining rights to a whole *cluster* of asteroids. They had every reason in the world to object, strongly, to anything that created a unified government for Vesy.

"Let me put something forward," she said, tapping the table. An uneasy silence fell. "This is the first system we have discovered that has evolved an intelligent race."

"Tadpole Prime," the Turk sneered.

"The Tadpoles discovered us, not the other way around," Joelle said. "Furthermore, *this* intelligent race is largely incapable of defending itself. The Tadpoles could tell us to go to hell and make it stick, if they liked; the Vesy can do no such thing. There is nothing they can do to stop us invading their world and enslaving them. How many books and movies have we seen where a more advanced race sets up shop on Earth and starts eating humans for lunch?"

She paused. "The only restraint on humanity, here and now, is humanity itself."

"A pretty speech," Rani said. "But it won't impress the *Vesy*."

Joelle ignored her, somehow. "We can agree, I believe, that we can have transit rights through the system without going anywhere near Vesy or its asteroid clusters," she said, softly. "There's no reason we can't set up a cloudscoop for refuelling starships in orbit around the gas giant - and there is absolutely no risk of sucking the gas giant bare. Hell, Saturn alone provides more than enough HE3 to keep Earth's civilisation going for millions of years.

"This system is *theirs*. We shouldn't plunder it, particularly when there's no *need* to plunder it - and for what? What can we find here we can't get at a million other star systems? Let us leave this system's resources in trust for the Vesy, when they finally climb up into space and meet us as equals. They can settle the question of who rules this system without our input."

The Turk scowled. "The precedent of Terra Nova..."

"The precedent of Terra Nova applies to a system that was settled from Earth, not a system that developed an intelligent race of its own," Joelle snapped. "There is nothing, save for their own disunity, that prevents the people of Terra Nova from developing their own space-based industry. They do not need to learn to understand the theories they need to understand the theories they need to understand how the Puller Drive works, let alone the drive fields we use to move ships from tramline to tramline. And, every year, thousands of them leave the planet for somewhere more congenial.

"The Vesy have none of those options. They will leave their planet, one day, and what will they find? They will discover that the resources they need to bootstrap themselves into a spacefaring race, an interstellar power, have been stolen by us!"

She looked from face to face, quietly gauging their opinions. "I understand that the World Court might have handled this situation badly," she added, addressing Rani. It was true enough; the World Court had wasted time trying to sort out who, if anyone, should be charged with breaking the non-interference edict, while the Indians and other minor powers had been plotting how best to take advantage of the situation. "But if you give a damn about colonialism, you should consider that perhaps the best response to the situation is to back off and let the Vesy sort things out for themselves."

Rani opened her mouth, but Joelle spoke over her. "And if you can't bring yourself to abandon your friends on the surface, even if we do the same, then at least consider leaving their asteroids and planets alone. Let them have their resources, their rightful inheritance, when they finally climb into space.

"We represent all the powers involved in the system," she concluded. "*We* can agree, now, that the asteroids are to be left alone..."

"My government will not accept that argument," the Turk drawled. "We claimed the asteroids first, Ambassador. I don't think we will merely abandon them in exchange for...what? What do you have to offer us in exchange for giving up our rightful claim?"

He went on before anyone else could say a word. "You are bringing this up now, I believe, because we did something you never thought to do," he added. "If you want us to give up our rights, you will have to pay for it. Your government can argue the matter with my government."

"It would seem to be too late," Rani said coolly, "to recognise that you *might* have made a mistake. You and the other Big Five put together an agreement without consulting us, then expected us to stick to it. India's position is, and remains, that we are not obligated to honour any agreement we did not sign. We signed no agreements with you, Ambassador, but we *did* sign an agreement with the Flowered Clans. Those agreements will be honoured."

Her eyes swept the room, then fixed on Joelle. "Your nation could have acted faster, if it had truly wanted to allow the Vesy to develop in peace," she pointed out. "You could have claimed the system for yourself and kept a firm quarantine in place. Instead, you looked for advantages, just as we did. Do not blame us, please, for doing the same. I am not impressed by your attempt to move the goalposts, as you would put it, when you happen to be losing the game. We have no intention of abandoning our claims on Vesy in exchange for vague pleasantries about the moral and ethical dilemmas faced by people unwilling to do what it takes to secure their positions of power."

"There is no way we can recognise your...*clients* as the sole rulers of Vesy," Joelle snapped.

"Agreed," Schultz echoed. "They do not even control a tenth of the land surface."

"They will," Rani said.

She rose to her feet, then nodded to the table. "I do not believe we will be having another pointless meeting, Ambassadors," she said. "Those of you who believe in upholding the non-interference edict wasted their chance to keep it firmly in place. But then, thanks to the Russians, the Vesy already knew we existed before our fleets arrived. Their culture was no longer uncontaminated."

Joelle watched her go, followed by the Turks. She cursed under her breath. Rani was correct, in a sense; the political manoeuvrings were designed to remove India, and everyone else, from Vesy. But it would be better for the Vesy, wouldn't it, if they had no further contact with humanity? Their society could be turned upside down.

No, she thought. *It has already been turned upside down.*

"She meant her clients would start invading the other city-states," Schultz said, quietly. "They have the guns, they have the men, they have the training too..."

Joelle nodded. She was no military expert, but certain things were universal. Attack Ivan's City, attack the other places that had contact with off-worlders, then move on to swallow up the rest of the planet. With everything the Indians had already given their allies - guns and radios, mainly - it would be easy for the Flowered Clan to overrun a vast empire. They'd be smarter than the God-King too, she suspected. Given careful diplomacy, they would probably be able to win hearts and minds too; they'd be offering advantages to submitting to their empire, not the slavery and worse the God-King had offered. It was possible they'd become overextended, she considered, but they'd still have too many advantages to lose quickly.

But one thing was certain. A great many Vesy were about to die.

"We need to counter this," she said. She could simply withdraw the mission - she did have that authority - but that would concede Vesy to the Indians. By the time the legal battle ended, the Indians would be more firmly entrenched than ever. "I propose offering an agreement of our own to our allies. Get them to form a...a Vesy-UN."

"The UN ended badly," Schultz pointed out.

"They need a united front," Barouche said. "But how far are we prepared to go?"

Joelle swallowed. The Indians had brought more weapons and tools to Vesy than anyone else, as far as she knew. They'd even set up factories to produce bullets and other basic equipment the Vesy would need...and the Russians, of course, had introduced the Vesy to gunpowder. What *else* would they introduce to the aliens? Armoured vehicles? Light aircraft? Long-range guns?

And even if she wanted to open the floodgates, she was damn sure the PM wouldn't agree to an unlimited arms race. Too many MPs would defect to the Opposition if he did.

The Indians might just have won, she thought, grimly.

"Give them whatever we can," Schultz said. "And pledge to defend them against the Indians, should they take an active hand in the coming war..."

"We can't keep that pledge," Barouche pointed out. "Between us, we have nine warships in the system. Seven if the Chinese don't get involved."

Joelle looked at the Chinese Ambassador, who shrugged. "My government has not issued any orders," he said. "I believe, however, that they do not consider Vesy to be a prime concern."

So they might have done some horse-trading with the Indians already, Joelle thought, coldly. China and India were neighbours, after all; they might have found a reason to cooperate, even though they distrusted each other. *If they don't give a damn about the Vesy, it would be quite easy to abandon them - and, in doing so, shatter the unity of the Big Five beyond repair.*

"The Indians have twenty-two warships in the system, plus a number of armed freighters," Barouche continued. "They have at least six thousand troops on the ground, going by my intelligence staff's estimates. I don't think we can keep them from driving us away from Vesy, if they feel like it."

"They couldn't win a war against the combined might of America, Britain, China and France," Schultz snapped. "They'd have to be insane to start one."

"Or crazy like a fox," Barouche said. "Are you so willing to break the Solar Treaty? To shatter the Earth Defence Organisation?"

"They're playing poker for very high stakes," Joelle said. Barouche had a point; the Indians might well be gambling that the Big Five wouldn't want to break the Solar Treaty, no matter what the Indians did. And they might well be right. "They could easily blunder into a war."

She rose. "With your permission, I will seek an interview with Ivan at once," she added. "If you talk to your allies, we can try to put together a united front. And hope that the Indians hold off long enough for the diplomats back home to sort things out."

"Really?" Schultz asked, as he rose too. "I had the impression they wanted *us* to sort things out."

CHAPTER
THIRTY ONE

"This could get interesting," Peerce muttered, as the small convoy approached Ivan's City. "And not in a good way."

Percy nodded. It was the first time they'd been allowed to take the AFVs out of Fort Knight, save for the training exercises they'd conducted with the Paras, and he was grimly aware that the Vesy were watching them through cold beady eyes. They didn't seem scared of the vehicles, merely contemplative; they'd not only seen them being deployed from the shuttles, but also taking the long way around to get to their destination. Going off-road slowed them down considerably.

We should have brought heavier tanks, he thought, grimly. The Bulldogs were, in theory, all-terrain vehicles, but they had their limits. *And perhaps some more firepower as well.*

"We couldn't get them very far into the city, sir," Peerce warned. "I'd hate to have to fight my way through the city, block by block."

"Yeah," Percy agreed. He'd done training simulations for urban warfare and they all agreed that it was nightmarish, with all the advantages of high technology cut down to the bare minimum. In hindsight, Penny and the Paras - including one who seemed to be well on the way to becoming her boyfriend - had been incredibly lucky. "We couldn't clear the whole city easily."

He keyed his radio as they approached the gates. "Stop well away from the walls, then dismount," he ordered. "We'll stick to the script."

The Bulldog lurched to a halt. Percy checked his rifle automatically, then jumped down to the ground, followed by five other Marines. Behind them, the Paras hastily secured the Bulldogs, then opened a hatch, allowing the Ambassador to climb out. She looked hot and sweaty, Percy noted; her shirt was clinging to her skin in all the right places. He looked away hastily, towards the welcoming party emerging from the gates. They couldn't afford any problems, not now.

"We greet you," the lead alien said. "We will take you to our leader."

The Ambassador's lips twitched. "It would be my honour," she said. "These men will accompany me."

Percy nodded to his men, then followed the ambassador through the gates and into the city itself. Ivan's City had always seemed odd, a combination of old structures and newer - human-inspired - buildings, but now it seemed on edge. Hundreds of aliens were watching them, standing by the roadside or staring from windows; he couldn't help feeling more threatened than he'd felt when he'd taken part in the attack on the Russian base. There were no weapons in view, but that wasn't reassuring. Normally, every alien in sight, apart from the slaves, would be armed with a sword. It was out of character for them and it bothered him.

The aliens were eerily silent as the humans approached the central building. Percy had dubbed it the Palace, even though he wasn't sure it was anything of the sort. Ivan wasn't a king or an emperor, at least as far as Percy knew; he was a strange cross between elected religious leader and professional politician. And he'd been a resistance leader, back before encountering the British. But the precise terms simply didn't translate very well.

He glanced at the Ambassador, whose face was pinched and drawn. She looked alarmingly like his mother for a long moment, in expression if not in appearance. Percy shivered, recalling his mother's expressions during the war, back when she'd come into his father's share of the prize money from the alien ship. Maybe he would have thought better of her, he knew, if he'd known she would be lost to him shortly afterwards.

They stepped into the palace, which was mercifully cool. Percy watched grimly as they were led down a long corridor, decorated with alien carvings, and into a giant ballroom-sized compartment. Hell, perhaps it *was* a ballroom. He had no idea if the aliens actually danced, but maybe they did. There was so little humanity truly knew about the Vesy.

Ivan was seated on a giant throne, flanked by a number of other aliens. Percy's eyes narrowed as he realised they came from different cities. He hoped the ambassador saw it, because he couldn't speak to her now. It would be undiplomatic.

"The guards stay here," the alien escort said. "The Speaker approaches alone."

Percy gritted his teeth, very aware that they might have walked straight into a trap, but did as he was told.

———

Joelle had never felt so pressured in her life, even when she'd just started out in the Foreign Office and her mentor had piled her with so much work - and pointless tasks - that she nearly broke under the strain. Sweat trickled down her back, alternatively hot and cold as gusts of air blew through the giant building; her back and buttocks ached after sitting in the cramped vehicle and trying to focus her mind. The alien escort stepped back as she approached Ivan, unsure - for once - just how to talk to him. This too was unprecedented.

They prefer us to be blunt, she told herself. It went against the grain - insulting a human leader to his face tended to lead to diplomatic incidents - but it would have to be borne. *It's the only way to deal with them.*

"The Flowered Clan have secured the open support of the Indians," she said, without preamble. "They have signed a series of treaties with them. One of those treaties grants them recognition as the sole rulers of the system."

Ivan let out a hissing sound. "They do not rule the world," he said. "Their allies know this to be so."

Joelle hesitated. The Vesy would be unimpressed by any assertion that recognising someone as having authority *conferred* authority. All that mattered to them was power and the will to use it to shape reality, not names. If they'd been ruling Britain in 1940, they would promptly have recognised Nazi Germany as the ruler of Europe, even though there were a number of free governments in exile. But it probably wouldn't have stopped them fighting.

Though we did get into trouble ourselves through recognising the wrong government, she thought. *That nearly cost us a war more than once.*

"They have a legal claim to large parts of your star system," she said. "This claim may well be upheld by human courts."

Ivan *looked* at her. "Your system makes no sense," he charged. "Why would human courts be involved?"

"Our weapons are terrifyingly destructive," Joelle said. By his standards, he had a point. The Vesy might be irked at the Turks - and everyone else - snatching asteroids, but they wouldn't waste time whining about the unfairness of it all. It was just what the powerful did when they had power. "We prefer to try to avoid confrontations that might lead to mass slaughter on both sides."

Absently, she wondered if the Indians had told the Vesy about the Tadpoles - or the First Interstellar War. Did the Vesy know that they and humanity weren't the only intelligent race out there? Or that a war between the other two had claimed literally *billions* of lives. More humans had died in the war than there were Vesy on Vesy.

"So they have an agreement with the Flowered Clan," Ivan said, after a moment. It took Joelle a second to realise he'd simply dismissed her words. "This is of no concern to us."

"It will be," Joelle said. "The Indians will use these agreements to assist the Flowered Clan to take over the entire planet. They are already preparing to wage war against you."

"We have already received offers to switch sides," Ivan said. "What do you intend to offer to counterbalance *their* offer?"

Blunt, Joelle thought. *Very blunt.*

"We can offer the same level of protection and support as the Indians are offering the Flowered Clan," Joelle said, simply. "They will be unable to provide direct assistance to the Flowered Clan."

"We are given to understand that they have more" - a word Joelle didn't recognise - "than you," Ivan said. "Can you keep your word?"

Joelle blinked. Did the alien mean *starships*? The Vesy weren't ignorant, by any means; they had telescopes and starships were visible from the surface, but how could they tell the difference between British and Indian ships? Coming to think of it, how could they identify a warship? It wouldn't look *that* different to a freighter if one didn't know what to look for...

Or someone talked to them, she thought. *Or the Indians simply did a little boasting.*

"They would start a general war if they decided to challenge us," she said, pushing the question aside for later contemplation. "It would be" - she searched desperately for an analogy that might make sense to the Vesy - "it would be like attacking a party of troops in unclaimed territory. There would be a general war once the survivors got home and reported in."

She hoped that made sense, although she wasn't sure. The Vesy didn't really seem to have fixed borders, not as humans understood the term. Each city-state had farmland, then grazing land, then land that remained largely unclaimed. Indeed, she had a private suspicion that some of the smaller settlements, positioned between two of the larger city-states, wound up paying taxes to both sides.

"We would also require considerably more support," Ivan said. "The Flowered Clan has received a great many items you never suggested were possible."

Joelle swore, mentally. What the hell were the Indians playing at?

"We will try to match what they have offered," she said, instead. "And there may be other things we can offer to you."

———

Percy couldn't help wondering, after the first hour became the second, just how long the Vesy intended to keep them in the city. The aliens watching them didn't seem restless, as far as he could tell; indeed, they stood so still they could easily pass for soldiers on their passing-out parade. It wasn't so easy for him, despite years of training. The crippling awareness that they were in the midst of a city full of heavily-armed aliens, aliens who could easily turn from friendly to murderous in a split second. By the time the Ambassador was finally released, he would almost have welcomed a fight, if only to break the monotony.

The aliens led them back out of the Palace, past the hordes of watching aliens, and out to the AFVs. Percy was amused to note that the Ambassador looked almost relieved to be back in the vehicle, even though he knew from bitter experience that they were hot, uncomfortable, smelly and impossible to escape if something punched through the armour before it was too late. But there shouldn't be anything on the planet that could do any real damage, he'd been assured...

But there was that damned rocket launcher, he thought, as he scrambled up onto the AFV, Peerce right behind him. Colonel Boone had told him, during his debriefing, to try and capture an intact launcher next time, if only so that they could figure out who to blame for giving it to the aliens in the first place. *What would that do to an AFV?*

He shook his head, then tapped his headset, telling the driver to take them back to Fort Knight. Bulldogs had the latest in light ablative armour; bullets would simply bounce off them, as would primitive antitank weapons. But plasma cannons and modern missiles would rip the Bulldogs open like tin cans, killing everyone inside before they had a chance to escape. Hell, if the vehicles hadn't been so light, they probably would have been removed from service long before the war. He grabbed hold of the railing as the vehicle lurched to life, then forced himself to relax. They'd be back at Fort Knight shortly and grab some downtime before they were expected to go back on duty.

"I don't think negotiations went well, sir," Peerce noted, through the radio. "The Ambassador didn't look pleased."

"Looks that way," Percy said. He kept a sharp eye on the alien countryside as the Bulldog continued to circle the jungle between Ivan's City and Fort Knight. "The Indians have stolen a march on us."

He felt a flicker of sympathy for Ivan. The alien was caught between two human powers, both of whom might abandon him in a split second. He had to worry about just how reliable the British were, particularly after Kun's stupidity. Ivan couldn't support the British openly as long as there were question marks over British interference in his society.

And Kun convinced many of them we couldn't be trusted, he thought, darkly. *God damn the bastard to hell.*

He ducked before his mind had quite registered the gunshot. A bullet pinged off the AFV, fired from the jungle. Percy closed and dogged the hatch, just before a hail of fire swept over the Bulldogs, glancing off the armour and spinning off into the tall grass.

"Contact," he snapped, keying his headset. "I say again, *contact!*"

"At least seven aggressors, hiding in the jungle," Peerce noted. "Do we return fire?"

Percy hesitated. So far, the attackers hadn't shown anything actually capable of hurting the Bulldogs…and he didn't want to make the situation worse by leaving a number of dead aliens behind him. But on the other hand, *not* making a vigorous response could easily cause more problems for Fort Knight. It might well be seen as a sign of weakness.

And they already see us as potential blasphemers, he thought. *It could get a great deal worse.*

"Swing the machine guns, then return fire," he ordered.

The incoming fire slacked off as the machine guns unleashed a long blast into the jungle, slicing through trees and bushes with effortless ease. Percy watched, waiting for the enemy to either run or return to the attack, wondering if they'd realised just how lethal machine guns could be against what the aliens normally used for cover. Trees that would stop arrows with ease would be ripped apart by the machine guns. A handful of shots rang out, then silence.

His headset buzzed. "Lieutenant, two assault helicopters are taking off now," a voice said. "Drones inbound; I say again, drones inbound."

"Hold the helicopters," Percy said. He peered into the jungle, wondering if he should dismount and give chase. Who had attacked them? A scouting party from the Flowered Clan? A remnant of the God-King's forces? Ivan, testing their willingness to defend themselves? Or someone else altogether? "The enemy appear to have broken contact."

Or are lying dead on the ground, his thoughts added, dryly.

"Understood, Lieutenant," Colonel Boone said. "Return to base; I say again, return to base."

"Yes, sir," Percy said. The Bulldog lurched back into motion, altering course to put more distance between the jungle and its armour. "We're on our way."

He linked into the live feed from the drones and swore under his breath. They were designed to look for humans, not Vesy; the lizard-like aliens didn't show up so clearly against the jungle. If there were any Vesy closer than a bunch of farmers at the edge of Ivan's territory, he couldn't see them. He shook his head slowly, then made a mental note to discuss the jungle with Colonel Boone. They'd need to give it a wide berth if they had to fight the Vesy on the ground, without help from the orbiting ships.

Fort Knight slowly came into view, surrounded by hundreds of alien buildings. A handful of humans could be seen, talking to aliens, as the Bulldogs drove past and through the gates, into the fort itself. It looked as though they were trying to buy native artwork, although Percy had a feeling that most of the purchasers were being taken for a ride. On the other hand, it *had* been produced by the Vesy, even if it *wasn't* their version of the *Mona Lisa*.

He clambered out of the Bulldog as soon as the vehicle lurched to a halt, then released the ambassador and handed her over to her aide. The ambassador had maintained her nerve, he noted; indeed, she seemed almost *pleased* to come under fire. Percy puzzled over that for a long moment, then dismissed it as unimportant. Instead, he joined Peerce in inspecting the outer hull of the Bulldogs. The paint had been scratched - it looked as though the aliens had used the Union Jacks as aiming points - but there was no significant damage.

"Good thing we didn't have a Whisper," Peerce commented. "It could have got us into real trouble."

Percy nodded. He'd never seen a Whisper, but he'd heard about them. In theory, their hulls acted rather like chameleon skin, allowing them to remain undetected at close range; in practice, the cells on the hull broke frequently, crippling the vehicle's ability to remain invisible. It was, he'd been told during training, another brilliant idea from some idiot in a lab that had never worked out in the field.

But that's why we don't use walkers either, he thought. *They don't work so well in real life too.*

"But we don't know who attacked us, or why," Percy said. By now, he was sure that any bodies would have been removed...and, in any case, it would be impossible to track down the people who'd sent the attackers. "And we don't know what they wanted."

"To test us, sir," Peerce said. He nodded towards the wall. "Out there, they're watching us; watching and assessing our strength. And if we look weak..."

Percy nodded. "They'll join the Indians," he said. Why would anyone side with the British when they seemed the weaker party in the dispute? "They're too pragmatic to do anything else, aren't they?"

"It looks that way, sir," Peerce said. He shrugged. "Quite admirable, in some ways. But not in others."

CHAPTER
THIRTY TWO

It would have horrified the Vesy, Anjeet was sure, if they had any idea just how capable human intelligence-gathering technology actually *was*. He'd been careful to ensure that none of his people mentioned microscopic bugs to the Vesy - for once, he knew he and the British were in agreement - or anything that might allow the aliens to deduce their existence. If the Vesy didn't even have a concept of *atoms*, how could they guess that humans could build machines little larger than an atom? Or machines that were literally flies on the wall? Or that those machines could remain silent, not transmitting anything, until a drone was close enough to pick up the low-power signal?

Of course, they might pick it up from some of their intelligence work, he thought, coldly. The British had been careless in allowing the aliens to establish so large a presence near Fort Knight. Anjeet knew, all too well, that the aliens had begged, bought, borrowed or stolen quite a few pieces of technology, including datapads loaded with human novels and non-fiction textbooks. And the NGOs had passed quite a bit of information over to the Vesy, often without considering what that information might mean for the human race. Who knew what fragment of data would give the Vesy an unexpected advantage in a bargaining session.

He pushed the thought aside as he studied the latest report from Ivan's City. The British - and their allies - were caught between a rock and a hard place. On one hand, they needed to back their alien allies to the hilt if they wanted to reverse the Indian coup; on the other hand, they simply didn't have the resources Anjeet and his men had brought to the planet. No matter what happened, the Indian-backed alliance was going to have the advantage for the foreseeable future. The Flowered Clans were unlikely to let the opportunity to establish themselves as the sole rulers slip past... and their rivals would know it. They'd be torn between staying loyal to the British and switching sides before it was too late.

It wasn't something the British would understand, not really, but Anjeet had done quite a bit of campaigning as a young man along the North-West Frontier. The tribesmen there respected both strength and the will to use it; they stayed loyal to the government only so long as the government showed its teeth on a regular basis. And it had to be regular, because the insurgents and terrorists who still infested the region that had once been called Afghanistan were savage, quite willing to descend on a tribal village and loot, rape and burn it to the ground. The government not only had to threaten the villagers, it had to protect them as well, or they would switch sides. It wasn't *evil*, although it had taken Anjeet years to understand; it was survival. The villagers cared nothing for global causes, or religion, or anything else. They just wanted to stay alive, raise their children and pass their village on to the next generation.

And the Vesy are very much the same, he reflected, as he reread the report. *If they doubt the British promises, they will not feel inclined to resist when they can have a place in our alliance.*

But that, he knew, wasn't the worst of it.

The message from the Prime Minister was completely innocuous, to anyone who happened to decipher the code and read the text. He had no doubt that the Great Powers - and everyone else who happened to have access to the latest generation of supercomputers - would be trying their hardest to crack the code; everyone did it, even with their allies. Indeed, there was a regular joke passed around the intelligence community that everyone should just send messages in clear, if only to save time. There were times when Anjeet figured they actually had a point. No one reading the message, in plain text or encrypted form, could guess at its true meaning. They didn't know the key.

But Anjeet did. And he knew it meant war.

It was a chilling thought. The plan had been devised years ago, shortly after the First Interstellar War. It was a gamble - it had always been a gamble - to force the Great Powers to accept that the so-called lesser powers were now their equals. The plan had been updated rapidly after Vesy had been discovered, pushing things forward a couple of years. Anjeet had agreed, when he'd been briefed, that the opportunity had been too good to miss. But the rising tension on the planet's surface could easily lead to a general war, rather than a stalemate. And if that happened...

We think we have the politics sewn up, he thought, *but what if we're wrong?*

Anjeet had seen war. He'd served against tribesmen who were the most brutal enemies of civilisation in history, then against the Tadpoles on two different worlds. Not, he had to admit, that there had been *much* fighting; the Tadpoles had largely ignored human settlements, save for ground-based defences and factories that could easily become a threat. But he'd seen the damage they left in their wake, during the Battle of Earth, and knew a second war could be even more devastating. And if the Solar Treaty collapsed...

That's the issue, isn't it? He asked himself. *We think no one would dare violate the Solar Treaty, we think everyone else would jump on whoever did, but we might be wrong.*

He shuddered, despite the warmth of his apartment. The Great Powers might have been soft, once upon a time, but they weren't soft any longer. No puny Third World state was allowed to defy them, let alone do anything that might pose a threat. Indeed, before the First Interstellar War, India and the other lesser powers had known better than to pick a fight. But now, the Great Powers were weakened, divided and focusing on their own recovery. It was just possible they'd accept the Indian demands without a fight...

...But what if they were wrong?

Anjeet looked down at his hands. They were clean, but he knew they were covered with blood - and they would be covered in more, if matters spiralled out of control and straight into war. His unit had pulled hundreds of thousands of dead bodies out of the sea, during the aftermath of the Bombardment; how many more would join them, he asked himself, if the human race fought a civil war? It wasn't as if they were alone, not any longer. What if the Tadpoles took advantage of the situation to restart the war? Or what if the other Great Powers joined the war? India would rapidly find herself outmatched.

And what, he thought he heard the Prime Minister say, *is the alternative?*

They won't grant us equality unless we prove we can take it, Anjeet answered, inwardly. The Great Powers were jealous of their status, jealous of the strength they'd shown, the innermost nerve, to hold together during the Age of Unrest. *We have to prove ourselves their equals...*

He looked at the message, one final time. It would be easy enough to back off, to defuse the crisis...except he knew it was already too late. The Vesy would fight it out on the surface and whoever won would be looking to their human allies for support. And India would get a great deal of the blame, and rightly so. Backing off now would mean exposing his country to the whims of the World Court, to the whims of a politically-driven series of charges that would leave them as exposed and isolated as the Russians. No, backing off was no longer an option. They'd been committed from the moment they'd decided to set up their own relations with the Vesy, rather than working through Fort Knight.

And if it be war, he thought, as he rose, *the country will not find us wanting*.

Bracing himself, he stepped through the hatch and walked down towards the conference room. Only a handful of Vesy had ever been invited into the base - Anjeet had a feeling the British were likely to regret allowing so many aliens to wander through their defences - if only to ensure that those who *did* receive an invitation treasured it all the more. Two armoured guards stood against the wall, a statement that the Indians took their guest seriously; humans might have been offended by their presence, but the Vesy were not human.

And that is something of the point, he thought. *Isn't it?*

He smiled, rather coldly, as the scent receptors confirmed the alien's identity. They might have been almost impossible for humans to tell them apart - it had always amused Anjeet that some Westerners believed the same of both Indians and Chinese - but sensors designed to detect approaching intruders through body odour had no difficulty telling the different aliens apart. Anjeet had never met Ivan before, not face-to-face, but he was quietly impressed with what he'd heard about the alien leader. Did the British realise, he wondered, that they were dealing with someone akin to Romulus, if indeed that legendary figure had lived at all? Moses, perhaps, or Daniel? Who in human history had lost one city, escaped slavery, fought a desperate insurgency in the jungle and finally found allies who had helped them to recapture and rebuild their city?

And all of Ivan's deeds are recorded, he thought, mischievously. The British and the NGOs had done a surprising amount of recording alien stories, including some that would have been unbelievable if they hadn't happened in living memory. *How much from our early history is nothing but legend?*

"I greet you," he said, in careful Russian. He had no idea if Ivan spoke Bengali or not, but he wasn't about to risk confusing the alien with a new language. It was annoying - the aliens all seemed to use the same language, even though it defied logic - yet he had no choice, but to tolerate it. "I bid you welcome to my home."

"I greet you," Ivan replied. The alien's Russian wasn't bad, just oddly accented. "I can speak in English, if you would prefer."

He may have been invited, but he knows he is a supplicant, Anjeet thought, coldly.

"It would be acceptable to speak with either," he said. "I speak both fluently."

Ivan's beady bird-like eyes fixed on his. "You invited me," he stated, flatly. "I assume you have something to say."

"I do," Ivan said. There was no point in beating around the bush. "Your allies have betrayed you."

The alien showed no visible reaction, but his scent changed noticeably. Anjeet wondered, absently, if the aliens had any form of control over their emotional displays, then decided it was probably unlikely. A culture that had built itself around brutal honesty could only have formed if lying directly was impossible. And it allowed anyone with the right technology to practically monitor their emotions without using any form of intrusive probing.

He knows, Anjeet thought.

"They have lied to you, several times," Anjeet continued. "They have no intention of defending you against the Flowered Clan."

He smiled, then leaned forward. "Kun is alive."

The alien rocked backwards, shocked. Anjeet wasn't surprised, not even slightly. If there was one thing humans and Vesy had in common, it was a shared urge to protect their children. Indeed, if the Tadpoles so clearly *hadn't* shared the same urge, he would have said it was a universal impulse. And the battle in City Seven had smashed dozens of eggs, killing children who would never be hatched. The media hadn't been the only ones to be shocked, then turn it into a deliberate mass slaughter.

But it helps to back the right media producers, Anjeet thought, coldly. It had been risky, sending the records home directly, but it had given them a chance to shape the coverage - and it had succeeded, remarkably well. *There isn't a story that couldn't be made to sound more dramatic - and to hell with whoever gets hurt.*

"They lied to you," he said. "Kun was shipped to orbit, then dispatched back to Earth along with the rest of his party. *That's* how little concern they show for your feelings - or for your position."

He watched Ivan closely, keeping one eye on the screen monitoring the alien's scent. Ivan knew - he had to know - that he had staked his position on the British keeping their promises, that he would lose his power and influence if the British proved to be weak reeds. There would be a party in Ivan's City ready to take over and make an agreement with the Flowered Clan, Anjeet was sure; hell, given how the alien politics worked, it was quite likely that Ivan had even *encouraged* it. If Ivan lost his power, the British alliance would be lost with it and the city would join the Flowered Clan.

It was fascinating to see just how swiftly the alien's emotions changed. Ivan didn't know it - no one knew, apart from a handful of researchers - but the Indians had purchased a number of slaves from the Flowered Clan and experimented on them. It wasn't perfect, not yet, but the monitors could tell roughly what the alien was feeling at any given moment. Ivan had already had his doubts - that was clear - and he was seriously considering throwing in the towel.

And what will happen to him, Anjeet wondered, *if he did switch sides?*

It wouldn't have mattered to humans, he figured. Humans could change their minds about anything, but Ivan had staked his entire position on a weak reed. Would he simply hand over power to the collaborationist faction or join them himself? Or would he be ritually killed for leading his people into a trap? The Vesy didn't tend to like incompetent rulers. Anjeet had heard stories of what had happened to the God-King's supporters, stories that would have made a tribesman blanch. Ivan might well have signed his own death warrant by working with the British.

"They had no intention of giving you weapons," Anjeet added. "It was only when we started to offer weapons to the Flowered Clan that they changed their mind. And even then, they didn't offer you unlimited ammunition or support. They don't care about you, not at all. All they care about is the system."

It wasn't entirely fair to the British, Anjeet knew, but he didn't care. *They* hadn't thought to bring along a handful of portable factories, even though - in hindsight - they had to be kicking themselves. Giving the Vesy weapons was one thing, giving them practically unlimited supplies of ammunition was quite another. Anjeet knew from bitter experience - and his British counterparts would know the same - just how rapidly ammunition stockpiles were burned through on active service. Having a factory ready and able to replenish those stockpiles would be decisive.

Ivan peered at him. "Do you have a better offer?"

"Join us," Anjeet said. Didn't the British recognise, honestly, what a treasure they'd had at their disposal? Probably not; their age of heroes was long gone. "Your city can join the Flowered Clan as an equal member, with the same level of access to weapons, support and training as the others. We would be honoured to have you."

"And what," the alien said, "would you want in exchange?"

And how, Anjeet added mentally, *are you planning to betray me?*

He smiled, inwardly. Ivan would have had problems wrapping his head around the concept of bare-faced lying, but once he'd gotten the idea it would probably have occurred to him that Anjeet could lie as easily as Ambassador Richardson. The Vesy did seem to place more weight on the word of a soldier, rather than a civilian, yet Anjeet knew better than to take that for granted. He might well be blinded by his own preconception that soldiers were inherently more noble than civilians.

And besides, he reminded himself, *just about every freeman in that city will be a warrior.*

"The Flowered Clans will want your support in destroying the British-led alliance," Anjeet said, flatly. It was true enough, but it would have the added advantage of making it impossible for Ivan to switch sides a second time. "Your city must join us in war."

"You speak of fighting a foe who can drop hammers from the sky," Ivan pointed out. "The Russians smashed walls with firebolts, the British stomped on the God-King so hard that the ground shook miles away. His forces were crushed. Who could fight such a foe?"

Anjeet swore, inwardly. Most of the Vesy he'd spoken to hadn't quite taken the concept of KEWs seriously. How could they when all they'd heard had been rumours? But Ivan had seen the Russians and British both use KEWs to great effect. He *knew* they were far more than just absurd rumours, rumours that had grown in the telling.

"They will be barred from deploying any such weapons," Anjeet said, simply. There was no point in saying anything else. "We will be extending our protective umbrella over you too. To drop rocks on you would mean a general war."

He wished, suddenly, for the ability to read minds. Emotions were one thing, but emotions could be controlled. Ivan had to know he'd been betrayed - and that the Flowered Clan was a mortal threat to his city - and yet, he might fear the consequences of switching sides. But if he didn't switch sides, and word got out, he would rapidly find himself replaced. His government, insofar as the term could be used, would fall.

"Then we will join you, on even terms," Ivan said. "What do you want us to do?"

"We welcome you," Anjeet said, without a trace of irony. He took a moment to organise his thoughts. "This is what we want you to do..."

CHAPTER
THIRTY THREE

"Captain," Tara said. "We just picked up a FLASH alert from the drones monitoring Tramline Three."

John blinked in surprise. Tramline One led - eventually - to Cromwell and Earth, while Tramline Two led to Pegasus, but the remaining tramlines were largely unexplored. No one who had jumped along them had reported back, at least to him. Chances were they had slipped back to Earth, if there was anything worth claiming, to lodge a claim with the World Court.

But a FLASH alert? That meant trouble.

"Yellow alert," he ordered. "Can you get me an IFF?"

"Not yet, sir," Tara said. "The newcomers probably wouldn't bother announcing themselves to the drones."

Because the drones are stealthy and meant to remain ignored, John thought. Placing them there would probably have annoyed the bean-counters - drones were expensive - if they hadn't just proved their value. *There's nothing to gain by signalling them.*

"Keep an eye on the tramline," he ordered, glancing at his display and running through some mental calculations. Assuming the newcomers headed straight for Vesy - the drone would send a second update soon, if it was close enough to track them - it would be at least nine hours before they reached orbit. "Let me know the moment we pick up either a sensor image or beacon data."

"Aye, sir," Tara said.

John forced himself to sit still, thinking hard. The drone had sent a FLASH alert, which meant that more than one ship had come through the tramline, but it hadn't sent an update. Had the drone been honestly unable to glean enough data…or had the drone been attacked before it could send a second message? Or was he just being paranoid? If someone was good enough to locate, then destroy the drone before it sent a second message the Royal Navy was in deep trouble. No known sensor array, human or Tadpole, could track the drones except at very close range…

They might be aliens, he told himself. It would have seemed unlikely, five years ago, but now two non-human races were known to exist. Why not a third? *Or the Tadpoles could have decided to pay a visit.*

He shook his head, after a moment. Vesy was deep within the Human Sphere; the Tadpoles could have come to investigate a whole new intelligent race, but they would have passed through human space and someone would have forwarded an alert to him first. Hell, given the growing tension, it might be the best thing that could happen. The EDO treaties would be activated and the human forces would band together, just in case. Who knew *what* the Tadpoles might have in mind?

"Picking up a second transmission," Gillian said, breaking into his thoughts. "Captain…I think you're going to want to see this."

"Show me," John ordered, feeling cold ice congealing around his spine. "Put it on my display."

He sucked in his breath a moment later as twelve icons appeared on the display. Seven of them were frigates, four were cruisers…and one was very definitely a fleet carrier. It wasn't transmitting any IFF signals, but the Combat Information Computer had no difficulty in identifying it as INS *Viraat*, the Indian carrier. Between the newcomers and the forces already in orbit around the planet, a good two-thirds of the Indian Space Navy had been dispatched to Vesy. John had known the other warships were badly outmatched, but this…he shook his head, unable to believe what he was seeing. The Indians had dispatched enough firepower to cause a great deal of damage to a seemingly unimportant star system.

There must be a link between Vesy and the Indian colonies, he thought, grimly. It was hard to predict the tramlines, but logic suggested that one of them might go towards a star that had a tramline to New Delhi. *They must have scouted out the system during their early explorations, then brought ships with alien-grade drives through the tramlines.*

"Send a priority alert to the relay ships," he ordered. The presence of the ships meant…what? A deliberate attempt to intimidate everyone or a mere coincidence? He had to admit the latter was possible. No one, but a complete idiot would attempt to coordinate a multipart operation over a hundred light years. "Attach the sensor readings and inform the First Space Lord that matters may be reaching their denouement."

We thought we had an advantage, John thought, as Gillian hurried to send the message. *The link through Pegasus should have let us get ships to Vesy quicker than anyone else. But the Indians may have their own pathway through the tramlines.*

"Then send a second priority alert to Ambassador Richardson and Colonel Boone," John added, feeling almost mesmerised by the tonnage bearing down on him. "Inform them that the Indians have raised the stakes yet again."

He glanced at the status board and swore under his breath. There were hundreds of tiny outposts on Vesy, not counting either Fort Knight or the Indian bases. Did the Indians believe they could seize the entire planet? Or were they just racheting up the tension in hopes of getting something out of it? They'd have to be mad to risk war with the Great Powers, even after the First Interstellar War…

"Captain," Gillian said, "I'm picking up a PTA burst from the direction of Tramline Three, with IFF signals attached. The Indians are requesting permission to enter orbit."

How very polite, John thought, sarcastically. The words of a very old joke ran through his mind. *Where does a fleet carrier-based task force sit? Anywhere it wants to.*

"Contact System Command and request that they assign the Indians orbital slots," he ordered. Maybe it was just a friendly visit after all. And if that was true, he added privately, he'd give up his command and go work in Sin City as a fucktoy. "And keep a sharp eye on them."

He gritted his teeth as he looked back at the drone's sensor images. The cruisers alone would be a nightmare, if the Indians did intend to chase them away from Vesy, but the carrier tipped the balance firmly in their favour. No one had actually *tested* one of the post-war carriers, not outside simulations and war games…he shook his head. The human race had learned a whole series of nasty lessons from the war and the Indians would be ready for anything he could do, if he had a chance to put up a fight. And he couldn't even leave orbit and prepare for a scrap without causing a diplomatic incident…

"Send a second message to Ambassador Richardson," he added. "Invite her onboard *Warspite* at her earliest convenience."

"Aye, sir," Gillian said.

John left her to get on with it, thinking hard. The Indians had raised the stakes once again, but why? What did they hope to get out of it? They already had a powerful alien faction on their side, with a guaranteed supply of weapons and ammunition to *keep* them on their side, and they'd created a great deal of disagreement among the ranks of the Great Powers… what more did they want? Why bring the carrier at all?

It couldn't be a coincidence. Fleet carriers were *expensive* to build and maintain; John knew, for a fact, that no British carriers had travelled beyond Britannia until *Ark Royal* had launched its first strike into alien space. Hell, even the Americans had been reluctant to send a carrier more than a tramline or two away from their claimed systems…and *they'd* been staring down the barrels of a war with China. The Indians were taking one hell of a chance sending INS *Viraat* so far from Earth. It *definitely* couldn't be a coincidence…

He swore as it struck him. There *was* something the Indians could do…and if they were lucky, it would allow them to walk away with Vesy, enhanced status and no threat of a general war.

"Mr. Howard, you have the bridge," he said, rising from his chair. "Inform me the moment the Indians come into sensor range. Gillian, get me a direct and secure link to Colonel Boone."

"Aye, sir," Howard said.

John stepped into his office, then sat down at the desk and waited, impatiently, for Boone's face to appear in the display.

"Captain," Boone said. He didn't sound worried, although Paras were notoriously phlegmatic. "I hear we have more guests."

"Enough firepower to kick the ass of anything smaller than a *Theodore Smith*-class carrier and escorts," John said, flatly. Perhaps Admiral Soskice's theories about the role of the starfighter in modern war were about to be tested. "But they may not be the real problem."

He took a breath. "I think you can expect a major attack soon, Colonel," he added. "Either on Fort Knight and the outposts, or on the cities supporting us."

Boone frowned. "Why?"

"The Indians would have to be crazy to start a fight here," John said. "It isn't just us, Colonel; they'd be picking a fight with the Americans and French, perhaps even the Chinese. And there are quite a few other smaller powers here too. The Indians could find themselves at war with *everyone* else."

"True enough," Boone said.

John met his eyes. "But they have an agreement with the Flowered Clan," he added. "They've agreed to defend them against any human attempts to intervene in their conflicts - say, by hammering advancing columns from orbit. They drew a line, Colonel, and they made damn certain we would *know* about the line. And what does that mean if the Flowered Clan launches a war against us?"

"We have the right to defend ourselves," Boone said, stiffly.

"But if we called on our most effective weapons, the Indians would be obliged to join the war," John said. "And they have enough firepower to rapidly wipe out everyone in orbit before we could make a real difference. I think they sent a carrier because they wanted to make it clear that any attempt to join the war would be an exercise in futility."

"They could pretty much win a war against us here, *on Vesy*," Boone pointed out. "Would they win a war against us everywhere else?"

John ticked off points on his fingers as he spoke. "Five years ago, they would have been swatted down long ago," he said. "Now, after the war, is that still true? Do we have the nerve to take them on, even though victory is certain? And it would come at a very high price, Colonel. We'd be weakening humanity's defences against the Tadpoles - or any other alien threat."

"And they'd be counting on the Solar Treaty remaining in force," Boone said. "We wouldn't be able to hammer their industries because they're orbiting the Earth!"

"Precisely," John said. "They could lose both of their out-system settlements, Colonel, but they wouldn't be *greatly* harmed."

"Then we bluff them," Boone said. "Tell them that we won't feel obliged to honour the treaties."

"They would call our bluff," John said.

And it *would* be a bluff, he knew. Eighty percent of humanity's remaining industry was orbiting the Earth, vulnerable to a war breaking out among two human powers. Britain couldn't take the risk of uniting the remaining nations against it, while the Indians *wouldn't*, not when it worked out in their favour to honour the treaties. The hell of it was that he could see it working, even if the Indians *did* manage to start a war with the rest of the human race.

They know we can't take risks with the industrial base we need to support another war, he thought, numbly. The sheer scale of the plan worked in their favour; hell, even *he* had trouble believing in it. *And that traps us into playing their game. Either surrender what they want and allow them to reap the rewards of boldness or fight a war that might have no real winners.*

"I see," Boone said, sourly. "What do you want us to do?"

"Prepare for attack," John ordered. He *was* the military commander of the mission, but he would defer to Boone on the ground. "Get as many people as you can into defensible positions and secure Fort Knight."

"I can try," Boone said. "Many of the NGOs aren't respecting our authority so much, now."

John groaned. The Indians had started to offer basing rights to NGOs, even ones that couldn't be relied upon to toe the party line. It had puzzled him at the time, until he'd realised the NGOs were largely working with Vesy cities that had already obtained weapons from the Indians. The arrangement suited both parties; the NGOs got to introduce new ideas to the Vesy, while the aliens got their weapons from third parties. Given time, the Flowered Clan would become the dominant force on the surface, while the Indians ruled the skies.

"Do the best you can," he ordered. "Have a word with the other military officers on the surface too. Their bases may come under attack."

"And none of them are as well-defended as Fort Knight," Boone finished. "And *we're* not as well-defended as the Indian fortress."

John sighed, bitterly. "Do the best you can," he repeated. "I'll speak to the Ambassador and get back to you."

"Understood," Boone said. "Have a good one, sir."

"Thank you," John said.

He tapped a switch, closing the channel, and then glanced at his updates. Ambassador Richardson had agreed to visit *Warspite*, but she needed to talk to two of the alien representatives first. John groaned, then forced himself to focus on writing out a report to the First Space Lord. It would be relayed to Earth before the Indian carrier entered orbit and then...

They can't spare anything capable of standing up to the Indians, he thought. The more he thought about it, the more he wanted to admire the Indian who'd dreamed up the whole scheme, to shake his hand and then strangle him. They'd taken the opportunities presented by Vesy and run with them, while the Great Powers had been arguing over just what should happen to the Russian deserters. *We need to take the initiative, somehow, but we can't. The bastards have boxed us in neatly...*

His intercom pinged. "Captain, a freighter just popped through Tramline One," Gillian said. "She transmitted a sealed message for you."

"Understood," John said. He wondered, briefly, if someone at home had *finally* realised that *Viraat* was missing. "Send it down to my terminal here."

The message, when it popped up on his display, insisted on a full series of security codes, fingerprint scans and DNA readings before it conde-scended to decrypt itself. John cursed inwardly - anything so sensitive had to be trouble - then swore under his breath as the message activated, displaying an image of the First Space Lord.

"John," the First Space Lord said. "The World Court, after weeks of arguing, has finally come to a set of decisions concerning Vesy. I'm afraid they won't make your position any easier. This message should be a day or two ahead of the official notification, assuming I've timed it properly. It's all the warning I can give you."

He noticeably took a breath, then went on. "There are a set of minor rulings, but the key one is that there is an immediate ban on selling weap-ons and ammunition to the Vesy," he continued. "You are *not*, under any circumstances, to supply the Vesy, friendly or unfriendly, with anything that can be used to wage war on their neighbours."

"Tell me," John snapped. "How the hell are we meant to keep their friendship if we leave them defenceless?"

The recording, unsurprisingly, went on. "This ruling is deemed to apply to every spacefaring human power, without exception," the First Space Lord said. "As such, the World Court will be pressing charges against anyone who breaks the embargo. They have also decided that the Vesy System is to be left undeveloped, held in trust for the natives. British claims to the asteroid cluster are to be abandoned.

"I believe they expect you to enforce these judgements," he concluded. "I..."

John paused the recording and swore, venomously. How the hell was he meant to enforce such a ruling with three ships against an entire Indian task force? Not to mention, of course, the other powers that might take exception to the World Court's decree? It would result in a battle shorter and more inglorious than the Battle of New Russia where, at least, one side hadn't known it was badly outmatched until battle had been joined.

He forced himself to calm down, then restarted the recording. "... Understand that you have too few ships to enforce the ruling," the First Space Lord said. "I have explained this to the PM and I believe he understands, but the media is producing a definite cacophony in favour of not making the situation on the planet any worse. For the moment, therefore, you are to do nothing but keep Fort Knight secure. *Do not* hand over any more weapons to the Vesy."

"And lose their friendship once and for all," John muttered.

"I'm trying to convince the PM to start the diplomacy to put together a multinational task force, but it's slow going," the First Space Lord concluded. "There are too many interests that aren't in favour of the ruling. If matters get badly out of hand, you are authorised to pull our people off the planet completely, by force if necessary. We can leave the planet to the Indians until we have a chance to put together a joint approach."

He paused. "You are also authorised to open Set #3 of your sealed orders," he added. "Good luck."

"Brilliant," John said, as the recording came to an end. He honestly couldn't remember feeling so screwed, even the moment he'd first laid eyes on the remains of HMS *Canopus* and known that Colin and he were stranded a very long way from home. "Now what?"

CHAPTER
THIRTY FOUR

"Fuck," Joelle swore. "Fuck, fuck, fuck."

"I hope that isn't the kind of words you use at diplomatic meetings," Captain Naiser said, as he passed her a mug of tea. "Blunt as they are, they are a tad undiplomatic."

Joelle smiled, rather dryly. "I would use nicer words than that at the table," she said. She took the tea and sipped it, gratefully. "All hell is about to break loose…"

She stared at the frozen image of the First Space Lord. The message was lethal, literally; she couldn't help wondering if the Indians had planned it that way all along. If the British didn't supply weapons and training, as they'd promised, the Vesy would switch sides openly and the British position would crumble without the Indians having to lift a finger. But if she defied the message and refused to carry out her orders, when they finally arrived, she would be fired and her replacement would do as she was told. The delay would be minimal.

"I don't suppose there's any room to manoeuvre," she said, although she already knew the answer was *no*. The flat ban on exporting any more weapons and ammunition to the aliens left no room for creative interpretation. "Is there no naval regulation you can cite to avoid having to carry out orders?"

"The orders would have to be illegal," Captain Naiser said. "That's very clearly defined in the book, Ambassador. I don't think that even the most cunning lawyer in the world could reasonably brand the orders as illegal."

Joelle considered it. "Couldn't we claim they were encouraging genocide on the planet's surface?"

"We'd have to be ordered to carry out the genocide ourselves," John
said, shaking his head ruefully. "Even then, there would have to be a complete shortage of mitigating circumstances. It wouldn't be the first time
a town or even a city was hammered from orbit for doing something we
disliked. Everything else…?"

He shrugged. "We're not being ordered to launch a coup against the
duly elected government, or to disobey orders from that government, or
to fire on British civilians without an extremely good reason," he added.
"All we're being ordered to do, Ambassador, is leave the Vesy to their fate."

"Fuck," Joelle said, again.

"They'll switch sides," John warned. "You know they will."

"Yeah," Joelle said. "And who could reasonably blame them?"

She cursed under her breath. The Captain's suggestion - that the
Indians had intended to create a situation where their allies could overrun
everyone else, without interference from outside - made a great deal of
sense. Indeed, keeping the human warships out of the fight definitely gave
the advantage to the Flowered Clan. They had a vast stockpile of ammunition, plenty of weapons and probably quite a few other advantages. Ivan's
forces were a great deal weaker and much less well coordinated. Orbital
bombardment would have altered the odds, but orbital bombardment was
off the table.

"I can't," the Captain said. "I don't think anyone *could*."

"The folks at home will," Joelle said, bitterly. "They won't understand
why we lost control of our allies."

She sighed in bitter frustration. The Foreign Office *tried* to make sure
its senior officials all had tours overseas, but not all of them made it. She
knew, all too well, that hundreds of people who had never left Britain
were going to be second-guessing her when the inevitable inquiry began.
Captain Naiser and she were probably going to wind up being turned
into scapegoats and then formally sacked for gross incompetence. Or
something.

Gritting her teeth, she thrust that thought out of her head. She could
worry about her career later.

"We need to get as many of our civilians out as we can," she said, sitting upright. "Not all of them will *want* to leave, but I'm going to put out a call. The ones who want to stay can take their chances."

"Put Fort Knight into lockdown again," Captain Naiser added. "Colonel Boone can make damn sure there are only a limited number of potential targets out there."

"I will," Joelle said.

Captain Naiser paused, then spoke. "Tell him to make sure that there are no aliens within the walls," he added. "If the Flowered Clan is planning an assault, they will probably try to make use of people on the inside. We suspect they probably had spies among the aliens who gathered around Fort Knight."

"That won't go down well," Joelle said. "But I'll tell him. I'll also speak to the other ambassadors - get them to do the same."

"If they can," Captain Naiser said. "Some of the NGO bases are practically shared between two races."

He shook his head. "The Indians won't honour the ruling," he added. He nodded towards the near-orbit display, which was showing the carrier holding position on the other side of Vesy. "I think that carrier is sending a message to the World Court."

Joelle nodded. "Oh, yeah?" She translated. "Make me!"

"Exactly," Captain Naiser agreed. "Indeed, all hell is going to break loose, ambassador, and that carrier is going to keep the orbiting ships from interfering."

"I know," Joelle said. She didn't know *precisely* what had happened on Earth, but she could guess. The Indians and Turks - and probably a few more lesser powers - had drawn a line in the sand, daring the Great Powers to assert themselves. And now the Great Powers were faced with the problem of doing just that. "You can't launch a first strike, can you?"

"It would start a war," Captain Naiser pointed out. "And even if we took out the carrier on our first attack, before it had a chance to launch starfighters, we would still be badly outnumbered. I have *three* ships, Ambassador. The Indians have thirty-four."

He sighed. "I don't think we have a military option here," he added. "Evacuation and then regrouping elsewhere would seem to be the best chance we have to salvage *something* from this disaster."

Joelle looked him in the eye. "What happened to the Captain Naiser who attacked a Russian base and a pair of Russian warships?"

"He wasn't so badly outgunned, nor did he have thousands of civilians at risk," Captain Naiser said, irked. "This is going to turn into a bloody mess no matter what we do, Ambassador, and we *cannot* win a fight against the Indians here. Our political leaders have just knifed us in the back. The Vesy will desert us in droves once the news reaches them."

"I see," Joelle said. "Do you see any hope at all?"

"We might be able to hold Fort Knight indefinitely," Captain Naiser said. "We might be able to point out that an assault on Fort Knight by the Flowered Clan would risk starting a general war, if you wish to do so. But for the rest of the planet? I think the Indians have established themselves so firmly that dislodging them would require a major commitment."

"And that isn't going to happen," Joelle said. "The PM wouldn't support something that would divert resources from Earth."

"No," Captain Naiser said. "He wouldn't."

Joelle winced, thinking of the millions of British civilians who barely had enough to eat, no matter how hard they worked. Britain had fed itself for centuries, ever since the Age of Unrest, but the bombardment had ruined a great many farms. The mere suggestion of shipping farming equipment to Vesy might start a political landside, perhaps even an insurgency or civil war. There were all sorts of rumours about what had happened to government inspectors who'd asked the wrong questions of angry refugees...

"We can't give them anything more," she said. Factories? They were needed at home to rebuild the defences, as well as the economy. Jobs? There would be a riot if British citizens thought their jobs were being given to aliens. Economic support? What did it matter if the Indians reaped the rewards. "There's nothing left to give."

"I'm afraid so," Captain Naiser said.

Joelle finished her tea, then rose. "I'll speak to Colonel Boone now," she said, flatly. "Let him know that all hell is about to break loose."

She sighed, then met his eyes. "Did we ever have a chance?"

"I think the Russians and the Indians, between them, ensured that we didn't," Captain Naiser said. "We couldn't outbid the Indians without pouring resources into Vesy. And now..."

He shook his head. "We can give up our own claim to the asteroids, Ambassador," he said, "but we don't have the firepower to force any of the other powers to abandon *their* claims. We might either wind up trying to force them out, once a multinational force is assembled, or trading something they want back home to convince them to give up their claims."

"Recognition as Great Powers," Joelle said, flatly. "There's nothing else worth playing for."

She wanted to grind her teeth together. It was generally agreed that the Great Powers worked together, recognising one another as equals; even when they disagreed, they stayed out of each other's spheres of influence. The Indians *wanted* such a status for themselves, even though they had been late to the party; the Turks, the Germans, the Brazilians...they too wanted that level of recognition. She made a silent salute to the Indians - they might get what they wanted, now they'd staked their claim so firmly - and then cursed them under her breath for what they'd unleashed. If one power succeeded in elevating itself to the ranks of the Great Powers, what was to stop others from trying as well?

And we're disunited too, after the war, she thought, bitterly. *The bastards might just win by default.*

"Thank you, Captain," she said, aloud. "Can I borrow your terminal?"

"It's on the desk," Captain Naiser said. "Just ask the communications operator for a secure line."

———

"Hey, Penny," a voice called. Penny looked up to see Allen Roebuck, an American reporter who had been attached to Fort Knight by CNN-FOX. They weren't exactly friends - she knew she was competing with him for scoops - but she liked comparing notes with him in the bar. "What's all this about?"

"I haven't the slightest idea," Penny said. "All I know is that everyone with an outside pass has been called to the briefing hall."

She sucked in her breath sharply as she followed Roebuck through the doors and into the hall. It was a large room, easily big enough to pass for a ballroom, and yet it felt cramped. The room was crammed with people;

Penny silently thanked her parents for her height, then peered towards the podium. It was empty, but a trio of armed Paras were clearly on guard, watching the crowd. Unfortunately, none of them were Hamish.

Or perhaps I should be relieved, she told herself. *What would happen if he had to drag me out for asking questions?*

"There's just about everyone here," Roebuck said, shouting to be heard over the noise. "I didn't know so many people wanted to get out!"

"It gets boring here," Penny shouted back. "Why stay inside the walls when you can visit the alien bazaar?"

She smiled inwardly at the thought. The aliens had offered to sell her everything from artworks to pieces of carved wood...and all they'd wanted in exchange was human money or technology. Penny had refused to give up anything, but she'd heard whispers that not everyone had stuck to the rules. Why would they, she wondered, when an alien-made carving would be worth millions when they got it back home? Or alien-produced alcohol...Vesy drinks tasted funny to her, but she'd drunk worse at Fitzwilliam Hall. Maybe they'd even start a new trend on Earth...

"It could be about the carrier," Roebuck speculated. "Everyone thinks the Indians are planning to invade."

"I doubt it," Penny said. "They wouldn't need a whole carrier to take this world from the natives."

"If I could have your attention, please," Colonel Boone said. He stood in front of the podium, wearing body armour that made him look hellishly intimidating. "We don't have much time."

He ignored the hail of shouted questions with the ease of long practice. Penny smiled to herself; she might have been embedded with the Ambassador, but she hadn't been able to get an interview with Boone... or Captain Naiser, now they'd arrived on Vesy. She rather suspected they had orders to refuse interviews, orders that had to have come from the Ambassador. Or perhaps they'd simply disliked the idea of being interviewed and their words taken out of context, then broadcast to the world.

"By order of the Ambassador, Fort Knight will be going back into lockdown, effective immediately," Boone said. "The gates will be closed. Anyone outside the gates will be allowed to return, but not to leave once again. If any of you want to go to any of the outposts, you may do so...on the understanding that we will not rescue you if you are not allowed to return. You will have to take your chances on the other side."

Penny gasped. She wasn't the only one.

"Colonel," a voice called. "Are you seriously saying that you will leave us to our fate?"

Boone glowered at the speaker, hidden somewhere within the crowd. "I am saying that we have very limited resources," he said, tartly. "It may not be possible to protect Fort Knight, let alone the rest of the outposts. If you do something that will make my task harder, expect to pay a price for it."

He paused. Everyone seemed too stunned to speak.

"In addition, we will be running shuttles to get as many people into orbit as possible," Boone continued. "We will not be *forcing* any of you to leave, but we strongly advise you to put your names on the list for evacuation. Should you miss your shuttle, you will be allocated to the next one… which may be too late. You have been warned.

"The situation is becoming very dangerous," he concluded. "We strongly suggest you remain within the walls and prepare for evacuation. All hell could break loose at any moment."

Ignoring the handful of shouted questions, he turned and strode out of the room. Penny watched him go, shocked. She'd been in dangerous places before, but she'd never been told so bluntly that she would be abandoned, if she insisted on putting her life in danger. Indeed, British forces had recovered more than one reporter who'd been kidnapped and held for ransom by local terrorists.

We had much more firepower there, she thought, as the crowd started to disperse slowly. *I wasn't at so much risk.*

"Penny," Roebuck said. "Do you think he was serious?"

"Probably," Penny said. There would probably be lawsuits, if not questions in parliament, if the reporters were abandoned. But it wouldn't help any reporter who was hacked to death by alien hordes. "I'm going back to my room. See you later."

She walked past Roebuck, out of the room and down towards her barracks. Somehow, she wasn't surprised to see Percy standing there, carrying enough weaponry to fight a minor war.

"Percy," she said. "Is this for real?"

"Yes," Percy said, flatly. Her brother looked her up and down. "Pen-Pen, I need you to put your name on the list for immediate evacuation…"

"No," Penny said, surprising them both. "I can't just cut and run…"

Percy took a step forward, then stopped himself with an effort. "Pen-Pen…"

"My *name* is Penny, or Penelope if you insist on being formal," Penny snarled. Being called Pen-Pen made her feel like a child, even though it had been cute and funny years ago. But they'd both grown up a great deal since then. "This is my great chance to…"

"Get yourself killed," her brother snarled back. He softened his voice with an effort. "Penny, the base could be in very real danger."

"So I gathered," Penny said. She waved a hand at the grenades on his belt. "Is that why you're walking around like Desperate Dan?"

"We could come under attack at any moment," Percy snapped. "Penny, *please* get on the first shuttle."

Penny shook her head. "I can't, Percy," she said. "How would your superiors feel if *you* got on the first shuttle?"

"I get paid to fight," Percy said. "You don't."

"I get paid to report on events of major importance," Penny countered. She took a breath, glaring at her brother. "This is my one real chance to make a name and a reputation for myself. I am *damned* if I'm going back to reporting on things that won't even make Page 10, unless it's a very slow news day. That's if I don't get sacked for running from the story!"

"Would your bosses rather you were dead?" Percy asked, angrily. "Your body buried in a makeshift grave on this shithole of a planet?"

"I won't leave," Penny said. She crossed her arms under her breasts, then glared at her brother. "Are you going to try to drag me off the planet by force?"

"I should sedate you and put you on the list for medical evacuation," Percy muttered, just loudly enough for her to hear. "Hamish would probably help, if I asked."

Penny sighed, then reached out and touched his shoulder. "I can't back away, not now," she said. She understood his feelings - it wasn't as if they had anyone else - but she wasn't his kid sister any longer. "I'll be fine, really."

"I hope," Percy said. He reached for her holster and removed her pistol. "One clip, just one."

"It's enough," Penny said.

"Draw more clips from the armoury before the rush starts," Percy snapped. "And really, try to stay out of..."

His wristcom bleeped. "Shit," he said. "I have to go."

"I'll be fine, really," Penny said, again. "Have a good one."

"You've spent *far* too long with that damned Para," Percy said. "Good luck, Penny."

He kissed her forehead, then hurried off into the distance.

CHAPTER
THIRTY FIVE

"Sir," Percy said, as he entered the office. Colonel Boone was seated behind his desk, with Ambassador Richardson and Grace Scott seated in front of him. "Reporting as ordered."

"At ease, Lieutenant," Colonel Boone said. "We have a mission for you."

Percy nodded, but didn't relax. It was rare for marines to be briefed in front of civilians, which meant...what? Was Boone showing off? It didn't seem likely. Or was he planning to raise concerns in a manner he couldn't be called on? Percy shrugged mentally, then waited. He'd find out soon enough.

"The Ambassador needs to be escorted to Ivan's City," Boone said. "You and your men will accompany her, providing a standard close-protection detail."

"Unfortunately, this mission may turn dangerous," the Ambassador said. She sounded as though she had bitten into a lemon. "We have to give the aliens bad news."

Percy frowned, biting down the question he wanted to ask. He had no idea how Ivan would react, if only because he had no idea what the bad news actually *was*? He'd heard nothing, save for the order to go armed at all times and prepare to man the defences if necessary. Part of him resented being left in ignorance, but he knew that was always likely to be the case. A young officer wouldn't be told more than his superiors thought he should know.

"In the event of trouble, two armoured platoons, four helicopters and a dozen Bulldogs are ready to pull you out," Boone said. "Keep the Ambassador safe, then hole up as long as possible; we'll have help on the way."

"Aye, sir," Percy said. He couldn't help feeling cold. *None* of this sounded good. "We'll do it."

He paused, then asked the question anyway. "Sir...what are we going to tell them?"

It was the Ambassador who answered. "The World Court has declared a general embargo on shipping weapons to the Vesy," she said. "We won't be able to send them any more weapons until the embargo is lifted."

Percy gaped. "They'll go mad," he said, forgetting himself. "We made promises..."

"As you were, Lieutenant," Boone snapped.

"I know," the Ambassador said. "But we have no manoeuvring room at all."

"Sir," Percy said, turning to Boone. "I think we should be delivering this message from a safe distance. They will *not* take it calmly."

"The least we can do is go to them," the Ambassador said. "They may desert us, but they're not likely to pick a fight."

Percy hoped she was right. Ivan knew more than any other Vesy about the power of human weaponry, but...how long would Ivan stay in power after this betrayal? The Vesy had a quaint custom, one he rather admired, of insisting that their political leaders were responsible for their decisions. Ivan, who had gambled everything on his alliance with Fort Knight, was likely to lose everything after his failure. And then...

Someone will come into power who doesn't like us, he thought. *And that someone will go elsewhere for their weapons.*

"It will be risky, sir," he said. He would carry out the mission, if ordered to do so, but it was his duty to make his superior aware of the risks. "They may turn on us."

"Yeah," Boone said, drawing the word out. "If they do, we can have reinforcements there quickly. Very quickly."

But will they be quick enough? Percy thought. It wasn't *far* to Ivan's City, not from Fort Knight, but it would still take time. *We could be overwhelmed within seconds.*

"Yes, sir," he said, out loud. At least he'd written a will…not that he had much to give away, apart from his share of his father's prize money and his banked salary. Penny would get it, as well as his other possessions. "I assume we have permission to use the Bulldogs to reach the city?"

"You do," Boone said. "Have a good one, Lieutenant."

Percy nodded. "Then I will brief my men," he said. He made a brief calculation in his head, then doubled it. "We will be ready to leave in twenty minutes."

"That will be fine," the Ambassador said.

Boone looked irked. "I suppose it will be," he said. "Watch your back."

Percy saluted, then turned and marched out of the room. It wasn't hard to work out what had happened, in the moments before he'd arrived. Boone had clearly argued against the mission, only to be overruled by the Ambassador. Percy had to admit she had balls, at least metaphorically; he'd known marines who would have hesitated to walk into an alien city and announce that the solemn treaties of friendship and mutual respect were going to be cast aside on the whim of REMFs back home. Ivan might let them go…or he might take his frustration out on them. Why not? By cutting him loose, the REMFs had doomed his political career…and, perhaps, doomed his city too.

"Sir," Peerce said, as he stepped into the ready room. The entire section was there, reading datapads or trying to catch a nap before the shit hit the fan. "What's up?"

Percy wished, suddenly, that he'd had a more normal career. He hadn't wished to be put in an awkward position on *Warspite*, he hadn't wished to be left behind at Fort Knight and he hadn't wished for promotion. No, that wasn't entirely true; he'd wished for promotion, but not responsibility. He would have sold his soul to be a mere private again, to know nothing more than what his officers told him…

"We're going back to Ivan's City," he said, simply. "Prepare the Bulldogs."

Peerce gave him a sharp look as the marines hurried to obey. "Sir?"

"They're going to betray our allies," Percy said, flatly. He felt numb, as if he couldn't quite believe what was happening. "And all hell is going to break loose."

Twenty minutes later, they were on their way.

———

"You passed on the message?"

"Yes, General," Rani said. "There's no way to trace it back to us either. The freighter that brought the news was kind enough to broadcast it all over the system."

Anjeet nodded, curtly. He'd known the World Court was moving towards an embargo - the messages he'd received from home had made that quite clear - but he hadn't expected them to move so quickly. The British should have vetoed it, he was sure; *India* would have done so, if her interests had been so badly exposed. But the British Government was a prisoner of its backbenchers…and the idealistic fools squatting in the House of Commons. They only saw the downside of selling human weapons to the aliens, not the simple fact that the Vesy fought each other as often as humans and *someone* might as well advance their interests by providing the weapons.

He glanced at the live feed from the orbiting satellite. Seven British vehicles, all Bulldogs, heading down towards Ivan's City. They'd be there in thirty minutes, he calculated, unless they ran into trouble. It wasn't too likely - every unit the Flowered Clan had dispatched had strict orders not to engage until they received the signal - but accidents happened. And sometimes they were even *real* accidents.

"The message is prepped, ready to go," Rani added.

"Good," Anjeet said. He swallowed, hard. "You may transmit it once the fighting begins."

He shook his head, mentally forcing himself to relax. Whatever happened, they were committed. There was no way he could pull back now. India, his India, stood on the cusp between apotheosis and nemesis. It had seemed a good idea at the time, he knew, but now…now everything was ready to go, he couldn't help feeling jittery. Too much could go badly wrong.

"And then we pray," he added. If everything went according to plan… but nothing ever did, he knew. "And hope we survive the coming months."

———

Joelle had rapidly learned to dislike the Bulldogs. They weren't the ambassadorial cars she'd used on her foreign postings, where the interiors were comfortable even though the vehicles were almost as armoured as a heavy tank; they were cramped, smelly and far too warm for her peace of mind. Sweat dripped down her back as the vehicle lurched onwards, making it impossible for her to concentrate on the coming meeting. The aliens *would* take it badly, she knew; nothing she'd seen or heard had made it possible for her to believe otherwise. Hell, a *human* would take it badly.

But we don't have a choice, she thought, even though she knew it was pointless. The Vesy would never understand if she tried to explain about the World Court, not when it was hundreds of light years away and well outside their frame of reference. *They will think we're lying for our own reasons.*

The vehicle lurched violently, then shuddered to a halt. Joelle swallowed, trying hard not to be sick, then let out a sigh of relief as the hatch opened. They might be at the outskirts of an alien city, on an alien world, but the air smelled better than the Bulldog. Too many hot and sweaty men in close proximity, she guessed, as she allowed one of the marines to help her out of the vehicle. Outside, the alien city gleamed in the sunlight, brilliant flickering light dancing over its stone walls. She could see a dozen aliens standing on top, looking down at the humans. They all carried human-designed weapons, ready to use them against threats to their city.

"Ambassador," a voice said. She looked up to see Lieutenant Schneider, holding out a set of body armour. "Might I advise you to wear this, please?"

Joelle frowned. She'd never liked body armour - it gave the wrong impression, she'd always thought - even when she was on Earth, where it was generally cooler. On Vesy, she suspected that wearing the armour for any length of time would leave her drowning in her own sweat. But the more she looked at the alien city, the more she felt that she was badly exposed. No doubt Schneider had waited for this moment to ask, just to make sure she *felt* the potential threat. She silently saluted him, then pulled the armour on over her shorts and shirt. It felt as hot and uncomfortable as she'd expected.

"Well," she said, once she'd buckled the armour into place. "Shall we go?"

Schneider looked nervous, but led her towards the gates. As before, the streets were lined with aliens, some staring with unconcealed interest, other watching dispassionately, as if they were merely standing there because they'd been *told* to stand there. Joelle couldn't help a flicker of disappointment. She'd been in countries where the locals had been gathered up and told to cheer loudly - and threatened with beatings or worse if they refused to comply - but she'd hoped it was a purely human shame. The idea that the Vesy, on some level, were no different from humanity stung.

The marines fell in around her as they walked in eerie silence towards the Palace. Joelle had the sense they were running a gauntlet, even though no one was hurling blows or firing guns towards them. Dark beady eyes watched their every move; Joelle still found it hard to read alien motions, but it was all too clear that the marines were nervous. She could only hope that the aliens weren't canny enough to understand human body language.

But they might have secured a few of our textbooks, she thought. It had surprised her to discover just how many people on the base were studying for degrees of one kind or another, or just how many datapads and datachips had gone missing. *They might even have studied our own works on how we think and act.*

She scowled, inwardly, as they reached the Palace and were shown through the massive doors. In hindsight, the mission might have been doomed from the start. It would have been easy to cut a deal with the Russians to claim Vesy, then supervise access to the system…but even so, the native culture had been badly contaminated. And the Russians would have demanded a high price for signing over their rights without demur. And not everyone would have accepted that the Russians *had* any rights. The Indians would certainly not have accepted their claims unless they were presented with a compelling reason to submit.

"Stay wary," Schneider muttered. She wasn't sure if he was addressing her or his men, but it was clear they were in danger. The corridors were lined with alien guardsmen, watching them with dark eyes. "Don't let your guard down for a second."

Joelle felt her heartbeat suddenly speed up as they stepped into the throne room. Ivan stood there, waiting for them, flanked by a handful of other aliens. But, unlike last time, the rest of the room was empty. She couldn't decide if that was a good thing or not. Maybe Ivan didn't want any witnesses to what was about to happen.

She looked into the alien face and *knew*, with a certainty so strong it surprised her, that he already *knew* why they'd come.

The Indians must have told their allies about the betrayal, she thought, numbly. *And those allies passed word to Ivan - or to their friends within his city.*

"I greet you," Ivan said, in English. "You demanded a meeting. Speak."

Joelle felt Schneider tense beside her. The aliens were blunt, but they were rarely truly rude...

She swallowed - her mouth was suddenly very dry - and then forced herself to speak.

"Our leaders back home have ruled that we may no longer give weapons to you," she said. She'd tried to think of a way to sugar-coat the message, but she hadn't been able to think of one. "That none of us humans may give weapons to any of you until we have sorted out our affairs. That..."

Ivan cut her off. "When you came, you assured us that you could speak for your people," he said, flatly. A strange scent filled the air as he leaned forward. "We made agreements with you in good faith. We have endured your people wandering through our cities and asking foolish questions in good faith. We allied ourselves with you in good faith."

Joelle felt almost as if she'd been slapped. "We don't have a choice," she said. On Earth, she would have found a way to sweeten the pill. Here...she doubted there was any way to make the Vesy feel better. "Our people..."

"The Indians have already made it clear that they are not bound by this ruling," Ivan said, flatly. "They are still providing weapons and ammunition to the Flowered Clan. We will soon be badly outmatched. You have betrayed us. You have betrayed *me*."

His flat tone made the accusation feel worse, somehow. Joelle wanted to argue, but he was right. Britain *had* made it harder for him to come to terms with the Indians, then dropped him like a hot rock. The weapons he'd stockpiled wouldn't last against a massed attack from a foe who had effectively unlimited ammunition. His city was doomed. And the coalition she'd hoped Ivan could build, to counter the Flowered Clan's claim to rule the entire surface, was lost. The Indians had effectively won the planet without firing a single shot.

"You will be held here," Ivan continued. He gestured; the doors slammed open to reveal a handful of alien guards. "You and your men will be traded back to your people, once Fort Knight has been removed from our territory."

"This is an act of war," Joelle said. "I…"

"You have betrayed us," Ivan repeated. "That too is an act of war."

"Get down," Schneider snapped. Joelle glanced backwards and saw the marines lifting their weapons, then threw herself to the stone floor. "Ivan, tell your people to back off! I can't let you take us hostage…"

A shot rang out. Moments later, all hell broke loose.

———

Percy had run enough close-protection exercises to know that allowing his principal, and his men, to be taken hostage was among the worst thing he could do. Hostage-takers were rarely rational; they might torture or kill the soldiers, while keeping the important hostages prisoner for years on end. The moment one of Ivan's guards opened fire, Percy pointed his rifle at the crowd, flicked the selector to automatic and hosed down the guards with bullets. It would have earned him a rebuke in training, he knew, as he hastily swapped out one magazine for the next, but he hadn't seen any choice.

"Call it in," he snapped. Ivan was lying on the ground, bleeding heavily. Percy took one look - the shot had gone right through his skull - and knew there was no point in trying to save the alien. The guards were a mangled mass of flesh and blood. "Tell the Colonel we need support, now!"

Peerce hastened forward and checked the door. "I hear more guards on the way," he said, sharply. "We can't stay here."

"Pick up the ambassador," Percy ordered. They'd have to get onto a rooftop and wait for the helicopters, again. It would be embarrassing, but he wasn't proud. "We need to get up."

"I think the guards are above us," Peerce said. "We may not be able to get to the roof."

"Shit," Percy swore. The Vesy weren't stupid. They'd noted what had happened in City Seven and taken steps to make sure it couldn't happen again. If they couldn't get up, there was no way they could be evacuated. "This was a *planned* ambush."

"Sir," John Hardesty said. "I can't get through to Fort Knight."

Percy blinked. "What do you mean?"

"There's no response to my calls, sir," Hardesty said. "They're off the air."

CHAPTER
THIRTY SIX

Penny had tried to interview a handful of people after the lockdown had been announced, but none of them had any real time for her. Ambassador Richardson was out on a hush-hush mission, according to her aide, while Colonel Boone was busy and most of his subordinates were occupied in planning the evacuation. One of them had even gone so far as to threaten her with arrest, if she continued to interrupt their work, and leave her in the fort's jail until she could be evacuated from the planet. In the end, she'd given up and returned to her barracks, where she'd lain down and tried to write another article. But it seemed pointless when there was no way to know what was going on.

Maybe we should have just interviewed each other, she thought, sardonically. *We could have written a set of articles about the lockdown and our reactions to it.*

She sighed as she leaned back on the bed, hearing the sound of another shuttle taking off and clawing for orbit. Her terminal had blinked up a whole string of reminders to book a seat on a shuttle, but she'd steadfastly refused to leave the fort. Percy would have been outraged - she had a feeling *he'd* been the one to put her on the priority list - yet she was definitely not going to leave, just because he said so. Indeed, why would she *want* to leave when she still hadn't got her story? Perhaps she should slip over to the Indian base and join the growing cadre of reporters there...

The entire building shook, violently. Seconds later, she heard the explosion, so loud it had to be far too close to her. She rolled off the bed and hit the floor before her mind had quite caught up with her, then grabbed for her pistol as she heard the sound of pieces of wood crashing to the floor in the distance. The barracks was a strong building, she knew, but could it stand up to a real blast? What had happened? She looked at the wall, just in time to see the picture of her family fall to the ground, then pulled herself to her feet. The terminal went blank, then blinked up an emergency alert, far too late to do any good. In the distance, she could hear the sound of shooting.

She looked up - the building was creaking alarmingly - and then opened the door, clutching her pistol in one hand. The sound of shooting was growing louder, but she knew she didn't dare stay in the barracks. It was evident the building was at risk of collapsing into a pile of rubble. She gritted her teeth - there was a very real risk of being mistaken for a threat and shot by one side or the other - and forced herself to move forward as she heard the sound of more timbers crashing down. Someone screamed in pain and she turned towards them, just in time to see yet another piece of wood falling to the ground. She hesitated, then turned and ran towards the door. It felt as though she was racing against time before the roof caved in on her.

"Get out," a voice shouted at her. "Get out and stay low!"

She ran out of the door, into a whirlwind of confusion. A giant plume of smoke was rising up from the direction of the north wall, where the aliens had built their bazaar; she cursed under her breath as the sound of shooting, also coming from the north wall, grew louder. Flickering lasers stabbed into the sky as mortar shells came crashing towards the fort, only to be intercepted and detonated high overhead. She kept low as a trio of armed Paras ran past her, one of them screaming into his headset. The ground shook as another explosion flared up in the distance, towards the helicopter pad. Had one of the alien shells actually managed to take out a helicopter? She had no way to know.

A hand caught her arm and she almost screamed, then spun around, ready to shoot. A young woman stared back at her in shock, her face pale; it was clear she hadn't been on Earth during the bombardment. It wasn't something Penny would have chosen to live through, if she'd been offered a choice, but it *had* taught her that the world could change and all hell could break loose at any moment. The chaos sweeping through the fort would claim hundreds of lives before the military reasserted control.

The woman gasped for breath, then spoke. "Where do we go?"

"I don't know," Penny said. Percy would have known what to do, or Hamish, but both of them were out somewhere, manning the walls. "Just keep your fucking head down!"

She thought as fast as she could, but drew a blank. None of the emergency plans she'd been briefed on had included a major attack on Fort Knight. They'd always assumed the Vesy would never dare to attack the offworlder base. She winced as she saw another spread of mortar shells wink out of existence overhead, then gritted her teeth as a single shell made it down and slammed into one of the prefabricated buildings. It didn't punch through the armour, but it left a nasty mark and shook up whoever was inside.

A dull clattering noise echoed high overhead as one of the helicopters took off, then swooped down to unleash hell on the attackers. It didn't look very coordinated, Penny thought, but it was hard to tell. She cheered, inwardly, as the incoming fire slacked off, then swore out loud as a single antiaircraft missile rose from somewhere beyond the walls and slammed right into the helicopter, blowing it apart into a billowing fireball. The Indians had given the Vesy antiaircraft weapons? Who else could have given them such weapons? Moments later, the incoming fire resumed, stronger than ever.

The ground shook, once again. She heard a final creaking sound from the barracks and crawled away as fast as possible, moments before the wooden building folded up and collapsed into rubble. A gush of water shot up from where the water tank had been hidden, then faded away as the building died. Penny thought, wistfully, of the photographs she hadn't been able to leave behind on Earth, then pushed the thought aside as another explosion wracked the base. Right now, she had worse problems.

She hesitated as the sound of shooting seemed to grow nearer, then made up her mind and started to crawl on her hands and knees towards the south wall. It seemed to be the safest, although it was impossible to be sure. A shell landed directly on top of the American barracks, blasting through the flimsy wooden roof and exploding inside, smashing the building into a hail of flying

313

debris. Penny hoped, desperately, that most of the inhabitants had managed to get out of the building before it was too late. What were the Vesy *thinking*? They had to know such an attack would provoke a heavy response...

Unless they think the Indians will cover them, she thought, grimly. She was no military expert, but she could count ships. *It makes sense...*

Gritting her teeth, she kept moving, praying they'd survive long enough to see the sunset.

———

There was always a time, Colonel Wilson Boone had learned long ago, when all hell had broken loose, the enemy were carving one's side to ribbons and the situation looked completely irreparable, as if all he could do was cut his losses and retreat. He'd been in them, back during the war and innumerable punitive actions, and he had learned that refusing to panic and maintaining a steady hand could help in regaining control of the situation. But this...he had the nasty feeling that Fort Knight was in deep shit.

"I just got a ping from Carver Outpost," Lieutenant Parry reported. "They're under attack too!"

"Never mind them," Wilson snarled at him. "Can you get me a link to the navy?"

"Working on it," Parry said.

Wilson cursed, vilely. The aliens had done something so simple it wasn't remotely cunning; they'd moved gunpowder up to the walls, hiding it within one of the buildings they'd built to sell supplies and trinkets to the humans, then detonated it before anyone had realised it was there. They'd succeeded, magnificently; the north wall was gone, a number of Paras had died before they'd even known they were under attack and their forces were storming the base. He'd managed to put together a defence line consisting of the reserves and a handful of small detachments from the other powers, but he knew it wouldn't hold for long. The aliens were draining his ammunition at a terrifying rate.

Damn diplomats, he thought. He'd wanted to move the aliens back from the walls, or go with the original plan and move most of their facilities to an island, but the diplomats had refused, pointing out that it would have insulted the aliens. Right now, he found it hard to care. *They left us exposed to attack.*

He pushed the thought aside, angrily. "Get Macintosh to round up as many armed civilians as he can, then start shuffling the rest towards the newer facilities," he ordered. So far, the Vesy hadn't shown any weapons capable of denting either the prefabricated buildings or armoured vehicles, but if the Indians had been mad enough to give them antiaircraft weapons who knew what *else* they might have given them? "Throw the armed civilians together into a scratch group; they're to form our last line of defence."

"Aye, sir," Lieutenant Yawper said.

"Then pull half the troops on the remaining wall back into a QRF," Wilson added. "I want them ready to block the aliens when they punch through the defence line."

He cursed as another red light flared up on his display. The attack had begun twenty minutes after Ambassador Richardson and her party had entered Ivan's City and he doubted that was a coincidence. He'd assumed the aliens would react badly, but he hadn't expected an all-out attack...clearly, the Indians had had a plan to take advantage of the embargo all along. Now, the Royal Marines were screaming for help... and he had nothing to send. Percy Schneider and his section were completely alone.

Shit, he thought, bitterly.

"Captain Yates has the Bulldogs on standby, ready to go," Lieutenant Yawper added.

"Then get them out and around to flank the bastards," Wilson ordered. Maybe they could drive the aliens away from the walls, giving him time to see to his defences. "Order the powered armoured units to back them up. Don't try to drive them through the fort..."

He cursed, again. The civilians had never realised, not really, just how weak the defences actually *were*. Fort Knight should have been built on an island, as per the original plan, not allowed to grow far too close to an alien city. But...

"And tell him watch his ammunition," he added. "We don't know when we will be resupplied."

Penny found herself hugging the ground once again as another hand-ful of shells broke through the defences and detonated within the base. The sound of shooting slacked sharply, then grew louder once again - and closer. She glanced at the girl behind her, then looked up as a handful of aliens came into view. Instinctively, she lifted her pistol and shot the first two, jamming her finger on the trigger time and time again. And then she ran out of bullets...she swore, hastily grabbing for the extra clips Percy had insisted she take, but it was already too late. The aliens charged her, grabbed her, searched her so roughly they left bruises and bleeding cuts all over her body and then tied her hands so tightly behind her back that her wrists began to cramp at once.

She tried to struggle as one of the aliens picked her up, only to be smacked in the face for her pains. Behind her, she heard the other girl cry out as she was subjected to the same treatment, then the alien twisted and started to carry Penny towards the wall. She glanced from side to side, hoping to see Hamish or Percy - she would even have welcomed the overly-officious aide who'd threatened to arrest her - but there was noth-ing, save for ruined buildings and flames licking through the wreckage. They'd driven the Paras back, she realised mutely, and swept up everyone they'd caught as they pushed forward.

Her captor ran faster as he darted through a steaming crater where the north wall had been, then ran through the ruined bazaar and down towards the jungle. Penny heard the sound of engines in the distance and prayed for rescue, but nothing materialised. She wanted to kick, to try to hurt her captor, but she knew it would be futile. All she could do was wait for a chance to break free.

They ran into the jungle, then stopped. Penny barely had a moment to realise what was happening before she was unceremoniously dumped on the ground, next to a handful of other prisoners. Two of them wore military uniforms, but they were so badly injured that Penny rather doubted they would last longer than a few hours, unless they received prompt medical treatment. The others looked to be civilians, including a couple of reporters and an NGO expert on farming Penny recognised. They were all bound

- their captors hastily chained their legs to make it impossible to move quickly - and some of them had been injured. There was no hope of escape.

The implants, Penny thought. She hadn't liked the idea of being implanted - the government would always know where she was, at least until the implant was removed - but it might work out in their favour, if the aliens didn't take them somewhere where the signal could be blocked. They might not know about the implants, but the Indians certainly would. *We might be found, if the base survives the attack...*

She glanced at her fellow captives, trying to assess their condition. The Paras were too badly injured to escape, even if they could move, while some of the civilians were in shock. Penny didn't really blame them. They'd gone from viewing the aliens as primitives ready and willing to welcome the human race's advice on how to live to seeing them as all-powerful captors. The others...Penny tested her bonds and groaned as she realised it was impossible to loosen the knots. She recalled the slaves she'd seen in alien fields and shuddered. The aliens had no shortage of practice in keeping people under control - and in bondage.

We're fucked, she thought, tiredly. *And if the military comes after us, we might be killed in the crossfire.*

———

Corporal Danny Hawkins rather liked the Bulldog, although he knew he was in the minority between people who preferred a full-scale Churchill tank and those who liked the lighter Hanover armoured car. It struck him as the ideal compromise between an ATV, which could go anywhere, and a tank, which might sink in the mud or become trapped in a canal. God knew he'd been on exercises, before he'd been seconded to 3 Para, where some luckless tankers had discovered the hard way that their vehicles might be largely invulnerable, but they were alarmingly easy to get stuck.

He smirked to himself as the Bulldog emerged from the south gate... and then felt his smile grow wider as bullets started to ping off the hull. It was possible, Captain Yates had shouted as they'd hurried to get the Bulldogs up and out of the fort, that the enemy had something that could penetrate their armour, but so far nothing had materialised. He gunned the engine and drove forward anyway, pushing into the bullets like a man might walk into a blizzard. The Vesy were standing there, shooting at him; they didn't really seem to understand the dangers facing them.

"Weapons locked," the gunner said.

"Give them hell," Danny ordered.

The Bulldog's machine guns fired once, sweeping bullets across the Vesy formation. Danny watched the aliens literally disintegrate as the bullets tore through them, ripping their bodies to bloody chunks. The incoming fire slacked off sharply, allowing Danny a chance to move out and around the fort. Most of the alien buildings assembled near Fort Knight were rubble now, either through the fort's return fire or through battles between the different alien factions. It was quite likely, Danny had been told, that some of the aliens might oppose the first group of aliens. But how was he meant to tell the difference?

Something smashed against the hull. Moments later, flames cascaded over the transparent window before fading away. Somehow, either by themselves or with Indian advice, the aliens had reinvented the Molotov Cocktail. It would have been a hazard to earlier vehicles, Danny knew, but it was such a common threat that the Bulldog was armed against flames and gas as well as bullets. More bottles crashed down around the advancing vehicles, only to be smashed uselessly against their armour.

"Got another team of aliens coming into view," the gunner said.

"Take them out," Danny ordered. There was less room to manoeuvre now they were pressing through the alien settlement. The flanking teams had spread out to try to prevent the aliens from sneaking up through the jungle. "I…"

He broke off as he saw the antitank missile being launched. The Indians had given the aliens antitank weapons…he swore out loud, then hastily reversed course as the gunner opened fire, wiping the team out of existence. But it was already too late.

The missile punched through the Bulldog's armour and detonated inside the hull. There were no survivors.

CHAPTER
THIRTY SEVEN

John had been half-asleep when the attack began, dreaming of the last moment he'd seen Colin alive. They'd both known the risks when they'd started flying starfighters, but neither of them had truly believed they could die. Or, if so, they would die together...

He jerked awake as the alarms sounded, bringing the ship to red alert. "Red alert," Howard said, his voice echoing through the cabin. "I say again, red alert! Captain to the bridge!"

John grabbed for his jacket as he rolled out of bed, then pulled it over his head and raced towards the hatch. It opened, allowing him to step into the corridor and then straight onto the bridge. The display glowed like a Christmas tree, showing dozens of red icons on the planet's surface. There didn't seem to be any orbital threat, but the Indian ships were clearly coming alive and preparing for action.

"Report," he snapped, taking his command chair.

"Multiple attacks on the planet's surface," Howard reported. "The situation is confused, sir, but Fort Knight is under attack, the Ambassador's party bleeped a distress signal and troops are pouring over the border from the Flowered Clan. Many outposts are under attack too; British, American, French...everyone, but the Indians and their allies."

They couldn't have put this together after they knew of the embargo, John thought. He wasn't a ground-pounder, but he'd worked with enough logistics headaches to know that putting together a coordinated attack on the fly wasn't easy. *They must have had this planned in advance, then moved it up to coincide with the attack on the Ambassador.*

"Clear the decks for action," he ordered, thinking hard. The Indians weren't doing anything *threatening*, but it was impossible to ignore their presence. "Can you get a tight-beam link to Fort Knight?"

"Negative, sir," Gillian said. "I think the transmitter on the ground must have been sabotaged or taken out in the first assault. There's no jamming, just no response."

The Vesy couldn't have done that for themselves, John thought, as he peered at the images from orbiting satellites. *Their allies must have helped them…hell, they provided the weapons and other equipment.*

He scowled. The Indians had created a major headache. If he intervened by dropping KEWs, the Indians would be obliged - by the treaty they'd signed - to come to the defence of their allies. The fact that the Flowered Clan had *started* the war would go by the wayside, John was sure, all the more so as no one inclined to disagree with the Indian point of view would survive. But he couldn't leave his people stranded on the surface…the evacuation had moved several hundred civilians to the freighters, but there were hundreds more trapped in Fort Knight.

And even if we could drop KEWs, we might have some real problems separating the good guys from the bad guys, he added, mentally. *We might wind up killing more of our own people than the Flowered Clan.*

"Continue to monitor the situation," he ordered, tersely. "Can you link to the Ambassador's party?"

"No, sir," Gillian said. "But Lieutenant Schneider transmitted a distress call before Fort Knight came under attack."

John cursed. *This* time, there would be no helicopters coming to the rescue. Percy Schneider and his force would be trapped, unable to fight their way out of the city or hole up and wait for rescue. The Vesy would dig them out, then murder them. And, by their standards, they had a very good cause. They *had* been betrayed by their allies.

But there *was* another option. "Major Hadfield," he said. "Can you and your company prepare for a drop into Ivan's City?"

"Aye, sir," Hadfield said. "We can get Percy and his team out, but escaping afterwards might be problematic."

"We can have the shuttles primed to pick you up once you escape the city," John said. It wasn't the best plan, but it was the only one he had. "In your suits, you should be largely invincible."

"Unless the Indians gave the aliens plasma guns," Hadfield pointed out. He sighed. "We'll be ready for the drop in five minutes."

"Acknowledged," John said. He closed the channel, then looked at Gillian. "Contact the destroyers. Inform them that I want them to be ready to drop their marines into Fort Knight, should the situation merit it."

"Aye, sir," Gillian said.

John nodded, reluctantly. He didn't dare send troops until he knew just what was going on - and if there was anything left worth salvaging. It didn't seem likely that Fort Knight was completely overrun, but the aliens had soundly hammered the defences, based on what he could see from high overhead. He needed to speak to Colonel Boone or someone else in authority before he committed himself...

"Captain," Gillian said. "I'm picking up a message from the Indian base. It's addressed to you personally."

John sucked in his breath, then nodded. "Put it through," he ordered. "Now."

"Captain," Ambassador Rani Begum said. Her dark face crinkled into a smile. "A pleasure to speak to you at last."

"I'm not feeling particularly diplomatic right now, Ambassador," John said, tightly. "Fort Knight is under attack and Ambassador Richardson is in grave danger."

"We know," Rani said. She gave him a wide-eyed look of innocence that was so exaggerated John *knew* it had to be manipulation. "We have been asked to pass on a message from our allies, the Flowered Clan."

"Your allies have launched an unprovoked attack and are butchering my people," John snapped. "You will excuse me, I'm sure, if I don't regard them very kindly."

Rani shrugged, her mask dropping just long enough for John to see a cool and calculating personality under the smile. "City One, the city you call Ivan's City, has formally asked for membership in the Flowered Clan," she stated. "The Flowered Clan has seen fit to accept the application. As part of the terms of membership, the original agreement that allowed you to build Fort Knight on their soil has been cancelled. They would like you to remove the base at once, without further ado."

John barked down a laugh. "That would be a great deal easier," he said, "if the base wasn't under heavy attack."

"They are prepared to offer a ceasefire on the understanding that you will withdraw all presence from the surface within twenty-four hours," Rani said, smoothly. "You would be able to save the rest of your people without trouble, Captain."

"I would be prepared to agree to a ceasefire in place," John hedged. "But I couldn't agree to withdraw completely from Vesy, Ambassador. Fort Knight is arguably not part of Ivan's City."

Rani's face hardened. "Let me be blunt, Captain," she said. "Your former allies have deserted you. They were betrayed and now they have betrayed you in turn. You have the choice between accepting my offer, which will allow you to save the rest of your people, or fighting it out on the ground with the Vesy. I will not permit you to intervene from orbit, as per our agreement with the Flowered Clan."

Her voice softened, slightly. "I don't expect you to concede anything, Captain," she added, solemnly. "It wasn't our intention to find ourselves backing an all-out assault on your positions. The diplomats on Earth can sort it out over the coming months. Get your people out, keep them safe… leave the rest to your superiors."

John thought rapidly. On the face of it, her offer was tempting…all the more so as the *Indian* version of the story would put all the blame for the crisis on Britain. He wasn't authorised to make deals on Britain's behalf, so - on the face of it - abandoning Fort Knight wouldn't be a problem. But the diplomats would see it as surrendering any remaining claims Britain had to Vesy.

"I'm sending marines to recover the Ambassador," he said, finally. "And if you try to intervene, it will be considered an act of war. We can determine the status of Fort Knight later."

He closed the channel, then looked at Gillian. "Anything from the surface?"

"Got a low-powered laser link," Gillian said. "Colonel Boone reports that the base has taken heavy damage, but he thinks he's on top of the situation now."

"Then drop the marines," John ordered. It was a gamble - the Indians might fire on the shuttles, or the Vesy might have antiaircraft weapons in place to protect Ivan's City - but there was no choice. "And then contact the freighters. I want every shuttle they have prepped and ready to go to evacuate Fort Knight."

Howard blinked. "Sir?"

"The base has become indefensible," John said. If they'd been able to use KEWs, he could have swept the surroundings clear of alien life, but the Indians would certainly interfere. It might not be wise, diplomatically speaking, to accept the Indian-backed ceasefire, yet he knew they couldn't hold the base, not any longer. "And Gillian?"

"Yes, sir?"

"Keep sending updates through the relay network," he added. "I want everyone to know what happened here."

———

Percy swore under his breath as a group of armed Vesy appeared, pouring down from a stairwell that should have led up to safety. He launched a grenade into their midst, blew them into bloody chunks and then swore again as a hail of fire poured down from further up the stairwell. The aliens had them neatly pinned down, unable to go up...

"We'll have to go down," he said. It was going to be a nightmare - there was no way they could hope to pass unnoticed in the alien city - but he saw no other choice. If no one was coming to get them - and they hadn't been able to raise either Fort Knight or the Bulldogs - staying where they were was suicide. "Sergeant, stay at the back; if anything happens to me you're in charge."

"Aye, sir," Peerce said.

Percy glanced at his men, then silently calculated their remaining ammunition supply in his head. It didn't look good, no matter how he ran the figures; they were likely to burn up their ammunition at a frightening rate, then get overrun by thousands of angry aliens. Ivan's death underlined just how badly the situation had fallen apart. If he was dead, the next ruler of the city would definitely not be pro-British.

"Keep trying to raise someone - anyone," he added. If Fort Knight was off the air…it spelled trouble, he was sure. There was no jamming, nothing that should have impeded the signals; the Bulldogs should have responded, even if Fort Knight hadn't. And that meant they'd walked right into an ambush. "Let's go."

He hefted his rifle and stepped forward, slipping past the blood and gore and down the corridor. Behind him, three Marines followed, weapons at the ready; behind *them*, two more half-carried the ambassador. The Sergeant and his men brought up the rear. Percy glanced into the first room, firmly resisting the urge to throw a grenade in first, then relaxed very slightly as he saw nothing. The room was empty, the walls carved with strange symbols that meant nothing to him. Perhaps, one day, he'd have a chance to work out what they really meant.

Unless they mean something like DEATH TO HUMANITY, he thought, as they inched down towards the next room. He'd served in places where threatening messages were written everywhere, from promising great victories against the punitive forces to threatening anyone who dared even consider collaborating with a toughly unpleasant and graphic fate. *The Vesy might have the same tradition of night letters.*

The next room was barren, completely. There were no carvings on the walls, nothing to draw his attention. He puzzled over it for a long moment, then led the way on to the next, slightly surprised that the Vesy hadn't mounted a counterattack yet. Had they assumed the humans would always go up and massed their forces accordingly? Or had they refrained from involving the entire city in the plot? There was no way to know.

He froze as he heard the sound of someone running towards them, then carefully hefted his rifle as a small alien came into view. Too small… it was clearly a child, wearing nothing more than a loincloth. Percy levelled his rifle, then hesitated as the alien came to a halt and then turned to flee back down the corridor. He'd been warned, more than once, that children could be turned into unwitting suicide bombers, but he didn't have it in him to shoot a child, not even an *alien* child. He just hoped the youngster - he hadn't been able to tell if it was a boy or a girl - wouldn't tell everyone about their presence.

And what would you do, his own thoughts mocked him, *if you knew he would?*

They kept moving faster now, moving past a set of rooms that seemed to have no logical purpose. Percy gave up puzzling over them as they moved closer and closer to the door, then froze again as he heard a force of aliens right in front of him. He lifted his rifle as the aliens came into view, carrying a handful of primitive swords and spears. If the Marines had been wearing their armour, he knew all too well, the aliens wouldn't have been any sort of threat. They could just have used powered muscles to push the aliens aside, breaking bones in passing…but they weren't. He cursed the diplomats under his breath, then opened fire. The aliens seemed to stagger to a halt as the front rows collapsed into bloody chunks, but the middle rows were pushed on by the aliens at the rear. He'd seen it happen before during urban combat training…

"This way, sir," Peerce called.

Percy glanced back, saw a door and motioned his men through it. He unhooked a grenade, threw it towards the mob and then ran after the Sergeant, slamming the door firmly closed behind him. The grenade detonated moments later, shaking the door badly, but it wasn't enough to discourage the mob. They started hammering on the door as soon as they recovered from the brief shock.

"Sir," Peerce said, a faint note of amusement in his voice, "I think we've just walked into the harem."

"Oh," Percy said.

He looked away from the door…and saw the aliens staring back at him, clearly wondering what they were. If he hadn't known what to look for, he would never had recognised the aliens as female; they looked practically identical to the males. Behind them, a handful of gelded males observed the humans with listless eyes. The scars he could see between their legs made him feel sick. Who would willingly agree to have their manhood chopped off - worse, for a Vesy - just so they could serve as a harem guard?

Maybe they were prisoners, he thought. The medics had speculated that the aliens lost the will to do anything, but follow orders if they were gelded. Indeed, most of the slaves he'd seen had been castrated before they were put to work in the fields. *Or maybe they saw it as their only chance of a secure place to live and work.*

He pushed down his rising gorge, then looked at one of the gelded aliens. "Is there another way out of here?"

The aliens eyed him, but said nothing. Percy repeated his words, making it a clear order, yet they still showed no response. He even threatened them with his rifle, but they did nothing. It didn't seem as though they cared if they lived or died.

"They may not understand you," Peerce said. "I don't think..."

One of the alien females rose and pointed a clawed hand towards a second door, set within the stone. Percy stared at her, nodded his thanks and then hastily led his men through the door, into another set of twisting corridors. By his estimate, there should be a way out, back into the city, if they walked around the harem. They moved rapidly down the corridor, weapons at the ready, and then came face to face with a bunch of alien guards. Percy gunned them down, cursing out loud. The noise from the brief one-sided fight would bring a whole host of other aliens.

"Shit," Peerce said. "Incoming, sir."

Percy looked back. Waves of aliens had charged through the harem and were running towards them, weapons in hand. There were too many of them...

"Use the gas grenades," he ordered. He'd brought them because the medics had speculated they would have a nasty effect on the aliens, but no one knew for sure. "Now!"

Peerce nodded, then unhooked one of the grenades and threw it towards the aliens. It detonated, spewing coloured gas everywhere. Percy watched, then smiled as the aliens staggered backwards, the mob coming to a halt as more and more of its members began to retch. The grenades weren't pleasant for humans, not by any definition of the word, but for the aliens, with their powerful sense of smell, they had to be an absolute nightmare. Percy took a moment to watch, then motioned for the marines to follow him. They weren't out of the nightmare yet.

His radio buzzed. "Percy? This is Hadfield."

"Captain," Percy said. He unhooked a second gas grenade and threw it as they stepped through the door and into the open air. "You have no idea how pleased I am to hear from you."

"Us too," Hadfield said. "We're inbound and armoured; coming down hard. All hell's broken loose."

"Tell me about it," Percy said. He watched the aliens retching, then cursed as he saw a new line of alien solders, well away from the gas. Two of them looked to be carrying primitive RPGs. "It isn't very pleasant here, either."

CHAPTER
THIRTY EIGHT

"The marines are jumping now," Gillian said.

John nodded. "Keep me informed," he ordered. There was no point in trying to micromanage from orbit, even if Hadfield had been inclined to allow him to try. "Let me know when they're ready for pickup."

"Aye, sir," Gillian said.

"Captain," Tara said. "A number of freighters are leaving orbit!"

John glanced at the display, then swore under his breath. Most of the ships breaking orbit and abandoning Vesy were civilian, but a couple belonged to various national merchant marines. He'd hoped to use them to transport refugees away from the surface, before they'd started to run. But even if he'd had the authority to stop them, he rather doubted they'd listen. With Fort Knight under attack and a giant Indian fleet in orbit, it looked as though their commanders had chosen not to run the risk of being caught in a war zone.

"Damn," he muttered. There was nothing else he could do. "Copy our records to them before they jump out through the tramline, just in case."

"Aye, sir," Gillian said.

———

Percy fought the urge to let out an unprofessional cry of delight as armoured marines plummeted from the skies, landing all around him and opening fire with plasma weapons on alien targets. The shuttles roared high overhead, launching missiles towards a handful of makeshift weapons emplacements, then turned and flew off to the south. He felt a hint of wistfulness at their departure, then pulled himself up and saluted as Hadfield landed in front of him.

"Lieutenant," Hadfield said. "Report!"

"Four men injured, but no one dead," Percy said. He glanced at Ambassador Richardson, still stumbling between two marines, and winced. "Ammunition frighteningly low. And one Ambassador in shock."

"Got it," Hadfield said. "Follow us. We'll cover you."

Percy nodded, then covered his eyes as the armoured marines opened fire again, spraying plasma bolts towards their targets. Most of the Vesy in view fled, trying to escape the hellish weapons; it was clear, he reasoned, that the Indians hadn't introduced them to *those*. It did make a certain kind of sense, he told himself. Plasma weapons could burn through armoured combat suits and the Indians might want to keep those in reserve.

He took a moment to check the Ambassador and swore, inwardly. She was remaining upright, somehow, but she was shaking so badly that he knew she needed medical attention. No matter where she'd been, she'd never been in the midst of a war zone, let alone forced to hide behind armed guards as they fought their way out of the trap. Percy felt a stab of sympathy, then turned to follow Hadfield as the marines made their escape. The resistance slacked sharply as they moved towards the gates, as if the Vesy were prepared to just let them go. Percy didn't blame them. They had nothing that could do more than dent the armoured suits.

They'll pay a price for what they did here, he thought, as they inched down the empty streets, watching for traps. Hundreds of bodies lay everywhere, including some that looked to have been killed by alien weapons. Not all of Ivan's faction had accepted their removal from power gracefully, he suspected. *But with Ivan dead, who's going to hold this city together?*

His headset buzzed. "Got a major troop movement crossing the border and coming towards the city," a voice said. "They're advancing at quite a clip too."

The joys of not being loaded down with more crap than a toilet cleaner, the irrelevant side of Percy's mind noted. Alien soldiers had one advantage, at least, over their human counterparts; their logistics were considerably easier. They only carried weapons, ammunition and a small pack of food. In the long term, they would have to develop Roman-style logistics - an army would rapidly eat its unwilling hosts out of house and home - but for the moment it gave them a definite edge. *How long until they're at the city?*

He frowned as he saw the gates; abandoned, but sealed tightly shut. Hadfield barked orders and five armoured marines walked forward and pressed their weight against the stone. There was a long pause, then the gates fell outwards, smashing to the ground with a deafening sound. The aliens would find that intimidating, Percy hoped, as the marines advanced forward, weapons at the ready. He swore bitterly as he realised the Bulldogs were nothing more than burning wreckage, their crews either dead or taken prisoner. Ivan had to have been in on the ambush all along.

"Check the Bulldogs," Hadfield ordered. "How many men did you leave with them?"

"Two each," Percy said. It was standard procedure; he'd seen no reason to change it. Two men in each vehicle should have been more than enough to stand off any reasonable threat, or simply move away and outrun it. "They were drawn from the Para supporting units."

He gritted his teeth, then peered into the wreckage. The faint stench of burning flesh rose to his nostrils - he had to force himself not to be violently sick - but the bodies were completely gone, unsurprisingly. Modern antitank weapons - nothing less could have smashed the vehicles so effortlessly - punched through the hull, then detonated inside. The bodies would have been reduced to atoms. He checked the other vehicles, but found nothing. There was no way they could take their bodies back home.

"There's nothing to salvage, sir," he reported. "Sergeant?"

"I concur," Peerce said. He sounded distant, as if he was replaying what had happened over and over again, looking for a way they could have changed things. Eight men were dead, eight men who'd served beside the marines. They'd deserved better than to die in a treacherous attack. "The Bulldogs are completely beyond repair."

"Then we leave them," Hadfield said. He glanced back as the sound of shooting broke out again, back in the city. "The Flowered Clan isn't *that* far away."

"We could engage them," Percy suggested. "They won't have anything that could harm the suits..."

"We have orders to avoid engagement, if possible," Hadfield said. He turned and led the way towards the fields. "Follow me."

The Ambassador groaned and slumped to the ground. Her escorts caught her before she could collapse completely, then exchanged glances with Percy. Percy sighed, stepped forward and hefted the Ambassador over his shoulder in a fireman's carry, then followed Hadfield. Behind him, a handful of armoured marines brought up the rear, watching for signs of attack.

Poor girl, he thought, even though the ambassador was at least a decade older than him. *She shouldn't have been caught in this position.*

He gritted his teeth as he fought to pick up speed. Ivan had betrayed them and that hurt; he'd liked the alien and he'd thought the feeling was mutual. But Ivan had always been fixated on defending his people, no matter how much he liked his British allies. Once the British had abandoned him, he'd had no choice but to seek the best terms he could from the Flowered Clan. And if that had meant luring a British party into an ambush...

Maybe he got sloppy deliberately, he thought. The alien ambush hadn't been *bad* - it was clear Ivan had hoped to take hostages, rather than killing them all in the first few seconds - but it had failed. *Maybe he wanted to give us a chance to escape.*

He shook his head, then glanced up as the shuttles roared overhead and then started to descend towards the fields. Percy checked around out of habit, but there were no aliens in view; he jogged towards the shuttles as soon as they landed, letting out a sigh of relief when he saw the medics emerging from the craft. He carefully unslung the Ambassador, then placed her gently on the ground. One of the medics bent over her while the others attended to the wounded marines.

"She's in deep shock," the medic said, pressing an injector to her neck. "She needs rest, really. Hopefully, she won't turn into a zombie."

Percy shivered. He'd seen zombies in the refugee camps, men and women who had been so badly traumatised by the bombardment that they'd effectively checked out of life and just shuffled around like zombies.

Most of them had died, unable to recognise that they needed to take steps to save their lives; others had wound up in rape camps or simply murdered by other refugees. There had been no way they could all be helped, then guided back to the mundane world. Resources had been very limited.

"I'm sure she won't," he said. He didn't know the Ambassador very well, but he had to admit she had nerve. "You'll give her some proper treatment, right?"

"Of course," the medic said.

"Percy," Hadfield said. "The wounded will go straight back to orbit. You and the rest of your men will accompany us back to Fort Knight."

"Aye, sir," Percy said.

"Reload on the shuttle," Hadfield added. "You will need more ammunition."

———

"They made it out of the trap, General," Lieutenant Ravi reported.

Anjeet nodded. In truth, he'd been fairly sure the Vesy wouldn't be able to keep the British Ambassador and her guards as hostages, although it had been worth the gamble to see if they *could*. The real purpose of the exercise had been to separate the ambassador from Fort Knight and, in addition, to underline to the British that they could no longer count on their alien allies. It would only add strength to those among the British ranks urging an immediate withdrawal from the system.

"Good for them," he said. He'd always admired the Royal Marines, even though he'd known he'd meet them as enemies one day. "Keep a sharp eye on their progress, but take no steps to intervene without my direct order."

"Aye, sir," Ravi said.

"General," Rani Begum said. "Did their ambassador survive?"

"So it would seem," Anjeet said. "Losing her would have been embarrassing, no?"

Rani shrugged. "Yes," she said. "I liked her enough not to want to see her dead."

Anjeet suspected she meant something entirely different. Rani was, after all, a woman in a society that was still largely male-dominated. She wouldn't have reached her post through sentimentality and warm sisterly feeling for other women. But there was a different concern, one that would be uppermost in her mind. Killing ambassadors would set a dangerous precedent - *had* set a dangerous precedent, back in the Age of Unrest. The gods alone knew how much blood had been spilled reiterating the lesson that, no matter the cause of one's upset, ambassadors and embassies were untouchable. He smiled at the double meaning, which would only really make sense to a Hindu, then dismissed the thought. The Vesy weren't human. No one truly expected them to play by human rules.

"Keep encouraging the other freighters to leave, Ambassador," he said, instead. "They need to understand this is our world now."

———

"Shit," Peerce said, as Fort Knight came into view. "It's a wreck."

Percy nodded in agreement, feeling a bitter pang of frustration. He'd organised the construction of the original fort, then watched as it grew larger and larger, accommodating parties from all over the Human Sphere. Now, the north wall was a shattered ruin, most of the barracks were on fire and the alien community that had grown up beyond the walls was a torn mess. The wreckage of a helicopter, burning brightly on the ground, bore mute witness to the inadequacy of their defence planning. How long had it been, he asked himself, since all hell had broken loose? It felt like they'd been fighting for hours.

Alarms sounded. The shuttle rocked violently from side to side; Percy cursed, grabbing hold of the railing and praying under his breath. If an antiaircraft missile struck the shuttle, they were doomed. He had no armour, no way to survive the fall even if the blast didn't kill him...

The shuttle rocked again, then plummeted towards the ground. Percy braced himself, an instant before the craft touched down with an impact hard enough to rattle him. He forced himself to his feet as the hatch opened, then followed the armoured marines out into the open air. The stench of burning flesh and wood greeted him as he lifted his rifle, his section forming up around him. Fort Knight was in so much confusion that he honestly had no idea where to begin.

"Percy, take your section to the south and link up with the Paras guarding the prefabricated buildings," Hadfield ordered. "Any Vesy within the walls are to be regarded as hostile; I say again, any Vesy within the walls are to be regarded as hostile."

Percy shuddered. How many Vesy had gone in and out of the base since it had opened for business? The NGOs, the religious factions… they'd all invited the aliens into the base, showing them the wonders and glories of human civilisation. And the aliens had used that knowledge to precisely target their attack. How much of it, Percy asked himself bitterly, was *his* fault? If he'd taken a tougher line with the aliens, he wondered, would they have dared to attack Fort Knight?

Of course things would have been different, he thought, sourly. *They'd have attacked and wiped out the last human presence on their world before we received any further word from Earth.*

He gritted his teeth, then led the way through a gash in the walls and into Fort Knight. The barracks the aliens had built, the barracks that had housed the reporters - including Penny - were nothing more than piles of debris. He shuddered as he saw a body, half-trapped under pieces of falling wood, then cursed as he realised the man was far beyond salvation. The face, by some dark miracle, was untouched, but Percy didn't know him. He took one final look at the body, then pressed on, lifting his rifle as he heard the sound of shots ringing out ahead of him. Moments later, they came face-to-face with a pair of armed Vesy.

Percy levelled his weapon and shot the first one through the chest; the second fell to Peerce's shot, right through the head. He took a moment to inspect the bodies, then walked on, leaving the Vesy behind. There was no point in picking up the bodies now, not when they had a mission to do. He kept a sharp eye out for Penny as they rounded a corner and saw a set of burned bodies lying on the ground, but they were completely unrecognisable. DNA analysis would be the only way to identify them, after the bullets had stopped flying.

He allowed himself a sigh of relief as the prefabricated buildings came into view, guarded by a number of Paras who'd hastily dug themselves foxholes and prepared for a long siege. Their positions were surrounded by a number of dead Vesy, who'd clearly tried to charge their enemies only to run into vastly superior firepower. Percy felt a glimmer of pride, mixed with sadness, then walked forward, careful to keep his hands in view. The Para in command stood up and waved back.

"Lieutenant Schneider, reporting as ordered," Percy said. There were only five Paras in the line, two badly wounded. "Where do you want us?"

"We're still holding this line," the Para said. He sounded tired, but proud. "The CO thinks the attack is slacking off. What's your ammo like?"

"Got reloads in the shuttle," Percy said. He keyed his radio. "Captain, we've linked up with the Paras."

"Remain there while we sweep the base," Hadfield ordered, coolly. "We'll link up with you afterwards."

Percy nodded, then dove into the foxhole as he heard the sound of incoming mortar fire. The aliens might have realised they weren't going to win, but that hadn't discouraged them from pressing the offensive anyway, even though it was pointless. Or perhaps it wasn't pointless, he thought; there weren't that many British troops on the planet, making every soldier killed or wounded at Fort Knight one the Flowered Clan wouldn't have to face later. The ground shook as the shells landed, then shook again as one of the shuttles launched a spread of missiles towards the mortar post. A hail of explosions billowed up in the jungle, silencing the gunners before they could launch another shell. Or so he hoped.

Standard procedure is to fire one shell, then relocate and fire again, he thought. *Did the Indians teach the Vesy to do that?*

Slowly, very slowly, the fighting died away as the last of the infiltrators were rooted out and killed. Percy found him and his men assigned to patrolling the outer edge of the walls, then pulling bodies out of the wreckage as the surviving civilians were urged towards the shuttles and dispatched to orbit. There were no shortage of bodies; indeed, he had a sneaking suspicion that they would all have to be buried on Vesy, rather than transhipped back to Earth. Or stored until a special freighter convoy could be arranged.

"Take some rest," Hadfield ordered, after what felt like hours. "But make sure you sleep with your weapons."

Percy was too tired to make the obvious joke. "Sir," he said. "Have you seen anything of Penny? My sister?"

Hadfield shook his head. "She's not on the list of known dead or people transported to orbit," he said. He sounded too tired to try to offer any real reassurance. "But she could be buried under the rubble somewhere and we'd never know until we started digging into the wreckage."

"I know, sir," Percy said. Penny had nerve, no doubt about it. She'd been so determined to win her story that she'd stayed on the base until it was far too late. He should have forced her to leave…but how? He wasn't her boss, nor was he in command of the base. "But…"

He shook his head. "I'm sorry, sir," he said. "I…"

"Don't worry about it," Hadfield said. "Just get some bloody rest. You need it."

CHAPTER
THIRTY NINE

"She deserved better," Grace Scott said.

John eyed her sharply. They stood together in *Warspite's* sickbay, looking down at the sleeping body of Ambassador Joelle Richardson. The doctor had prescribed rest and relaxation for the ambassador and told them that she would be kept under for at least another couple of days, long enough for the shock to wear off. John knew better than to try to argue with the doctor. He still owed the man his regular check-up.

"She will recover," he said. Shock could be nasty - he'd seen people stumbling around like drunkards after being badly shocked - but the ambassador was tougher than she looked. "I have no doubt of it."

Grace said nothing as they walked back through the corridors and into John's office. John took advantage of the quiet to study her, wondering just what was going through her mind. She'd been an idealist, of sorts, when they'd first met; she'd even taken him to task for daring to consider the Vesy as anything other than human. But since then, she'd learned hard lessons. The Vesy simply *weren't* human and couldn't be judged by human standards.

Not that that would stop people trying, he thought. The steward brought them both mugs of coffee, which he sipped gratefully as he glanced at the latest updates from the surface. *If they're prepared to try to judge the Tadpoles by human standards, why not the Vesy?*

He sighed, inwardly. Seven hours after the attack had begun, Fort Knight was still being sniped or mortared, while most of the outposts were simply gone. There was no way to know what had happened; hell, he didn't even have the manpower to send recon missions to the bases to see if there were any survivors. The Indians had been loudly offering to do just that, citing their ties to the Flowered Clan; a handful of minor diplomatic representatives had agreed, despite the risk. John ground his teeth in bitter frustration, then concentrated on his coffee. It was just a shame the steward hadn't put something stronger than coffee grains into the machine before making the drink.

"Ambassador Richardson is currently...out of commission," Grace said, once she'd drunk her coffee. "I believe that puts me in command of the mission."

John considered it for a moment. Grace was right, technically, but the appointment was something of a poisoned chalice, under the circumstances. Besides, Ambassador Richardson had never commanded the military side of the mission. His orders were purposefully vague over just how much he was obliged to listen to her, let alone follow her lead. But then, he'd seen enough of the inner workings of the Admiralty to know that if he'd failed, he would be blamed for misunderstanding or outright disobeying his orders. Admiral Soskice was just waiting for the chance to stick a knife in his back.

Life was so much simpler, he thought, *when we only had to worry about the enemy in front of us.*

He pushed the thought aside, then nodded. "You have certain limited powers, yes," he said, flatly. "I don't believe that *all* Ambassador Richardson's powers devolved on you."

Grace shrugged. "I believe the mission has failed," she said. "Fort Knight is a ruin, the outposts are gone and hundreds of people are dead. Would you disagree with this assessment?"

The Indians have us in check, John thought. The Vesy-UN was deader than the alien leader who'd trusted the British Government to keep its word. He suspected the demand that the British evacuate Fort Knight would be backed up by the Indians, sooner rather than later. *But they have to know there will be consequences for this.*

"Provisionally, I will agree that the mission has hit a major snag," he said. "I don't think we've lost yet, just..."

"I do," Grace said. Her voice rose, sharply. "We have stumbled from disaster to disaster, Captain. Our influence with the aliens has fallen to the point they're prepared to take the risk of waging war on us. The Indians have outsmarted us right down the line. It's time to pull out and rethink our approach. Let the Indians have the planet if they want it so much!"

John eyed her, sharply. "Are you suggesting we cut our losses and abandon the planet?"

Hypocrite, his own thoughts mocked him. *Wasn't that what you wanted to do?*

He ground his teeth. *I wanted to remove the civilians*, he told himself. *Too many people were caught in the middle for us to risk pushing matters.*

"Yes," Grace said. "The only things of real interest here are the tramlines and…well, we can agree to abide by the *Indian* proposal of free navigation."

"The Prime Minister might have other ideas," John said. He knew word was already heading back to Earth, but it would be at least a fortnight before a response reached them, if it was relayed up the chain. A physical message would take a great deal longer. "Shouldn't we wait for orders?"

"There's nothing we can do here, save for serving as a punching bag," Grace snapped. "I can only advise that we leave, then have a rethink."

John scowled. The hell of it was that she had a point. Fort Knight was vulnerable, with most of its population heading to orbit; the outposts were gone. Worse, the Flowered Clan was steadily absorbing the alliance of cities Ivan had painstakingly built, then lost when the British Government had betrayed him. Colonel Boone might be able to dominate the surrounding territory, but only until he ran out of ammunition. The fort's stockpiles were already dangerously low.

And they just have to keep wearing away at us until we collapse, John thought. *The Indians have created a situation where the only rational choice is to concede defeat and abandon the planet.*

He sighed, inwardly. It wouldn't go down well on Earth. The last count claimed that over three hundred British soldiers and civilians were dead, along with at least fifty-seven foreigners. God alone knew how many people had died in the various outposts. If a number hadn't been evacuated just before the shit hit the fan, it would be a great deal worse. And quite a few humans remained completely unaccounted for. No matter what excuses the Indians offered, it might well mean war.

"We need to finish locating the missing - or the dead," he said. "Miss Scott…"

Grace shook her head. "We don't have the time," she said. "Captain, in my post as current head of the ambassadorial party, I am ordering you to withdraw everyone to orbit and then return to Earth."

John gave her a long considering look. "Do you have the authority to issue such an order?"

"I believe I do," Grace said. "We leave the planet, salvaging what we can, and then sort out what to do next."

Like finding ways to punish the Indians for this, John thought. *Get the civilians out of the zone, then start putting together a coalition to sanction the Indians…*

"Very well," he said. "But I hope Ambassador Richardson will understand when she wakes."

He keyed his wristcom. "Mr. Howard," he ordered. "Contact Colonel Boone and inform him that he is to evacuate the remainder of Fort Knight. I say again, that he is to evacuate Fort Knight. I want every last one of our remaining personnel off the surface as quickly as possible."

He scowled. "You do realise that a number of our personal may have been taken hostage?"

Grace blinked. "I thought we'd all been implanted," she said, rubbing her upper arm. "Travis told me that we could be found, if we were kidnapped…"

"Yes," John said. He met her eyes. "And those transmitters would still be working, even if the people carrying them were dead. We should be able to locate their bodies, but we can't."

"And so you think the aliens have them," Grace said. She stared down at her hands. "I can speak to the Indians…"

"Better make it convincing," John said, tiredly. The Vesy had nothing capable of blocking the implant signals, unless they took the prisoners so deep underground that they were surrounded by miles of solid rock. But the Indians could easily put together a jammer, if they wanted to help the aliens take hostages. "They won't want to commit themselves to anything."

———

Percy jerked awake as Peerce shook him. "Sergeant?"

"We've just received orders from the Colonel," Peerce said. "We are to transport everyone back to orbit at once, then shut down Fort Knight. We're leaving the planet."

"Shit," Percy said. He wasn't too surprised at closing down Fort Knight - the base's defences were ruined, providing an excellent excuse for moving operations elsewhere - but abandoning the planet? The Indians would take the entire world, if they cared to. "What about the missing?"

"Still missing," Peerce said, sympathetically. "There's nothing we can do."

Percy cursed under his breath as they stumbled outside, then grabbed for his terminal and checked the records. Everyone who'd landed at Fort Knight had a locator implant, something the Vesy couldn't begin to imagine, let alone remove safely. The search and recovery crews had found dozens of bodies, from defenders caught in the open to civilians cut down as they tried to run, simply by tracking the implants through the drones. But a number of people remained unaccounted for...

Penny, he thought, bitterly. Where *was* she? Even if she'd been blown to bits, the implant might well have survived. Hell, the Paras had found a couple of implants in the crater where the north wall had been, where several Paras had been literally disintegrated. *Where are you?*

Hadfield met them outside, still wearing his suit. "The civilians need to be escorted to the shuttles," he ordered. "They are not to bring anything apart from the clothes on their backs; if they try to bring anything else, take it off them and leave it here. There just isn't the room."

Of course not, Percy thought. *Half the freighters that should have offered berths for civilians have buggered off through the tramlines.*

"You may tell them that they will be heading to Cromwell, rather than Earth," Hadfield continued. "We may not have the life support to get them all the way home. Do not listen to any arguments they may offer, just get them into the shuttles as quickly as possible."

He broke off as a trio of shuttles flew overhead, dropping down to land just outside the remains of the fort. "Use whatever force is necessary to get them onto the craft," he concluded. "You may secure them, if they refuse to listen to reason."

Percy nodded, then led his section towards the prefabricated buildings. Most of the surviving civilians - he felt a stab of hatred for them, merely for not being Penny - had been gathered there, watched by the Paras. He exchanged a brief word with the Paras on guard, then opened the hatch. The civilians were lying inside a hall, looking tired and dazed. Some of them were asleep, others clearly wishing they were.

"On your feet," he snapped, taking command right from the start. "We're going to the shuttles. Leave bags and everything else behind, just take the clothes on your back…"

A burly man stumbled to his feet, clutching a heavy carryall. "I can't leave this here," he protested. "It's mine…"

"It's staying here," Percy said, feeling his self-control starting to fray. He hadn't felt so tired since the first week of training, when the Drill Instructors had pushed them right to the limit, just to see who would break under pressure. They'd been sadistic bastards, he'd always thought, but they'd never included a genuine threat to his sister. Maybe he *would* have broken if one had been offered. "Leave the bag here, *sir*, or it will be thrown aside."

The man saw his expression - Percy was sure he looked tired and murderous - and dropped the bag with a clatter. There was no time to feel relief. Percy hastily assessed the civilians, then sent the women ahead first, escorted by Peerce and a handful of marines. No one objected, although there were several sharp glances from those who remained behind. They had to be wondering if they were going to be left behind, if the occasional bombing and sniping managed to take out a shuttle.

"Sir," a voice said. "Where are we going?"

Percy turned to see a middle-aged man, wearing a torn and bloodied suit. Had he been hit and refused medical treatment? Or had he tried to help someone else? There was no way to know. Instead, he forced himself to speak calmly. It wasn't easy.

"Cromwell, apparently," he said. There was no point in mentioning problems with the life support. "It's the closest inhabitable world."

We could take them to Pegasus instead, he thought. It made sense, in theory, but practically it would be a major headache. Clarke III didn't have the living space for thousands of additional colonists, while Wells was nowhere near terraformed and wouldn't be for at least a hundred years. *At least Cromwell has a breathable atmosphere and food supplies.*

He smiled, remembering their last visit there. *And the locals would be delighted to have an influx of women.*

It took longer than he'd expected to finish emptying Fort Knight. Several civilians refused to leave and had to be secured, then dumped into the shuttles. Others tried to argue, insisting they could carry datachips; one researcher even insisted that she could strip naked and carry the datachips instead. Percy fought down the temptation to agree - she was pretty and his tired mind thought it would be funny - and told her to transmit her research to the ships before she boarded the shuttles. Everything was meant to be backed up in orbit anyway.

"There's no sign of her," Hadfield said, as the final shuttles were loaded. "I'm sorry, Percy."

Percy winced, bitterly. He wanted to stay behind, to search for his sister…but he knew he couldn't. A marine went where he was told to go and they were *all* leaving the planet. And besides, where would be look for her. Bitter rage and helplessness welled up in his chest. If only he'd knocked her out and shipped her to *Warspite*…she would never have spoken to him again, yet at least she would be alive.

"Thank you, sir," he said, numbly.

"I don't think she's dead," Hadfield added. "The implant would probably have survived, even if she had died."

"And if she's a hostage," Percy asked, "would she be better off dead?"

"Maybe not," Hadfield said. "This isn't Earth."

Percy nodded. There were thousands of horror stories about what could happen to hostages on Earth, once the kidnappers realised that no amount of threats would make the British Government bend. But the Vesy, at least, wouldn't want to gang rape the hostages, or torture them to death. Hell, even a relatively unsophisticated human could teach them a great deal...

"I hope you're right, sir," he said. "I hope you're right."

He turned to take one last look at the remains of Fort Knight, the base he'd commanded for nearly six months and then stepped into the shuttle. Somehow, he had a premonition that he would never return. Vesy was unimportant, in the light of the war the Indians might have just begun...

And all he could do was pray for the missing.

———

"The last of the shuttles has returned to the ship," Howard reported. "Major Hadfield reports that his men have evacuated the entire base and destroyed all sensitive materials."

"Tell him to report to me once he's seen to the final evacuees," John ordered.

"Aye, sir," Howard said. "The ship is crammed, sir. It may be some time."

John nodded, watching the Indian ships on the display. True to their word - and in a manner that showed they'd plotted the whole affair from the beginning - there had been no attacks on the evacuating shuttles. Indeed, the Flowered Clan had pulled back to make *sure* there were no incidents that could mar the evacuation. John couldn't help thinking of Hitler's famous *halt* order at Dunkirk, another evacuation that had changed the course of human history. The enemy, for reasons of his own, had made the evacuation possible.

Wars are not won by evacuations, he thought, remembering Churchill's words. The true test of Britain's strength, and determination to resist, had been about to begin. Now, he couldn't help feeling that history was repeating itself. *We're not going to let the Indians get away with this.*

"Good," he said. The remainder of the tiny flotilla was already heading towards the tramline, unimpeded by the Indians or anyone else. "Take us out of orbit, standard cruising speed."

"Aye, sir," Armstrong said.

"Deploy stealth drones once we're out of sensor range," John added. If he'd had more ships, he would have left one in place to watch the Indians, but all three of his warships were crammed with refugees. "I want them programmed to monitor the system through passive sensors, drawing no attention to themselves."

"Aye, sir," Tara said.

John nodded, then looked towards the large red icon on the display. The Indian carrier was holding position, as if her crew cared nothing for the departing British. He knew, he thought, what they were thinking. They'd won. Vesy was theirs now, their alliance holding the planet's surface firmly under control. And, no matter what they'd said in the diplomatic meetings, they would try to use it to maintain control of the tramlines. They would gain a controlling interest in the entire sector.

But it isn't going to happen that way, he thought, coldly. There was no way the final insult could be ignored, despite the risks of a general war. *We'll be back.*

CHAPTER
FORTY

"Success, then," Rani said. "Vesy is ours."

"Don't count your chickens," Anjeet said, as the last of the British ships entered the tramline and vanished. He'd been careful, so careful, to avoid a final slap in the face, but he knew the matter might not be over. "The diplomats will have to patch together something that will prevent war."

He sucked in his breath, sharply. "And the hostages?"

"Safe and well," Rani confirmed. "They will be handed over to us, as per the agreement."

Anjeet nodded. Allowing the aliens to butcher any humans they captured might have served as a rallying cry, if the British Government needed one. The hostages would be treated well, then returned to Britain as swiftly as possible. Unless, of course, they chose to stay...he shook his head, firmly. No one, no matter how idealistic, would look at the Vesy in the same way after the attack on Fort Knight.

"Very good," he said. The Flowered Clan had the dominance they wanted over the surface - and India ruled the system beyond. They'd won what they wanted; now, he knew, all they had to do was keep it. "You *do* realise we're going to be doubling down?"

The Prime Minister had discussed it endlessly with him, when he'd been fully briefed on the whole operation. Vesy alone was important, but they couldn't take the risk of allowing the British to mount a counterattack. The fleet would be securing both the direct tramline to Vesy and Pegasus, trapping the British between a humiliating surrender and an uncertain war that might weaken the entire human race. No, it *would* weaken the entire human race…

"I know," Rani said.

"Good," Anjeet said. He held up his hand, then make a throwing motion. "The die is quite firmly cast."

———

Penny had hoped, when she'd left the refugee camp, that she would never have to endure such a place ever again. After a week in alien captivity, kept tied and chained almost constantly, she would have been quite happy to return to the refugee camp. The food had been appalling and her body had ached so badly that, when they'd finally been handed over to the Indians, she had needed help to stand upright. Hell, she'd been relieved to see the Indians. At least they knew how to take care of human guests.

"Your government will be informed we have you as soon as possible," Rani Begum told her, after a doctor had checked her over and prescribed painkillers and a long nap. "I believe we will probably return you to them once we've made arrangements for a safe handover."

"Thank you," Penny said, gratefully.

The hell of it was that she *was* grateful. She had no idea what the Vesy would have done with her, eventually, but she doubted it would have been pleasant. Maybe they would have scarified her to their gods. The thought made her snicker, inwardly. If they happened to need a virgin sacrifice, and they might, they were going to be disappointed. She'd lost her virginity before the bombardment.

"There is a second option," Rani added. "You can stay here as an embedded reporter, under the standard international protocols."

Penny hesitated. She could remain with the Indians and her boss wouldn't object, but she'd had quite enough of Vesy. On the other hand, it was the story of a lifetime; she'd have a chance to write out her impressions of the attack on Fort Knight, then send them home to be published. But what if the Indians decided to edit her stories before sending them on? They were in a very good position to ignore the standard protocols and make her look like yet another hired shill.

"I might," she said. "Can I think about it?"

"You have until we make an agreement to decide," Rani said, simply. She made a show of looking around the hospital ward. "A room has been assigned to you, for the moment, but we will need an answer sooner rather than later."

"Thank you," Penny said. "I…do you know if my brother survived?"

Rani made no pretence of being surprised by the question. "We believe he was one of the Royal Marines who escaped City One," she said. "A number of those marines were injured, but none were killed as far as we know. He's also not one of the dead bodies we pulled from the remains of Fort Knight."

Penny winced. She'd seen some of those people die.

"The bodies will also be returned to your country, or to their nation of origin," Rani added, softly. "For the moment, they will remain in storage here. The Vesy did nothing to harm them."

"Apart from attacking Fort Knight," Penny said, bitterly.

"A natural consequence of your government's blithe disregard for their point of view," Rani said. She rose. "The doctor will show you to your room, Miss Schneider. There's a terminal there, if you wish to write a report, and a bed. I believe the doctor ordered rest, but…work is sometimes a good antidote to sorrow."

Penny scowled at her. "Thank you," she said, tartly. "I'll do my best to rest."

———

"I couldn't save her," Percy said. "Admiral, I *couldn't* save her."

"You followed orders," Admiral Fitzwilliam said. They stood together in an observation blister on Nelson Base, staring down at the planet below. "I don't think you could have stayed on Vesy."

"I should have," Percy said.

"You're a Royal Marine," Admiral Fitzwilliam pointed out, dryly. "If the concept of obeying orders bothers you, hand in your resignation and try to book passage to Vesy on a civilian ship. I dare say the Indians will be glad to scoop you up."

Percy scowled. It had taken a month for *Warspite* and her flotilla to make it home, but word had rocketed ahead of them. Earth had been arguing over the meaning of it all for three weeks, by the time they'd arrived; they'd been ordered to remain in orbit, denying all requests for interviews, until the Admiralty had had its say. The only good news in all the darkness had been a note from the Indians that the hostages had been handed over to them and would be shipped home as soon as possible. Penny was alive, merely...

A prisoner, he thought. Did the Indians plan to stall? *They could have shipped all of the hostages to Cromwell by now, if they'd wished.*

"There will be a great many hard questions for you in the future," Admiral Fitzwilliam added, after waiting for Percy to say something. "The attack on Fort Knight...well, certain elements within the Admiralty will want someone to blame. You're the one who designed the fort..."

"I worked with what I had," Percy said, stiffly.

Admiral Fitzwilliam shrugged. "One thing you will learn, as you climb up the ranks, is that the people at the rear know very little of what is going on at the front, but they won't hesitate to carp, criticize and claim that *they* would do better, if only they were in command," he said, dryly. "A few of them may even, with the benefit of hindsight, have a point. Mostly, though, they won't understand the limitations faced by those at the front. It wouldn't be the first time some elaborate plan was discarded in favour of something more suitable to the situation."

He met Percy's eyes. "You may wind up with a black mark on your record," he added, "although I will do my best to ensure you don't. I doubt you will be given any independent commands in the foreseeable future, though. The problem with shit is that the smell tends to linger, even when the shit itself is wiped off."

"Yes, sir," Percy said.

Admiral Fitzwilliam slapped his back. "They'll want to see you soon," he warned. "Try and prepare yourself as best as you can. It won't be a fun debriefing."

———

"It is to be war, then?"

"It looks that way," the First Space Lord said. "The latest report has Indian ships moving into both Pegasus and J-25. They pulled a fast one with that carrier, John. MI6 assumed she was going to New Delhi and they were right, but she didn't stop there."

"Yes, sir," John said.

The First Space Lord sighed. "The Prime Minister is playing his cards close to his chest, but there's no way we can let the Indians get away with this," he admitted. "They're making a big song and dance about how their claims are reasonable…and they might even have a point…yet we cannot just concede anything, not to this. Everyone will try to get in on the act if the Great Powers just roll over when someone deliberately sets out to get our people killed."

"Good," John said.

The First Space Lord lifted an eyebrow. "I hope you understand that a war, even a localised war, could be disastrous for *all* of us," he added. "We can't fight here, because of the Solar Treaty; the worst we could do is take both of their major colonies and Vesy. At which point…the war stalemates. We'd either have to occupy their worlds permanently or hand them back. Oh, they've created a situation where there are no good options."

"We could also ship their settlers elsewhere," John pointed out.

"The logistics would kill us," the First Space Lord said. "And the media would crucify us in the courts of public opinion. The Indians have laid the groundwork very well."

He cursed, just loudly enough for John to hear, then looked up. "Admiral Fitzwilliam has been drawing up a plan to recover the lost systems and evict the Indians from Vesy," he continued. "You and *Warspite* will have a role in the operation."

"Thank you, sir," John said.

"Don't thank me yet," the First Space Lord warned. "The media storm this time is bigger than the last one. And…your judgement has been called into question. Yours, Ambassador Richardson's, that damn aide of hers… lots of people just trying to throw mud everywhere, just to confuse the issue."

He met John's eyes. "But all that really matters is that we're not going to let this pass," he added, sharply. "We're going to strike back."

To Be Concluded In

A Small Colonial War

Coming Soon!

APPENDIX:
GLOSSARY OF UK TERMS AND SLANG

[Author's Note: I've tried to define every incident of specifically UK slang in this glossary, but I can't promise to have spotted everything. If you spot something I've missed, please let me know and it will be included.]

Beasting/Beasted - military slang for anything from a chewing out by one's commander to outright corporal punishment or hazing. The latter two are now officially banned.

Binned - SAS slang for a prospective recruit being kicked from the course, then returned to unit (RTU).

Bootnecks - slang for Royal Marines. Loosely comparable to 'Jarhead.'

Fortnight - two weeks. (Hence the terrible pun, courtesy of the *Goon Show*, that Fort Knight cannot possibly last three weeks.)

'Get stuck into' - 'start fighting.'

'I should coco' - 'you're damned right.'

Levies - native troops. The Ghurkhas are the last remnants of native troops from British India.

Lorries - trucks.

Rumbled - discovered/spotted.

Squaddies - slang for British soldiers.

Stag - guard duty.

TAB (tab/tabbing) - Tactical Advance to Battle.

Walt - Poser, i.e. someone who claims to have served in the military and/or a very famous regiment. There's a joke about 22 SAS being the largest regiment in the British Army - it must be, because of all the people who claim to have served in it.

Wanker - Masturbator (jerk-off). Commonly used as an insult.

Wanking - Masturbating.

Made in the USA
Middletown, DE
15 July 2015